Cyril Cook was born in Easton, Hampshire, but at the age of five was brought to live on a farm in Mottingham, Kent. Educated at Eltham College, he matriculated in 1939, joined The Rifle Brigade in 1940, and was commissioned and transferred to The Parachute Regiment in 1943. He saw considerable service in the 6th Airborne Division in Europe and the Far East where for a period he commanded, at the age of 22, a company of some 220 men of the Malay Regiment.

His working life was spent mainly as the proprietor of an engineering business which he founded, until he retired to start the really serious business of writing the six volumes of The Chandlers.

By the same author

THE CHANDLERS

VOLUME ONE – THE YOUNG CHANDLERS
Published in 2005 (Vanguard Press)
ISBN 1 84386 199 2

VOLUME TWO – THE CHANDLERS AT WAR
Published in 2006 (Vanguard Press)
ISBN-13: 978 1 84386 292 5
ISBN-10: 1 84386 292 1

VOLUME THREE – THE CHANDLERS FIGHT BACK
Published in 2006 (Vanguard Press)
ISBN-13: 978 1 84386 293 2
ISBN-10: 1 84386 293 X

THE CHANDLERS

VOLUME 4

The Chandlers Grieve

Cyril Cook

THE CHANDLERS

Volume 4

The Chandlers Grieve

*To Margaret & Ray in Tunbridge Wells with all best wishes
Cyril.*

*Cyril Cook
11. July 07.*

Vanguard Press

VANGUARD PAPERBACK

© Copyright 2006
Cyril Cook

The right of Cyril Cook to be identified as author of
this work has been asserted by him in accordance with the
Copyright, Designs and Patents Act 1988

All Rights Reserved

No reproduction, copy or transmission of this publication
may be made without written permission.
No paragraph of this publication may be reproduced,
copied or transmitted save with the written permission of the
publisher, or in accordance with the provisions
of the Copyright Act 1956 (as amended).

Any person who does any unauthorised act in relation to
this publication may be liable to criminal
prosecution and civil claims for damage.

A CIP catalogue record for this title is
available from the British Library

ISBN-10: 1-84386-294-8
ISBN-13: 978-1-84386-294-9

*Vanguard Press is an imprint of
Pegasus Elliot MacKenzie Publishers Ltd.*
www.pegasuspublishers.com

First Published in 2006

**Vanguard Press
Sheraton House Castle Park
Cambridge England**

Printed & Bound in Great Britain

This book is dedicated to my five brothers who served in World War Two.

Arthur who tramped the length of Burma fighting the Japs.

Alec who was in the 8th Army in the desert fighting the Afrika Korps, then Sicily and Italy.

Jack an anti-aircraft gunner in The Blitz on London, then an anti-tank gunner in Europe.

Jim with combined-ops in North Africa.

Peter with the tanks of The Staffordshire Yeomanry, among the first to go ashore in Normandy on D Day.

By some miracle we all survived.

MAIN CHARACTERS AND EVENTS FROM BOOKS ONE AND TWO AND THREE

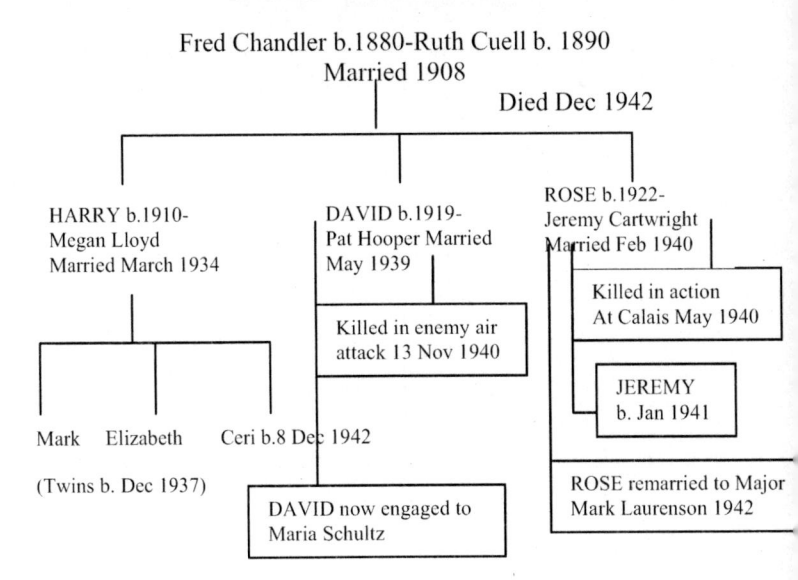

Fred Chandler b.1880 - Ruth Cuell b. 1890
Married 1908
Died Dec 1942

HARRY b.1910-
Megan Lloyd
Married March 1934

Mark   Elizabeth   Ceri b.8 Dec 1942

(Twins b. Dec 1937)

DAVID b.1919-
Pat Hooper Married May 1939

Killed in enemy air attack 13 Nov 1940

DAVID now engaged to Maria Schultz

ROSE b.1922-
Jeremy Cartwright
Married Feb 1940

Killed in action At Calais May 1940

JEREMY b. Jan 1941

ROSE remarried to Major Mark Laurenson 1942

OTHER FAMILIES

JACK HOOPER Pat's father. Divorced Pat's mother. Married MOIRA EVANS, Megan's Aunt. Moira is a Top Civil Servant involved in the Atom Bomb project. Son JOHN born August 1937.

TREFOR LLOYD and Elizabeth. Megan's parents.

BUFFY CARTWRIGHT and Rita. Baby Jeremy's grandparents.

KARL REISNER Refugee from Nazi Germany. Father of ANNI married to ERNIE BOLTON, David's friend from boyhood and now Works Director at Fred and Jack's Engineering company Sandbury Engineering.

DR KONRAD VON HASSELLBEK
and wife. Parents of DIETER, David's great pre-war friend now in a panzer division of the German Army and all fervent anti-Nazis. Also daughter INGE, ardent Nazi married to Himmler's nephew. DIETER married his cousin Rosa in April 1940.

CECELY COATES with children Oliver 16, Gera 14 in England from home in Malaya when Japs invaded. Husband NIGEL and brother-in-law JUDGE CHARLES COATES presumed in Japanese camp if still alive. Brother-in-law James is a Captain in British Army.

LORD RAMSFORD Brigadier controlling David's operations overseas. Father of Charlie Crew, a great friend of David and the Chandler family, and son of the Earl of Otbourne.

Chapter One

It was the 7th day of January 1943. After the last of the mourners had left Chandlers Lodge following the funeral of his beloved wife Ruth, Fred Chandler sat for a while on his own in such despair that he could see no way in which he could face the future. He had fought in the South African War at the turn of the century, then in the bloodbath of the 1914-18 War – the war to end all wars! – and had witnessed more death than any man should be called upon to experience, but the loss of his Ruth at only fifty-two, when they should still have had years together to watch their grandchildren growing up was almost beyond his ability to bear. The door opened silently.

"You alright Fred?"

It was Jack Hooper, his long time friend, who as he phrased the enquiry was telling himself 'what a bloody silly question.' It was an opening gambit however, so often used when little else could be thought of to say, to imply appreciation of the pain another was feeling, to bridge the gap, or attempt to bridge the gap, between being inconsolable and having to face a different life from now on.

Fred looked up. "I didn't know we had so many friends," he said, "I am so shattered that the boys were not here."

"It will hit them hard too when they are eventually notified."

Harry, the elder son was in the jungle in Malaya. David his younger brother was with the partisans in Yugoslavia. It was not going to be easy to get the bitter news to either of them. When it did arrive they would suffer grievously, and with no other members of the family to support them the tragic tidings would be doubly difficult to bear.

The sombre silence was broken by Rose entering with a struggling Jeremy trying to break away from her. He was just two years old, a sturdy lad, the image of his father who had been killed in action at Calais in May 1940.

"You're not to bother granddad."

Fred turned. "Come on old son, come and give me a left and a right."

These two were always sparring with each other. Rose let him go, but instead of pretending to box, he threw himself on to Fred's lap and hugged him round the neck as if he knew that his grandfather needed to be comforted. Rose and Jack watched, half smiling, until Rose said quietly

"Now say goodnight to granddad."

Reluctantly the little lad let go his hold, slid down off his grandfather's lap, bade him and Uncle Jack goodnight, and made a chattering exit, hand in hand, with his mother.

On Thursday evening 7th January, Harry sat on the veranda outside his room in Camp Six in the high jungle of Johore in Southern Malaya talking to Matthew Lee, a fourth year medical student who was the camp doctor to the sixty odd Force 136 men based there. The monsoon had been particularly vicious for the past three days, constantly finding new places in the atap roofs through which to spring leaks, in the process washing out sundry unwelcome guests in the form of foot long centipedes, even the occasional tree rat which had taken shelter there; along with the ubiquitous little lizards they called chit chats.

"What would the weather be like in England now?" Matthew asked, looking out at the solid wall of saturated darkness. As another moth incinerated itself against the Tilley lamp hanging to the side of them and fluttered to the floor Harry thought for a moment.

"It would be cold, probably even snowing. People would be dressed in heavy overcoats, wearing thick gloves, woollen scarves around their necks, and a hat of some sort or another. Some January days are very beautiful where we live, with snow on the hills and settled on the trees and roofs of the houses, particularly if there is winter sunshine to add to the picture. You must come and see it after the war, come and stay with us, my mother and father would be delighted to meet you, as would all the family."

At that precise time, due to the time difference, the coffin of Ruth Chandler was being carried from the ancient church of Sandbury to its resting place in the new section of the churchyard, to be interred next to her beloved daughter-in-law, Pat, David's wife, so cruelly killed in an enemy air attack two years ago.

"Well, I think I'll turn in, we've got the strategy meeting tomorrow, not that much can be done in this weather, perhaps it'll start clearing up a bit soon. Goodnight Matthew." Harry turned and went into his room, lit the Tilley lamp, then Matthew heard a loud "Bugger!" He poked his nose in the doorway to see Harry standing by his soaking wet bed, this surmounted by a saturated mosquito net and a hole above in the roof as big as a dinner plate. They pulled the bed to one side, got a couple of dry blankets from the store along the veranda, put a bucket under the hole, deciding that was all they could do until the morning when hopefully the weather would ease up a bit and allow them to make repairs.

On the evening of the 7th of January, Major General Mutsumi Takahashi sat in his comfortable sitting room at his headquarters in Kluang having dined sumptuously, now taking his ease with the aid of a liberal measure of the newly arrived supply of saki sent to him from his home in Togitsu, a little town near Nagasaki in the southern island of Kyushu in Japan. Although he told himself he would much rather be fighting on the Pacific Islands or in Burma or back in China again, he nevertheless thoroughly enjoyed his present luxurious lifestyle, good food, absolute power at his command, civilised entertainment on the radio, and at the end of the day the comfort of that particularly delightful Korean comfort girl he had chosen from the new batch which had recently arrived to staff the senior officers' brothel.

However, there was a small, but ever increasing, blight on his otherwise attractive landscape. Over the past few months a gang of renegade guerrillas holed up in the high jungle had attacked targets in his command area and caused a number of casualties to his occupation forces. At a meeting with General Yamashita in Singapore the previous week, he had received a forceful directive to do something about it. He had put the point of view that seventy five percent of his command was either almost impenetrable jungle, or mangrove swamp, the force was obviously small and would soon die off from natural causes. No one could live in the jungle for more than a few months without suitable food and medical attention: they therefore would be extirpated in due course by the grim forces of 'mother nature' – he could play a waiting game. However, so as to show he was doing something about it, he contacted his local air force commander and asked if he could provide some spotter planes to systematically search, area by area, territory which would take months for him to cover with foot patrols. The air force commander had dined with him that evening and agreed to do just that.

The major-general took a final swallow of his saki, and with a grunt, heaved his fifty-five year old carcase out of the cane armchair making his already half-aroused way to his bedroom where the young eighteen year old so recently kidnapped off the streets of Pusan would be waiting for him. He saw no conflict between his Samurai honour and the rape of a Korean slave, for that indeed was what she was, nor lamentably would he ever be called upon to pay for this crime.

On the evening of the 7th January, David Chandler and his comrade Paddy O'Riordan, his one time batman, now a company sergeant major but still insisting on 'looking after the Major,' sat by a roaring log fire enjoying the comfort of being warm, well fed, and louse free after campaigning with the partisans in Bosnia over the past three months. Sadly they knew they would be leaving their friends in two days, to journey south-east to join a brigade on the borders of Serbia and Montenegro, a distance as the crow flies of some 250 miles, but nearer 400 on the ground. They were delighted to have been told they, and their two guides and an interpreter would be given horses, although the mountainous terrain was such that a good deal of the journey would inevitably be on foot. It was still bitterly cold – it was not going to be a picnic by any manner of means. They were there to assess the strengths and fighting ability of the partisans so that a large British military mission planned to visit Marshall Tito at the end of April could be reliably informed of the needs of his forces and, in particular, whether whatever was provided would be efficiently used. So far in the north they had been overwhelmed by the courage, discipline, ability to improvise, and high morale of the partisans, less than half of them communists, and some twenty per cent of them women and boys. In two days they would be off.

"I wonder what's happening at Chandlers Lodge at this moment Sir? They will be upset at no Christmas cards from you."

"Your new wife will be missing you Paddy – that's for sure." David paused, "when we get back and get some leave will you take her back to the honeymoon cottage in North Wales again?" It was a standing joke between them that during the seven-day honeymoon Paddy and Mary had enjoyed at Bangor; they only emerged twice from the cottage to buy milk and bread from the corner shop.

"I thought of letting you and Maria have it Sir, since I've assumed you will be getting spliced when we get home."

"Always assuming we do get home."

"Oh, we'll do that alright Sir, though I must say I'm not looking forward to the journey locked in that bloody submarine from here back to Alexandria."

"We've a lot to do before that happens."

On the evening of the 7th January 1943 Mark Laurenson, Rose's husband, sat in a tent in the Libyan Desert talking to Charlie Crew. They had just received the news of Ruth Chandler's death, although it was not unexpected since letters from Rose to them both had kept them informed of her sad condition. Their division, in reserve after being in the van of those chasing Rommell's Afrika Korps back towards Tripoli after the great victory at El Alamein, now were enjoying a well earned rest whilst their vehicles were being serviced and repaired ready for the next dash westwards.

Ruth had meant a great deal to each of them, having acted almost as a surrogate mother to Charlie whose own mother deserted him when he was a child. To Mark she had given guidance and support when he had fallen in love with Rose. She being still in a state of some confusion of loyalties as a result of losing her husband, killed in action only two years before, felt it so difficult to give her heart to someone else. Ruth had bridged the gap for which Mark would be eternally grateful.

"I feel so helpless, stuck here in this fly-blown wilderness," Mark complained. Charlie remained silent for a while.

"Sir," he began. Despite the fact they had close ties, Charlie never took advantage of that fact and always addressed Mark, his company commander after all, as 'Sir.'

"Sir, I don't often say any prayers, but do you think I could say one now?"

"Of course, Charlie. What had you in mind?"

Charlie bowed his head. "Dear Lord, our dear, dear friend Ruth Chandler has joined you and we shall miss her so much. Look after her for us, and above all, look after the lovely people left behind at Chandlers Lodge, and David and Harry as well of course, and know that of all the people who deserve to be welcomed into your presence no-one merits it more than our dear Ruth. Amen."

Mark repeated the Amen slowly and thoughtfully. He waited a short while.

"Come on Charlie, let's go and get some cordon bleu corned beef hash."

Chapter Two

Gradually a new routine established itself at Chandlers Lodge. Mrs Stokes, their daily help, whose husband was serving in Palestine, said that now her two youngsters were old enough to take care of themselves without getting into mischief, she could work full-time during the week, including getting the evening meal ready at the end of the afternoon and leaving it in the Aga. Rose would, in addition to looking after Jeremy, play her part by carrying out her share of the household chores as she had when her mother was alive, in addition to being 'chief cook and bottle washer,' as she put it, at the weekend. Through most of the war they had had officers billeted on them who were either involved with the army camp out on the Maidstone Road, or on Sandbury airfield on the outskirts of the town. The camp had been empty for some while, except for a handful of maintenance and security troops, but rumours had been going around the town that it was soon to be re-occupied. It was no surprise therefore when, on a cold, grey, rainy day at the end of January, a convoy of some twenty-odd vehicles, some laden with contents securely sheeted down against the weather, others filled with probably a hundred or so soldiers, snaked their way through the mighty metropolis of Sandbury – it took them all of five minutes – and out onto the Maidstone road, leaving the denizens of the town to assume the first of their new neighbours had arrived.

The next morning Friday 22nd January, an army car crunched up to Chandlers Lodge just as Rose was taking in the milk off the front step. It was a funny thing about the war; everything seemed to be getting more and more egalitarian. Before the war, the milkman always walked around to the back door and left the milk there. Other tradesmen delivered to the back door and would not dream of knocking on the front door. Now the milkman left his milk on the flagstones in the front porch and tradesmen in general no longer delivered anyway. The world was changing in many seemingly insignificant ways which would ultimately precipitate a different Britain altogether compared to before the war.

The arrival was the area-billeting officer, an old friend of Ruth's.

"Good morning major, you've made an early start."

"Yes Mrs..." he hesitated, "I'm terribly sorry. I don't know your name."

"Laurenson, but Rose to you please."

"Thank you Rose. I hardly know, in view of your recent sad loss, whether to ask you this, but are you still able to billet a couple of officers who will eventually be going into the Maidstone Road Camp?"

"Yes of course we are. Have you any details about them? When they will arrive and so on?"

"The advance party is already there. I understand the train bringing the rest of the battalion arrives at Sandbury station mid-afternoon tomorrow, so they could be with you at any time after. Names, by the way, Majors Wrighton-Browne and Rees-Evans."

"They sound frightfully posh."

"It's a battalion of The Welsh Guards – very – very posh," he joked. "As long as they don't go around singing Cwm Rhonda at six o'clock in the morning they shouldn't give you any trouble. Right, I'll be on my way, and once again my sincere condolences regarding your mother. I have met many lovely ladies in my long and not uneventful life, but Ruth Chandler was way at the top of the list. Bye-bye now Rose."

His driver whisked him off as Rose stood on the steps, still holding the milk bottles, wondering what the two new majors would be like, and then considering what her rifleman husband, her rifleman brother, and her dear rifleman friend Charlie Crew would think of their entertaining GUARDSMEN in their house. She smiled fondly as she thought of them and what their reactions would be. Redcoats would be bad enough – marines only marginally more acceptable – but GUARDSMEN? There were no clubs in Sandbury where the officers could while away their time leaving the N.C.O.s to run the battalion, as was believed to be the case by the rest of the army of the way a guards battalion was organised. Still, London was only an hour away on the train, so they would probably be hijacking the first class compartments in the evenings from now on.

She went back into the house, shivering a little from the cold air on the front porch. Ten minutes later Mrs Stokes arrived and was told the news.

"We'll put them in where the marine gentlemen were shall we Mrs Laurenson?"

"Yes, though what David and his rifleman friends will say about our having guardsmen around I'm sure I don't know."

"Any news from Mister Harry or Mister David?"

"No, nothing."

"Well, I'll get on and get the beds made up and have a quick dust round before I start down here."

"Thank you Mrs Stokes."

After spending a few minutes on the telephone telling her father and Ernie Bolton at the factory of what was going on, she got on with the daily routine. With a child to take care of and a house now to look after she had little time to be consciously lonely. When, however, she had time to think, she had difficulty in not sinking into depression. She was only twenty-one, she had lost her first husband when she was only nineteen, her second husband had been snatched away from her after only two weeks of marriage to fight in the desert, her mother, the solid rock of the family, had just been taken from her, and her two brothers, she had good reason to believe, were in constant danger. Their family doctor, Doctor Power, not only their doctor but also a good family friend, and fellow Rotarian to Fred, was very well aware of the situation. He was somewhat unique among G.P.'s of the period in recognising not only that depression was in itself an illness, but also in analysing circumstances surrounding a patient which could trigger the disorder. Whereas most family doctors relied on a bottle of 'tonic' and a few cheerful words, he devoted time – he had few medicinal aids to offer – or at least as much time as he could, to getting to the basics of the patients' problems. In Rose's case he knew all the factors which could possibly induce melancholia in her. So far no symptoms had shown themselves, but he knew full well that such symptoms frequently only show themselves when the sufferer is alone. Fortunately in Rose's case those periods during the day were infrequent in that Anni, Megan and Cecely were constant visitors to the house with their children. At night it was different. She lay awake some nights physically aching at being alone, remembering the tragedies she had already endured in her young life, Jeremy, Pat, her Canadian friends Tim McEwan and Jim Napier, killed on the raid on Dieppe last year, and her husband in constant danger so many miles away to whom she was unable to cling for comfort. Doctor Power therefore was pleased to hear of the arrival of the new guests. Not only would it require further activity on her part, but would provide added interest to her life, both of which was, in his opinion, good sound therapy. During the afternoon he called in at Chandlers Lodge, and said to Rose, "I was on calls in the area, thought I would scrounge a cup of tea, shan't charge you for the call, wanted a quick word about your father. He tells me he is as fit as a fiddle, but I know what a lying so and so he is. Does he complain of anything? Aches and pains, breathlessness or things like that? I know he's got creaky joints. All of us who slogged around in waterlogged trenches for years in the last lot have got those."

"Which of your innumerable questions would you like answering first?" replied Rose.

"Anything that comes to mind. I only came in for the tea anyway."

They laughed and chatted. He made a fuss of young Jeremy, letting him scribble on his prescription pad – with a pencil; he would deny anyone the use of his precious Conway Stewart pen, even his wife. He told his friends his wife could put her hands on anything he'd got – except his fountain pen. When he left he felt happier about Rose. With spring not so very far away, and with the life it gave to everybody after the long, cold, wet, blacked out nights, she should be back, or nearly back, to the sparkling Rose of yore.

Half an hour before the troops train arrived, two motor coaches of bandsmen arrived at the siding, the people on the platforms being entertained by the cacophony of sounds of scales from instruments as diverse as piccolos, trombones and tubas, as the bandsmen, in their woollen gloves, some with fingers uncovered, started to breathe or blow life into cold unresponsive instruments. At three o'clock the train pulled in, was diverted to the siding, the men in response to innumerable shouted commands from the N.C.O.s, fearsome looking people with the peaks of their caps flat to the forehead and almost obscuring their eyes, fell in in ranks of three in their respective companies. Five hundred odd men, in full marching order, out of the train, on to the hard standing ready for the next move, in under ten minutes. While all this was going on, a cluster of officers stood to one side indicating that this initial argy-bargy required no intervention on their part. When all the companies 'fell in,' the R.S.M., all six feet four of him, marched up to the commanding officer, saluted, "Parade ready to move off Sir."

The C.O. ordered, "Fall in the officers," at which they each took their pre-ordained places. The drum major at the front of the band which had now positioned itself at the leading off point, kept his ears strained, and gave the 'Band Ready' command. He had his back to the colonel who would be behind the band but leading the main body. However it was not totally unknown for a colonel to give the order 'Quick March,' at which the band should strike up, to have his voice drowned by the whistle of a passing train or some similar hazard. That, of course, would never happen in the Guards.

The parade through the town was the talking point of the clubs, pubs and homes of its citizens for a long time after. The guardsmen, marching to attention with rifles at the slope, were immaculate in their precision. Fred, who had come into town from the factory to see Reg Church their accountant, watched from the window of Reg's first floor offices overlooking the town square, where they held the weekly market and acknowledged, "Well, you've got to admit they know how to do it." Knowing Fred Chandler, his friend accredited they could receive no higher accolade.

As the parade reached the centre of the town, and the band struck up the Regimental March, The Rising of the Lark, a fifteen hundred weight truck drew up outside Chandlers Lodge, disgorging two soldiers, one of whom, seeing Rose appearing on to the porch, sprang to attention, saluted and said "We have the officers' kit here madam," in a profound bass voice Rose could imagine forming the depth of any male voice choir from the valleys. "We are their servants, madam, I am Davies 309 and he is Davies 432."

A totally bemused Rose asked "Why the numbers?"

"There are a lot of Davies in the battalion, ma'am."

"But don't you have different Christian names that you can be called?"

"Not in the army, ma'am – at least not in the Guards. Maybe they do in some of the inferior regiments. Anyway Davies 432 here and I have the same Christian name as well. We are both Idris." Rose put her hand to her forehead and smiled.

"I shall have to find a way around this I can see. Come on in and I will show you their rooms."

The two men, in their late twenties Rose judged, seemed an amiable couple, joshing each other as they carted the somewhat extensive cargoes of kit up the broad stairway. When all was safely delivered and they started to unpack, Rose asked whether they would like some tea, which invitation was received with open arms.

"Well, I'll call you when it is ready – then come down to the kitchen."

She sat at the big deal table waiting for the kettle to boil on the Aga, thinking of the different people who had congregated around this centre point of the house since the Canadians first came at the Christmas of 1939. And not only them but others too – all welcomed here as a result of being thrown together by the war. As the kettle began to sing, she heard the back door latch rattle and her father came in. Being Saturday, the factory closed down at four o'clock, giving him and Ernie an early day plus a whole day on Sunday not devoted to the hustle and bustle of running what was now a sizeable undertaking. As the door opened she espied the familiar frame of Ray Osbourne following him, jumping to her feet she ran and hugged him, giving him a welcoming kiss on the cheek.

"You smelt the tea," she laughed.

"I though I'd pop over and see you all today, I go for my final medical on Monday, then I shall swiftly become Mister Ray Osbourne."

"Mister Ray Osbourne M.C. and bar," Rose added, "they will never take that away from you."

"You can still be known as Captain Osbourne can't you?" Fred asked, "even though you are demobbed?"

"That's a bit of an affectation though isn't it? I know after the last lot that captains who had never set foot in a trench came back requiring to be addressed as captain this or captain that. I don't think it will happen this time."

As they were talking the two guardsmen appeared through the doorway. They instantly froze to attention as they saw the officer, dressed in ordinary battledress with the purple and white Military Cross ribbon on his chest, this containing the silver rosette which indicated he had been decorated twice for gallantry.

"Come in and sit down," Rose invited them. They remained standing where they were. Instantly she sized up the situation. Men in the ranks don't sit down with officers, particularly in the Guards she speculated. To Ray and her father she said "These two men are Davies 309 and Davies 432 – have I got the numbers right?"

"Yes ma'am," they chorused.

"Right, well this is my father Mr Chandler, and this is Captain Osbourne, so now you know each other you can sit down and have your tea." Hesitantly they did as she asked, accepting gratefully a piece of homemade cake she proffered each of them. "These two young men" (they were years older than she was!) "are looking after the two majors who arrived today. They will be here later this evening."

"You will be having a house full again then," Ray commented.

"Not quite full," Fred answered quietly and sadly.

"Of course not, how stupid of me," Ray was embarrassed at his own lack of thoughtfulness.

To the puzzled guardsmen Rose explained, "We lost my mother on New Year's Eve."

The two men expressed their condolences, 309 adding, "Well, you are very brave taking people in, very brave, so soon." Finishing their tea and cake, the two men stood up, thanked Rose, clicked to attention to Ray, turned about and went up to finish their work.

At around nine o'clock that evening a P.U. pulled up outside. The two majors had arrived. Fred let them in, closely joined by Rose emerging from the sitting room where she had been writing a letter to Mark, telling him of the new 'lodgers' and accurately forecasting the substance of the reply she would get regarding this intelligence. The two men were very similar in build and appearance. Tall, of course, a little over six feet, not heavily built, both early thirties, both wearing wedding rings Rose speedily noticed, both with very well tailored battledresses – if they're as posh as that in battledress what will they be like in service dress, or mess dress come to that was Fred's immediate thought. They each had the K.G. V Jubilee and K.G. VI Coronation medals, which indicated they were regular officers; even Fred was a little in awe of these military aristocrats.

Shaking hands with Fred and then Rose, the first major announced, "I'm David Wrighton-Browne – this is Dafydd Rees-Evans."

Rose, totally un-awestruck asked, "Since your first names sound almost the same, how are they different?"

David explained that his home was on the English borders, hence the English sounding name. He continued, "Dafydd has the Welsh version, he comes from Carmarthen. There is no 'v' in the Welsh language, hence the letter 'f' is pronounced 'v', and the 'a' is pronounced as in 'bat.' So Dafydd is almost the same as David, except for the 'a'."

"If that explanation was designed to de-mystify me I'm afraid it hasn't succeeded," Rose laughed, "but come on in and I will show you your rooms. Oh, and by the way, my sister-in-law Megan comes from Carmarthen, or at least a mile or two outside on the Tenby road."

"What's her family name?" asked Dafydd.

"Lloyd, her father is Trefor Lloyd, a farmer."

"Shall we be meeting her?"

"Yes, she will be here with the children tomorrow. She speaks Welsh, but I imagine she will be a trifle rusty by now. She has been here for some years."

"Well, we will put our gas masks and stuff into our rooms and come down again if we may."

"Oh please do – come into the kitchen – everybody congregates in the kitchen, it's by far the warmest place in the house." Rose led them upstairs.

Ten minutes later they re-appeared. They still had the clipped accents and superior attitudes of peacetime guards' officers but looked a little more ordinary in the sloppy pullovers they had each pulled on. Fred opened the proceedings.

"Do guards' officers sink to the level of drinking beer?" Fred asked, "I'm afraid my scotch ran out a week ago."

"A glass of beer would be most acceptable," David replied. Whereupon Fred withdrew to the cupboard under the stairs, which all visitors to Chandlers Lodge speedily became aware was the repository of a stockpile of liquid gold, namely Whitbreads' Light Ale. He extracted two quart bottles from a crate and took them back to the kitchen, decanted the nectar into thin pint glasses and handed one to each of their new guests.

"Cheers."

"By jove" Dafydd exclaimed, "I swear this is the best I have ever tasted."

"It's the Kentish hops, best there are."

They sat talking for an hour or so, the two officers then going off to bed. Fred's comment to Rose as he got up to lock up was "Looks as though they will fit in."

The next morning, Sunday, Fred was about early; he had a Home Guard parade at 9.30. Just as he was about to leave at 9 o'clock, the two Majors appeared. Fred was second in command of the Sandbury company, a captain. Seeing him the two majors stopped in their tracks, looking at Fred's medal ribbons indicating past campaigns on the North West Frontier, in the South African War, and the Great War of 1914-18, these campaign ribbons preceded by his O.B.E. awarded the previous year, and his Military Medal won in the trenches, or to be more exact, attacking from the trenches. David pointed to them.

"Mr Chandler, you didn't say a word about all this. You know more about soldiering than we two put together."

"I suspect gentlemen you've got a great deal of soldiering to do in the near future and not on this side of the Channel either."

"From what I know, and from what I suspect, it will never be as horrific as you chaps had on the Western Front."

"I'll remind you of your saying that in a couple of years' time," Fred laughingly replied. He was not to know that this short meeting imbued a respect in them for their host which totally neutralised the innate superiority they automatically enjoyed in being officers of His Majesty's Foot Guards. Later in the day they were able to meet most of the rest of the family, they being much amused by the short bursts of Welsh between Dafydd and Megan, who it transpired, were almost neighbours back home, although neither of them for obvious reasons saw much of their homeland. As Megan said to Rose and Fred later, "I say we are more or less neighbours, except that the Rees-Evans family own half the county compared to our thousand acres." The general opinion was that the two majors were not as 'toffy-nosed' as they might have expected – once you got to know them!

The next morning 24th January, the eight o'clock news broadcast to a jubilant nation that the 8th Army had entered Tripoli led by the 27th Armoured Division, of which Mark Laurenson and Charlie Crew were part. This latter fact led to Rose receiving two very unexpected telephone calls, the first from Charlie's father, Lord Ramsford, during which conversation Rose asked whether he had heard from David in Yugoslavia. He had not, but said he would make enquiries and ring her in the next day or so. Casually – very casually – he asked after "your friend Mrs Coates, was she and the children well?" Rose, a great 'fixer' replied by giving his Lordship Cecely's day-time telephone number at the shop so that he could 'ask her himself.' He laughed a trifle sheepishly at being caught out, but thanked her nevertheless. 'The shop' was a boutique, 'County Style,' originally owned by David's wife Pat. Pat was killed by enemy aircraft whilst driving a canteen on the Sandbury aerodrome, the shop being now managed by Pat's original assistant Mrs Draper, helped by Cecely who needed something to occupy her.

The second call was from Lord Ramsford's father, the Earl of Otbourne, Charlie's grandfather. Rose had stayed at Ramsford Grange with David, Pat and Charlie, the Earl having visited Sandbury on a number of occasions. He had a long chat with Rose about the exciting news from Africa, about little Jeremy and whether she had heard from Charlie and Mark. "I get one four page letter from that blighter Charlie every month," he complained, "and he doesn't tell me much." The Earl had secretly hoped that Charlie and Rose would get together, he was very fond of her, but when Laurenson came on the scene, he realised his hopes would not materialise.

And so the dismal grey month of January passed. The price of coal, strictly rationed, went up by a shilling a ton, Herman Goering decided not to bother them for a change, the guardsman settled in at the camp and so far had caused no disturbances in the town. The two majors gradually became part of the family; the two servants came and went, looking after their officers quietly and efficiently. The news was getting even better with the advance of the 8th Army continuing towards Tunisia and the 1st Army moving eastward along the Algerian coast, the R.A.F. increasing their pay-back offensives, and above all the steady advances of the Russians, the great victory at Stalingrad being expected at any moment. The icing on the cake was the announcement that the Americans had launched their first bombing raid, on Wilhelmshaven, the precursor of a day-by-day assault, which along with the R.A.F. at night was to create havoc in German war production. However, with the resurgence of the hopes and aspirations of the thinking population was the knowledge that sooner or later, sooner if the Russians were to have their way, we and the Americans had to cross that narrow strip of water called 'The English Channel' and thrust bayonets into German bodies once again.

Chapter Three

Harry Chandler sat at the mess table with Major Clive Hollis, Captain Robbie Stewart and Ang Choon Guan, the communist camp leader. Clive was to outline their strategy for the next three months. He commenced by telling them they were to have a visit from the officer commanding the six camps of Force 136 in the next few weeks, who would, he was sure, be very pleased with what they had achieved so far. In their six operations in the last six months they had caused considerable damage, killed upwards of forty Japanese for the loss of only two of their own comrades and had become, if not masters of the jungle – no man would ever master the jungle short of cutting it down, even then it would grow again as soon as he turned his back! – if not masters of the jungle at least they had learnt how to live in it and fight from it. He spread an Ordnance Survey map on the table.

"Our first objective will be the Rest House near Batu Anam."

He pointed to it on the map.

"It is some five miles south of the town, so will be much easier to attack than if it were in the centre. Only officers use it. We shall march due north to this point, then turn west to hit the trunk road where it crosses the main tributary of the Muar river, by this means we shall have good cover all the way, and the Rest House is only about a quarter of a mile up the road. There is a problem. The bridge will be guarded. The two men we sent to reconnoitre this bridge before Christmas say there is a sentry at each end, but the guard itself is a mile away in the outbuildings of the Rest House. The sentries tend to wander up to each other at one end of the bridge or the other and have a chat. We have got to eliminate them without making a noise. This is where you come in Mr Chandler. Do you think you could eliminate them with your blowpipe?"

When Colonel Llewellyn had visited them some months ago he had, as guides, two of the aborigines whose forbears had lived in Malaya for thousands of years before Stamford Raffles first arrived. Harry had befriended them, as a result they had taught him how to make and use the bamboo blow pipe which fired a dart, poisoned with resin from the indigenous Ipoh tree, to kill their prey, birds, monkeys, tree rats and so on. Unlike curare, used by similar people in Borneo and South America which paralysed the victim when hit, the Ipoh resin killed in seconds. When the orang asli left, Harry had made a couple of blowpipes and practised with them every day until he was deadly up to thirty or forty yards. So far he had not used the poison, but the aborigines had shown him where there was an Ipoh tree not far from the camp from which he could tap his deadly liquid.

Harry answered the major. "I could do that Sir," – although he and the other four Europeans were normally on Christian name terms when together, in front of Choon Guan and the other Chinese they always addressed each other by their rank, Harry being a warrant officer class one, i.e. an R.S.M., was addressed as 'Mister.'

"I could do that, although of course it would have to be in daylight, and I would have to get within thirty or forty yards of them."

"Well, we've got to polish the plan up, but in general terms it will go like this. We will move you close just before dawn and park you in the beluka at the south end of the bridge. You will then play by ear, or rather by eye as to when it will be the right time to liquidate them. The second they are down we will move up to the Rest House, kill the guards and officers there who will be asleep and hot foot it back to you, where you and your party will be positioned to cover us should anyone come in pursuit. There will be no one on the road because of the curfew, but that would not include the possibility of an army truck coming along. Once we're all back in the beluka they will never find us. I want the whole operation from the time you despatch the sentries until we get back into the beluka to be over in fifteen minutes, we shall practise that on the ground here until the men are sick of it. Fortunately one of Choon Guan's men used to work in the Rest House before the occupation. Since we have a plan of every room, we shall not waste time going through unnecessary rooms. Any questions so far?"

Robbie Stewart asked the question which had already presented itself to Harry.

"Sir, supposing the Japs have women in bed with them."

"Our men will be given orders to do all they can not to harm women, or Malay servants they may encounter. However, they will be given very strict instructions indeed that they are in no way to jeopardise the operation, or any part of it, if women attempt to interfere or do not instantly obey the orders of our men. They too will be shot. As Choon Guan has said to me when I raised this with him, the Japanese killed millions of women when they captured Nanking so that the gutters ran with blood. Our Chinese comrades will not forget that."

There were no further questions; the answer just provided giving the group a very sobering aspect to their previous ebullience.

"Right then, when this bloody rain eases off, we will mark out the plan on the parade ground and start our practising until we could almost do it blindfold."

Harry went off to his rooms to find his friend Matthew Lee, and another of the Christian Chinese just finishing off the repair to his roof.

"Since when did doctors become roofing specialists?" he asked. "Thanks anyway, I was not looking forward to that job – too many creepy crawlies up there for me, that is if they have not all been drowned."

"Well, we did find a small python up there," Matthew replied, "but he was only about twelve feet long, and as he was asleep we left him there."

"God, you are joking I hope, the very thought of the possibility of it gives me the willies."

The small Christian community centred around Matthew's treatment room which was so different to the main bulk of the communist guerrillas in the barracks, mainly, Harry thought, because the communists were constantly being bombarded with exhortations, lectures on political correctness, the party line, Marxist philosophy and so on to the extent that their faces were one continuous picture of proletarian gravity. The Chinese were generally a race easy to amuse, ready to see the funny side of things. The picture of the 'inscrutable oriental' was usually gained by some western idiot shouting at them or endeavouring to show his or her superiority in some way. Now their collective communist face was being changed by the commissars to be equally as inscrutable as the rickshaw coolie being told he was not going fast enough up the Orchard Road in Singapore. Matthew's little band of six kept on good terms with the communist block; some of whom they would have known in peace time, but kept their distance from them. As one of his not quite so religious friends adjudged "They are a miserable lot of sods."

The next day they had several dry hours which enabled them to mark out the layout of the Rest House in the surface of the parade ground. It was a single story building with twenty bedrooms plus the usual dining and recreation rooms. The garages at the rear which used to house overnight the Rolls Royce's and Morris Oxford's of the travelling wealthy had been partly converted into a barrack room for the guard of six men and an N.C.O., two of whom would be on a four hour stint on the bridge a short distance away. They went into every smallest detail they could, which way the door was hinged, which ones would be locked, any good hedge cover to conceal them from the road in case a military vehicle came long, and so on. Whilst the layout was being prepared every man was told to think and make suggestions, one small observation now might save a man's life later, even save the operation.

The next two days were closed down again by the rain, but on the Monday they were able to redraw the plan in the parade ground earth and have two further days' practice until Clive was happy with both the plan and the method of operation.

Harry, in the meantime, was practising hard with his blowpipe and had reached a pitch of near perfection. He still had yet however to get his 'ammunition' from the Ipoh tree, about an hour from the camp. He had made a cylindrical container from a piece of hollow bamboo and fitted it with a very tight stopper kept secure by a 1½" screw scrounged from the two navy radio operator types with them. Lieut Joe Rogers and Chief Petty Officer Terry Martin had been with them from the beginning but were not called upon to take part in operations; they were responsible for base defence and of course communications. The brass screw was drilled through the top of the stopper and matching holes in the tube, and fitted with a wing nut to make it easy to unscrew. Harry was not entirely happy with this arrangement, although it was, to all intents and purposes, leak-proof. He felt as though he would be carrying a mini time bomb around. *If* it leaked, *if* he had a cut anywhere and *if* it went in the cut, he would be up there harping – he didn't fancy that at all. Joe Rogers came to the rescue. He had a small silver hip flask which carried a couple of double whiskeys and which had a cap designed to keep secure the most precious liquid known to man, namely usquebaugh, the water of life. He gladly lent it on the understanding it was washed out thoroughly afterwards! "We'll blow steam into it from a kettle," Harry promised.

All being ready they moved off on Thursday 14th. It would take two days to reach the bridge, using mainly game trails. Clive had had parties over the months they had been in Camp Six charting all the game trails, which by their very nature were more or less permanent. Very faint sometimes, but rarely did they get grown over so completely as to be unrecognisable to what was now the professional eye of the guerrilla. They could now go over a days' march from the camp in more or less any direction using the maps they had compiled, which was a big advantage over having to march entirely by compass.

They reached the bridge late on Friday and camped in the jungle about a mile away. The Saturday was spent in careful reconnaissance of the bridge, and the Rest House itself through field glasses. They had chosen a Sunday attack, firstly there would be little, if any, traffic on the road at dawn when they intended to strike, secondly the Rest House was known to be well patronised at weekends, with officers bringing their popsies out of town, up into the hills, from Kluang and Malacca.

Clive was quite happy with the plan but he did realise there was one weak point – getting rid of the sentries. Suppose they didn't both come to the south end of the bridge so that Harry could pot them? Suppose only one came? The land either side of the river was marshy, thick with reeds and all manner of large rhubarb like spiky plants. It would be impossible to wade through that lot to swim across to the north side, and God knows what was lurking in the river itself. He had a contingency plan in that if they could not despatch the sentries he would march upstream to a point where he could cross and come down on the north side, but after a further look at that line of approach he concluded it would be impracticable due to the numerous obstacles on that approach and the fact they would have lost the element of surprise. The success of the venture therefore depended on the sentries being in the right place at the right time and on Harry being a crack shot. He sweated at the thought.

At 3 a.m. on Sunday morning they moved out. Every man was tense at the thought that in an hour or so they would be slaughtering their loathsome enemy. Harry led the way with his section of eight men who would, when he had killed the sentries, form the covering party to stop the unlikely approach of enemy from the south, and then, should they need it, to give covering fire to the raiding party, retreating from the north. He would, he put to himself, be first in and last out – what have I done to deserve this?

Half an hour before dawn Harry reached the edge of the beluka. They were only thirty or forty yards from the end of the bridge. He signalled those behind him to stop. Clive moved noiselessly up to him. The land between them and the road was covered in bushes some six feet high, interspersed with grasses beaten down by the heavy rain which had fallen in the previous days. Harry whispered, "I'll go forward now, and give you the signal when I've taken them out."

Clive nodded in the dark, "Good luck Harry." With one of the Christian boys, Peter So, who was carrying a torch which he would flash back when the targets had been eliminated; Harry slowly made his way forward. He could not, as yet, see the sentries as he was somewhat below the level of the bridge. As they got nearer he could pick out the first one, standing in the middle of the road, looking up at the stars, eastwards, obviously waiting for the dawn to come up. Where was the other one? He moved forward very carefully until he was only ten to fifteen yards from the end of the bridge. He could now get a clear view down the road but could see nothing moving in the dark. Where the hell was the other bloody sentry? He could feel himself becoming agitated, recognised the signs and consciously took a grip on himself. It would start to get light in about twenty minutes, and once it started it happened very quickly.

Suddenly he nearly jumped out of his skin. From no further than five or six yards away on the edge of the road, the other sentry emerged, talking loudly to his companion. He was pulling up his braces obviously having been what squaddies euphemistically refer to has 'having been attending to the call of nature.' Harry immediately noted he had no rifle with him, he had either left it with his companion or leaning against the bridge. Harry raised his loaded blowpipe. The two would be together in another yard or two, as they met he puffed at, what to him now at ten yards, was an unmissable target. As the dart winged its way, Harry dived into his quiver for the second dart, then carefully but speedily loaded it. Taking a second aim he saw the slow motion death throes of his first quarry. He had grasped the shoulders of his comrade, and in doing had knocked his rifle from his shoulder. As it clattered to the road, his mystified compatriot was trying to hold him upright, asking what was wrong with him, had he been bitten by a snake? Was he having a heart attack? As he became, literally, dead weight, the other sentry dropped him, presenting Harry with another perfect target. He too went to his maker not knowing what had hit him. Harry turned to Peter So. "Flash the light," he said harshly, he had far from enjoyed killing in this manner, although as he had moralised to himself on many occasions before, there was no difference between eliminating your enemy, especially this bestial enemy, with a poisoned dart that there was with a .45 Tommy gun bullet. In Harry's code of fair play however, it was way below the belt.

Clive led the men up, seeing the bodies in the road hugged Harry. "Bloody marvellous. We've got a quarter of an hour before dawn, we shall get there, get it done and be back before they know what hit the bastards." They ran off in a long stream, keeping on the side verges; Harry was surprised how quietly forty men could move.

Quickly he organised his own little party.

"Drag the bodies off the road. Take up your positions." They had barely carried out these orders when all hell was let loose a few hundred yards away. It went mostly according to plan. Only fourteen of the twenty rooms were occupied, one of those by a Swiss Red Cross worker and his wife – at least I suppose it was his wife, Clive surmised later. They were unmolested. Since the Japanese officers were in what militarily speaking could be described as 'undress order,' it was difficult to establish what ranks they were. They had trouble with only one of the women companions. She, a Chinese, was so in love with her bow-legged little companion that she jumped out of bed after him when they first heard the noise and wrapped herself round him, her arms round his neck, her legs around his belly. They didn't know whether she was trying to protect him or whether she couldn't leave him. It mattered little. He threw her off to try and get to the chair in the corner of the room where his revolver was hanging in its holster. The two guerrillas cut him down, then executed the woman without any compunction whatsoever.

The complete action had taken only a little over ten minutes. Some Malay staff, the Red Cross people, and a Sikh jagger or night-watchman, were driven into the front garden, several well placed phosphorous bombs were thrown into the buildings, Clive blew his three-blast whistle signal and they moved off up the road to the bridge. They estimated that including the guards, two Jap orderlies in the cookhouse, and the officers, they had eliminated over twenty of the enemy. Harry gave the main party five minutes before he followed, first pulling the darts out of his victims and throwing them in the river, having arrived at the conclusion it would do no harm for the Japs to be confused as to how the men had died.

The long uphill journey back was a nightmare in that the monsoon deluged them every inch of the way. They had no sleep on Sunday night because of the weather despite their tiredness, so that by Monday midday the unit began to struggle badly. Under normal circumstances Clive would have called a halt and bivouacked, giving himself an extra day to make the trek, there were however two men who were beginning to look very sick, and they were all out of food. He gave them a half hour break, on moving out put Harry and Robbie at the rear to keep the tail from falling back, and walked up and down the line wherever he could encouraging, goading, heartening them, and in the process, covering twice the distance the men themselves were having to cover. They staggered into Camp Six four hours after dark, welcomed by the cheering base unit with Tilley lamps. As they eventually formed some sort of formulation in front of the company office Clive stood in front of them, silence fell.

"You know what is coming next. Weapon inspection in half an hour. Parade, fall out!!"

Wet, cold, miserable, hungry and desperately tired, there was not one word of dissent, the men turned away, the two sick men, now very sick were led away by Matthew and a half hour later the weapon parade was held in the huts, so that at long last the men could dry off, put fresh clothes on, eat the meal prepared for them and fall into a sleep of exhaustion before a late reveille on Tuesday morning.

At six o'clock on Tuesday morning Matthew went to Clive's room, with great difficulty managing eventually to awaken him.

"Sir, the two sick men are very ill, they have all the symptoms of tick-typhus. I have done everything I can to keep the fever down but I'm afraid I am losing the battle." Clive immediately jumped out of bed, pulled on a pair of shorts and sandals and hurried with Matthew to the medical room. The men were lying flat, sweating profusely, showing the tell tale eruptions of purple spots, already in a state of semi-delirium.

"We shall keep them isolated and keep a very watchful eye on the remainder, Sir, but I have little here with which to treat them, and even if I had, it would not be very helpful."

"Do your best Matthew, do your best, that's all you can do."

Despite his best efforts, which he would be the first to acknowledge were vestigial by any description, the two men were dead by mid-afternoon. Graves were dug for them at the corner of the parade ground, into which they were placed by Matthew and two of his helpers. A firing party was paraded, which simply pulled the triggers of unloaded rifles, they could not afford gunshot noises, they had no doubt they were being looked for now with a vengeance. They were not mistaken. Back in Kluang Major General Takahashi had that afternoon had the dressing down of his life from an irate General Yamashita in Singapore. It was a wonder the wires had not melted down, such was the ferocity of the castigation, the two main areas of attack being he had made no move against the bandits and secondly one of the officers killed in the Rest House was a nephew of one of the generals on the Imperial General Staff, known personally to the Emperor himself. Takahashi endeavoured to excuse himself by saying he had arranged for the search to begin but the monsoon had grounded the two captured British Tiger Moths which were to be used for the purpose. At this Yamashita nearly exploded.

"Find them," he had screamed, "find them even if you have to go after them bare-footed yourself," and with that he slammed the field telephone down, leaving an extremely shaken major-general standing to attention and wondering what the hell to do next. He was in a quandary really. He had ordered no army men to go after them; there was therefore no one at whom he could scream. The air force friend with the Tiger Moths, was doing him, or would be doing him, a favour; therefore he could hardly scream at him. It must have been the only time in his illustrious career he had been unable to scream at, or slap, a subordinate for some real or imaginary misdeed. It was an upsetting experience. It did, however, galvanise him into organising a two-pronged combing of sections of the jungle. These being in the order of some seven hundred square miles, with the possibility firstly of the camp being anywhere in that area, and secondly so well concealed a searcher could get to within two hundred yards and probably not see it, made the task virtually impossible. After a month having not covered a tenth of it, and with men falling sick by the score, he gave up, having in the meantime applied for a transfer to the Philippines.

On Sunday 24th January they had a coded radio message to say 'Sunrise' would be visiting them in a few days. This was the code name for the new C.O., Colonel Ransomes. This message was followed by a second message, which when C.P.O. Terry Martin finally decoded it, put him into a quandary. It ran:–

From: Brigadier Lord Ramsford

To: Officer Commanding Ops Force 136

Please advise W.O.I. Chandler H. that with deepest regret we have to inform him of the death of his mother Mrs Ruth Chandler on 31st December. The Duke and I tender our condolences and are keeping in close touch with the family.

Ramsford.

Terry was undecided as to whether he should take it direct to Harry or whether, as was the case with all incoming messages, he should present it to Clive. He decided on the latter course. Clive read it, sat back with a look of great sadness on his face and asked Terry if he would find Harry and get him to come in. He found him talking to Matthew in the medical room.

"Will you go and see Clive please Harry?" he asked.

Harry's inevitable reply was, "Certainly, what have I done now?" adding "or not done as the case may be?" He received no answering grin from Terry, which although the non-acquiescence in the little joke on the radio-man's part failed to register with Harry, it registered immediately with the perceptive Matthew. With Harry gone and in response to Matthew's raised eyebrows Terry told him of the cable.

"He is going to need us over the next few days," Matthew stated in a cheerless voice, "being so far away and unable to take part in the mourning will be very difficult for him.

And difficult it was. Harry came away from Clive in a daze, walked to his room, sat on the edge of his charpoy, where in a minute or so Matthew joined him.

"I am going to lead prayers this evening for the repose of the soul of your dear mother," he told him, "the major and the others are coming, do you think you will feel up to being with us?"

"Yes, of course. I'm very grateful to you. She was a very, very special lady."

"Now, tell me something about her which I can bring into the short homily I shall give."

"I didn't know you were a preacher."

"I was training as a medical missionary to go into China in a couple of years' time."

"The war has ruined all our lives."

"Not necessarily ruined them; maybe taught us how grateful we should be for what God has given us, and furthermore persuade us to overcome evil in all its forms. Perhaps then, when we take up our lives again, we shall be more tolerant, more compassionate, more understanding. There now, I'm practising my preaching again!" Harry gave him a trace of a smile and squeezed his arm.

It was a simple, fifteen minute service, after which Choon Guan came from the main billet, shook hands with Harry, a thing he had never done before, and told him, "All the men have heard of your great loss and we are sad for you. We know you are a very brave man and that you will bear this sorrow. Be sure our thoughts are with you," and with that he turned away leaving Harry with the thought that communists can't be all bad! However his brief flirtation with flippancy soon left him and he continued to suffer that bitter feeling of loss, the gripping pain in the pit of the stomach, the sickening sadness that he would never see his mother again, the thought of what the rest of the family so close to a home without his mother in it, were suffering and suddenly – where was David and did he know? When he went to bed that night he found an envelope on the table by his bed, with two tablets in it, on the outside of which Matthew had written, 'if you need them.'

"I don't take tablets," he told himself, but on this occasion, as midnight came and he tossed and turned, he did, and slept until his batman awakened him at eight o'clock, when the rest of the camp had been about for over an hour. He went about his tasks that day mechanically until he was jolted out of his languor by the faint sound of an aeroplane engine. This being the first clear day for some weeks Takahashi's air force friend had at last got his Tiger Moths cruising over the jungle canopy. Harry, stung into action, yelled for all to get on parade to cover the emergency. They had considered the likelihood of being spotted from the air would be remote, firstly because the aircraft the Japs had in Malaya were either transport or fighter planes, certainly not spotter planes, secondly the area they would have to cover was so enormous as to make the observation of one relatively tiny speck 'somewhere' in it to be very unlucky indeed. Nevertheless, although the huts were concealed by the overhanging trees, the patch which was the parade ground could possibly encourage the pilot of a small manoeuvrable plane like the Tiger Moth to come down and have a closer look. Prepared for this contingency Harry had organised piles of mainly evergreen vines and branches all along the edge of the open space which now this emergency had arisen the men responded to his yell by pulling over the sandy space. With forty men moving, as Harry described later, 'like the clappers,' the space was covered in a couple of minutes at which they all retired to the forest cover and told not to look up if the plane flew directly over. Although they could hear it cruising around for some little while, it did not fly directly over and even if it had done, the general consideration was it would see 'bugger all.'

Three days later the new colonel arrived. He brought with him two very pleasant surprises, and to Harry a piece of astonishing news.

Chapter Four

They were two days out of Bihac. Apart from being saddle sore and 'cold as charity, and that's pretty chilly, but it's not as cold as my poor willie,' as David put it, he and Paddy were making good progress to the south for the second part of their assignment of assessing the quality, efficiency and effectiveness of the Yugoslav partisans. The three months they had spent, mostly in the front line in Bosnia, had already convinced them of the superb organisation and fighting spirit of these men and women – twenty percent of the force was female – now they were to spend two months or so with the brigades on the borders of Montenegro before being taken off by submarine back to Alexandria and then on to Cairo. Their journey would take them entirely through what the Germans called 'Tito territory.' The huge swathe of mountainous country running down the centre of Yugoslavia was garrisoned by partisans, largely clothed and armed from the Italian and fascist militia prisoners taken in ambushes. So secure was this central ground that the large town of Uzice, in Western Serbia, which before the war was the main armaments manufacture of the country, was now securely partisan and turning out the standard Mauser previously used by the Serb army. It was to Uzice that David and Paddy were being conducted, prior to being sent off to the field brigade. Uzice was a journey of some two hundred miles. The weather, fortunately, was in the main good, in that they had no further blizzards, but the going was often bad, sometimes dangerous. However, they covered the distance in ten days, sleeping at night in barns and being fed either by local partisan units or the peasant farmers. At Uzice they said goodbye to their guides and were handed over to the southern area commander, an ex regular soldier named Pero Bozovic, a tall, distinguished looking man in a pre-war officer's uniform, but surmounted now with the Tito forage cap with its red star on the front. They gave him an immaculate British open handed salute, which he returned with the clenched fist salute to the forehead which had now become the standard among the partisans, inherited from the anti-fascist fighters in the Spanish Civil War. He spoke fairly good English.

"I welcome you to Uzice Major Chandler and Sergeant Major O'Riordan," he had considerable difficulty with 'O'Riordan.' "However, before I let you go I have a sadness to carry out. I have received a radio message sent to you at Bihac from Cairo which they have sent on to me as you travelled. He handed it to David.

David's shoulders visibly shrunk. Paddy noticing this asked "Something wrong Sir?" David handed him the Message Form. It read:–

INFORM MAJOR CHANDLER. BRIGADIER LORD
RAMSFORD REGRETS TO INFORM YOU OF THE DEATH
OF YOUR MOTHER RUTH CHANDLER ON NEW YEARS'
EVE. OUR SINCEREST CONDOLENCES
HOPGOOD BRIGADIER.

From force of habit from his Catholic upbringing, Paddy crossed himself. There was a silence for a number of seconds, broken by Paddy saying to the commandant, "She was a wonderful lady Sir, so she was." The commandant remained silent. David lifted his eyes.

"Thank you Sir for passing this information on to me."

"Now, if you go and rest and see me tomorrow morning I will tell you your plan of action at that time. All my staff are pleased to see you here and will help you all possible." He shook hands with them again; they saluted and followed his aide to their room where two comfortable beds awaited them. David sat on it, his face drained of colour.

"I can't imagine the world without my mother," he told Paddy. "She was never flustered, always had a solution for any problem whether it was romantic, physical or even financial. My father will be absolutely lost. Although to the world he appeared the head of the house he relied on her advice and common sense to the extent that he would not do a thing without getting her opinion first. Nearly all the officers we have had billeted at Chandlers Lodge have, at one time or another, come to her for counsel. Charlie Crew and Kenny Barclay loved her – she was really the nearest thing to a mother they ever had. Why should a loving decent person like that be taken so young? She was only fifty-two. That's no age these days. And now she won't be at my wedding. I wonder if they have laid her next to my Pat. I do hope so. Pat thought of her as her mother as well you know."

Paddy let him talk on without interruption.

"Jack Hooper will be devastated. It was because she was so kind to Pat when she was a thirteen year old that Jack became so fond of her and got to like us all. And poor Megan. She was like a mother to Megan, or perhaps a big sister, with Megan being so far away from her family. When I was younger I used to notice they had sort of womanly secrets together by the way they used to stop talking when I appeared on the scene. And Anni too. She was a real mother to Anni when we got her out of Germany. God Almighty, all the good she has done to be taken away from us like this." He threw himself on the bed burying his head in the clean linen covered pillow. Paddy just sat still and waited for him to regain his composure. After a while he sat up.

"Thanks for listening." Paddy gave no reply, just a fractional shrug of the shoulders.

The next morning they had a meeting with the commandant's chief of staff. "I am Branco Nedic. I have just heard that a big offensive is taking place against our brigades around Bihac, from whence you have just come." The chief of staff's interpreter, a former correspondent of the London Times newspaper spoke faultless English.

"This offensive is being carried out by the crack German SS Mountain Division, 'Prince Eugen.' They are completely ruthless, take no prisoners, and kill all the wounded, men and women." David and Paddy had the same thought going through their minds – the safety or otherwise of their friends Livia and her commandant, Todor Mavric.

"Now, your programme. You are to proceed to a brigade at Novi Bazar on the Montenegro border. They are facing German and Bulgarian troops on the east and Italians between them and the coast. I wish you good luck and thank you for all you have done and are doing for us."

They shook hands and for the rest of the day prepared themselves for an early start on Thursday morning. They were given good horses and were guided for the first day by a young boy, no more than twelve years of age but clad in a motley uniform with the inevitable red starred cap and carrying a captured Beretta submachine gun. He spoke no English but by this time David had picked up a considerable vocabulary of Serbo-Croat language. He had a gift for languages which had stood him in good stead on a number of occasions already during this war. At the end of the day they were handed over to a young woman to take them the remainder of their journey. That night they stayed in a peasant's barn, overrun with rats and accommodating two cows and a goat. A combination of scurrying noises from the rats, it seemed almost continuous ploppings from one cow or the other, the pungent smell of the goat tethered only six feet away and the particularly vicious biting of voracious fleas gave them little sleep. They were glad to be up at day break and on their way, scratching themselves continuously until they reached their destination, thanked their guide, then stripped down for the most assiduous of all flea hunts.

"Did you notice Sir; the bloody fleas didn't seem to have a go at her at all?"

There was no answer to that.

The area commander here passed them on to a field commander with whom they would operate until the end of February when they would begin their journey to the coast. He was a lean, cheerful man – "Just call me Stjepan," he said, they did not query this but assumed although he was a partisan he was no communist and did not much like being addressed as comrade. He had a young girl, probably sixteen or seventeen they thought, who was introduced as his daughter, and also spoke good English, which she said she had learnt at school.

"On Monday we are moving out to attack a village a day's march away occupied by Italians. We are hoping to replenish our food and ammunition as well as kill a few fascists. However, although they cannot dig in because the ground is too rocky, they have built strong points from rocks and have lots of barbed wire around them which stops us from rushing them. What we do therefore is to fire on them from an angle while our smallest people crawl under the wire and lob grenades into the defences. Some of the Italians fight hard; others hate the Germans as much as we do and if they are not well led swiftly put their hands up. They know we will only take what we need and go, we do not kill Italian prisoners."

"What about German prisoners?" David asked.

Stjepan looked at his daughter and replied, "There is no such thing as a German prisoner, or Bulgarian or Hungarian."

They rested over the weekend and checked over the kit they would carry for the three-day operation through the mountains to the borders of Montenegro. When they moved out they were struck by how young Stjepan's troops were. He had probably a hundred and twenty men for this attack, very few of whom were much over twenty years old. They moved in the typical two-file mountain warfare column, scouts two hundred yards ahead. These lads have obviously been well trained David and Paddy agreed. Although there was snow underfoot the going was quite good and they reached a small hamlet about three miles from their target late in the afternoon. While a meal was being prepared Stjepan and his second in command stated they were going forward to reconnoitre. David said that he and Paddy would join him if he had no objections. They had only half an hour of daylight at a bluff overlooking the little village, during which time Stjepan made a sketch of the defences, the barbed wire enclosures, and in particular any likely lines of approach for his grenade throwers. While he was doing this he asked David and Paddy if they could make a careful search to establish whether there were any minefields in the wire entanglements. They would be anti-personnel mines of course – the partisans had no tanks. David and Paddy made a careful search through their binoculars for any sight of tell-tale trip wires, but could see nothing. This did not mean there were no mines there, they may have been sown without trip wires relying on an attacker to tread on them, but trip wires attached to them greatly enhanced their effectiveness. On the balance of probability there were therefore no mines.

That evening Stjepan made his plan. There were six stone emplacements, each about six to eight feet in diameter each connected to a wooden hut where the section garrisoning that strong point lived. The hut and the short access path to the hut were further protected against rifle fire by stone walls some five to six feet high. In the centre of the village would be the officers' quarters and the stores. They had calculated from previous observation there would be a full company stationed here, something like one hundred and fifty men. Hearing this David's eyebrows rose at Paddy. To attack a strong point with one hundred and fifty defenders with only around one hundred and twenty very young, relatively untrained, amateur combatants was to say the least, brave to the point of foolhardiness. Stjepan obviously thought differently. He announced his plan. Six parties of six would crawl under the wire with grenades to the edges of the stone enclosures; on the way carefully emptying the stones out of the tin cans the Italians had hung on the wire in the hope that a prospective attacker would rattle them. They would wait for the signal. Six more parties of six riflemen would be positioned to cover them from outside the wire. This left the remainder with the one machine gun they possessed, a Czech ZB27, the forerunner of the famous British Bren Gun, to storm the entrance to the village, fired in by the ZB27. As in all operations in the dark – the attack was scheduled for half an hour before dawn – over unknown or little known country; all sorts of things could go wrong. A dog barking a warning could render the most careful planning useless. A partisan with a head cold sneezing at the wrong time, or falling over a tree root, and so on and so on, could all precipitate disaster. The one factor in their favour was the Italians would much rather be back home in Italy and leave the Germans to get on with their war, in which the average Italian had never had a lot of interest, nor enthusiasm for.

They moved out a little before two hours before dawn. The six grenade parties all got into the wire and got up against the stone emplacements without incident. This in itself was, David considered, something of a miracle. Thirty-six men crawling around a camp undiscovered for up to half an hour without something untoward happening certainly would not be something you would bet your last fiver on. They obviously knew what they were doing, and did it well.

A quarter of an hour before dawn, the Italians left their guard huts and stood-to, chattering away together, some pointing their rifles over the stone walls, oblivious of the grenade throwers huddled against the emplacements immediately below them. Five minutes later Stjepan blew his whistle and all hell was let loose. The grenadiers let the safety levers fly off, counted two, lobbed them into the enclosures and flattened themselves away from the rock walls – the last thing they would want would be to have a loose wall fall on them. By letting the safety levers go, the grenade would explode within a second of hitting the ground thus giving the defenders no time to throw them out again.

The covering parties now opened up. They were so sited that although they fired over the enclosures, they were aiming at the central group of buildings. In the meantime the assault party, which included David and Paddy, under the cover given by the ZB27, stormed the double barbed wire gates and fortified guardhouse. There was little resistance. The fact that a well choreographed attack had taken place on all the strong points was enough for the Italian captain to immediately wave a white flag from the central building, and all firing ceased.

While the second part of the plan was put into effect, namely the 'requisitioning' of the food, clothing and ammunition, including, they were extremely pleased to find, four mules, David and Paddy approached the officer. They had replaced their combat hats with their red berets, seeing which the officer sprang to attention, saluted and asked, "English?"

David replied, "Yes."

The captain spoke no English, but being in a mountain regiment from the Austrian border, he spoke quite good German. He told David the men were sick of being here, they could see no merit in fighting Germany's war. David asked him why it was then that Mussolini had taken possession of parts of Slovenia and Dalmatia as integral parts of metropolitan Italy now, as well as putting a governor in Montenegro and annexing Kosovo. "Mussolini," the captain answered slowly "is so puffed up with his own vainglory he must have an Empire, like England. He has lost his empire in Africa; he must have one in Europe to take its place." He obviously thought very little of his Duce. He paused for a moment. "Perhaps he will not live much longer to enjoy it."

"Do you mean there is a plot against him?"

"I am much too junior to know anything about it, but my uncle is on the general staff and I know from hints he made to me when I was on leave six months ago that if we were driven out of Libya he would not survive for long, we have lost nearly a million men – and for what purpose?"

As he finished the sentence they heard three blasts on Stjepan's whistle, which meant all outlying picquets to rejoin for the return journey, less a rearguard to cover them for an hour before they too quickly returned to base.

David asked the captain's name and for some reason his family address – "You never know, we may meet again."

"Yes Sir – if we both survive." He shook hands with them both and saluted. It seemed odd that had he been pointing his revolver at them only a few minutes ago, they would have killed him, now they were shaking hands. War is a funny thing. An even funnier thing was that in a few months time when Italy signed an armistice with the allies, that complete division took up arms with the partisans.

Stjepan had lost two men killed. He asked David to ask the captain if he would bury them for him, to which the captain replied they would be having a service of committal for his own fallen and would include the two adversaries.

They reached their base in the early hours of the following morning after a long and gruelling march. Each man, in addition to carrying his normal compliment of equipment, rifle, ammunition, water bottle etc, was laden with around twenty kilos of food, equipment or ammunition. The mules were loaded with four captured machine guns and their ammunition, as well as rolls of blankets and waterproof capes. It was testimony to their fitness and discipline that none fell out. The half dozen men who had been wounded were not so incapacitated they could not walk; nevertheless, they were placed around the mules so that they could hang on to their loads and by that means be helped along. David and Paddy each took a load, they too by the time they reached camp being, as Paddy put it, "as knackered as I've ever been," to which David replied, "But does that include Bangor I wonder?"

In early February news came of a major defeat of the partisans on the River Neretva by a German S.S. mountain division, assisted by Russian Cossacks who had defected from the Red Army. Ten thousand partisans were trapped in the valley of the river, which ran more or less east to west. On the western end there was savage fighting between the two forces, but the Germans meanwhile had gone up into the mountains on either side of the river, moved eastward inland in parallel columns and then after advancing for some ten miles had turned inwards to meet each other down in the valley producing a cul-de-sac completely surrounding the partisans. Stjepan's brigade, with others, was ordered forward to cover the retreat of the Neretva forces and to keep the passes back into the mountains open so that the wounded could be evacuated. Nearly five thousand were lost, but it was here that David and Paddy found themselves fighting Germans, for the second time in David's case. Time after time the partisans, in groups of about a hundred, outflanked the German positions and kept them pinned down whilst their comrades struggled through the holes in the cordon which had surrounded them. On four separate occasions they stormed German defences, overcame them, thereby providing yet another sector through which the beleaguered partisans could filter out of the net, carrying as many as they could of their wounded with them, knowing that any left behind, and many had to be left behind, would be butchered.

For five days the battle raged. They had little sleep. The Germans had brought up mountain artillery, the shells from which caused more casualties as a result of hitting rock and sending splinters far and wide than they did by impact. However they were vulnerable in that in the wooded country partisan snipers were able to work around them and pick off the gunners. At the end of the five days the S.S. Division withdrew, wisely deciding not to follow the partisans up into the mountains. They had inflicted a major blow on Tito's forces in that part of Yugoslavia, but the five thousand that did get away would live to fight another day.

Three days after they got back to their base, David and Paddy were asked to go with Stjepan to a command post in a neighbouring village some three miles away. On arrival they were surprised to see several vehicles, some motorcycles and as David and Paddy swiftly observed, a much better standard of dress than that which obtained in the field brigades. They were met at the H.Q. building by an officer with the new badges of rank on his uniform – these had not yet filtered down to the field brigades – two red bars surmounted by a red star on each cuff, the equivalent of a major. He led them in to an inner office where, to their surprise, they were introduced to Comrade Tito himself. They immediately came to attention and saluted, the salute being returned in the British fashion as the smiling partisan leader walked across the bare boarded floor to meet them, his hand held out in greeting. Shaking hands vigorously he said, his words being interpreted by the A.D.C. who had met them, "I have heard some stories about you and your comrade major. You were sent here to observe, but I understand you have been killing all sorts of fascists as well in your spare time." He roared with laughter at his joke.

"Well Sir, we had to keep our hand in," – the interpreter had some difficulty with that expression.

He sat them down and ordered coffee and for a little over an hour questioned them about their experiences, their observations on the content, operation, discipline and morale of his forces in comparison with British troops, and a dozen other aspects of their fight against the fascists. He studiously drew Paddy into the discussion, saying that he knew the backbone of the British Army was the professional soldier of Paddy's calibre. He went on to express his gratitude for their coming

"And trust you can persuade your superiors that aid in the form of heavy weapons, tanks, even aircraft, will not be wasted. We are even now pinning down some fifteen to twenty divisions here. With support weapons we could annihilate them."

David explained to him that their terms of reference were to establish whether the sending of a large mission to his country to quantify the aid would be expedient. His report would wholeheartedly recommend this, not only material aid, but aircraft training, commando training and training in armoured warfare. "We are now quite good at armoured warfare as the Afrika Korps has now found out," David concluded.

Before they left the presence of this redoubtable leader – later to be the only communist leader to stand up to Stalin and win – he presented them with honorary badges of rank in the National Liberation Army of Yugoslavia, to give the partisans their full and proper name. David received brigade commander, an inverted V containing the red star, and Paddy received the badges carried by the A.D.C. namely two horizontal red bars surmounted by the red star.

"We shall honour these all our days Sir," David told him, "and will always remember all those very brave men and women we have lived and fought with."

When they rejoined Stjepan outside they discovered the interview had been scheduled to last only ten minutes – it had stretched to one hour and ten minutes – "You must be very important people," he joked.

Two days later they left Novi Bazar and their new friend Stjepan after much hugging, handshaking and back slapping. It is a feature of war that you meet someone, or a group of people, possibly for only a few days, yet your association is so concentrated that you remember them for the rest of your days. As Comrade Tito had commented, they were supposed to be there as observers, in fact they saw more direct action in those few weeks than many people saw in the whole war.

The plan was to journey to Kolasin, some sixty miles, the first part on horseback through friendly territory. At the river Lim they would part with their horses, be ferried over the river, and then journey on foot to the coast through Italian held territory. At the end of the first day they reached the river, were ferried over and accommodated overnight. The next morning they climbed back into the mountains, a party of five altogether, keeping a wary eye open for Italian patrols about which they had few fears having been told they were very thin on the ground and generally content to look the other way should they bump a partisan patrol. They slept the night in a somewhat decrepit and therefore draughty shepherds hut in a temperature of -5°C, the next day covering the final twenty miles to Kolasin.

They waited until after dark before moving into Kolasin and the safe house there, where they would be lodged until they received radio instructions about moving to the coast. The comrades in this outpost made them very welcome, affording them the unbelievable luxury of a bath in really hot water. Except for one occasion, they had forgotten where, for the past months, they had had to make do with an all-over wash, and that usually in the cold with only barely warm water. They were there for four days before the order came to move to the safe house on the coast north of Castel Nuovo. This was a distance of sixty miles on the map, but by virtue of the fact they had to make detours and trek over little used mountain tracks across the two ranges between Kolasin and the sea meant they had to allow for up to eighty miles, or four long days.

On the second night they moved at dusk into a largish barn, a short distance from a small farmstead. The danger in this situation was to know whether the farmstead was occupied by its owners, or by an Italian standing patrol, or even both. Draza, one of the party, handed his weapon and equipment to Paddy and indicated he was going to check it out. To their surprise, watching him through slits in the board walls he walked up to the back of the house bellowing the equivalent of 'Anybody home?' The back door slowly opened and an elderly lady appeared, dressed in black, with a headscarf to match almost obscuring her face. After a short conversation he turned to them waving them to come on. She led them into a largish kitchen where, to their utter astonishment, sat two large, amiable-looking Italian soldiers who, on seeing the newcomers, stood up smiling in welcome.

"What the hell's going on Sir," Paddy asked David and the world in general. Draza, who spoke German having worked in Austria for several years, told David the two soldiers came up to the farm from the camp every two or three days to collect milk, hated the Germans, came from Bologna where they were all communist anyway despite Mussolini and his black-shirts, taking four churns on their two mules back to the contingent in the valley after milking in the morning. As this explanation was forthcoming two rather plump young women, obviously daughters of the older lady came in from a side door and stood by the two Italians, each of whom automatically slipping a proprietorial arm round the adjacent somewhat ample waist.

"It's not only the bloody milk they come up for by the look of things," was Paddy's observation.

The Italians looked at Paddy and David. "You English?"

By this time in his long years of service to the Crown of the

United Kingdom Paddy had overcome the urge to answer this question with 'No, I'm bloody not,' since such a retort invariably resulted in trying to explain to foreigners how it was that although he was in the service of His Britannic Majesty he was not, repeat not English. "Must be the same with the Scots and Welsh," he had reasoned to David in the past. Paddy therefore nodded. At once the two Italians ceased their respective secondary sexual encirclement, got up, shook hands vigorously with the two Englishmen, turning to the others saying "England – good, German, no good."

David looked at Paddy, Paddy looked at David. "We should be killing these bastards; instead we'll be getting invited to the bloody weddings if we stay long enough."

Before they left the next morning they breakfasted well on ham, eggs and fried potatoes that the old lady cooked for them, and were on their way by daybreak. They would have roughly ten hours of daylight before they again had to halt for the night. They saw two patrols in the distance during the day's march, otherwise it was uneventful. They slept in a barn again that night, looking forward to perhaps a proper bed at the Castel Nuovo safe house the next night. Before that they had to meet up with their guide. There was a large monument on the hill overlooking the town where it had been arranged, on the radio, that he, or she, would visit every half hour from three o'clock onwards to meet them and when dark to take them two miles along the cliff to the safe house. There was a copse of closely planted trees near to the monument where they could wait if they were early, and after they had made contact wait until dark. It was nearly four o'clock before they saw the monument in the distance, some mile or so away, but between them and the rendezvous was very open ground until they reached the copse, what was worse was that there were three largish buildings, although some distance away, overlooking this open space. David spoke to Draza. "I think it will be best if you go on, one person will not attract attention, and then as soon as it gets dark we will join you." Draza left, the remainder lay in the hedgerow out of sight; the last thing they wanted to happen was to be caught out on the final stage of their journey. In David's previous training before he went to France for a spell with the Resistance it had been drummed into him that so often agents slipped up by being careless in the final stages of an otherwise successful and well carried out operation. It was not going to happen here.

When it was fully dark David gave the order to move. Reaching the copse they were met by Draza with the guide, who to their astonishment looked like a twelve-year-old girl. "What have we got here?" he asked Draza. The girl, for that was what she was, and it transpired was only eleven years old, spun round, obviously frightened by hearing the two men speaking German.

"It's alright; these two men are the English officers."

David and Paddy shook hands with her. "You, comrade, are a very brave girl," David told her. Draza translated. David had got used to calling everyone comrade by now, communist or not!

They reached the safe house without incident where the girl said goodbye. When they left Stjepan they had given him all their spare clothes they had brought with them, travelling to Castel Nuovo in what they stood up in, plus of course their weapons, ammunition, water bottle and blanket. As the young girl said goodbye David took his service wristwatch off and gave it to her. "Souvenir," he said, "but do not wear it in public until the war is over." This being translated into German for Draza to translate back to the girl, she put her arms up around his neck and kissed him on his stubbly cheek, looked excitedly at the watch, then running to a smiling Paddy benignly looking on, she repeated her thanks by giving him a smacker on his even stubblier cheek, much to the amusement of the three partisans, and away she went.

The safe house might be safe but David's thought of the possibility of a comfortable bed took a resounding nosedive when he viewed the accommodation. The building itself was part of the remains of an old monastery. It lay back some quarter of a mile from the cliff edge in a hollow. The living quarters were a small cellar about fifteen feet square containing some very ancient plank beds and nothing else. Although it was not as cold as it had been up in the mountains it was still decidedly chilly, a fire being out of the question since the smoke might very well attract attention.

"How long have we to stay here Sir, do you know?" Paddy asked.

"What's the date today?"

"God knows Sir; I don't even know what the month is."

"It must be the twenty-sixth of February – is that right Draza? – Is today the twenty-sixth?"

"Yes comrade Major, the submarine will be here on the evening of the 28th."

So they spent their last two days in Yugoslavia in a cellar living on the remains of the food they had brought with them, augmented by the bread the old lady with the two prospective Italian sons-in-law had given them. On the evening of the 28th, as soon as it was dark, they picked their way down a steep and non-too smooth path running to the sands below and hid in a cave tucked away beneath the cliff. At ten o'clock Draza sent a signal from his flashlight, repeated it at 10.15, again at 10.30, and at 10.40 they saw a dingy being rowed by two sailors bouncing over the small breakers. The partisans ran to hold it while their two erstwhile comrades climbed in. Before the arrival of the dingy David and Paddy had given Draza their Tommy guns and blankets, along with such ammunition as they had left, after which Paddy had said to him, "I bet you a fiver Sir, the bloody quartermaster at Cairo has got a list as long as your arm of everything we took with us. I bet the bugger will try and make us pay for all the deficiencies."

"How can he do that – it was all lost either on the drop or when we were heroically fighting for our king and country wasn't it?"

"So it was Sir, so it was."

Draza and his two companions waved to Paddy and David until their craft had broached the breakers and moved away into calmer waters. Paddy repeated to David his previous feelings about being incarcerated in a submarine.

"You know Sir; I'm not looking forward at all to being battened down in one of those things."

As it transpired he had good reason for his misgivings.

Chapter Five

At Sandbury February 1943 started off bitterly cold. A northerly wind blowing straight out of the Arctic, bringing with it from time to time flurries of snow, made life very unpleasant for those who had to work, or go to work in it, as well as inducing those who did not have to brave the elements not to wander too far from the fire. The troops manning the anti-aircraft, guns, listening posts and on general guard duties on Sandbury airfield had had their duty times altered to one on, two off, from the usual two hours on, four off. Although the air temperature was around 22°F that is ten degrees of frost; with the strong wind blowing across the flat expanse this was reduced to around twenty degrees of frost. Cecely and her companion, driving the canteen vehicle which David's wife Pat had driven the day she was killed by a lone German fighter, were heading for their last port of call, a Bofors gun emplacement, before calling it a day. They had volunteered to do the Wednesday and Sunday morning runs after the vehicle had been put back into service, this being the Sunday duty.

Each time she left the Bofors emplacement she looked across the open expanse of fields beyond the perimeter from which that airplane had appeared, and thought how terrified Pat and her friend Lady Halton must have been when it started to fire at them, and for some reason coaxed a little more speed out of this somewhat sluggish vehicle. She drove back to the garage in town where the canteen was housed and by noon had finished all the 'tidying-up' chores, leaving the vehicle ready for the afternoon run with two other volunteers. Saying goodbye to her colleague, she turned towards the town centre to see coming from that direction none other than David's brigadier boss, Lord Ramsford, accompanied, to her even greater surprise, by Oliver and Greta, both home from school for the weekend.

"What a lovely surprise. How did this come about?" she asked.

"Well, I had a day free so I thought I would take the train down to see the Chandlers," was the somewhat mendacious reply. As Henry IV would have said, he told himself:–

'For my part, if a lie may do thee grace,
I'll gild it with the happiest terms I have.'

Hugh Beresford Ramsford loved his Shakespeare!

"I arrived early and went to church with the Chandlers, less Mr Chandler who is on Home Guard parade, and Rose suggested we come along after the service to meet you after what must have been a decidedly chilly outing on your part."

"It certainly was. There is no heater in that Bedford as you can imagine – my feet are only just beginning to thaw out." And she then added as every woman would, "Oh and I must look an awful sight, all blown about."

"She looks utterly pleasing, does she not?" he asked the two youngsters.

They looked at each other for a few seconds until Greta agreed – "She always does."

"Well then," Hugh continued, "I asked Rose if the Angel did lunches on Sunday. She said they did but one had to book and as she knows John Tarrant very well – it is John Tarrant isn't it? she would telephone as soon as she got home and use her charm on him to fit us in. So off we go hoping she has performed the necessary, but firstly putting you outside a nice measure of brandy to warm you up."

John Tarrant, swayed no doubt by the fact that a real live Lord was seeking refreshment in his hostelry, did manage to squeeze another table into the restaurant. Furthermore he performed the miracle of "finding" a glass of brandy for Cecely, literally smuggled in under a white napkin – it would not do for everyone to see the distinctive glass and demand one! With the two youngsters there the lunch was a jolly affair, albeit the food was not exactly cordon bleu since the most a restaurant was allowed to charge for a meal was five shillings plus a modest cover charge. Whilst they were drinking their coffee, Oliver, who had been quiet for a while, suddenly burst out, "Mother I want to join the army." Hugh immediately realised a family issue had arisen, one which had arisen many hundreds of times in many hundreds of families up and down the country over the past three years. He therefore kept his own counsel; he was not part of the family.

"But you are not old enough."

"I shall be seventeen and three quarters in a month's time, then I shall be."

"But I thought you wanted to stay at Sevenoaks and get your Higher Schools before going to university."

"Yes, but things are different now, and anyway we cannot possibly afford for me to go to university."

Cecely looked at Hugh, with a suspicion of tears in her usually bright intelligent eyes. "What can I say?" she asked. Hugh paused for a moment or two.

"This is a family matter, and one upon which I can only give the opinion of an outsider. You have to take into account that if he is not going to university he will be called up when he is eighteen anyway. If he goes in at seventeen and three quarters he is more likely to get a choice of which regiment or corps he would like to join. I've no doubt you have many friends who could help and advise on that particular point."

They sat silently for a few moments.

"Alright, I'll not stand in your way. Now, since you have been giving this matter considerable thought, upon which arm of the service are you intending to bestow the benefit of your talents?" his mother enquired.

"I'd like to go into a tank regiment."

Hugh smiled at Cecely. "They are awfully smelly things you know, and very noisy. I always think being in one of those contraptions is not really a gentlemanly occupation."

As quick as a flash Oliver replied, "Ah, but then you're a guardsman, you're a race apart." Lord Ramsford was a Grenadier.

They all laughed at this quip, which broke the tension of five minutes ago.

"Have you been in the O.T.C. at Sevenoaks?"

"Yes, I'm now a Sergeant."

"In which case you would go to the basic training unit, I believe they call it the General Service Corps now. You spend a couple of months there, most of which will be a complete waste of time since you know it all from O.T.C. anyway. You will be asked your choice of regiment and provided it is not too selective they will pack you off to a depot, or straight to O.C.T.U. if they think you are up to it. So it will be all down to you. Have you decided on which tank regiment you would like, or just take pot luck in the Royal Armoured Corps?"

"My friend Fotheringham at school wants to join as well. He is the same age as I am. His uncle is in the Kings Dragoon Guards. We thought we would try for that."

"The K.D.G. eh? A very good outfit – used to be terribly expensive before the war when they were cavalry. Had to have at least two parade horses and so on, plus polo ponies. In the Guards, once you became a field officer – a major – you could just about live on your pay, but you certainly couldn't hope to in the K.D.G. or the Lancers, or any of that ilk. Different now of course! They are of course very selective – father to son and so on – so it depends on how many junior officers they need as to whether you get in or not. Anyway, no harm in trying, you've a number of hurdles to overcome first anyway, recruit training, officers selection boards and so on."

During these exchanges Greta, fifteen in a couple of weeks, had sat without interrupting the others. Suddenly she blurted out, her eyes full of tears, "And supposing you get killed? Daddy has been taken from us, Uncle Charles as well, and now you are going."

Oliver was the first to respond. "But Greta, I have to do my bit. You wouldn't want me to slope off to university and get out of it would you? And anyway, we don't know about Daddy and Uncle Charles. They are civilians; the Japanese would not ill-treat European civilians."

Greta wiped her eyes and mumbled, "Sorry," seated as she was between Hugh and Cecely they each took one of her hands to comfort her.

They walked back to Chandlers Lodge, the two youngsters walking more quickly, swiftly moved ahead. When they had got some way on Hugh said, "I've been trying to get some sense out of the Red Cross in Switzerland through one of my chaps there." Cecely immediately noted that he spoke of 'one' of his chaps and wondered how many there were in total, further pondering on the fact that this comparatively ordinary looking man in his weekend tweeds and brogues walking the by-ways of Sandbury held so much responsibility for the lives of men and women scattered all over she knew not where. He continued.

"Apparently, the Japanese, despite continual pressure from neutral sources, refuse to give the names of the civilian internees they have in the lands they have conquered. In fact it is known that large numbers have been moved back to Japan as slave labour. However, a glimmer of hope showed itself this week. They have allowed a small contingent of Red Cross officials into Malaya. What they will discover no one knows, but it is a start. As soon as I hear more I will contact you. Secondly Force 136 in Malaya is to be asked if some of their Chinese can start finding ways of collecting names. I don't think that is too hopeful, the Force in my opinion is there to fight not to act as secret agents, and one operation could easily jeopardise the other. Anyway, be assured they are not forgotten anymore than you are." He paused for a moment, then addressing no one but the passing breeze added, "Which would be totally beyond the bounds of possibility in any event."

Cecely squeezed his arm and said "You are very kind," and wondered, as David's Pat had done two years ago, what it was that caused a woman to leave such an accomplished and charming man and run off to Kenya with someone else as his wife, Charlie's mother, had done. 'I wonder if she ever regretted it,' she asked herself 'someone as flighty as that would probably tire of the new man in her life pretty quickly and be out of the frying pan and into the fire. Look at Mrs Rowlands in Malaya; she left Jack Hooper, another wonderful man.'

"You're quiet," said Hugh, a remark half question, half statement of fact. She squeezed his arm again.

"I was wondering about what sort of accommodation they would give the internees," she fibbed. It was fortunate she did not know, nor even guess at the degradation, discomfort, hardship and brutality being inflicted upon men, women and children, in camps all over the Greater East Asia Co-Prosperity Sphere, the hideous reprisals being taken for the slightest misdemeanour, the mass murder of innocent Chinese in the cities and in the countryside. It was a mercy she had no knowledge of this evil hegemony, how then would she sleep at night.

Reaching Chandlers Lodge and having thanked Rose profusely for 'organising' John Tarrant, they found Ernie Bolton there, with Anni and her father Karl. Anni's second child was due in June, so her 'bump,' as she and Rose, who shared her first pregnancy always cited it, was now beginning to show. Karl felt immensely privileged when in conversation with a member of the aristocracy, and the two generals and their 'Lady' wives, who were visitors to Chandlers Lodge. During his head to head with the brigadier he asked whether his knowledge and expertise as a clock maker could be put to use. He had been making sophisticated clockwork mechanisms all his life; surely someone could make use of his talents? Hugh took his arm and led him away from the general throng, which by now included Jack and Moira, Megan and the children.

"Mr Reisner," Hugh began.

"Please, call me Karl. That I would like better."

"Karl it is. Karl, this is not my particular department, but I do know a man who could possibly use your expertise, particularly with your knowledge of German. I will have a word with him, but you do understand that if they recruited you, you would undergo all sorts of examination under the Official Secrets Act, down to how much money you have and how often you change your underpants even." He paused, smiling. Karl immediately saw the joke, laughed merrily and replied

"I must remember to have a good clean answer to that one, nein?"

From across the room Anni and Rose, as near to being sisters as any two women could be, noticed them laughing together.

"I wonder what they are cooking up." Anni reflected, "I know my father has been anxious to help win the war against Hitler ever since he was released from internment. He does not consider it traitorous to fight against Hitler in any way he can, since by helping to defeat him he considers he would be liberating the German people."

That evening Anni asked her father what he and the brigadier were talking about.

"I asked him if my expertise in clockwork mechanisms could be of use, he said he would enquire. However, there is a problem. I would be thoroughly investigated before they would be able to employ me, supposing I could be of use, particularly as to friends, family, und so weiter – and so on. He said that Ernie would be alright because he has already been cleared, but he was not too sure about you."

They had been listening so far in all seriousness to what he was saying, then realising he was indulging in one of his rare leg-pulls, Anni picked up a cushion to throw at him. Quickly he threw up his hands.

"I surrender." He paused for a moment or two, and continued, "I do hope they find me something."

A little over a week later Karl received a telephone call from a Claude Roberts of the Ministry of Supply who wished to come and see him. It was arranged for Wednesday morning 17th February, Karl automatically reminding himself he had better be sure he changed his underpants that morning. Mr Roberts arrived, a nondescript looking gentleman who would not excite a second glance in a crowd, or out of one for that matter. He was accompanied by a somewhat sprucer looking gentleman whose card read 'John Smith, Special Branch.' "I would have thought he could have chosen a more original pseudonym than that," were Karl's first thoughts, which were quite unfair really, since it was in fact his real name.

For an hour they discussed Karl's origins, his internment, his views on the National Socialists and so on, all of which Karl was reasonably sure they would have been well informed already. Karl then suggested perhaps they would like some coffee – "Only bottled coffee I'm afraid" – which offer they gratefully accepted. They then asked if they could see some of his work. He took them into his workshop, provided each with a watchmakers' eyepiece and pointed to a bench where he had laid out clockwork mechanisms he had made from units several inches across down to the tiniest units, to study which they had to use the eyepiece. Karl noticed the ministry man used the aid as expertly as he himself would have done, the Special Branch man having a little difficulty in fitting and focussing his.

"And you made all these with the equipment you have here?" Claude asked.

"Yes Sir, of course in Germany I had more sophisticated apparatus so could work much more quickly than with these simple tools, most of which I made myself."

"Well I think you've done bloody miracles," he replied, looking at John Smith for agreement. "Right now. Let's go back and sit down."

Being seated he continued. "Now, John here will want to know where you bank, and will require your authority to study your bank accounts for the past three years. We shall want the name of your solicitor, accountant, and any other professional person you have dealt with in the past three years, again with authority to be given such information as we may require. Beyond all that we shall require three referees, not to include any immediate family, people of substance in the community who have known you continuously for the past three years. Having received all that information, proved it to be totally satisfactory, you will then be called upon to sign the Official Secrets Act before we invite you to the next stage of our enquiries at the research station with the technical boffins. Have you any questions?"

As he was informing Karl of these requirements, John Smith took a sheaf of half a dozen papers from his briefcase.

"It's getting on for lunch time," he said, "if you would like to read these, complete and sign them, we will, in the meantime, wander off to that rather attractive looking pub across the market square and have a pie and a pint. We will then collect them and get the train back to the Smoke." Karl was a bit puzzled about 'the Smoke' – I must ask Fred what that is or where that is, this evening.

The papers were various authorisations to people and organisations to issue to those who may lawfully request them, details of the affairs of Mister Karl Reisner. They included not only the Inland Revenue and other people already mentioned, but also the superintendents of the two internment camps at which he had been held. "It's a good thing they are unable to contact my old headmaster, I would never get the job," ran through his mind as he sat down to sign, then he thought, "but I don't even know what the job is yet."

The family that evening all wanted to know how he had got on. They were all very pleased at his obvious enthusiasm at hopefully being able to aid the war effort of the country which had saved his daughter's life and given him sanctuary, he was further relieved to know the meaning of 'the Smoke,' which unknown factor had stayed in the back of his mind all day until Fred laughingly put his mind at rest.

The next day, 16th February, the House began the debate on one of the most momentous projects ever to be brought before Parliament, namely the Beveridge report. It was a single coherent plan of Social Insurance which would affect the lives of every person in the United Kingdom for all time. It provided family allowances, comprehensive medical services, housing benefits, among other things; everyone would be looked after from the cradle to the grave. It had opposition of course. The conservatives made the point that vast sums would be paid out in family allowances alone to those who had no real need. A man earning a thousand pounds a year, for example, had no requirement for assistance in bringing up his children. The debate dragged on for three days, each evening the country, including the Chandlers and their friends and family, sat with ears glued to the wireless to learn more of this proposed legislation. That it should be presented in the middle of an unresolved war was in itself a miracle. The fact that poorer people, and this included many hundreds of thousands of wives of serving men in the forces, would not need to look into their purses to see if they could afford to go to the doctor or dentist if they needed to, gave a tremendous boost to the morale of the nation, even though it was 'jam tomorrow' – the legislation would take some while before it was put into effect.

On Saturday 20th the Labour Party held a conference. Harry Pollitt, General Secretary of the Communist Party of Great Britain had applied for his organisation to be affiliated to the Labour Party. Jack Hooper's view on the subject was expressed in the phrase "They've not got a snowballs' chance in hell," and so it proved to be. When war broke out on September 3rd 1939 the communists were violently opposed to the U.K. Government being part of it, and this remained their active and vociferous view until Russia was invaded by the Wehrmacht in June 1941. They then performed the most prodigious somersault of all time pronouncing we should give massive help to our Soviet allies, open a second front and in short do everything they had been voting for us not to do for the past two years. The Labour Party executive formally rejected the application for affiliation. The communist party was to be marginalized, eventually to disappear completely.

The Beveridge Report in particular received a good deal of discussion on that Saturday evening, Megan being asked how the proposals would affect the hospital service. She had to admit that they knew so little of the mechanics of what was to happen she was as much in the dark as anyone else. However, from what she had gleaned from discussions with the senior staff and management committee more people would be using the hospital and hopefully government money would remove the constant need for the fundraisers to get their begging bowls into the community to keep it going. Like many local hospitals they lived on a shoestring, not helped by the fact that nursing staff were all to get a pay rise next month. However, all conversations inevitably included the unanswerable question – as to where David and Harry are tonight? – they usually knew roughly where Mark and Charlie were. David was on the last stage of his marathon trek with Paddy to the safe house, and Harry was preparing for another mission. It would not be long, hopefully, before they saw David again, having Harry with them again was an entirely different kettle of fish.

On Sunday 21st February, Moira and Jack were invited, among hundreds of others of the good and the great, to Buckingham Palace to commemorate the great Russian victory of Stalingrad, generally accepted later by historians as the real turning point of the war. The King had had fashioned a magnificently jewelled sword to be called 'The Sword of Honour to the People of Stalingrad.' In the presence of this distinguished audience it was presented to the Russian Ambassador in the much bombed house of the King and Queen and their family, as a tribute to the Russian people, to be hung in the new city hall of Stalingrad when it came to be rebuilt. The strange thing was that although the newsreels around the world showed this ceremony, held in a bombed palace in the middle of a war, nothing of it was shown in Russia! One wonders what happened to the sword of Stalingrad when eventually the Russians changed the name of the city and began to revile the name of Stalin.

On the following Thursday, Karl received a telephone call asking whether he could be available to visit the Royal Ordnance establishment to further discuss his application. Having acknowledged he was available at any time he was told a ministry car would collect him at eight o'clock the next morning. Quickly he asked how long he would be away, whether he needed to take overnight things and so on. A laughing Mr Roberts said, "No, nothing like that, we are only twenty minutes away from you."

A thoroughly mystified Karl wondered where on earth an ordnance factory could be located twenty minutes from Sandbury. "If anyone knows, Fred will," he thought, but here he drew a blank. As an afterthought Fred wondered whether it was a place called Fort Malstead situated in a private road, manned by War Department police, in the thick wooded country on the top of the downs. "It can't be a factory," Fred continued, "or they would be drawing people from Sandbury to work there and I have never heard it mentioned by my Home Guard chaps, and between them they know everything that's going on."

"Well, tomorrow I shall know."

The car, a black Austin 16 with civilian number plates, arrived five minutes before it was scheduled, the chauffeur standing by the rear door preparatory to opening it for Karl when he emerged from the house. He was greeted with a polite, "Good morning Sir," but that was all he said on the journey to what Karl eventually established as being exactly that which Fred had guessed, namely Ford Malstead. It was probably the most inaptly named site, Karl determined, he had ever known. There was a small brick building, single storey, surrounded by a number of Nissen Huts, the only 'fortifications' in evidence being a single, very high, wire fence with highly visible high voltage warning signs at intervals. He further noted two dead foxes outside the wire who obviously could not read.

The superintendent, Henry Gee, who received him was a genial, long haired gent, somewhat scruffily dressed, possessed of a pair of percipient eyes which Karl immediately registered with the thought, 'he doesn't miss much.' After the formalities of signing the Official Secrets Act, Mr Gee told him what their job was. "We make all sorts of bits and pieces for the various military intelligence people – they have a dozen or so different departments besides M.I.5 and M.I.6 – as well as all manner of special gadgets for our special operations people, air crews, and of course the services generally. For example, in your particular discipline, we may get a requirement for a watch to be made with a compass built into it, or even a space for a cyanide pill. Our embassies all over the world call for all sorts of gadgets, some of which we can make here. The ordnance people often call for minute special clockwork systems, shock proof systems and so on. The torpedo people are always wanting something or other: the list is endless. The fact that you can actually make items of this nature was the factor which recommended you to us. We can get as many watchmakers as we want who can take a timepiece to bits and put it back again, we need someone who can actually fashion something from what is nothing more than a requirement, in other words you would be responsible for designing and making whatever is called for. If you need specialist help you see me and I will organise it. If you feel a requirement cannot be met, we have a daily refusal meeting after which we can usually suggest to the customer a different line of approach, or tell him to jump in the lake if he becomes too difficult – and some of the top brass, up to and including the P.M. himself are very huffy if we tell them a pet scheme won't work."

Karl took all this in in a state of inner excitement he nevertheless did not allow to surface. Henry continued.

"I understand you made all the tools in your workshop at Sandbury?"

"Most of them yes."

"That's another thing we are called upon to provide, all manner of miniature specialist lathes and so on. Well now, any questions so far?"

"I am not a draughtsman. I can do sketches, make micrometer measurements and so on, but I am useless as a draughtsman."

"We have draughtsmen and tracers. They can work from your sketches."

"There is a problem with how I get here, there would appear to be no buses running here, and although I could buy a second-hand car, I have no licence, and presumably petrol would be a problem. Even my friend, Fred Chandler who owns Sandbury Engineering goes to work on a bicycle through shortage of petrol."

"We have a bus, painted a nondescript green which goes around the villages each morning. It would collect you at eight o'clock at Sandbury War Memorial, leaving here at 4.30 in the afternoon. In the event of a special need for transport should you be held up here on an assignment we would provide a ministry car to get you home."

For the next two hours Karl was given a conducted tour of various Nissen huts ending with lunch in the staff canteen – an above average meal as he later imparted to the folks back at Chandlers Lodge. He apologised for not being more forthcoming about his visit other than telling them where it was, his hours, travel arrangements and so on, due to his having to sign the Official Secrets Act – "And you wouldn't want me put in the tower would you?" They understood completely. Fred, Jack, Ernie all had the same restrictions, but none of them knew secrets as dreadful as those Moira carried with her all the time. She had been involved in the U.K. and in America, in the atom bomb project since its inception. She knew of its dreadful power, she also knew that Russia and Germany could well be working on a similar project at that very moment. She lived with the fear that one or the other could be a month ahead of Britain and America, and there was no doubt in her mind, and in the minds of most of the top few politicians who knew of the weapon that if the Soviet Union got it first there was no telling whether they would remain our allies or not. The general public looked at the valiant Russians through rose-tinted glasses, but those in the know were more than well aware of the Soviet avowal of world revolution, world communism. With that weapon they really could rule the world – or destroy it!! As for the Nazis???

Chapter Six

'Sunrise' – Colonel Ransomes, their new overall commander, arrived with a small coterie of bodyguards, and, to Harry's great pleasure, his old friends Bam and Boo. He hugged them both, much to the bemusement of the colonel's men who, whilst they recognised the skills possessed by the two trackers, would certainly not think of being familiar with them in any way. It was approaching darkness. The party had a welcome shower and got into clean clothes for the ones they were wearing to be washed. The two orang asli curled themselves up on Harry's veranda after they had been given food, Harry again providing them with blankets as he had done at their first visit. The talk that evening in the 'officers' mess' was general, the colonel saying they would have a formal meeting in the morning when Ang Choon Guan, the communist Chinese leader would be invited to join them. However, in the meantime, he casually announced during the conversation, "We have a friend of yours at Camp Four Harry." Harry immediately started a race through his mind as to who the devil that could be – Colonel Deveson? Nigel Coates? it would not be the judge; he would be too old for this lark.

"I can't think who that could be, Sir."

"A lady friend in fact."

"The only lady I know is safe in England as far as I know. Anyway Sir, what on earth is a lady doing in a camp like this?" punning the old phrase.

Clive began a leg-pull. "We always guessed there was more to Harry than met the eye. He obviously kept a fancy woman up at K.L. or regions adjacent."

Robbie joined in. "Or even a mother and daughter, Harry likes a bit of variety so I understand."

"Well, you met this lady at a party," the colonel continued, "and you made such an impression on her that she has not been able to get you out of her mind since. She wakes up in the night thinking of you apparently – your virile charm, your masculine magnetism – or so I am given to understand."

"Sir, you are extracting the urine, if I may be allowed to say so." Everybody laughed uproarishly; it was not often they had heard a colonel being quipped in that manner.

"Well, I will tell you who it is – it is a lady known as Mrs Rowlands. I believe the daughter from her first marriage was married to your brother until she was tragically killed by enemy action."

Harry was silent for a few moments. "I did meet Mrs Rowlands.

She left one of the finest men I have ever known, with a six-year-old daughter, to come out here with the bastard Rowlands. What is she doing at Camp Four Sir? You know Rowlands is a traitor and should be shot?"

The mood at the mess table where they were seated had changed abruptly. From the joviality of the leg pull the mood had shifted to suspecting there was a serious, a very serious undertone to the colonel's news. Harry had put so much venom into 'the bastard Rowlands' and that 'he should be shot,' quite out of character to his normal breezy, good humoured self, they knew intuitively something had offended him way beyond the trivial.

The colonel apologised immediately for bringing up the subject in the middle of what had been a convivial get-together. He continued:–

"Harry is quite right on all accounts. Mrs Rowlands has told me her full story and that if she could make amends she would, knowing full well that that is impossible. In the meantime she is doing great work at Camp Four, both practically in the sick bay, where she has had to cater for a veritable epidemic of dysentery, the cause of which we are urgently trying to find, and in the planning of their operations, where her knowledge of the overall layout of tin dredging plants is invaluable." He paused for a moment. "You know, you can get a good idea of a person's moral fibre when they are up to their elbows in other people's crap day after day." He paused again. "As for Rowlands, he is in our sights. If we do not get him now we will get him after the war. We have so much on him that added to the evidence Mrs Rowlands has given us, a hanging in Outram Road Jail will be too good for him. You see, she was prepared, as many women stupidly are, to put up with his numerous infidelities. That was something between him and her. However, to betray his country, to conspire with the Japanese thereby causing the deaths of his fellow countrymen, his Malay and Chinese workers, is something which has instilled a great hate in her."

There was a silence around the table. Their normal conversation was usually either light-hearted, or deeply technical regarding operational matters. Although the people being discussed were unknown to them, the combination of love turning to hate, of initial family betrayal being succeeded by service to one's country, the expectation that a wrongdoer would ultimately be called upon to pay the penalty for his moral turpitude, were subjects outside their day to day chat. These were things that happen in the real world they had left behind, a world they rarely thought about if they could avoid it, a world where pumping poisoned darts into people was beyond the pale, not events to be rejoiced over.

The colonel sensed the turn in the conversation was making them introspective. "Well, I'm for bed," he announced. "I do hope you are not plagued with kraits as they are up at Camp Two. The nasty little buggers are everywhere – you certainly don't walk around barefooted up there." Kraits were small but venomous, fast moving snakes, which are often concealed in vegetation or under rocks. At the height Camp Six was situated they were fortunately almost unknown. As he got up he said, "Till nine o'clock then gentlemen, when I hope I shall be able to give you some good news." Turning to Terry, the radio operator, he said, "That message we discussed should be in by midnight or just after. Sorry to give you a late bedtime – goodnight all."

Harry wandered out to give Bam and Boo a cigarette each, then he too went off to bed thinking firstly of what the surprise was the colonel was going to spring on the morrow and how Mrs Rowlands had ended up at Camp Four. He resolved to question the colonel further when he could get him on his own.

The message came through at three o'clock in the morning. A dozing Terry Martin was jolted awake by the shrilly repeated call sign superimposing itself on the constant night time symphony of the honking of the frogs and the constant chirping of the cicadas. Terry had often wondered at the noise the jungle produced at night and how quickly you accepted it, then ignored it so that you slept soundly despite the continual commotion. He took the rather lengthy message down, then spent the next hour decoding it and making four handwritten copies. It was five o'clock before he snatched a couple of hours sleep.

At nine o'clock they sat around the mess table again, joined by Choon Guan. On the table the colonel had spread firstly a general map of central Malaya, and on top of that a large scale, one inch to the mile, Ordnance Survey map of their immediate district. This latter was mainly of little use other than to show contours and river positions. Carrying out a survey in the jungle is an extremely approximate science.

"Right gentlemen, first the good news received by our wide awake Terry in the middle of the night. We now have the occasional use of a Liberator."

"And what, Sir, may be a Liberator may I ask?" Clive enquired.

"A Liberator is an American bombing aircraft which, suitably adapted, can fly very long distances. We therefore are to be supplied with ammunition and other stores from a base in Ceylon, which will be parachuted to us on predetermined dropping zones. These will include mail from your families, although I am afraid we still have not found a way to get mail out to them. However, Colonel Llewellyn has been invalided home, or will have been if the submarine collecting him has yet arrived, and will be contacting all Force 136 families as quickly as he can when he gets to the U.K. Now, first things first. We have to decide on a dropping zone which will be pinpointed by the Ordnance Survey reference number. We will talk about recognition factors and so on later." He leaned over the O.S. map. "To your east and to the south, you have high jungle – no good for a drop zone. To the west you slope down towards the main trunk road and railway line, where I understand you carried out a very satisfactory operation last year. You are there running dangerously close, in aircraft terms, to civilisation – something to be avoided at all costs. It therefore leaves the land to the north. Some twenty miles to the north there is a plateau at a height of some fifteen hundred feet." He pointed to the general area on the map. "Now, do you know what the country is like there?" Clive looked at Harry.

"You have been up there when you blew up the power lines, can you answer that?"

"Yes Sir, there's a considerable area of rock with some trees and a few small streams coming down off the mountains to the east. It's fairly flat and not heavily forested."

"Right, well that seems a good drop zone, but you do have the disadvantage of firstly, porterage for twenty odd miles, and secondly, making matters worse, having to climb two thousand feet to get back up here into your eyrie. On the other hand it being well away from your camp is a good thing."

Clive looked at the excited faces seated around the table. "I reckon we can put up with that," he stated, as much a question to the others as a statement of fact.

"Right, any questions thus far?"

Harry chipped in, back to his previous good humour, "Can you tell me what shape of container the whisky will be put in Sir?"

The colonel laughed. "Actually you will not be far out. There is an allowance for a rum ration. Now, we have drawn up a code number for all the items you are likely to need. You will be notified, again in code, of when the next drop will be, and given at least ten days' notice, sometimes more. You then send off your shopping list which we pass on to the Kandy people who get it made up into suitable loads. If you over order, preference is given to ammunition and weapons – I warn you about that. The aircraft will make drops to three camps in each run, you should get a drop every two months or so."

This announcement had caused great excitement among the officers around the table. They led an extremely lonely, cut-off existence, the prospect of this aircraft bringing them a lifeline from the outside world was psychologically the greatest thing to have happened to them. They had the excitement and boost to their morale at the success of their various operations, but that evaporated after a while to the recognition they were imprisoned in this all encompassing green hell, containing ghastly creatures small and large, capable of doing them harm, with no prospect of an end in sight. The aircraft therefore was a step forward to the time when they would be released from this incarceration. To live in the hope of getting mail, however little, from their loved ones, was, in itself, such a miracle as to almost wipe away the terrible despondency they sometimes suffered at being apart from them.

The colonel continued. "Regarding post. I can take two letters from each of you back with me. We have a submarine coming in up north with a replacement for number one camp commander who died recently from peritonitis. The boat will take a small sack of mail back for us. I have therefore to ration mail to two letters per person. They will not, of course, be censored here, but nevertheless you must be incredibly careful as to what you put in them in case I should be shot up on the way back and they fall into the hands of the little yellow bastards." Harry had a feeling the colonel was not greatly enamoured of the soldiers of the Rising Sun. "They will of course very probably be censored in Ceylon." The knowledge they were going to be able to contact those at home doubly increased their high spirits. If they could have presented the colonel with a marble statue they would have done so. The fact was the colonel was an old campaigner. A subaltern in the trenches in the Great War, wounded twice, soldiering on the North West Frontier in the 1920's and in Palestine in the 1930's he knew the value of the sending and receipt of mail to the morale of the troops – at all levels. That and a plentiful supply of tea, a beverage of little nutritional value, but of inestimable worth to the average soldier's well-being, out of all proportion to its health-giving properties. These soldiers had now been locked in the jungle for a year, they seemed very well adjusted, working as comrades together, but the colonel who had had long spells with a small nucleus of men in strong points up in the Himalayas knew that whilst familiarity did not necessarily breed contempt, they could, to use a well known army metaphor, get on each others tits. This raising of the morale, introducing a new factor to life, could prevent that from taking place.

"Now finally," he continued, "operations. Your area operations will continue to be under your own control. However, I want you to do a combined operation with Camp Five. About eighty miles north of here the Pahang River runs west to east out into the China Sea. At Kampong

Bintang," he gave the Ordnance Survey reference number, "they have built a very large rubber godown complex using both civilian and P.O.W. slave labour. From the estates to the north and the west they are bringing in loads of rubber which will then be taken down the Pahang River by lighters to the port of Pekan at the mouth, loaded on to ships and taken to Japan. In a month's time the godowns will be full. Camp Five have several mortars and a good stock of incendiary bombs, so the outline plan is that you will meet at this point on hill 2101, Camp Six force will eliminate the guard detail consisting of some twenty to thirty Japanese then withdraw while Camp Five burn the place down. Camp Six will cover their retreat from any interference coming up from the river and when they are clear both lots will bugger off home. I suggest both units meet the day before so that a visual reconnaissance can be made from hill 2101 which overlooks the Kampong and the river. As with all these operations, final plans have to be made on the spot. Any questions?"

There were numerous questions, but they were all fired up with the thought of hitting the Japs again. The fact they were having to trek for sixty odd miles, largely through jungle, and then sixty odd miles back again was accepted without trepidation. They were becoming professionals in their own right.

Before the colonel left three days later, he asked Harry to show him his skill with the blowpipe. This he did by placing a four inches wide, five feet high, piece of timber in the ground and at thirty yards put four darts out of four in a neat group about a foot from the top. The orang asli, watching excitedly, clapped and stamped their feet as each dart went in, showing their pleasure at the success of their apprentice. Finishing the shoot, and having been congratulated by the colonel, Harry turned and put his arms around the shoulders of his two friends, hugging them to him, of which event the two aborigines never hesitated to tell the members of their tribe over and over again when they eventually got back up to Cameron Highlands.

When the colonel had departed they started to list what should be in their first drop. Robbie's first question was "What number is the whisky?" He was unlucky, but found to his partial delight as the colonel had indicated, rum was listed! "Any port in a storm," he commented. Clive had decreed that ammunition; explosives and medical supplies must head the list, after that they could sort it out among themselves! Toilet rolls, toothpaste and writing paper came high up on the various officers' schedules of necessities, although as Robbie remarked – he had been delegated to make the final tally – they had been without them for a year or so how could they be a necessity?

Before the colonel and his party left, Harry had written his two letters, the first to Megan of course and the second to Rose and his father. In both he had shown how heartbroken he was at the loss of his mother, asking them to thank the brigadier (no name mentioned) for getting the cable to him. Apart from saying his camp was quite comfortable, which when the letters were received at Sandbury brought the comment 'well he would say that wouldn't he,' he found it difficult at first to find things to say. Like most forces people who had to suffer the indignity of a superior officer reading their letters home, intimate correspondence was muted through sheer embarrassment at the thought of some gormless base-wallah having a laugh at declarations of love, remembrances of past passions and statements of everlasting devotion. In fact of course, the people who handled this chore became quickly experienced at skimming over the luvvy-duvvy and even occasional plain pornographic sections, picking out straight away blue pencil material. Once you have read a couple of hundred letters written by other people, it all becomes a blur until you instinctively spot something which should not be there. Unfortunately the letter writers did not know this to be the case, and even if they had been told it to be true, would not have believed it.

During the first week in February Clive and Harry with Choon Guan made several forays north to plan their drop zone. Each recce lasted three days. A day to get there, a day to carry out a search and to establish exactly where they were on the ground, this determined by taking reverse compass bearings on the various peaks of mountains they could recognise from the ordnance survey map. Drawn on the map these lines should run back and cross at the point at which they had been taken. They never did of course, exactly, but they provided usually a small triangle which would be designated a drop zone and which would be lit up by flares on the night of the drop. Eventually they decided on a flat expanse of scrubland some two miles long running north to south by half a mile wide, situated in a depression so that nothing could be seen from the west, which was the only direction in which there was civilisation, and that was thirty miles away.

On the 14th February the message came through to rendezvous with Camp Five on Friday 26th February with the operation to take place at dawn on Sunday 28th February. Clive divided his force into five columns, one of which included the navy men and Matthew Lee and his section who would stay behind, along with some four or five sick, to guard the camp. Matthew suggested that he should come, along with a medical orderly, to attend to any wounded. Clive had to remind him that, apart from superficial wounds which the men could attend to themselves, there would be no wounded. There was a silence until Matthew asked, "And who would be delegated to despatch the more seriously wounded?"

Clive replied, "Choon Guan and myself will attend to it." Up until now their operations had been concluded without this macabre task having to be performed, but there was bound to be a time when they would be called upon to carry out this awful undertaking. It would, in fact, challenge them in the very near future.

On the early morning of February 22nd, the four active columns moved out soon after dawn. Once they left the game trails and high jungle of their home territory they came to the wooded plateau where eventually they would hopefully receive their air drop. They had lived in the expectation of receiving the ten day notice by now, without its having been realised. "The Liberator probably has a puncture or something," was Harry's professional opinion! They made good time and had covered some twenty miles – very good going in that sort of terrain. They did equally well the next day, but on the third day, having to cross a small river, the Keratong, at a point within some six or seven miles from one of the very few Kampongs up here on the plateau they did not do quite so well. It was therefore almost dark on the 25th February that they approached the rendezvous area. It was too late to send out patrols to endeavour to contact the Camp Five force; they would be most likely to find them in the dark, to say nothing of the possibility of their getting lost in the process!

The columns were looking forward to a rest day on the morrow, although the column leaders would have to go forward, once they had met up with Camp Five, to carry out the reconnaissance of the target. They stood-to at dawn after which three two-man patrols were sent forward to find Camp Five. In the meantime Camp Five commander had sent three two-man patrols to find Camp Six, the patrols missed each other completely, not difficult even in light jungle conditions such as they were in, but each in turn found their opposite main bodies. At eight o'clock therefore Camp Six moved forward about a mile to join their comrades. It was now quite a formidable force, some one hundred men, well armed for their task and ready to go. Charles Grenville, a major in the Malay Regiment, the commander of Camp Five, had been designated the officer commanding the operation. He had two white officers and his communist camp leader who along with Clive and his column leaders, he now led to a scrub covered bluff overlooking the wide, winding Pahang River probably two miles away. On either side of the river were endless paddy fields. At a slight angle to their right they would see a large lake which fed into the river, at the side of which was the Kampong Bintang, mostly huts on stilts. To the left of the Kampong was the target, six large godowns, from the centre of which a newly made road ran for some half a mile to a jetty which would appear to be not completely finished. To the left of the godowns there were two largish huts with atap roofs, one surrounded by a mesh fence with barbed wire coiled around the top, the other obviously the guard's quarters.

There was, at first, little movement until the double doors on the guards' hut were thrown open and to the surprise of the officers peering through their binoculars, a motley crew of Indian soldiers emerged and lined up in two ranks in front of the building. An N.C.O. called them to attention, at which a short, plump Japanese officer and a Japanese N.C.O. appeared from a separated room at the end of the building. Even at that distance the watchers gave a little chuckle. The officer's legs were so short his sword was literally dragging the ground, he was walking along like a little plump turkey, all puffed up with his own importance.

"Jifs," said Major Grenville to Harry standing beside him.

"What are Jifs Sir?" Harry asked.

"Japanese Indian Forces. A number of Indian troops who were captured were induced to turn traitor and serve with the Japanese army. I don't think they will cause us much trouble."

As they were watching this mini-parade, the wired-in compound opened its doors. Out straggled some thirty to forty men, mainly Indians, but among them they could distinguish four white men. The Jif parade being dismissed, the gates of the prisoner compound were opened and the inmates marched off by them along the road to the jetty for the days work, less a section of about ten men, including the four whites, who were marched to the nearest godown, presumably to stack the rubber as it arrived. The watchers were interested to note that although the Indians were armed with rifles, they appeared to have no ammunition pouches or bandoliers. Presumably therefore they just had five or possibly ten rounds in the magazine, if that. "I suppose, being out here in the back of beyond with as many guards as there are prisoners, they hardly need more than a round or two for emergencies," was Harry's professional opinion, "that or the Japs don't trust them with too much ammo."

The next event was not quite so comforting. Both up and down–river they knew from their maps there were sizeable Kampongs. The upriver one some fifteen miles away, the downriver one about ten miles. With the first barge carrying rubber arriving at the jetty they were somewhat perturbed to observe it was being followed by a sizeable motor launch with a medium machine gun mounted on its foredeck and a group of eight or nine apparently Japanese soldiers aft. Again Major Grenville studied them carefully, then announced, "Japanese officer and crew, Korean troops. I wonder how long they will stay; they will probably go back up to their kampong later."

But they didn't. At midday they moved off down river, leaving the force officers somewhat unhappy that they might return. Attacking a force backed by a machine gun of that calibre would not be a picnic. Harry put forward a suggestion.

"This river, according to this map, is navigable for close on two hundred miles, and scattered along it, with no roads leading to them there are Kampongs about every fifteen miles. I would hazard a bet they are based down at Pekan on the coast and cruise up the river as far as they can go every now and then to show a presence. If this is so they are probably heading to base as fast as possible ready for their Saturday night booze up and Sunday off."

"I sincerely hope you are right," was the acknowledgement from Major Grenville.

Whilst Clive added, "Harry's not often very far wrong."

The next day the force spent relaxing, checking weapons and finally listening to the plan of action. To the close cover on the bluff, parties of ten at a time were brought forward to get a clear view of the target and to be shown their part in it. They were all anxious to get the job over, if only to rid themselves of the voracious mosquitoes which seemed to have found them and telegraphed up and down the river for reinforcements. An hour before dawn on Sunday 28th February they moved out to engage in a well planned attack. The problem is that things don't always go according to plan.

Chapter Seven

The small dinghy slowly made its way towards the submarine David and Paddy could now see outlined ahead. The first word to describe it that went through David's mind was 'sinister.' It was probably that knowing its purpose as he did, with the fact that it appeared a menacing black colour added to the general aura of malice which surrounded the sleek outline of this aquatic weapon of destruction – so powerful that even the mightiest battleship or aircraft carrier would be helpless once in its sights. He and Paddy were most apprehensive of travelling in this submersible coffin. How did they get volunteers to crew them, he asked himself? They must be stark raving mad. The amusing thing was that when it was known in the ward room they were paratroopers, the same thing was said about them. Reaching the boat they could recognise that in fact it was not black as it had appeared in silhouette, but painted a pale blue.

They clambered aboard, their boots, now having been re-soled by the partisan cobbler with bits of rubber tyres, slipping on the wet superstructure of this ominous looking cigar, up into the conning tower, where they were greeted by the skipper. Here they received their first surprise. Expecting to be met by a bearded character of the stamp of Jack Hawkins, they were in fact saluted by a genial young man, manfully it is true trying to grow a beard; singularly it would appear, unsuccessfully, as far as they could tell in the night light.

"Welcome aboard Thunderer gentlemen. I am Lieutenant Gates, known to all as Rusty. I will see you later. Number one; please take our guests down to the wardroom."

Number one, who introduced himself as Gus Clark was, if anything, marginally younger than the skipper. They negotiated the ladder inside the conning tower swaying gently with the movement of the boat in the gentle swell, and found themselves in the control room. It was called a room, but the two newcomers were soon to find there was no such thing as 'room' on a submarine. Every single nook and cranny was used to store something or other. Food, clothing, even books and magazines tucked away everywhere. David and Paddy were both big men, Paddy even bulkier than his officer, they were to find down here in this maze of pipes, cables, valves, cable trays, out-jutting pieces of original fabrication, sudden reduction in ceiling heights and innumerable other hazards, it would have been better had they been born of a more abbreviated stature. Passing a rating coming from the opposite direction frequently involved a pressing together which in a shopping aisle in Oxford Street would end in being charged with gross indecency.

The wardroom, when they reached it again, proved the point that had already registered with them. It was, to all intents and purposes, an overgrown cupboard, fitted out with bunks with curtains hiding the sleeper from the passers-by needing to move backwards or forwards along the boat. They sat down, looking around their new quarters.

"Not much like the Queen Mary eh Sir?" enquired Gus.

"Now look here Gus, we are guests of yours, so lets cut out all this 'Sir' lark. I'm David and this is Paddy – OK?"

"Yes righto – jolly good." He sounds exactly like another version of Charlie Crew, David thought; with a smile at the remembrance of his dear old chum.

"One good thing, you are both travelling very light I notice. We wondered whether you would be bringing tons of kit, in which case where the hell could we put it."

"We left everything we didn't stand up in including our overcoats and gas capes with the partisans," David replied, "they have so little they even have to sole their boots like this." He lifted his foot up to show the rubber tyred re-sole.

"By jove, won't the others be fascinated to hear of your adventures, you will have to write a book you know."

"Has it ever occurred to you that you might write a book about your adventures?" Paddy asked. "I would bet a months' pay you get some excitement one way or another when you come on these trips, or whatever it is you call them."

"Patrols, we call them patrols. Can be anything up to thirty days."

"You mean you live in here for a month without seeing the outside world?"

"Well, some of us see it at night time. During the day we stay submerged, particularly here in the Med. Too dangerous up top. Most of the engineering people, wireless ops, we call them telegraphists; and so on, rarely go up onto the bridge.

Paddy's reply said everything, "Bloody hell."

"Right, you must be hungry. I'll get some snorkers and haricots musicalles rustled up for you. No bread I'm afraid, that all went mouldy a week or more ago.

David and Paddy looked at each other, grinning widely at the exuberance of this slightly built cherub, at times in control no doubt of one of the most lethal killing machines used in the war.

"What the hell are snorkers and ... what was the other gastronomic masterpiece?"

"Haricots musicalles – baked beans. Snorkers are tinned sausages.

The Ritz can provide nothing as delectable as our snorkers I can tell you." He paused for a moment. "Mind you, when you have them twice a day for a week, they do tend to become a trifle uninteresting."

"To us," replied David, "they will be manna from Heaven," his stomach rumbling in anticipation of the consumption of real English sausages, tinned or no. The main problem they were to find with all the food in a submarine was that, tinned or not, it tasted vaguely of diesel.

The number one having departed, David and Paddy looked at each other and both burst out laughing at the incongruity of their sitting in this little steel enclosure amid the constant thud of the huge diesel engines providing the motive power and charging the batteries which would take over the propulsion when they dived just before daylight. They became more and more aware of the pervading smell within the boat, a mixture of diesel fumes, cooking odours, mildewy clothing, and 'gash,' the submariners' term for the garbage that piles up and has to be carried up the ladder in the dark to the bridge to be dumped overboard. As their food arrived so did the skipper.

"We're off now. We've secured the dingy under the grating on the foredeck. I thought I would just show you our course." He unrolled a map. "At about three o'clock tomorrow afternoon, we shall be keeping a keen watch out. Ships from Valona in Albania to Otranto in Italy and vice versa cross at that point right across our path. We may be lucky enough to get one; we've still four torpedoes left out of our original sixteen. Further south the Otranto to Corfu and Greece mainland are routed, we may get one there. Normally we would hang around a bit, but seeing we have such vitally important cargo to get to Alexandria, if we don't use our torpedoes we shall take them home."

"How far is it to Alexandria?" asked Paddy.

"About a thousand nautical miles. Say an average of ten knots – one hundred hours or thereabouts. All things being equal, should be in early on Friday. Right now," he continued, "you can use these two bunks. We serve breakfast before it gets light, so you can eat it and go back to sleep again. Have you walked far?"

"Eighty miles in the last four days."

"Well, have a good lie-in, you can do with it, then we'll have another chinwag, let you have a look at the jolly old periscope and so on – you get a marvellous view of the tops of the waves but not much else."

"Our last question, captain: whose bunks are we appropriating?"

"Mine and number one's, but don't let that worry you. We'll hot-bunk with two of the others."

"What on earth is hot-bunk?"

"When one officer is going on watch, the one coming off uses his bunk. As it is still hot ..."

"Who are the other officers?" David asked.

"Gus is the Jimmy – first lieutenant. Then Oscar is the navigating officer. Joe is the engineer officer, he smells of diesel much more even than we do, and Taffy is the exec officer."

"Hot bunking – God, what things I shall have to tell my grandchildren about," David exclaimed.

"One last thing – very important. Has number one told you how to use the heads?"

"What are the heads for goodness sake?" asked a mystified David.

"The lavatory, the bog, the loo, or whatever they call it in the army."

"Latrines," interposed Paddy.

"I'll send number one down, then he can take you and show you how they work."

As he made his way back to the control room Paddy inquired of no one in particular, "Surely to God we know how to pull a chain?"

Gus arrived and led them to the heads. "Now this is very important," he commenced. "Although we are on the surface the outlet from the heads is under the water. Therefore we need compressed air to evacuate after you have evacuated, if you follow my meaning. At periscope depth the outside pressure is about forty pounds to the square inch. Now this reservoir bottle is connected up to the boats' main compressed air ring main. You charge the reservoir with the pressure you need, according to the depth of the boat, and once that is done you pull the lever and away it will go. Now that isn't all. We'll assume you have the correct pressure in the reservoir, now you must ensure the 'discharge-to-sea' valve is open, and this sequence of events must be carried out in the right order."

The expressions on the faces of the two soldiers were pictures to behold.

"Do you mean to tell me you need to go on a course just to learn how to have a crap?" Paddy asked. Gus roared his head off.

"It's not as bad as that," he laughed. "However, this is the bit you have to remember, we call it 'getting your own back,' If, when you bend over to push the lever, you have not carried out the right sequence, or you have the wrong pressure in the reservoir, the pressure from the water outside the boat causes the contents of the pan to be blown back at some considerable velocity into the face of the flusher."

"How the hell can I go four days without having to go to the bog?" asked Paddy, not expecting a reply to his question.

"Well, when you have been, I'll show you how to do it."

"I never thought the day would come when I would need to have someone to take me to the toilet," was Paddy's final word.

Having finished their meal and operated the heads successfully they turned in, both wondering how they were going to sleep with the infernal noise going on, the rush of the air down the conning tower to feed the diesels being only part of it. The diesels required huge quantities of air to operate, the only way to feed them was from outside, down through the control room to the main engine room. Fortunately the wardroom was forward of the conning tower so the gale did not actually rush past them, nevertheless, since you were never far away from any other part of the boat in a submarine, the noise it generated made its presence clearly felt. Despite the noise, the movement and the smells, they both were asleep in no time, mainly because the bunks were very comfortable compared to most places they had slept in over the past six months.

The next morning they had their first experience of submersible travelling. Apart from the fact it was a good deal quieter it was also a good deal smoother, not that it was rough when they were on the surface, but a noticeable swell still moved the thousand odd tons of hardware. "What would it be like in a gale," David wondered, "they would have to surface presumably, to run the engines." He made a mental note to ask Gus about that later on.

During the morning they were taken individually through the boat, clambering through hatches hardly big enough to fit in a chicken house, being Paddy's comment later. They were given their promised look through the periscope. It was surprising how far in fact you were able to observe – "I feel a bit like Clark Gable in one of those heroic underwater films," David joked.

"Ah, but then you have to put your cap on back to front and throw your arm around the crosspiece," Gus laughingly replied, "they all do that on the films."

At about midday, the captain came down to them. "We're approaching a danger point now" he said. "We are opposite the heel of Italy where there are several airfields and they patrol this narrow strait – it's only fifty miles wide. If they spot us, and it is not difficult on a fine day in these clear waters, they can either attempt to bomb us, or if they are fighters they can call up Italian destroyers. A destroyer can travel three times as fast as we can underwater, so can get here fairly speedily. We may therefore have to go deeper," he grinned at them, "I understand you have had instruction in the gentle art of using the heads? Well don't forget the deeper we go the more pressure you need. Conversely if you get your own back the return is considerably more forceful." He laughed heartily at the joke as he wandered back to the control room.

"They've got a funny bloody sense of humour in these sardine cans, haven't they Sir?" commented Paddy.

At 3.50pm they were attacked. The officer slowly moving the periscope around 360 degrees suddenly called out "Enemy aircraft on starboard bow," followed by "Torpedo-carrying aircraft." The skipper immediately ordered the helmsman to go hard to port, and at the same time to go down to one hundred feet. At one hundred feet they resumed their original course and waited for an attack although an aircraft cannot see them, even in the clear blue Med at 100 feet. It was at this point that David had a clear perception of what it was like to fight blind. In fact, as he could immediately realise, you cannot fight at all, all you can do is to move as fast as you can, and in a submarine that is dreadfully slow, away from where you have been detected, in the hope that a destroyer or surface chaser of any sort will not pick you up with its sophisticated tracking gear.

The aircraft's torpedo was either not loosed, or if it was, it passed over or missed the boat. However, if the message of the presence of a submarine had been passed to Otranto, and if an attacking craft was ready to sail or already on patrol it would take an hour or so for it to reach their location. Instead therefore of proceeding directly into the Ionian Sea, the skipper decided to head due east and then move down the narrow strait between Corfu and the mainland. By the time they reached there it would be dark, they could surface and move back into the main ocean to resume their course. It was as this was being decided and the helmsman being given his orders they heard the first depth charge. Rusty gave the order to go down to two hundred feet, once levelled off he turned east ninety degrees again. The second and subsequent three further depth charges were no closer, but by now the two soldiers, and probably most of the sailors too, were aware their hunter had not lost them. A further realisation was that at two hundred feet they could hear strange squeaking noises from the steelwork of the pressure hull which had not been apparent at the surface and at one hundred feet. Rusty ordered a further $90°$ turn to port which took them back northwards. It was now nearly five o'clock. If the skipper of the Italian destroyer had not yet twigged the direction of their escape, or if he had a hot date in Otranto that evening, or if he had used up all his remaining depth-charges, or if? Suddenly there was no question of 'if.' The pinging of the Asdic in the control room worked its way up to a crescendo and a resounding crash turned the boat sideways through some thirty degrees before it righted itself. A few seconds later a similar blast repeated the movement, but from the other side. David and Paddy held on to an upright stanchion and looked at each other.

"Sod this for a lark Sir."

"It's not very pleasant is it?"

The things people say to each other as they consider the possibility of a watery grave!!

"Down to three hundred and stop motors," Rusty commanded. He knew their pursuer was aware they were still around, but to do any real damage, his depth charges would have to explode fairly close to his target. This meant they would have to be timed to detonate at a certain depth as well as in a certain area. He too, despite his sophisticated sonar gear was to a certain extent fighting blind.

They stayed where they were for three hours; hearing occasional depth charges at sundry distances from them, with some too close for comfort. They all ceased at seven o'clock. After another hour Rusty gave the order to start motors and carried out a semi circular movement to get back on his original course, hoping the destroyer captain really had given up the ghost and was not sitting up there waiting to pounce again. They went up to periscope depth, the telegraphist listening in to establish whether there was any radio activity nearby. After half an hour or so at periscope depth they surfaced, the first man up into the conning tower getting the usual soaking as he opened the top hatch. The diesels were started by the shattering roar of the explosive cartridge used for this purpose, and gradually the boat became vented with fresh air – vented being a somewhat optimistic term, it seemed nothing could remove the everlasting smell of diesel fumes and sweaty bodies. Submarine humour was reflected in their own proprietary songs:–

> If you go down in the washroom,
> All the boys declare,
> You'd better not take
> Any soap in there.
>
> <u>Chorus</u>
> For I don't give a damn wherever you have been,
> Nobody washes in a submarine.
> The Navy thinks we're a crabby clan.
> We haven't had a wash since the trip began.
> We've been at sea three weeks or more
> Now we're covered in shit galore
>
> <u>Chorus</u>
> For I don't give a damn wherever you have been,
> Nobody washes in a submarine.

> Our feet are black where they once were pink,
> Three blokes already have died of the stink.
> We hid them in the fore-ends where they couldn't be seen
> For to throw them in the sea meant they might have got clean.

Rusty asked if they would like a fifteen minute spell in the fresh air. Paddy went first, joining the Jimmy and two lookouts, each scanning their segment of the horizon continuously with their extremely powerful night glasses. After a quarter of an hour he came down and David took his place. It was an exciting and unusual experience for these two landlubbers to be standing on the bridge, an experience they would never have dreamt would come their way, and which a few hours earlier they could have done without.

Half an hour before dawn, breakfast was served after which they submerged without further irritation from Italian captains trying to make a name for themselves. They had expected to make Alexandria in the early hours of Friday. As it was, because of the delay caused by the attack in the Strait of Otranto, they arrived just before eight o'clock, or 0800 hours local time as Oscar, the navigating officer put it.

Slowly the boat manoeuvred itself alongside the jetty, seamen at either end waiting to receive lines to secure the craft. The Med being virtually tideless, they would not have to worry about the rise and fall of its moorings. Once secured, Rusty called down for the two passengers to come up on to the bridge. They had said their goodbyes over the past half hour to all down below, they now hugged Rusty and thanked him for, as they put it, the experience of a lifetime, promising him that when he was back in Blighty they would take him up in a Whitley and show him how to jump out. His answer could be classified as being a coital impossibility, no matter how double-jointed one might be.

"Your carriage awaits my Lord," he continued after having made it very plain his antipathy to jumping out of aeroplanes, pointing to the dockside where a Humber staff car waited, with a trim M.T.C. corporal immaculately dressed in khaki drill standing by.

Rusty added, "Though what she is going to say when she smells you, God alone knows, especially when the sun is really up and putting the temperature up inside to over a hundred degrees." He started to laugh until his sides ached. "Perhaps she will tie you on the luggage grid at the back. I'm going to get my binoculars to clearly see her face when she gets the first whiff." David could see his point. Not only were they dressed almost in rags – they had left their best stuff behind, and their boots looked like tramps footwear, but they had also snagged both their upper garments, and their battle dress trousers in various places on the boat. To put it in a nutshell, they were at the moment the two scruffiest soldiers in His Majesty's Forces – bar none! To make matters worse they were journeying to Cairo in the heat of the sun in their cold weather clothing which would increase their sweat rate and intensify their odour factor.

"I've come to the conclusion my dear Rusty that it is her problem, not ours," with that they shook hands again, David leading the way up the dockside wall ladder. Standing on the dockside they turned and gave an impeccable army salute to this valorous young man and the dozen or so seamen working on the craft. Rusty called them all up to attention and returned the salute, following with a parting wave, echoed by the matelots who then returned to their tasks.

Sadly Thunderer was lost with all hands six months later. Of the 54 T Class boats, 16 were lost, of the 16 S Class at the beginning of the war, only three survived to the end. The men on those boats earned their extra pay, or hard laying money as they called it for service in submarines, which amounted to the princely sum of the equivalent of fifteen pence per day.

They walked to the car, the driver affording them their second immaculate salute of the day.

"Major Chandler Sir? I am Corporal Patterson. I have to take you both to Brigadier Hopgood in Cairo G.H.Q."

"Thank you Corporal Patterson, but first perhaps you will take us to Hotel Rameses so that we can get bathed and changed. As you can see we are a trifle, what you may say, unkempt at the moment."

By this time they were standing close to the impeccably spruce, trim young figure of their chauffeuse to be. She instinctively moved back a pace, looked at the two dirty, unshaven, ragged apologies for British soldiers, lank hair hanging beneath the rim of their berets, boots filthy, apparently with half the soles hanging off, and above all emitting such a disgustingly unwholesome odour that the whole tableaux sent her into hysterics. David looked at Paddy, Paddy looked at David. "It looks as though we have another Amanda here Sir to deal with." Amanda was their driver at the Parachute Training School at Ringway who drove them from their billet at Wilmslow to the aerodrome each day, always putting the wind up them as to what they were going to have to do next.

The Corporal eventually regained control, "How did you know my name was Amanda?" she asked through her tears.

Paddy replied that as far as he was aware all corporal drivers allotted to them had to be named Amanda. They forgot all other names. This started her off again.

"Why are you laughing so much Amanda Two," David asked.

"Well Sir, it cannot be said in more gentle terms but you two gentlemen pong the place out, and in a place like Egypt that takes some doing." She was off again, continuing with, "I was just picturing your entry into G.H.Q., which you will know is almost antiseptic in its cleanliness. What the sanitised young poofters who inhabit the building will do as you pass them by I can't imagine – be off to the M.I. Room to get inoculated I should think." She was off again.

"Then why can we not get decontaminated?"

"Because the brigadier has to be on a plane at three o'clock. We've a hundred mile journey to Cairo dodging camels, goats, and children all the way so it could be midday before we reach Cairo, and then it is at least another forty five minutes to get through the Cairo traffic to G.H.Q."

The journey to Cairo was uneventful, only one goat and three chickens being transported to that heavenly animal sanctuary in the sky, although as David mused, presumably the chickens would have their own aviary, then he further mused, chickens don't live in aviaries, so what the hell would they have. Paddy asked, "Thinking about something Sir?" David explained his quandary regarding the provision of a heaven for the chickens Amanda Two had obliterated. The two discussed the problem, in depth, in the hearing of their driver, who continued to wonder what sort of nuts she had been obliged to collect.

"Amanda One would have had an answer," Paddy conjectured.

"Definitely," agreed David.

Amanda Two took this as an invitation to join in this deeply profound intellectual discussion.

"Chickens live in henhouses; therefore they would have heavenly henhouses in the sky." She then realised the ridiculous position in which she had placed herself – she was as much round the bend as they were. Like the smell which had wafted around her for the past one hundred miles she was now permeated by their zany humour, as a result she burst into a mild state of hysteria which, in the course of trying to control, she nearly hit an obstreperous camel, eliciting a volume of doubtless obscene vituperation from its driver, all adding gaiety to the proceedings.

The military policeman at the barrier to G.H.Q. came out to inspect the pass handed to him by Amanda, put his head partially into the staff car to check there were three occupants as described on the form, and very swiftly withdrew it. They heard him mutter Paddy's favourite expletive – "Bloody Hell," but seeing that, at least according to the schedule, one of the passengers was a major; he gave the customary military policeman's salute and waved them on.

"I wonder why he didn't want to see your identity documents," giggled Amanda, and continued, "I've to park the vehicle and take you direct to the brigadier's office."

She led them up the front porticoed steps into the main hall, heading for the main stairway. A voice from a sergeant behind an important looking desk roared, "Where do you think you're a-goin' of then?"

They turned, David walked to the desk and replied very quietly and politely, "Where do you think you're a-goin' of – SIR."

Amanda hurriedly showed the pass to the guardian of the inner court who immediately blustered "Well I wasn't to know you was officers, Sir, was I?"

"Well, perhaps not, but perhaps in future you might establish who people are before you start bawling at them. It lowers the whole tone of the place." The subtle mickey-taking, totally lost on the sergeant's sensitivities, brought on another fit of giggles to Amanda, which was still in evidence when she knocked on the brigadiers' door and was called to enter. As they passed through the doorway the brigadier got up and came round his desk to greet them, shaking hands vigorously with both of them.

"Right corporal, you go and get some lunch – be back in an hour – OK?" Amanda saluted, and went off to the canteen.

"Let me look at you. What a sight! What a bloody pong! I've got to have a photograph – Algy!" The yelled-for Algy ran into the room through a connecting doorway. "Algy – have you got your camera in your desk?"

"Yes Sir, and a film in it."

"Right now. This is Major Chandler and Sergeant Major O'Riordan. I would be grateful if you would take a full film of them together, apart, their boots, everything you can think of. Unfortunately we cannot get a record of their unique odour – that would be worth a fortune!"

Algy, having shaken hands with the pair and then wishing he hadn't in case he had caught something, went off, returning with a very nice Kodak Retina camera with which he took twenty four photos. At the conclusion he said, "I understand you two gentlemen will, in due course, be made life vice-presidents of the new Yugoslavia if the reports from Comrade Tito's headquarters over the radio are anything to go by."

David looked at the brigadier. "They do appear to be of the firm opinion that the sun does in fact shine from up your fundamental orifices. However more of that later. I have one hour to tell you about immediate requirements, then I shall be away for ten days. When I return we will go into the question of leave and so on. And, David, I was so sorry to hear about the loss of your mother. It must have been a real body blow to receive news like that stuck away out in the wilds, we, all of us here, felt bitterly for you."

"Thank you Sir, thank you very much."

"Right, let's get down to it."

They got down to it, 'it' providing more surprises ensuring there's was not to be a quiet life in the foreseeable future by any manner of means for either of them.

Chapter Eight

When Dieter von Hasselbek returned from his leave to join his new unit in General Guderian's army north of Kalinia on the Moscow Front in November 1941, he found his warnings to the staff at the conference he had attended at Stuttgart-am-Main, firstly to have been more than timely and secondly not to have been acted upon. The panzer unit to which he had been posted, as second in command, with the rank of major, despite the temperatures on some nights plummeting to minus 30°c, had still not been issued with winter clothing. Neither had they been provided with special equipment to deal with the effects of the intense cold on their vehicle engines, suitable footwear for mud, snow and ice, nor a sufficiency of shelter in a country known to have suffered from the scorched earth policy of the retreating Soviets who had not left a single building standing to house the invaders.

Despite the conditions, the Wehrmacht pushed on towards Moscow, at one point getting patrols into the city to where they could see the spires and domes of the Kremlin, but then Stalin threw crack Siberian troops into a major offensive – it was the nearest the German army was to get to Moscow.

Dieter presented himself to his new chief, Colonel Metzner, with a correct military salute, to be answered by, "Thank Christ you're not one of those arm raising morons we see so much of – though not as far forward as this as a rule I must say." Dieter grinned in reply. Guderian, the colonel, and he would appear to be on the same wavelength.

"I haven't seen any tanks Sir."

"No, they are not due until January, but we have three prototypes which we can look at tomorrow. I understand from the general you have been active since the beginning? You have come here highly recommended." Dieter replied with a shrug.

The colonel proceeded to outline the duties he had allocated to his second in command, which were, to summarise, sort out the officers as they arrived into squadrons and a good H.Q., get a training programme out utilising the three tanks they already had, and then as swiftly as possible be ready to move into action. "Right now," he concluded, "let's go and have a look at these beauties." They trudged through the snow to a large prefabricated building, the sliding doors of which seemed to take up half the side of the structure. Stepping through a personnel door Dieter took his first look at three monsters lined up.

"God Almighty – what are they?" he asked, breathless with excitement.

"They, my young von Hasselbek, are Tigers, the new Tiger tank. It weighs over fifty tonnes and has an eighty-eight millimetre gun on it. There is nothing in the world, Russia included, than can match it."

"And we are to have a regiment of them?"

"Yes, in due course. We shall not be fully established until the summer; in the meantime General Guderian will use us for specific tasks. Anyway I will leave you here to crawl over them. We shall eat in my quarters tonight and tomorrow you can start on all the paperwork." He turned to go; Dieter gave him a 'Potsdam' salute which was precisely returned.

For the next hour he examined every facet of this new monster. It is amazing how attached a fighting man can become to whatever type of weapon of which he becomes the master. It is an old saying that an infantryman's best friend is his rifle. Dieter had now, for several years, grown to love his Mark IV panzer. He always said it was like a woman, fast, manoeuvrable, difficult sometimes to handle, but lovely to sleep with. This Tiger was slower but it packed the punch of a heavyweight. It will blow the Russian T34's out of the ground.

The troops arrived in dribs and drabs from the railhead two hundred odd miles away, several officers among them. He quickly delegated the formation of squadrons and troops to the more senior ones, most of whom, to their surprise, being older than he was. The unit was gradually taking shape.

On the 12th of December a runner arrived at his office in the tank building, warmed by a huge pot-bellied wood burning stove which he was reluctant to leave, asking him to report to the colonel, who he found to be in a grim mood.

"I have just heard our esteemed Fuhrer has declared war on the United States," he told Dieter.

"Well Sir, I presume it was inevitable as soon as the Japanese came into the war."

"He's an idiot. Left to their own devices the Americans would have stayed out of the European conflict to concentrate on the Japs. Now that he has done this we shall not only have the US Navy fighting our subs in the Atlantic, but also they will open a second front in the west. We shall then be fighting on two fronts – we can never win in that situation, we cannot possibly match the war production of the United States and British Empire combined." The colonel thought for a few moments and then said in a low voice, "We must get rid of him." Realising what he had said he turned to Dieter. "Forget I said that von Hasselbek."

To which Dieter replied, "You have my word Sir, I heard nothing."

When Dieter went to bed that evening, fully dressed, as always, he was long in getting to sleep. Firstly with regard to what the colonel had said. The colonel was a first class, thoroughly patriotic German. There were many like him including a number of his superiors. People like Guderian for a start. Suppose they hatched a plot between them? Where would he stand if asked to join? But he would probably be too junior to be involved. Suppose he was, how would he react? A plot that failed would mean certain death. His mind switched to Rosa. Had she stopped her anti-Nazi, anti-war activities? She said she would. It would only mean one little slip or being given away by a fellow conspirator under torture and she would be put to death. Surely to God fighting the Ivans was complicated enough without introducing all these other entanglements. Particularly when you are thousands of kilometres away and up to your balls in snow.

The thoughts went through his mind over and over. He had the feeling that no matter how he worried about the situation, there was absolutely nothing he could do about it, except once again to write a guarded letter to Rosa at the first opportunity reminding her of what he had begged her – guarded because no one in Germany, particularly families of people at the front, was secure from the prying eyes of the censors, the Field Police and finally the Gestapo in Germany itself. If they would only put all these parasites together they would have another two or three divisions to fight with, not that they would be any use doing a real man's job – or so was the general belief.

Rosa, in the meantime, had thought over the admonitions David had made to her, becoming deeply divided in her desire to conform to the wishes of her darling husband, against the violent feelings of fighting the evil Nazi system, a system she had seen at first hand in the concentration camp at Mauthausen, on the periphery of which she worked as a doctor in the staff hospital. She was part of a group of like-minded people, mainly students, who opposed the war and left leaflets stating their views in telephone boxes all over Munich and elsewhere. She decided she would stop doing it at the end of the year. On Christmas Eve she and her mother left Munich to stay with Dieter's parents in Ulm for a few days, returning to Munich on the 29th. On New Year's Eve one of the students took a bundle of leaflets to a party at one of the biggest 'bierkellers' in Munich, where at midnight she hurled the cascade of leaflets from a balcony on to the crowds milling below, expecting to slip away through a side door, down the stairway into the street. She was unlucky. A Hitler youth leader, standing a few yards away, forced his way through the crowd and grabbed her and held her tight, whilst the people in the immediate vicinity promptly looked away, evaporating swiftly to another part of the building.

The police lost no time in taking a witness statement from the Hitler Youth, then promptly removed her to the Gestapo H.Q. – it would be their job from now on – 'poor bitch' as the Sergeant said to his accompanying officer.

The young woman was very brave, but very few people were brave enough to combat the vicious depravity of these monstrous people, most of whom, after the war ended, melted back into society unpunished – in fact many of them became policemen again in the new Federal Republic. One hopes that in later life they would at least suffer sickness of conscience at the wickedness they had carried out, but that, realistically, is just wishful thinking.

When arrested, she was not roughly handled, which surprised her, knowing the reputation of the police in general and assuming the Gestapo would be even heavier handed. She was taken down into the basement of the police headquarters and put into a room, not a cell exactly, but a room with just a solitary chair in it. They had allowed her to keep her watch, although they had taken her purse, and some letters she had in an inside pocket of her topcoat. It was 1.15am. It was very cold in the unheated room. One comparatively small bulb which stayed on all the time was the only lighting. She sat on the chair and waited, getting colder and colder despite still wearing her coat. From time to time she got up and ran up and down the small room in order to get warm, she carried out simple callisthenics for the same purpose, then she tired, sat back on the chair, got cold again, the whole cycle then being repeated.

At 6am a small hatchway opened in the door and a tray with a mug of water and a thick slice of black bread appeared. Removing these items from the tray, the tray was removed and the hatch fastened outside. Not a word had been spoken; neither could she see who it was who had brought her this sumptuous meal.

On New Year's Day she was left alone all day, getting sleepier and sleepier, but only being able to have catnaps sitting on the chair. At 6pm the hatch opened again and a repetition of the feast presented in the morning was offered her. During the day she had badly needed to go to the lavatory, but although she shouted no one answered her, and at long last she had to find a place in the corner of the room to relieve her bowels and bladder. She felt dirty and ashamed.

Another night was spent as she had the previous one. A succession of trying to get warm, looking at her watch, catnapping on the chair and finally and disgustingly having to relieve herself again in the corner. At 6am she was brought bread and water again. She was waiting for the hatch to open, immediately shouting to whoever was out there she must go to the lavatory. There was no reply as the hatch was slammed down and latched.

At nine o'clock she heard heavy footsteps outside. The door opened and a heavily built woman, thirty five-ish appeared, followed by a huge man in dungarees. He had a vacant, mongoloid appearance, obviously a Russian prisoner now working for the Germans. On entering, the woman immediately put a handkerchief to her nose, pointing to the mess in the corner she told the Kapo, "Clear that up," then turning to the prisoner she said in a kindly voice "I'm sorry about that, they should have left a lidded bucket for you, being new year it must have been overlooked." As she spoke, two more men arrived carrying a table with another chair lodged on it, placing it in the middle of the room. "Bring your chair up and sit down," she asked, still using a friendly conversational tone of voice. The mess having been cleared up, the Russian stood in one corner whilst the two women sat down facing each other at the table.

"Now, what is your name, and how old are you?"

"I am Gabrielle Schlicter, a student at the university, I am twenty years old."

"Now, I have a written deposition from a reliable witness who saw you throw a number of these leaflets onto people in the central bierkeller on New Year's Eve. Similar outrages occurred at other festive occasions which shows there is an organised group of you. This is an offence against the state, which, as you must know, could carry the death penalty." She was speaking in a soft, friendly voice. "Now I have investigated your family background, your parents are prosperous people who own a cinema in the city centre, your father is a party member, your younger brother is in the Hitler Youth. With that background I am sure you have been led astray by others. Now, all I want to know is the names of those others and you will be free to go and to resume your studies in the new session."

She opened a notebook.

"Well?"

"I'm sorry, I don't know any others. A woman gave me the leaflets and asked me to throw them at midnight."

"Did you not read the leaflet?"

"No, I just threw them."

"Look Gabrielle, I am a very friendly person. Sooner or later you will tell us who these other people are. I quite understand young university students latch on to crazy campaigns like this," she looked at the leaflet, "wanting to kill the Fuhrer indeed!"

"It doesn't say anything about killing the Fuhrer."

They looked at each other. Gabrielle knew she was caught. She was tired and she had been led into an elementary trap. There was no going back.

There was an edge on the woman's voice as she continued; "Now Gabrielle, we both know where we stand. My first offer is still there, you tell us of the others and you can go, if you don't, there will be other methods used – do you understand? I don't want that, I have a young sister of your age; I would not want her to be dealt with in that way. Now, write down here the names of the rest of your group." She pushed the notebook over to Gabrielle.

"I can't do it." She was thinking furiously, even if she gave the names there was no certainty this woman would keep her word. In fact it was probably just a wicked ploy; she probably did not have the authority to offer such terms. They will probably try and beat the information out of me – God, how I wish I didn't know who the others were, they could kill me then and I would not tell.

Her inquisitor sat back looking at her steadily. "I am sorry you said that. I will give you one last chance. You will die in this building if you do not tell me what I need to know. That is not all. Before you die terrible things will be done to you, why don't you see sense!" The last words spoken very loudly, making Gabrielle jump, and causing the jailer to move from his torpor in the anticipation of pleasures to come.

"I'm sorry, I can't do it."

"Very well, I did not want to have to use Ivan, but you leave me no choice." Thus cleansing whatever little conscience she had she looked at Ivan and nodded towards the door. Ivan went to the door reappearing with a vicious looking cane.

"Bend over the table." Gabrielle hesitated. Ivan moved with astonishing speed for such a big man, pulled her up by her hair, kicked the chair away and bent her double over the table. The inquisitor pushed down on to her shoulders whilst Ivan beat her on the buttocks with terrible ferocity a dozen times. She screamed with the sudden agony, when he stopped she lay sobbing across the table.

"Now will you tell me?"

"I can't."

Ivan repeated the punishment, Gabrielle by now lapsing into a state of semi consciousness as a result of the searing pain spreading through her body. Again she refused to tell. The inquisitor nodded again to Ivan, who went to the door returning with another similar cane, this one having one end split down in several places. He rolled Gabrielle over on the table on to her back, undid the buckle on her skirt and pulled it down, pulled her knickers down, rolled her back on to her stomach and bared her backside. Standing away he brought the split ends down on to her buttocks again, some seven or eight times with such force that the skin was broken in numerous places, as a consequence at the last two strokes the inquisitor herself was spattered with Gabrielle's blood. After a second session of this she was almost unconscious with the pain. The inquisitor called a halt. Again, lifting Gabrielle by the hair Ivan sat her back on the chair, her pain being so great she hardly noticed the extra agony of being seated.

"That will be all – today. Gabrielle, listen to me." Gabrielle looked up through tears of pain and outrage.

"Are you a virgin?" She nodded in the affirmative.

"Well tomorrow I shall have Ivan re-arrange all that for you. Ivan loves to de-flower German girls." Ivan, standing beside her, was making obscene gestures with his right forearm and wiping the saliva from his mouth with his other hand.

"So I shall ask you for the names in the morning. Remember, we have only just begun."

With that, the evil pair left, leaving Gabrielle crumpled on the chair, sobbing with terror and desperation, shivering with the cold on her half naked body. Slowly she gathered her faculties together, levering herself off the chair, in the course of so doing inflicting further agonising pain on herself, she stood leaning on the table until she found the strength to dress herself again and to recover her coat which her tormentors had thrown in the corner of the room. With the marginal recovery in her bodily comfort she began to reason what she could do. She could give half a dozen false names and addresses, but that would mean only a stay in her ordeal whilst they were checked out, and who knows what sort of distress would be inflicted on the people living in the addresses she gave. She could, and no one could blame her, give the names of the people with whom she had been associated. She ruled that out straight away, she could not live with herself afterwards if she did, and anyway they were probably going to execute her – they would never release her to tell others of her experiences. She steadily gained control of her thinking. There was only one way out. Before those two depraved cretins returned in the morning she would have to do away with herself. But how? Hanging was out of the question. Even if she could tear her clothing into strips to make a rope, there was absolutely no projection anywhere from which to suspend it. Even the window, small as it was at the top of the end wall, was in the form of solid glass blocks; it had no frame and was not covered by bars. Sobbing quietly to herself she wondered if she could use the electric light socket to electrocute herself, but even though she could reach it by standing on the table left behind from the morning's inquisition, the bulb was concealed in a heavy glass cover screwed into a metal ring flush with the ceiling, and anyhow she reasoned it would only be 110 volts, not enough to kill anyone unless they could hold on for a time, and since she would have to push her fingers into the socket that would not be practicable.

Exhausted by her constant hurt she sank back on to the chair only to cry out with the further agony of being seated on the hard wood. She laid her arms on the table and her head on her arms and quietly sobbed herself into a sleep, disturbed by the arrival of the inevitable slice of black bread and mug of water. She slowly made her painful way to the door, trying to get a glimpse of whoever it was out there.

"Who are you?" she asked in a broken, tearful voice. There was no reply. She took the bread and water. Washing the water around her mouth, dry with fear and with the constant breathing through it while her nose was blocked, she saw immediately what she could do. It was a tin mug, once upon a time enamelled probably, but with now most of its colour chipped off. The walls of the cellar were rough untreated sandstone. If she rubbed one part of the rim of the mug against the sandstone wall it would gradually become sharp, bit by bit, she would be able to turn the mug to obtain a two inch section honed like a razor. She would then cut her wrists.

The horror that struck her at the solution at which she had arrived sent her again into sobs of fear and total despair. Gradually she recovered, examined the wall for a fairly smooth piece of stone, reckoning this would give her a smoother, finer blade, and proceeded to move the mug rim laterally backwards and forwards until she had sharpened a small section. Repeating this, after nearly an hour she had achieved her goal, at the same time her mental demeanour had calmed to a steely determination to go through with this great sacrifice.

Gabrielle Schlicter was a deeply religious Catholic girl. Up until now the thought of the great sin she was to commit in taking her own life had not presented itself to her. But now, as the moment approached when she was to go to meet her maker she had fears of the purgatory she would surely endure. In great pain, she sank to her knees against the chair and prayed.

"Dear God, forgive me this great sin I have to commit. If I live until tomorrow I am sure the abominable torture I shall receive will result in my giving the names of my friends who have worked with me in opposing this dreadful war. They too will then perhaps name others I do not know when they too are tortured."

She paused for a few moments, crying silently.

"Dear God, take care of my dear mother, father, brother and sister upon whom I have now placed such anguish and distress. Comfort them in their torment, soothe their heartache, and bring them peace."

She was silent again for a short while, and then raising her face to Heaven, concluded her prayers:–

"Dear God, I entreat you to absolve me from this wrongdoing and accept my soul into heaven."

Lifting herself from her knees, she gradually lowered her suffering body on to the chair, placing her arms uppermost in front of her on the table. Sobbing quietly, and very afraid, she cut first one wrist and then the other. Softly she began to sing a song she used to sing in her school choir and which she had always loved so much. It was about a young man telling how his loved one had pledged her devotion to him with the gift of a ring, but then had gone away from him, the ring then breaking in two.

> *In einem kuhlen grunde, da geht ein Muhlenrad*
> *Mein liebste ist verschwunden, die dort gewohnet hat*
> *Mein liebste ist verschwunden, die dort gewohnet hat.*
>
> *Sie hat mir treu versprochen, gab mir ein ring dabei*
> *Sie hat die treu gebrochen, mein ringlein sprang entzwei*
> *Sie hat die treu gebrochen, mein ringlein sprang entzwei.*
>
> *Ich mocht als Spielman reisen, weit in die Welt hinaus,*
> *Und singen ...*

Beginning the third verse the sweet, sad haunting Schubert melody faded away as she lapsed slowly into unconsciousness. Fifteen minutes later her soul left her.

There is a horrific sequel to this evil event. When the inquisitor arrived with Ivan the following morning they found the girl dead. Ivan displayed such rage at being denied the prospect of ravishing this beautiful young woman that he stormed around, his face seething with hatred of she who commanded him. As a result, since she now feared she could no longer control him, she had him returned to the Russian Asiatic prisoners' compound at Mauthausen. Ivan was well nourished after his months at Munich. The night he arrived they set on him. He was a match for any one of them but not for all of them. They killed him and ate him. They were starving. Cannibalism was not uncommon among the Asiatic prisoners.

Chapter Nine

It was at ten o'clock or thereabouts on the morning of Sunday 28th February when the telephone shrilled at Megan's house. Megan had been on night duty all the previous two weeks, arriving home at a little after 6.30 that morning, then deciding to have a little blitz on the children's clothing before going off to bed, the children being with Nanny at the Hooper's. It was strange how the word 'blitz' was creeping into the language. After the 'blitzkreig' by the German Wehrmacht in France in 1940, followed by the "blitz" on London, the word had begun to be used commonly to describe any sustained action against a job that had been needed to be done for any length of time, hence her blitz on the children's washing.

"Who on earth is ringing at ten o'clock on a Sunday morning?" she asked herself, as she stopped hanging the newly washed clothes on the overhead drier in the kitchen. Although it was a fine day for the end of February, it was Sunday, and no well brought up housewife would hang her washing in the garden on the Sabbath.

"Sandbury 742."

"Is that Mrs Chandler?" It was a cultured voice, but one Megan failed to recognise.

"Yes, can I help you?" She thought it could, perhaps, be a visiting member of the medical staff at the hospital, but before her thoughts could speculate further she received the surprise of her life.

"I am Colonel Llewellyn. I have, until recently, been with your husband in Malaya."

"With Harry? Oh colonel, thank you so much, so very, very much for telephoning me. How is he? Is he well? What is he doing? Could he be coming home? I'm so sorry, I'm so excited." She was sounding more and more Welsh with every phrase she uttered.

"Well Mrs Chandler, I can tell you he is very well and doing a most marvellous job with people he has known for some while and with who he is on the very best of terms. Now, I am coming down to Canterbury on Tuesday to my depot, I am now posted to the Buffs. If it is convenient I could come over and see you any day after that and have a chat with you and the rest of the family. It won't be the same as your seeing Harry, but at least I can tell you what he is up to."

"That would be absolutely marvellous. I think it would be best if we met at Chandlers Lodge, then everyone can be there. If you came on Tuesday could you stay overnight?"

"Yes, I could manage that."

"I have to advise you in advance they have two majors in the

Welsh Guards staying there," she said laughingly.

"Well, since they are both presumably Welsh and we are both Welsh, I can't see there would be a problem. Now, if they were Scots or Irish we might have to ask them to retire to the breakfast room or something. After all, one has to maintain a certain degree of exclusivity don't you think?"

Colonel Gareth Llewellyn arrived on Tuesday afternoon at around four o'clock, driven by a smartly turned out lance corporal from the Buffs. Fred had taken time off to be there at his arrival, the factory presumably still functioning for an hour or two during his absence. The colonel was in civilian clothes, medium height, probably about forty but as grey as a badger as he was later described by Jack Hooper to Moira, who was away at an ordnance factory in the North East. Having descended from the Humber and been introduced all round; he reached back on to the rear seat and produced two large bouquets, one for Megan and the other, he explained, to be put on Harry's mother's grave. "Harry still had a fiver tucked away – I don't know where after all he had been through, but he insisted I took it and bought flowers for his wife and mother, which I was delighted to be able to do."

Megan thanked him profusely for taking so much trouble saying, "If we are to take the flowers to mother we had better go now or it will be dark." Although during the war, summer time carried on through the winter months – there was even _double_ summer time in the summer! – it would still be getting dark by half past five. It was decided therefore that the colonel, Fred and Megan would go to the churchyard while Rose and Anni got the tea ready.

When they returned from the churchyard they found the two majors had arrived, as also had Jack. The colonel dismissed his driver after confirming it would be in order for him to return and collect him at four o'clock on the morrow. Having each been given tea, an expectant hush fell on the gathering, broken by Fred who said, "Now, colonel, fire away."

"First of all I must tell you what I am doing here." He went on to explain how he had become the unwelcome host to a parasite which had settled in his liver. If they could not have got him away for treatment at the Hospital for Tropical Diseases in London, the only establishment having the necessary expertise in treating this very rare disorder, he would gradually get even more yellow than he is at present and be pushing up the daisies, except there are, as far as he knew, no daisies in that part of the world. "I have had my first consultation, they have carried out tests, they have told me quite frankly it is going to be touch and go, with the balance of probability on my side. Now, back in Malaya." He then gave them an outline of what was going on in the various camps. As he started this, Cecely arrived, along with Karl, as a result he went over the few sentences about the camps again, telling them how the various bodies, mainly manned by Chinese communists but led by British officers, were keeping substantial Japanese forces tied down in Malaya when they could be used to better effect, from Mister Tojo's point of view, in Burma or in the Philippines.

"Now Harry's story."

Fred interrupted him. "Colonel, do you think we could have dinner now, then we have the rest of the evening to hear the remainder of your story. However anxious we are to hear everything we must not overtire you." Fred had noticed that the colonel was beginning to perspire a trace, and that his voice was beginning to sound a trifle less robust.

The three girls had prepared soup and steak and kidney pie. Inevitably this was accompanied by Fred's elbow-bending commodity from the nether regions of Chandlers Lodge stairway, it was virtually impossible to buy wine, except cheap Australian or from on the black market. After the meal they settled down again to hear about Harry. They were told of his gallantry at Muar, of his flight as a tapper, of his exploits against the Japanese, and particularly of his friendship with the orang asli. At no time did the colonel exaggerate the dangers; he stressed the great comradeship between the men at Camp Six, the degree of comfort they enjoyed and how Harry was a tower of strength in his ability to maintain the morale of both officers and Chinese troops. He concluded with, "They are doing a marvellous job, working strictly on the basis of 'strike and away,' no heroics. The divisions they are keeping bogged down could make all the difference if they were available on other fronts. Now, can I answer any questions?"

Cecely tentatively raised her hand.

"My husband and his brother, Judge Coates, are in a camp, we know not where. Do you have any information on civilian internees?"

"I'm afraid I cannot help at all there Mrs Coates. My wife and two children are also in that position. They were taken at Singapore whilst I was upcountry. I have tried without success to trace them but the Japs will not allow Red Cross people in I understand, neither will they provide lists of those civilians held."

"I believe there is a possibility of the Red Cross soon being able to go in. colonel I am terribly sorry to hear of your family being interned, you have a great burden to bear," Jack commented.

There was a sympathetic chorus of agreement from the others.

Other questions followed. What did they live on? How were they re-supplied with ammunition etc? How did the British members get on with communists? And, of course, the question going through the minds of all of them, how did the Japs capture Malaya in such a short time? The colonel's answer to this latter question being that he could, under no circumstances, answer that in polite company. He summarised it as being one of the most disgraceful episodes in British history. He would, indeed he could not, in view of his seniority, go any further.

It was getting late. Fred arose, inducing general silence.

"I would like to thank the colonel on behalf of us all for taking the time to come and see us. I feel, and I am sure you do too, that somehow he has provided us a closeness with our Harry that has been missing all these months since Megan first received those telegrams. We all believed Harry could take care of himself, that was the first thing that anybody who knew him said about him. Now we know that to have been the case again in Malaya as it was in France. We do not miss him any the less knowing now of what the colonel has told us about him, but I am sure we are all a great deal happier in our minds as a result of what we do know.

To the colonel I extend our heartfelt good wishes in the treatment of his illness and to assure him a welcome to come and stay here at any time should he not have family connections in the U.K."

As Fred concluded his little speech there was a burst of applause, followed by the colonel thanking them all for their kindness, remarking that Mr Chandler had 'sort of hit the nail on the head.' Like so many colonials, he being an officer in the Malay Regiment all his service, they often had different groups of the family scattered all over the world. His only relative in England, his younger sister, was killed in the Blitz on London; he would therefore very much like to keep in touch with them all.

The next day he visited the factory and met Ernie Bolton and Ray Osbourne. Momentarily flummoxed by Ray offering his left hand he swiftly sized up the situation, asking, "What happened to you?"

"I had an argument with a German fuse," was Ray's joking reply.

"This bloke," Fred added clapping Ray on the shoulder, "has got two M.C.'s – if I don't tell you he certainly won't. He is now supervising our Hamilcar project.

"And what the devil may I ask is that?"

They took him around to the new Hamilcar shop where one of the gigantic gliders was almost completed.

"By God, does that thing actually fly?" asked the colonel.

"Towed I believe by a Halifax or a Stirling it will carry a small tank – ideal for our airborne people."

"Do you know, after the absolute bloody balls-up by the brass in Malaya, seeing that one object is beginning to instil in me a belief that there are still a few people left in the upper echelons of the military who are using their bloody heads." The others grinned. The pent-up feelings of the people on the ground in the Malayan fiasco were being expressed in unequivocal terms by their spokesman in the unlikely confines of a Kentish factory. It was the first time he had been able to get it off his chest other than to a very few of his military colleagues. He continued, "Do you know, there was not a single tank in the whole of Malaya. Ninety per cent of the troops, a hundred per cent of the Indian troops, had never seen a tank. They were scared out of their wits when they heard these roaring, clanking objects coming at them, and having nothing to fight them with. It was no wonder they turned and ran. Still, if I start off on that tack again we shall be here all day."

After a pleasant lunch at the Angel they returned to Chandlers Lodge to rejoin Megan and Rose, Anni having to go to the clinic that afternoon, and Jack having to be in town. His driver having arrived, at four o'clock they waved him off with requests that he keep them posted regarding the results of his medical tests and eventual treatment, and the renewed offer he should come and stay when he was able.

The days passed quickly. On the Friday after the colonel left, Megan had a pleasant surprise in the form of a pay increase. As a senior hospital sister she would now earn £180 per annum, furthermore night duty was to be restricted to a maximum of six months in any one year. Students entering the profession also benefited in the new pay structure in that they would no longer be required to pay initial fees to become probationers. They would now actually receive a salary – 'what's the world coming to?' was the view of the majority of the senior staff.

Although it had been a bad winter, spring began to show itself. Karl received a letter of acceptance and waited for his bus at the War Memorial, only a few yards from his front door. There were two other people waiting, a man and a woman, both, he imagined, around the forty mark. (He was getting to think colloquially nowadays!) When the bus arrived they climbed on, showing their passes despite the fact the driver knew them almost as well as he knew his own family. As Karl told Anni, that evening "Regulations are regulations I suppose." Karl had to show his letter, which the driver checked against a pad on his dashboard. All things being in order, the bus drove off, its departure as anonymous as had been its arrival.

When he arrived back at Sandbury at about five o'clock that afternoon, Anni was like a cat on hot bricks to find out how had he got on? Were the people nice? Was the work difficult? Did he have a nice lunch? Did the people on the bus talk to him? Did he now have a special identity card? – She even asked if he would get a holiday in the summer! Karl burst out laughing at all this, realising as he did that this display of cross-examination was the result of her pent-up feelings of excitement and pleasure at the thought of her father's inner pride of being able to work for the country that had given him and his daughter sanctuary. He answered all her questions, showed her the identity card with the embossed photograph on it taken at Fort Malstead, about which she declared – inevitably – "It's not a bit like you," ending up with "how about some tea then for a working man?" She hugged him and literally danced into the kitchen to put the kettle on.

On Tuesday 16th March Megan received her second great surprise of the month. A wonderful, wonderful, wonderful surprise, as she excitedly told Rose over the telephone. A letter from Harry!! It had taken a month to arrive, was stamped 'A.P.O. Colombo – Passed by Censor,' but had not been opened, presumably because on the reverse it had the sender's name. W.O.I. Chandler H. MBE, Force 136.

"They probably thought a bloke like that can be trusted to the hilt," Fred had guessed, and that in fact was what had gone through the censor's mind when he had picked the envelope up. Fred continued, "Well, read it to us, leaving out the luvvy-duvvy bits of course."

Megan scanned the letter and replied after a few seconds. "Give my love to the family."

"Do you mean to tell me that in all those half a dozen pages that's all he has to say?"

Megan teased a little more.

"Well he does say he has written to Rose and included a line or two to you."

"You mean we are getting a letter as well? I wonder how they have managed that – must have been collected by submarine, there is no other way it could happen. You know, the things that are going on that we know nothing about. Lord Ramsford's organisation, people operating behind the lines in Burma I've no doubt, Harry's lot, David and Paddy's lot and so on. The government asked everybody who had taken photographs at the French seaside during their visits before the war to loan the pictures. Most of them will be of little use; others will be invaluable for when we open the second front. I bet even now we have small navy and marine parties reconnoitring beaches over there under the very noses of the Jerry guards. Anyway enough of all that, what does he say?"

Megan read out the bits about living conditions, what the jungle was like and how you learnt to live with, and in it, after a while. There were no gory details of course, that would not be Harry's way, but there was, to Megan's sixth sense, a deep longing to be with his wife and family again although it was not expressed directly, he would not want to inflict conscious melancholy upon his Megan. The exciting news in the letter was that they could now write to him. It would reach him spasmodically, but at least it would eventually arrive.

"They must be going to use air drops to reach them," was Jack's view, "but where from, by whom, and with what sort of aircraft I cannot imagine. They are a very, very long way from anywhere else, and it would not be practicable to continually send submarines to them, either from the operational point of view or the risk Force 136 must run in coming out of the jungle to meet them on the beaches. "Well," he concluded, "we shall know all about it one day I dare say."

There was general discussion for a few moments, interrupted by Jack.

"Oh, by the way, I had to go to the ministry today and I learnt the most staggeringly important piece of news affecting all male civilians."

The chatter ceased immediately in order to fully comprehend this momentous, far-reaching news, of such gravity that Jack had to hold the floor to articulate it. He continued, "Mr Dalton, the Minister for the Board of Trade, announced in Parliament that he was rejecting, absolutely, demands for the removal of the ban on trouser turn-ups. He stated that millions of yards of cloth had already been saved by not having turn-ups, therefore the ban will continue." There was general laughter at this with Jack following up with, "But do you know, they debated this for over thirty minutes!! Arguing about trouser turn-ups in the middle of the biggest war ever known! The funny thing was I had to see him later – I was allowed five minutes then thrown out, but I did get a suggestion in – why doesn't he insist on everyone wearing shorts? Dalton doesn't often smile but he did a bit of a grin at that."

Rumours were circulating that Winston Churchill was very ill. How they leaked out is anyone's guess, but leak out they did. There was a feeling of great anxiety in the public as a whole, and certainly in the Chandler community at Sandbury. There was an almost universal connection in the peoples' minds between the health, and therefore the leadership, of Winston Churchill, and the winning of the war. Illogical? Probably. A fact? Indisputably. There was no one else of his stature who could have led the nation out of the chaos after Dunkirk, the nail-biting result of the Battle of Britain, and the Blitz on London, and still convince the battered people of these islands we could win.

On Sunday the 21st March the nation was unburdened of the fear of his ill health by a strong forthright speech in which he described he had been struck down with a fever for two weeks, but had been kept well informed of what was happening in Parliament, particularly with regard to the Beveridge report. He stressed very strongly that the Beveridge report, and all the benefits it would bring to the people, would be put into effect WHEN PEACE COMES. "We must not think the war is over," he boomed, "we have, with our allies, a long way to go, before that day comes, not only here in Europe but also against that formidable foe in the Far East."

The speech was received with relief and enthusiasm by his listeners, not so much, one might suspect, for its content, but for the fact that he was up and about again and still carrying the fight forward.

The next day Harry's letter arrived for Rose and Fred, with love and best wishes appended for everyone else he could think of! Explaining he was only allowed four pages he had made the writing so tiny they could hardly read it without a magnifying glass – that in itself is a work of art considering the very elementary pen and ink he had scrounged from Matthew Lee. The letter however, served as a direct connection with him, flimsy it was true, but the best they could hope for. At least they could write to him now, that was a step in the right direction; hopefully 'they' would find a way to get letters from him sometimes in the future. Unfortunately that would not be possible for another two and a half years.

March ended with another great victory in the desert. Monty had attacked the Mareth Line, the gateway into Tunisia. In the meantime an armoured force, which included Mark and Charlie, made a daring left flank movement around the Line to ten miles behind the German defenders, who fought valiantly to prevent being cut off, a number getting through to fight again, but the majority were overcome and taken prisoner. The Mareth Line battle was a classic, opening the way to finishing the Afrika Korps for good.

On Monday 29th March two things happened. At a little after ten o'clock Megan received a telephone call, accompanied by the usual 'who's that I wonder?'

"Mrs Chandler?"

"Yes, Megan Chandler speaking." She had always answered, 'Megan Chandler speaking' so that she should not be confused with Ruth or Pat. Now both Ruth and Pat were gone, the habit still remained, despite the fact she had told herself time and again she should just say 'Yes,' or 'Speaking,' as ordinary people do. Somehow or other she couldn't bear to part with the memory of those two people she had loved so much, by not answering 'Megan Chandler speaking' she would, somehow, in some convoluted way, be being forgetful of them.

"Mrs Chandler, this is Captain Reed, the adjutant at the Buffs Depot at Canterbury. I am afraid I have some bad news for you."

"Oh no, not Colonel Llewellyn?"

"I'm afraid so. He died of his liver complaint on Saturday night. He has left a letter here to send to you in the event of his death, which of course I shall do." Megan cried quietly for a few moments, the news being so unexpected on this bright spring morning. The adjutant waited, then continued, "We shall be having a military funeral here a week today in the garrison church followed by the interment in the military section of the city cemetery. If you and members of your family would like to attend we shall be most pleased to have you collected from Canterbury station, and to join us for lunch in the mess after the service." He paused again. "I'm sorry to be the bearer of such bad news. Perhaps you will be able to telephone me in a day or so to let me know the details of the number of your family attending, and the time of your arrival." He then gave her his number, and rang off, leaving Megan very depressed. Megan was used to death. She had seen it every week for years in the hospital, young children, accident cases, elderly folk, she had seen them all, to her it was never 'part of the job,' she felt a loss at every one. And now the colonel was to be buried without the presence of one person who loved him or whom he had loved. It was so sad.

Whilst Megan was talking to the adjutant, Oliver Coates and his friend Fotheringham were getting on the train for the short journey to Maidstone. They went straight to the recruiting office, were given a medical examination which comprised it seemed:–

"Strip off.

Can you see the letters on that board?

Bend over.

Cough."

And they were in – subject to parent's permission, being under eighteen. They were out in forty minutes exactly according to the big town hall clock and would receive their calling up in about a month. It was a bit deflating really, no welcome, no thanks, no King's shilling, no nothing. They looked at each other and laughed their heads off, much to the amusement of the passers by of the City of Maidstone, then walked into the nearest pub to celebrate with a pint of best bitter, feeling very manly since they joined the army.

When Karl had been catching his bus each day for a couple of weeks, Anni noticed than on a number of occasions he had mentioned 'Mrs Gordon said so and so, Mrs Gordon has a cat, Mrs Gordon is away this week.' At last Anni's curiosity got the better of her.

"May I ask who is Mrs Gordon?"

"Oh, didn't I tell you?"

"No, you jolly well did not. You are not having a paramour tucked away that Ernie and I know nothing about I hope."

"As the English say – I should be that lucky. That is what they say isn't it?"

"Come on, who is Mrs Gordon?"

"She is a lady I meet on the bus – I don't work in her section, I just meet her on the bus. You see we are the last to get on. All the others seem to always sit in the same seats, which leaves us to sit in the double one at the back, so when we are coming home we sit there also."

"So I suppose it could be described as your being thrown together by fate in the back of the bus where nobody can see what you are getting up to?"

Karl looked at her, was just about to protest when he stopped and said, "You are doing, what they say – taking the micky, nicht war?"

"Just a little Daddy dear. Now tell me about your paramour at the back of the bus."

"Well, Mrs Gordon lives down by the Crown and Cushion. She is a widow, her husband died in 1938. I would say she is about forty years old, perhaps a little more. She is bright and cheerful, has a daughter of seventeen and a son of fifteen, both of whom go to grammar schools in Maidstone. Tell me, what is a grammar school?"

When Ernie came home that night and they were snuggled up in bed, Anni said, "I think my father's got a lady friend."

"Good for him, come on tell me everything."

"Well apparently they snog on the back seat of the bus to and from work." The thought of that made Ernie jump with laughter, to the imminent danger to the contents of Anni's very noticeable bump.

The next morning at breakfast, after Ernie had taken tea and toast up to Anni, he casually looked across the breakfast table to his father-in-law and asked.

"What's all this I hear about you snogging on the back seat of the works bus?"

"Snogging – what is snogging? I do not know snogging. Ah, now I know, that Anni has been telling stories nein?"

"Telling the truth more likely. Anyway we shall have to meet her to make sure she is a suitable person for you to know."

"You too are taking the micky, ja?"

"No, not really. Good luck to you. It would be good for you to have a nice friend."

But the ways of friendship never run entirely smoothly especially if some members of a family insist that no German could be a friend – there was no such German as a good German!

Chapter Ten

An hour before dawn on Sunday 28th February the combined forces of Camp Five and Camp Six moved out of their bivouac area overlooking the rubber godowns of Kampong Bintang moving in open order columns towards their objectives. Camp Six was to capture the place and eliminate the defenders; Camp Five had the equipment to burn the place down. Clive, leading the assault section reached the guards' compound just as dawn was breaking. He was surprised to find there were no sentries; presumably the Japanese commander considered they were in such an isolated spot, approachable only from the river, that they were unnecessary. As Clive began his assault on the guards' quarters, so Harry and his section doubled past to defend the landing stage area nearly half a mile down the newly made road, and Robbie led his section to the godowns. As Clive and his men burst in on the still sleeping Jifs, not a man put up any resistance. Two problems flashed through Clive's mind: firstly where are the two Japs they saw with the Jifs; secondly, what the hell do you do with thirty-odd Indian mutineers, standing at that moment with their hands straining hard towards the heavens in order not to give an excuse for someone to despatch them to that great curry house in the sky, or wherever the hell it is they go to. He ordered their weapons to be collected and taken outside then told them to lie on their beds and stay there, leaving two guards to watch them. They hunted through the adjacent lean-tos but could find no trace of the Japs.

"Probably have women in Kampong Sir," Choon Guan suggested.

"I didn't think of that. Still if they make their way here Captain Stewart will soon see to them."

"What do we do with the prisoners Sir?"

"I'd like to shoot the bastards, but of course we can't."

"No Sir, of course," but behind that apparent agreement Choon Guan was formulating other plans.

In the meantime Harry and his party were trotting on, when about 150 yards from the jetty they came to a very precipitate halt. So far they had heard no shooting either from the guard's quarters or the godown area, he assumed quite rightly therefore they had been taken without resistance. He now, as he described it later, very nearly had a baby!! There, outlined in the breaking dawn, tied up to the jetty, only its top half visible above the river banking, was the bloody motor launch, complete with medium machine gun pointing straight down the road at them. There was no one about on it as far as he could see, but with dawn breaking there certainly soon would be. As this thought went through his mind a man emerged from the deckhouse, then stood and peed over the side into the river. "They will all be doing that any minute. If we rush them now it's going to take us only a minute or so and we shall be in amongst them before they know what's happening." The man on deck, in the meantime having found sweet relief, disappeared below.

"Right, let's go," he said in a loud whisper. They raced for the boat, cocking their weapons as they ran. Harry waved three of them to the aft well, told three others to stand on the jetty, whilst he and the others jumped on to the front of the boat and into the wheelhouse. Immediately they started firing through the openings leading below, hearing screams of pain from those being hit. On the far side of the boat Harry saw a small galvanised chimneystack which obviously came up from the galley.

"Everybody off," he yelled, "throw grenades in," and with that he took a grenade from his pouch, let the safety clip fly and dropped it down the chimneystack. The second he jumped off on to the jetty the others threw their grenades into the well of the boat and down the hatchway, none losing any time to then put as much distance between them and the boat as they could before they threw themselves to the ground.

Three or four simultaneous roars went off at which the boat seemed to split lengthways disgorging bodies, bedding, kitchen utensils, boxes of ammunition for the machine gun, life belts, and all the paraphernalia a small boat with a dozen men on board would carry. As soon as all the airborne bits had landed the men looked at the havoc they had induced, when to their astonishment a Japanese, clad only in a pair of underpants, blood streaming down his face and arms, carrying a sub-machine gun, fought his way through the corpses and other debris intent on taking on his attackers. The way he kept brushing his eyes indicated the head wound was almost blinding him, yet still he came on. The men watched him in silence until, at last, he spotted a target, raised his weapon, at that point half a dozen Chinese took revenge for all the massacres his race had inflicted in the land of their fathers, blasting him off the side of the boat into the murky Pahang River.

The boat itself was settling into the water as a result of splits in the hull. Harry ordered two of his men to strip the machine gun and throw the bits into the river; he wanted to prevent the Japs from being able to use that one again even if they did have plenty more tucked away in the Imperial Armoury. The men looked at him in some discomposure. "We don't know how Sir."

"That makes three of us," Harry replied, jumping down on to the foredeck. Although he had, on occasion, been on the receiving end of one of these playthings he had never actually seen one close up, let alone learnt how to strip it down. The men had followed him on to the deck.

"Just pull out any pins that will pull out, unscrew anything you can unscrew, and if nothing still comes apart we will tie a couple of grenades to the working bits and run for it."

The two Chinese grinned and began their examination, the boat slowly sinking all the while. More by luck then judgement one of them found out how to remove the firing mechanism and other assemblies around the breech. "Right, that's enough," Harry ordered as the pieces plopped into the water. "Now, run for it, I'll leave a grenade at the breech end. It won't be much good after that." The two men leapt up on to the jetty and legged it without being ordered twice. Harry took a grenade from his pouch, looked round to confirm his line of retreat – he would have only four seconds to get on to the jetty and throw himself flat, and you don't go far in four seconds when you are cluttered up with military equipment. He jammed the grenade into the opening where the firing mechanism had been, took the safety pin out, let the firing lever fly and was away. "One, two, three," he counted and threw himself on to the jetty. Nothing happened. Too old a hand to sit up and see what was happening he began to crawl along the jetty until he could shelter behind a substantial teak upright about twenty yards away. And that was the sight that met Clive's eyes as he appeared down the road having left Choon Guan in charge of his group whilst he came down to see what all the noise was about in Harry's theatre of operations. As he arrived and for the first time got a good view of what was happening, he saw a smoking boat slowly sinking into the river. Half a dozen men concealed behind any cover they could find, Harry crawling along on his belly, and no sign of any enemy anywhere.

"What on earth is going on?" he asked himself, not exactly in those words it is true, but to that general effect.

Harry spotted him. "Take cover Sir," he called out.

"What the hell from?" he yelled back, still walking towards the prostrate Harry. As he spoke he found out. The grenade went off. It not only went off, it had fallen on to a box of ammunition at the side of the gun, which began to explode, for the next five minutes giving a display that would not have disgraced Crystal Palace on firework night, except that each explosion was accompanied by the discharge of an extremely lethal projectile whistling and cracking through the air whilst the immediate examples of homo sapiens were fervently desirous of being elsewhere. Gradually the boat sank beneath the water and the fusillade ceased, they all emerged from their various hidey-holes, standing on the jetty together regarding the results of their handy work.

"Do we get a special bonus for sinking ships of the Imperial Japanese Navy Sir?" asked Harry in front of a grinning audience."

"You chaps have done a marvellous job, absolutely marvellous, attacking a boat head on with a machine gun pointing straight at you, bloody marvellous."

As they stood there they could see the first plumes of thick black smoke coming from the godown area. "Right, I must get back. Draw back to cover Camp Five, retreat when you hear the whistle. See you later." "Bloody marvellous," they heard him say as he trotted away.

Harry disposed his small force to positions watching up and down the river. Half an hour later, the smoke having increased to such an extent it almost blotted out the newly risen sun, he heard the three long whistle blasts from Clive which told him to retire to the camp area to take up positions with the rest of Camp Six force to cover the withdrawal of Camp Five personnel. As they retired he wondered what would happen to the prisoners they had seen during their reconnaissance the day before – "God, was that only yesterday?" – among whom there were four white men. Come to that what would happen to all the prisoners once the Japs arrived, or for that matter would the Jifs take it out on them for the humiliation they had suffered? He discounted the latter, they would only do what their masters told them, which meant that if the Japs were feeling particularly bloody at the loss of their boat, their men and their godowns they could very likely tell the Jifs to kill the prisoners, particularly the white ones. In any event he could do nothing about it.

When he arrived at the compound he found the decision had already been made. The four white men, all Australian, would be taken to Camp Five, it being nearer than Camp Six, in the state they were in they would never make the eighty miles up to Clive's hideout. The others, a mixture of Malay, Chinese and a handful of Tamils would have to be left. The Jif's rifles were all smashed so that they could not use them, and the bolts thrown down a well. There was nothing more they could do.

As Camp Five moved off, Major Grenville shook hands with all the Camp Six personnel, congratulating each one for an excellent operation. When he came to Harry he said, "Clive has told me of your dash and the sinking of the gunboat with all its occupants. We have agreed we should recommend you for a decoration, not," he added, "that you will hear about it I don't suppose for another twelve months or more. You see, the more Japanese we kill, and the more damage we do, the more help we shall get from the powers that be. The sinking of that boat put the gilt on the gingerbread on what was already a very successful operation," he then added thoughtfully, "provided we get away alright." With that they shook hands and he moved off.

An hour later the four groups from Camp Six moved out at fifteen minute intervals to rendezvous at their previous overnight bivouac area, Harry's group being the last to go. Harry was puzzled that no one yet had shown a face. The prisoners were keeping a low profile in their quarters, the Jifs likewise, not a soul was to be seen in the direction of the Kampong, it was quite eerie. In the meantime the flames were reaching hundreds of feet into the air from the burning rubber; the smoke by now must have been seen from miles away. He reasoned that since the only access to the Kampong and the godown area was from the river it would take a couple of hours for troops travelling on the river to get to them from anywhere approaching civilisation. He could not have been more mistaken. A little over twenty miles due east at Kampong Terlang the Japs had taken over a small airfield originally built for the R.A.F. from which it carried out reconnaissance flights looking for allied submarines in the South China Sea. One of these aircraft returning from a dawn patrol was redirected to take a look at the source of the enormous conflagration producing this huge column of smoke. The first Harry knew of their unwelcome visitor was a twin-engined aircraft appearing from behind the smoke, at very low level, clearly showing six small bombs fitted to exterior racks beneath the wings.

"Don't look up," he yelled, but the damage had already been done, as not only was everybody already looking up, but two of the more excitable members of his party were already standing up and firing at it with their rifles. It was lucky that his men were well spread out. The aircraft had a tail gunner who, spotting the two men being so impolite as to direct fire at his aeroplane, gave them a burst from his four machine guns, with which it was impossible to miss.

Harry yelled, "Get into the ditch under cover." They spread out, each getting into foliage of one sort or another to become totally concealed. The pilot turned, came back over the area where the two dead bodies lay in the bright sunlight raking the ground with its multiple machine guns. Although there were some very near misses, including a hit on the butt of Harry's tommy gun lying on the bank beside him which tore a chunk out of the woodwork, there were no further casualties. The plane then circled to the north, came back over them at which they found themselves on the receiving end of two of the bombs, which fortunately landed in the soft paddy a hundred yards away. Turning again he came back and dropped two more. One fell some twenty yards from Harry's far right wounding the guerrilla nearest to it, whilst the other hit the end of the building housing the Jifs. As the Jif's poured out, waving to the airplane in an endeavour to get it to stop, or at least not to bomb them, the gunner saw them as another target – they were obviously not his fellow compatriots – and gave them a burst or two.

Turning again, they dropped two more bombs, killing another of Harry's men, and finally came back to drop their last two which did no damage. It droned around for another twenty minutes or so, but not spotting any more targets, went home, having told his control what the situation was and they in turn having organised another boat to come up from Pekan.

Gradually the wind changed round blowing the smoke back over Harry's now very small force, giving them the opportunity to slip away across the paddy into some sort of cover until they reached the rendezvous point. Before they went, Harry was faced with the situation he had dreaded might confront him one day. The wounded Chinese was totally incapable of mobility of any sort. One leg was unrecognisably crushed, his back pitted with pieces of metal and stone. He moaned quietly with the pain, his hand being held by a comrade who had been his friend since they were young boys together at the infants school in New Bridge Street in Singapore.

"Right, move away across that paddy to that tree over there. I will catch you up."

The remaining six men from his squad moved as ordered, knowing what Harry had to do. He let them get a fair distance, then drew his revolver, lifted the back of the recumbent soldier and shot him through the back of the head. Looking down at what he had had to do he felt violently sick. He had killed many men so far in this war, and would likely kill more, at no time had he lost sleep over it. However, this killing would wake him often in the nights to come, and too, in the years to come.

They reached the bivouac area, Clive coming out to meet them. Harry told him briefly what had happened, Clive putting an arm around his shoulder saying, "Harry, I'm so sorry, I'm so sorry." Seconds later he ordered, "Right, move out; let's get into some cover before the bastards come back."

That four day march up into the high jungle seemed endless to all of them, particularly to Harry and Choon Guan. At the end of the second day they both developed dysentery. Having to stop at the beginning of the attacks every half hour or so, this deteriorated into fifteen minute gaps, then almost every five minutes. Accompanied as the discomfort was by knife like pains, only supreme will power kept them going. Eventually they had to walk without trousers, both feeling humiliated at the filth running down their legs on to their boots. Their equipment was taken from them and shared among the remainder. At the end of the third day they camped near a stream and were able, with help, to wash the filth off. When they eventually struggled into camp on the fourth day they both collapsed and were put to bed by Matthew Lee, who stuffed them with dozens of a sulpha drug, each tablet the size of a shilling. In a couple of days they recovered sufficiently to go to their own quarters in Harry's case being greeted by Robbie, "Well, you certainly pong a bit better now!"

Good news followed at the weekend. A signal received by Terry in the middle of Saturday/Sunday night, having been de-coded, informed them their supply drop would be made the following Sunday morning at 0300 hours. There was some discussion over a last minute problem which had not previously been considered, namely, what to do with the parachutes? They would not be able to leave them lying around, they would be white in colour so that they showed up at night, but would stick out like sore thumbs to any aircraft flying over in the daytime. They would not have time to bury them even if they could find suitable places in that rocky terrain to dig holes. They would be reluctant to carry them back to the camp, although they could make good use of the material in them if they did, since each chute weighed about thirty pounds – almost a one-man load.

"How many loads do we get?" Clive asked Terry.

"Since they are dropping to three camps I would think about half a dozen."

"Right. We take six extra men to carry the chutes back. Now, if they get hooked up in trees, how do we get them down?"

During the following week they manufactured two extending poles from female bamboo, whilst the camp blacksmith made some grappling hooks and a razor sharp fifteen-inch knife to fit on the end of the pole or poles when extended. The men detailed to carry the chutes would carry these poles and fitments, assemble them on site, and drag or cut the chutes down. As Clive remarked, "Necessity is the mother of invention." Another invention they had to perfect was the flare path they were going to have to provide. In the end that was not too difficult. Although the nearest rubber was a day's march away, there was always the odd self-seeded tree in the secondary jungle. Latex therefore was gathered, soft wood soaked in it for several days and presto! You have a torch. In one or two cases they over-egged the pudding and found themselves with a mini bonfire!

At dawn on Saturday morning they moved out to be in position before dark that evening. Everything now depended on the weather. It would be just their luck, Robbie contended, for heavy rain to come down at the crucial time and totally blot out what should be the moonlit dropping zone. They would, in that case, in addition to getting very wet, have the disheartening sound of their goodies, including their mail – and the bloody rum Robbie reminded them – wending their way back to Kandy, wherever the hell Kandy was!

As it was, the weather held, the aircraft was on time, that is "on time" in R.A.F. terms – only twenty minutes late. Twenty nail biting minutes in which prayers went up even from the communists who, until then had forgotten how to pray. The flares worked, only two chutes were stuck up high trees, quickly recovered by the 'Extendable-Grappling-Equipment Parachute Recovery Party,' as Harry had christened them, this name causing much hilarity in an already worked up assemblage.

It took longer than they had calculated to break down the loads into portable packs, an hour after dawn they still were not ready to move out. With the noise of the aircraft presumably being unrecognised as one of their own it was, they considered, highly probable the Japs would send a reconnaissance unit up at first light to see what, if anything, was going on. They need not have worried, there was no reconnaissance unit anywhere for miles, and anyway the plane had flown more or less the length of the spine of the Malay Peninsula so the Japs would not know where to look first. Eventually the packs were made up and the long crocodile made its way off the plateau up into the high jungle. They had an hours' break at midday, then pushed on to arrive to an enthusiastic welcome from the camp defence section just before dark.

Joe Rogers, the navy sub-lieutenant, had been appointed 'Drop quartermaster,' as well as the rum issuer. He had two Chinese storemen to assist him in unpacking, logging and issuing the goods, checking what they received against what had been asked for, as a result nothing would be available until the morrow – except, that is, the mail from the U.K. This he delivered in person to each of the officers. There were a few for Clive, most of his relatives being colonials; a handful for Robbie who had few contacts outside Malaya; Terry received a goodly number in what seemed to be a variety of female hands, about which he made no comment. Harry had an armful deposited on his bed, with the parting comment from Joe – "That'll keep you out of mischief for a while." Harry looked at the heap of battered, crumpled mail and was so overcome with emotion the tears streamed down his face. It was a full ten minutes before he could begin to sort them into piles, from Megan, first of all, then Rose, then Anni, then Fred, then Jack, and last but not least, what he called the 'miscellaneous file,' David, Cecely and Greta – there was even one from Karl. Megan had numbered her letters on the back of the envelope, the original idea being he would know if one went missing, although as he had originally told himself 'What the hell he could do about it Lord alone knows.' He set about putting them in order. He set to reading one, then another, but found what he was seeing was not really registering. He had been awake now for nearly forty-eight hours, had marched around forty miles in that time, he still had not fully recovered from the debilitating effects of the dysentery he had suffered the previous week, he was dead on his feet. Reluctantly he gathered his precious letters together from his bed, pulled down his mosquito net, checked it was properly tucked in, checked there was no unwelcome visitor inside it and collapsed into a sleep so deep it was known by these warriors, who had to stretch their endeavours at times to such an incredible extent, as a 'short course of death.'

The next evening they all had their first rum ration. With the combination of their first tinned 'M and V' – steak and vegetables, and the tot of rum their morale was such they would have taken on the whole bloody Japanese army on their own. As far as they were concerned, this was the turning point of the war, that one air drop proving they were not alone, that one air drop had shown the Japs were not invincible, they certainly had no aircraft to compare with that Liberator, and with the news they gathered from the half a dozen copies of The Times of India dropped to them, the Germans were on the run in North Africa and the Russians were giving them a bashing on the Eastern front. It was automatically assumed that once the Jerries were knocked out, the Japs would get their comeuppance. Clive let them enjoy their current euphoria knowing only too well they had a long, long way to go yet. He would give them a couple of weeks light duties before they carried out 'the big one.'

Chapter Eleven

In the hour David and Paddy had with Brigadier Hopgood before he had to fly to London, they were told what he required of them before he returned in ten days' time. Firstly they were to go to the hotel they were billeted in before they went off on their holiday to Yugoslavia and get themselves decontaminated – he had already arranged for a platoon of the Pioneer Corps to come in and fumigate the conference room they were using. Secondly they were to provide as accurate an account of their day to day movements with the partisans as they could, noting any particular difficulties they had encountered, any general antipathy to Britain that might exist, the causes thereof and so on. He gave David a sheet with various headings for guidance. After a number of other sheet headings to do with present equipment, discipline, military skill, the officer corps and finally the reasons David would, or would not, recommend a full mission to visit the partisans were presented, he concluded by saying, "Right, I'm off. Have a rest, get all that done and then if you want to sightsee Algy will arrange for Corporal Patterson to drive you."

Later they asked Algy what had happened to Toby, the brigadier's A.D.C. when they were here last year. "Sent home in disgrace Sir, I'm afraid; dipping his wick with one of the embassy wives I'm given to understand.

"What will happen to him Sir?" asked Paddy.

"Be promoted to major I expect, provided he promises to keep his trap shut."

Paddy looked at David. "You might make general Sir if you stay here long enough."

Amanda Two took them to their hotel saying, "I shall be interested to see what you both look like when you are civilised Sir."

To which Paddy replied, "Well now if you come and scrub our backs for us you would soon find out."

"She can't do that, we're both spoken for."

"So we are, so we are."

"I could put my very dark sun glasses on."

"What an accommodating lady she is Paddy, is she not?"

"Yes Sir, but with very dark sun glasses on she wouldn't be able to see what we look like when we are civilised would she?"

"Perhaps that's as well, she might die of laughter."

"You mean she would know the naked truth then Sir?"

Amanda Two broke in. "When you two gentlemen have finished your discourse, may I ask if you have Captain Finney's extension number so that should you require my services you know where to contact him?"

"Require her services Paddy? As I said, we are both spoken for."

"So we are Sir, so we are."

"Oh no, not again! Sir, don't you think you and the sergeant major should go and get unpolluted before it settles in for good? If I hear on that wireless tonight there is a main drainage problem in the city I shall know what has caused it."

"We shall do that Amanda Two, we shall do that straight away, and then sleep, lovely sleep until noon tomorrow." Amanda Two gave them a smart salute as they wended their way into the hotel to the reception desk, where an incredibly pretty receptionist acknowledged their bookings, called a boy to take them to their rooms, smiled beatifically, and not once registered disgust at the malodorous hum they had brought with them. 'That's what I call a professional,' David thought to himself. Reaching their rooms they were both surprised to find they had been allocated an Egyptian bearer, their clothes laid out ready for them, their baths quickly run and a Hessian sack on the chair in the bathroom to take the garments they stood up in, and which, in fact, almost stood up of their own accord when they were taken off.

The next evening, having slept until noon, visited the hotel hairdresser and been somewhat shorn compared to their coiffure for most of the previous six months, drunk a pint of ice cold beer with their meal and feeling, in general, on top of the world, David got down to the report with the occasional helping hand from Paddy. It took three days to finish. During that time they had a visit from Algy carrying a shopping bag with a couple of dozen letters for each of them. On the evening of their arrival they had both sent cables home saying they had returned to base and would be writing, both finding when they did put pen to paper they hardly knew where to start, and there was always the bugbear of knowing that some crap-head in G.H.Q. would be censoring their feelings of love and devotion.

Having finished the report and having taken it to Algy to have it typed they were free to do a little sightseeing. Amanda Two took them to the bazaar area to buy presents to take home, they paid a further visit to the Cairo Museum, drove out to see the Step Pyramid at Sakhara, lunched again out at the Pyramids where David said, in absolute awe as he viewed them from different sides as they drove around, "You know, I could come and look at these every day and never tire of absorbing their grandeur. They can't surely just be tombs, they must mean something else, they must have been built for a purpose. I wonder if we will ever know." Amanda Two, herself a highly intelligent young woman was left with the feeling there was a great deal more to this young major than the amusing, comical tramp she had collected at Alexandria. She was beginning, in fact, to be very envious of the fortunate young lady by whom he had pronounced he 'was spoken for' to the extent of saying to herself, 'God, some girls get all the luck.'

The colonel arrived back on the 16th March, came to their hotel that evening for dinner, and promptly told them they had to stay in for another ten days to meet the brigadier leading the mission to meet Comrade Tito, then, he added, we shall get you on the first plane to Blighty.

David's meeting with the mission brigadier passed without incident other than a total of two hours of questioning by various members from different parts of the services, an air force wing-commander, an armoured corps lieutenant colonel, a commando major, an ordnance corps colonel and a major from the medical corps. How will that lot get into a submarine, David asked himself. It transpired they were going to make the journey on a destroyer – a fast one – meeting the Yugoslav hierarchy on the off-shore island of Vis on the Dalmatian coast which, after the successful conclusion of the task, would, for the remainder of the war, remain the partisan's headquarters. From there the direction of the campaign to drive out the Germans would be conducted, with the aid, it must be said, of a complete Italian division which went over to them. The Yugoslav partisans were the only resistance movement in Europe which drove the Germans out of their country without the help of allied troops, although of course they received very considerable arms and logistical assistance from the British which made it possible.

After the meeting with the mission, time hung heavily on their hands, despite the fact that the Gezirah Club allowed them to use the swimming pool. Technically Paddy was persona non grata, not being an officer; Brigadier Hopgood had given him an introductory letter to the secretary naming him as Mr O'Riordan. The secretary assumed therefore he was a civilian with a very acceptable recommendation from a brigadier no less; the brigadier had no conscience about it since sergeant majors are called 'Mister' anyway, so everyone was happy. As David commented, "Thousands of people being killed every day and we have to connive to get you a swim." At midnight on 2nd April the hanging about ended very abruptly with Algy banging on David's bedroom door with the totally unnecessary question "Sir, can you be ready to move in one hour?"

"I could be ready in ten minutes if necessary," was David's immediate reply.

"Right, Corporal Patterson will collect you at 0100 hours and take you to the airport. There is a V.I.P. party going to Northolt in a York. It's got a couple of spare seats so I've got you on."

"Algy, you are the world's greatest. I shall definitely remember you in my will. Now tell me, what the hell is a York?"

By this time, Paddy had heard the commotion next door and had joined them.

"A York is the latest luxury transport plane, four-engined, fitted out to take top brass and government wallahs on their innumerable, and usually totally unnecessary little jaunts around the world. You will, I guarantee, go neither hungry nor thirsty if what I hear is anything to go by."

"Algy, you're a gem, you really are."

Algy's natural flippancy subsided for a few moments. "If people like you, dropping into places you've never seen before and doing the sorts of things you've had to do, can't get a comfortable ride home I'm buggered if I know who should." He continued, "Anyway, it's been great meeting you both, good luck in your next little party, the car will be here at one sharp."

They shook hands warmly, with the parting comment from Algy, "I'll cable Lord Ramsford your E.T.A."

They were ready and waiting when Amanda Two arrived. With their new suitcases containing the goodies they had purchased to take home safely stowed, they climbed in for the half hour journey to the airport.

"I'm sorry you are missing your beauty sleep on our account Amanda Two," David apologised.

"Well Sir, I'm sorry you are going. It has been great fun driving you both around. The majority of people I have to look after are either frightfully boring or trying it on. You've both really been such enjoyable company, I shall miss you."

David paused for a moment. "That was a most kindly thing to say Amanda Two. And despite the fact we both are, as we have joked, 'already spoken for,' we too shall miss you and remember your kindness and personality always."

"That goes for me too," added Paddy.

Arriving at the airfield they were directed to the York. About the same size as a Halifax – in other words, BIG, inside it was different altogether. Plush reclining seating, a conference table for eight, overhead lockers, stewards galley at the forward end, toilets toward the rear, it was an eye-opener for the two paratroopers used to sitting on their backsides on an aluminium floor or at the most occupying a canvas seat strapped to the fuselage frame. An R.A.F. corporal led them to their seats at the rear, passing half a dozen civilians, a couple of whom nodded to them as they passed, the others too busy chatting to each other in exaggerated Oxford accents to even notice their existence. The corporal informed them that he would bring them drinks as soon as they were airborne. As they settled in their very comfortable seats David was heard to say, "Drive on, driver."

In a few minutes the senior ministry men arrived to occupy the front seats, acknowledging neither the junior staff already referred to, ignoring completely the two military people at the rear since they were obviously not generals, or anything like it, and talking to each other in even louder and more exaggerated Oxford accents than even their acolytes had affected.

With stops at Malta and Gibraltar, the three and a half thousand mile flight back to Northolt began to pall, despite the frequent visits with lubricating fluids and ministry standard food by the R.A.F. corporal and his two minions. At last they were informed they would be landing in thirty minutes, 21.30 hours B.S.T. The landing was faultless, they taxied to the main reception area where they espied a long line of ministry Humbers waiting to convey their illustrious passengers to heaven knows where. As David said to Paddy, "I wonder how much this little junket has cost, and what they did to justify it."

Because of the suddenness of their departure from Cairo they still wore their khaki drill uniforms, although Algy had thought to bring them each an army greatcoat. Up until the time of landing at Northolt these latter items had been rolled up in the locker above their seats. On being removed and made ready to be worn it was discovered that Algy's estimate of the cubic capacity of the frames of Major Chandler and Sergeant Major O'Riordan was sadly adrift, so much so that when they attempted to 'slip' the coats on they were found to be suitable, in their opinion, for short-arsed A.T.S. girls, certainly not for a pair of bulky riflemen. Although it was early April it was still very chilly at that time in the evening, particularly on an airfield where, from their previous experience at Highmere, they knew it was always chill, and in this case, having spent a month in the heat of Cairo, the contrast was even more marked. They were the last to alight, being greeted at the bottom of the steps by an R.A.F. flight lieutenant, one Harry Oxford, as he introduced himself.

"You are staying here with us overnight, gentlemen. Your driver is here and will be taking you back to Wilmslow in the morning." He then realised they were in tropical gear.

"Have you no battledress uniforms?" David replied.

"In a word, no. At the moment one set from each of us adorns a partisan, the other set ended up in an incinerator."

As the young airman looked so mystified David continued. "It really is a long story; we have to get new as soon as we arrive at Wilmslow."

"Well look, I'll scrounge you a couple of pullovers and an extra vest each if you like, though I must say you will look a little odd in R.A.F. blue pullover, khaki slacks and red berets."

"Not half as odd as we have looked at times over the last six or seven months I can tell you Sir," Paddy chimed in.

"Right then, I'll show you to your rooms. Do you want anything to eat or drink?"

"We're full to bursting," was David's reply "but we would like the use of a telephone apiece if that is possible."

"There are two booths on your landing. Have you any money?"

"No, but we can reverse the charges."

"Jolly good. Now breakfast is at 0730. You leave at 0800. OK? Do you need your cases? If not I'll have them put in your vehicle."

They made their way to their rooms, dumped their hand baggage, then speedily took possession of the telephone booths. Being late at night David got through to Sandbury quickly to an excited Rose, telling her he would telephone again tomorrow from Wilmslow when they knew what their programme was likely to be. After the initial, inevitable animation, David asked how everyone was at the loss of their mother, whether she had suffered too greatly and so on – words always so difficult to find Rose said that, as was so often described, their mother's life really did pass peaceably to its close, and that she was laid to rest next to Pat. "We will go and see them when you come home," Rose said and after a pause for a moment or two, "Now, have you phoned Maria?"

"No, I thought I would wait until tomorrow, she's probably not home anyway, but since she always telephones Chingford on Sundays I can at least leave a message there, then she can phone me."

Coming away from the booth, David felt very drained. A combination of travel weariness, sadness at the renewal of the knowledge of the loss of his mother, being in another strange place and with another strange bed to look forward to, all combined to make him feel dejected. "I'll feel better tomorrow," he told himself.

And he did when he found their driver in the morning was none other than Amanda One – now a full corporal and almost dancing with delight at seeing them both again. Her first words were, "You're both thinner and you do look funny in those clothes."

Paddy hugged her up. "Our lovely Amanda One, what a great

surprise."

"Amanda One? What's Amanda One?"

"Well, you see, my dear full corporal, as I notice you now are, when we were in Egypt our driver there was also Amanda, so she became Amanda Two. Now, tell us everything that's been happening with you in the last seven months during which we have not been able to keep an eye on you."

They climbed into the Dodge, making a leisurely journey back to Wilmslow, stopping at a roadside pub at around 12.30 for a snack, and eliciting curious gazes from respectably dressed Sunday lunchtime drinkers at the peculiarly garbed strangers in their midst. The one point of interest about which they were most pleased to hear was that Amanda was going steady with a lieutenant in the Canadian paratroops who she met when he came to Ringway to do his jumps.

"Steady that is, at arm's length," she explained, "he's stationed on Salisbury Plain so we only see each other at rare intervals. He came on leave a month ago and stayed with my parents and I managed to get a long weekend. Those four days are the longest we have been together, but we got on very well, and my parents liked him."

"Where is your parents' home Amanda?" Paddy asked.

"In Blackheath, South London. My father is a police inspector at Greenwich, although he is expecting to be promoted at any time, in which case we shall have to move most likely. They were bombed out twice during the Blitz, there is nothing left of the home I was brought up in, the furniture and so on, so they have got used to moving you might say."

"A pretty grim way of getting used to something I must say," David commented.

Arriving at Wilmslow at around four o'clock they found the place absolutely deserted, no receptionist in the hallway, not a soul anywhere.

"Scout around and see if you can find anyone," David asked Paddy.

"I'll do it – you get the stuff out of the back Sir, if you will, those gold bars in the cases are very heavy," Amanda suggested, laughing at Paddy, who was still not used to being called 'Sir' by the rank and file. She ran up the stairway to the first landing, banged on a couple of doors without result, then looked through a window overlooking the rear of the house to see Robin practising putting on the rear lawn. She ran back downstairs to tell David, in the meantime Robin had caught a glimpse of her as she turned and, dropping his putter, hastened back into the building to warmly greet his two emissaries.

"As Handel would have put it, 'See the conquering heroes come'."

Then as an afterthought he remarked, "Actually it wasn't Handel – he wrote the music but Thomas Morell wrote the libretto as I recall." Paddy looked at David wondering what the hell he was talking about; David again marvelled to himself how cultured a man Robin was. "Anyway, it's marvellous to have you back in one piece, your fame has preceded you, you know, Lord Ramsford and I have been dining out on your exploits in the company of some very highly placed individuals."

Paddy looked at him and grinned.

"Does that mean we shall be getting a couple of weeks leave Sir?"

"Three weeks actually, starting on Wednesday," he paused for a moment and continued "They tell me it is very pleasant in North Wales at this time of the year." David looked at Paddy, Paddy looked at David, they roared with laughter.

"Right now, the corporal here will take you over to Saughall to the Royal Artillery depot there to get you both kitted out again tomorrow morning – a special indent has been sent to their Q.M. Lord Ramsford will be here on Tuesday morning to discuss your future programme and as at present you go on leave on Wednesday for three weeks, made up by two weeks entitlement and one week disembarkation leave so I am reliably informed."

"I find the words 'as at present' a trifle minatory," David detected.

"If I knew the meaning of the word minatory I would answer that," Robin joked.

"And in answer to that I would suggest that if anyone in this county is better aware of its meaning than you I would be surprised indeed."

Robin grinned, Paddy and Amanda looked at each other with raised eyebrows, David enjoyed the little intellectual repartee.

"I say as at present," Robin continued, "because in this lark, as you know only too well, anything can happen and frequently does. However, risking my pension, as I probably am, I would think you will be on leave, on Wednesday, without doubt."

That evening, being Sunday, the lines were not busy, the telephone booths, as Paddy described it, took a fair old bashing. David phoned Chandlers Lodge to ensure no buckshee Canadian, Australian or South African was currently occupying his bed. He then phoned Mr Schultz to ask if he would get Maria to contact him, since he would be unable to get in touch with her, and received the good news that she was, in fact, home on a special forty-eight-hour pass to compensate for some extra duties she had been involved in during the previous month. She was out at the moment but would be back in about an hour. The hour stretched to an hour and a half with David nearly biting the tassels off the carpet – at least he would have been biting the tassels off the carpet had there been a carpet, however the owners from whom the War Department had requisitioned the premises had wisely removed such easily swipeable articles as carpets, he therefore had to bite on the carpet metaphorically speaking.

They had a long talk together, David telling her that he was to see Lord Ramsford on Tuesday, after which he would have a clearer picture of his future movements. He would be home on Wednesday night if she would telephone Chandlers Lodge they could make arrangements for the weekend. He went to bed that night, his head in a whirl, very tired after the past days travelling yet finding it difficult to get to sleep. Niggling away at the back of his mind was what Lord Ramsford had up his sleeve. As far as he understood, he and Paddy would now be allowed to go back to their unit, but knowing the noble Lord, there could well be an enticing little venture dangled before his eyes that he would find difficult to refuse. And their wedding. He had made no definite plans with Maria over the telephone, in fact they both seemed a little reticent to formulate dates and times, on his part because of the uncertainty surrounding his forthcoming meeting with the brigadier, and on her part because of her natural modesty preventing her from being too assertive.

They made an early start for Saughall in the morning, replacing all the items they had used up, or left behind in Yugoslavia. The Q.M., an elderly captain, ex regular R.Q.M.S., in the gunners for thirty five years, pumped them about their exploits in Yugoslavia, avidly listened to with bated breath by Amanda One receiving her baptism of knowledge of real war at first hand. The story of the submarine and how they landed at Alexandria smelling the place out was received in uproar, as three of the Q.M. staff had latched on to the telling of the tale to join the audience. David then took Amanda One and Paddy to lunch at the Grosvenor, mentally noting that they could well be seated at the same table as his mother and father had occupied such a relatively short while ago. Two tables away a colonel, a major and a lofty looking civilian looked at a major, a sergeant major and a female corporal laughing and joking together and wondered what the bloody hell the army, discipline, and class consciousness was coming to.

They drove back via Tatton Park and watched some balloon jumps and a couple of sticks from Witleys, feeling very superior at their seniority in the craft. "I've got a funny feeling we haven't seen the last of this place," David said – and he was jolly well right!!

Chapter Twelve

Dieter von Hassellbek sat at his small camp table looking at his three Tigers. It was the first day of February 1942. He and his colonel were most depressed. As a result of the Wehrmacht's failure to take Moscow, beaten as much by the weather and their lack of equipment to combat it as much as for any other reason, the news had come through that Hitler had sacked their general, General Guderian, the army commander Von Bock and others. As a result, the chief of the general staff von Brauchitsch resigned, Hitler himself taking over as commander in chief of the army. It was this latter state of affairs which concerned them most. The Austrian corporal now the absolute ruler of the army – what the hell was the world coming to?

The weather had been so bad that neither side had been able to move so far this year, apart from local skirmishes. The German supply lines were so long they had difficulty in getting food, clothing and ammunition up, and from Dieter's point of view his promised Tigers to bring him up to half strength by March were nowhere to be found. The more he looked at the three he had, the more he became concerned about their weight. His Mark IV panzer had weighed twenty tonnes but even then he had had the occasional problem of reaching a bridge which patently would not carry a dead weight of twenty tonnes, ways having to be found to get round or, or engineers called up to strengthen it. He pushed his chair back and made his way to the colonel's office.

"What can I do for you?"

"Sir, I'm worried about the weight of the Tigers. At fifty tonnes I doubt if there is a bridge, outside those in the big cities, that could take the weight, and I should hate to end up in a stinking Russian river."

"Well, as our beloved commander in chief would say – you know the problem, solve it."

"I thought I would pick your brains Sir."

"Now don't you start your clever tricks on me," the colonel replied with a grin. He paused for a moment, "Go and ask the C in C – he will know, he knows everything."

Dieter laughed. "What I was wondering Sir is whether we could have a permanently attached assault engineer battalion with the regiment once we are up to scratch. They would trail behind carrying bridge reinforcing equipment and when we are stuck go forward under cover of our firepower to strengthen any crossing point. It occurred to me Sir, that when my next three tanks arrive perhaps we could lay on a little demonstration for the divisional and army staff – when they see our Tigers they will give us anything."

"By God, von Hassellbek, you're right. You know when General Guderian recommended you to me I thought what does a bloody twenty-three year old know about organising a heavy tank battalion. If it had been anyone else I would have told him – correction – I would have suggested he go and jump off the Kremlin wall. Right, now, the thaw will start to set in soon, your new tanks will be here soon, plan out what you are going to do, and in the meantime I will see our new general about the engineer unit."

As the thaw set in, Dieter started to plan his full exercise. Six more Tigers had arrived. He had some carcases of the Soviet KVI heavy tanks, knocked out before the Christmas offensive, towed to a target area. They were thickly armoured – he aimed to show how accurate his 88mm gun was and how they would penetrate the thickest armour the Ivans would present to them. By the end of March he was ready. The new army commander General von Weichs, along with Guderian's successor, came to see the demonstration, which exceeded all expectations, at the end of which von Weichs called Dieter forward and invested him with the Knight's Cross, the next higher gallantry award above his Iron Cross First Class. This was, he was told, for his gallantry in attacking three T34's in October, knocking them out at point blank range, thus saving an infantry and artillery position from being overrun.

When he reached his quarters late that afternoon overjoyed at the success of his new Tigers, and of the utterly unexpected award of the Knights Cross, he found a letter from his sister Inge. This in itself was a rare treat. Although he and Inge differed diametrically regarding National Socialism they were very close as brother and sister. However Inge was a 'bit miserly with the writing paper,' as Dieter had often expressed it to Rosa and his parents – one letter every blue moon. He opened it with a smile, which very speedily left his face as he read the first lines.

'My dear Dieter,

I am sorry to have to tell you that Rosa was arrested, along with six other young women in Munich, for distributing literature condemning the actions of our great National Socialist state in pursuing this just war against the Bolshevik menace.'

She's covering herself here – me as well probably in case this was censored, were Dieter's first thoughts. Then it struck him, she's so indoctrinated she almost certainly believes it. The letter continued:

'As a result the six have been executed for treasonable activities, but I was able to speak for her, in particular confirming that although leaflets were found at her house she had not in fact distributed them. This was accepted by the tribunal, as a result she has been sent to

Ravensbruck for six years.

I shall do all I can to ensure she is employed in as favourable circumstances as possible. You will not, of course, be able to visit her should you come on leave.

I am sorry to be the bearer of such bad news; it was a very silly thing for her to get involved in. I realise, *absolutely* that you had no idea whatsoever of her activities, your war record indicates fully your love for your Fuhrer and your country.'

God Bless you Dieter
Your loving sister
Inge
Heil Hitler

Dieter, having read the letter three or four times, his head in a whirl, decided to take it and show it to Colonel Metzner. The colonel read it, then read it again.

"The bastards."

He paused for a while. "Just between us, did you know she was doing this?"

"Yes Sir, when I was on leave she told me. I told her she was to stop immediately, that's probably why they found the leaflets in the house, otherwise they would, I imagine, have been distributed.

"Right. Under no circumstances are you to tell anybody – not anybody do you hear? – that you had an inkling this was happening. There are one or two of the new officer intake who would dearly love your job. If they could suggest to the Gestapo you knew about this, Knight's Cross or no Knight's Cross, you would be in trouble. You know what it's like – one person piddling in the soup – that's all it needs."

"Thank you Sir, thank you for your advice."

As he left the office, the colonel thought to himself, "I think we have another good man positively committed to our cause."

The reception at army H.Q. of the request for an engineer assault unit by mid-summer was well received. The position at this part of the front had reached stalemate. By the end of April, Dieter had eighteen Tigers and knew that the divisional commander would not let a force like that sit around doing nothing for very long. His gut feeling was far from wrong. He was called into the colonel's office and told to be ready to move with twelve of his tanks at dawn the next day. The infantry were to attack once more two hillocks about a mile apart, which although not very high, enjoyed complete surveillance over the flat steppes where the Germans were dug in. Two attempts to dislodge them had already been made, but the Russians had T34 tanks hulled down on each crest, each able to knock out the assaulting Mark IV panzers. The Tigers were to take the two strong points after a heavy artillery barrage, closely supported by a Waffen SS Brigade who would finish off with the bayonet.

Dieter was excited at the opportunity to put his new animals to the test. Those commanding the exercise knew they were in no position to mount a surprise attack, on the other hand, not knowing if they had any heavy anti-tank guns on the objective – they thought not, only the tank 76mm main armaments which in themselves were heavy enough! – they put heavy smoke down for a mile or so either side of the objectives.

Those Russians with bitter experience of tanks coming at them, dug in on the forward slopes, heard and recognised something much more menacing even than the clattering, stomach churning noise of the panzers they had faced up until now. The engine roar was deeper; it was louder, the screeching cacophonous slamming down of massive steel tracks on to the hard earth literally shook the ground in which they were entrenched. This was something new, something terrifying. As the Tigers hit the edge of the objective the smoke lifted, at which the Russian T34's began to fire, or at least some started to fire. Others, seeing these new monsters appearing out of the smoke, realised they were no match for them, reversed out of their hulled down positions and made a run for it. They stood no chance. The weakest part of a tank is its rear. They were at once on the receiving end of 88mm shells that eager gunners were itching to let loose. One by one they were brewed up.

Those that did put up a fight now found themselves in the same situation in which the Mk IV panzer commanders were when they first ran up against the T34's. The armour on the Tigers was such that hits either bounced off, or at the worst caused steel splinter wounds inside the tank, but did not stop it. Six Tigers had been allotted to each hillock, they destroyed some twenty of the enemy between them, only half a dozen escaping to tell the tale of these giants which had fallen upon them. To the soldiers on both the Eastern and eventually the Western Fronts the name 'Tiger' was synonymous with being invincible, as indeed it was for the next couple of years.

The tanks were pulled back and Dieter and his crews returned to their laager. A letter of congratulation had been received by Colonel Metzner from the general – as he said to Dieter, "Another one of these and you will get me my oak leaves," referring to an even higher grade of Iron Cross than the one he held already.

After the modest celebration that evening, Dieter returned to his bunk and wondered as he did every night when he went to bed what sort of indignities, suffering even, his darling Rosa was enduring. He assumed, as probably the majority of German civilians presumed, the concentration camps, as opposed to the extermination camps, of which they knew nothing, were a harsh extension of the prison system. Many of the inmates were set to work in factories in the town near which the camp was situated. They did hard manual work, operating machines, doing assembly work, filling coal wagons if they were near a mine, mending roads, clearing bomb damage and a host of other tasks. The Germans and Western nationals were supposed to receive the same amount of food as the German worker, but rarely did. They worked a twelve-hour day and lived in large dormitories sleeping on board-based bunks with only one blanket. If they succumbed to the harsh regimen they were speedily replaced.

Rosa's first task at Ravensbruck was as a machine operator in a large electrical components factory. The work was light but dreadfully monotonous. She would stand, feeding strips of steel or other metals into the automatic stamping machine which pumped out the component into a bin, which in turn was collected by a masculine looking female Russian slave worker, one of eventually millions abducted from the conquered eastern territories to feed Hitler's war machine. The machinery was not as well guarded as would become the norm in the post-war years, but as Rosa had been told by a friendly trustee when she first arrived, "Keep your head down, trust nobody and for God's sake never complain." As a doctor she had received basic training in the requirements of safety devices on machinery, so from the beginning of her being put to work in the stampings shop she could see glaring examples of what would not be accepted with normal workers. She remembered her advice – never complain.

One day the Russian woman collecting the bin, which she would wheel away on a trolley, tripped and fell against the stamping arm as it came down. It hit her elbow with great force, fortunately not trapping the forearm. She screamed with pain, falling to the floor alongside Rosa. It was obvious to Rosa she had a fracture of the forearm, but the force of the blow had disjointed her upper arm. Two or three other operators left their machines to see if they could be of help, Rosa in the meantime getting them to hold the unfortunate woman down whilst she used all her strength to pull on her upper arm and get it back into joint. This done she swiftly got two pieces of wood from one of the boxes the metal strip came in and set up the woman's forearm as best she could in splints, binding it with pieces of rag used as cleaning rags for the machine, finally tying the arm in a sling using the woman's own jacket. The woman, in great pain, but stoically enduring it, took Rosa's oily hand and kissed it.

Just as they were lifting her to her feet the floor supervisor, a vicious hard faced bitch of a woman arrived, accompanied by a slim, middle-aged, well-dressed man in a white coat.

"What is going on here?" the virago shouted.

"This lady fell against the machine," Rosa replied.

"Well, get back to work, all of you." They all moved away.

"Who attended to her?" the man accompanying her asked.

"I did Sir, I am a doctor." He turned to the overseer.

"What is a doctor doing operating a machine when we are desperate for medical personnel in the main block?"

"I don't know what they are Sir, I get workers given to me, I put them to work, if they won't work, or are no good at the work they go back to the camp – God knows what happens to them then."

"What is your name?"

"Von Hassellbek Sir."

If the prefix 'von' struck him as being out of place in the name of a concentration camp prisoner he did not show it.

"Take this prisoner to the medical block and hand her over to the overseer there. Take the Russian to have a proper splint put on the broken arm, then give her work here she can do with one hand."

"Yes Sir."

For the rest of 1942 into 1943 Rosa worked in the medical block, attending to accidental injuries and emergency illnesses sustained by the workers. In a plant of some six thousand men and women, a third of whom were concentration camp prisoners, a third slave labourers living in their own barrack blocks on the perimeter of the factory, the other third being Germans, most of whom had worked in the factory before the war, these provided a steady flow of people to the understaffed medical facility. In addition to the first aid work the block housed a small crèche where German staff could leave their children under five years of age whilst they were mainly employed in clerical work. There was no call-up system for women in Germany during the war. Hitler had laid down that the German woman should be at home having babies to further the cause of the Reich, rather than be involved in industry. This was one of the main reasons so many slave workers had to be imported, and his tunnel vision prevented a totally untapped labour market from providing a significant addition to the war effort.

Rosa had to fall in with the other workers at six o'clock having had a breakfast of plain bread and awful ersatz coffee before walking under guard the two miles to the factory. At the factory she shed her striped uniform – the hallmark of the camp prisoner – and put on medical overalls and a small round cap to cover her shaven head. Sometimes she was able to sneak an all over wash in warm water, a luxury for which others in the camp would have sold their souls. The regimen was not severe. The overseer, herself an ex-doctor and camp inmate, allowed a certain leniency as long as, in no way, it prejudiced her comfortable job. There were three other camp inmates in the centre, the other two staff being German civilians, the overall controllers, a frosty faced German male doctor who had been brought out of retirement to head the small group. The camp inmates did get one little perk to which the two German civilian women turned a blind eye. The children were fed a meal at midday. On occasion they would not eat it all. The leftovers were taken to the pantry whilst the prisoners in turn ate what was left, a watch being kept for any intruders. Even the overseer had her share, which probably explained her exceptional tolerance.

Nothing lasts forever. In March 1943 the R.A.F. turned the factory into a heap of rubble, one bomb dropping in the concentration camp, marginally increasing the normal monthly death toll. Two weeks later Rosa and about one hundred and twenty others were on the march, whipped in by vicious S.S. guards with even more vicious dogs, going they knew not where to do they knew not what. For three weeks, in the bitter cold, sleeping at night in barns after a meal of a bowl of cabbage soup and a slice of bread, they staggered through snow and rain, carrying their few possessions, until at last they came to a large brickworks and were pushed into a long unheated shed containing bales of straw which, laid on the cobbled floor, was to be their bed. They were strangely quiet, the quietness of total despair, total exhaustion, a total lack of the will to live. Some died that night, and the next, and the next. For those that lived, life from now on would probably be hell on earth. Rosa was among that small group.

Chapter Thirteen

Fred, Jack, Megan and Rose attended Colonel Llewellyn's funeral at Canterbury and were entertained to lunch afterwards in the officer's mess along with a handful of senior officers who had served with the colonel from time to time over the years. It was so sad that no one present was related to him, but at least he was not laid to rest without friends, old and new, who would mourn his passing. The military funeral, a mixture of regimental precision, perfect discipline, along with the final volley over the grave, exemplified his service to his king and country, whilst the oration from the senior chaplain of Southern Command, himself an old friend, spoke of his courage, his courteous manner and his love of his profession. It was a sad day, yet each of the Sandbury group had a feeling of inner contentment they had helped to provide a suitable parting for a gallant gentleman. Funerals are funny things!

That evening they were all eagerly waiting to hear from David. Soon after dinner he rang to say he would be home the next day sometime in the afternoon. He duly arrived soon after four o'clock, the taxi laden with all his kit, plus the suitcase of goodies he had bought in Cairo. Before it got dark he made his pilgrimage to the churchyard with flowers for his mother and for Pat. He was glad it was getting dusk, he had the feeling that he was being clothed in a silent world alone with the two people he had loved most in all the world, so close he could feel their presence encompassing him. He walked slowly home, despair in the pit of his stomach. Rose, understanding how he would be feeling, hugged his arm, saying, "The children want to see you," and led him into the sitting room, where he was set upon by young John Hooper, Megan's twins, and last but by no means least by young Jeremy and Anni's David. It was a clever move on Rose's part; it shook him out of his despondency as nothing else could have done.

The main question the family asked him was of course what was he going to do now? When he saw Lord Ramsford at Wilmslow, that was the question uppermost in his mind. It was settled more speedily than he had anticipated. Lord Ramsford came straight to the point.

"David, you've got the choice of three courses of action. One, you can stay on in my firm. Two you can rejoin your regiment, by that I mean the Rifles, or three; you can join a new airborne division being formed for the invasion of the continent. If you decide on options two or three you will retain your rank and will therefore command a company in one of the new parachute battalions or in the Rifles.

"Sir, as you know I have wanted to get back into a regimental unit for some time now. If I elect to go to a battalion, what happens to Mr

O'Riordan?"

"I reckon you know the answer to that as well as I do – he will almost certainly want to go with you – he will keep his rank of course."

"Then I think Sir, I would like to go to the airborne division and take O'Riordan with me."

And that was how it was settled. They would go to the Rifles depot at Winchester after their leave period, and wait to be posted to the airborne soon afterwards. When David told Paddy of the plan, telling him he could change the arrangement and go to the Rifles or stay with Lord Ramsford if he preferred, Paddy enthusiastically agreed with David's proposals.

However, the family were, to say the least, a trifle apprehensive about this new venture. Jumping out of an aeroplane to be welcomed by resistance fighters or partisans was one thing, jumping out of an aeroplane on to angry Germans with quite another. David's answer to that being, "Well, someone's got to do it."

This was met with the inevitable and universal "Why you?"

At nine o'clock Maria rang, telling David she was on a course this week, ending on Saturday afternoon, could he therefore meet her in Dover on Sunday. By then she hoped to have an answer to her request for leave from Friday 16th for ten days. She could envisage no problem in this respect as she had purposely delayed taking her leave entitlement to fit in with David's arrangements. "But how can I wait until Sunday?" was David's plaintiff reply, "that is four whole days, ninety-six hours, hang on a bit and I will work out the minutes. It's cruel, it's unfair, it's unjust, it's against all human nature, I shall never survive." All he received in answer was a tinkling laugh, a laugh he loved so much. They made arrangements in which hotel to meet – "I don't want you waiting on some street corner for me with all those blasted sailors making suggestive remarks to you. Neither for that matter would I myself, want to be waiting around when doubtless they would be making similar remarks to me, as is, I believe, their wont." More laughter.

Thursday, Friday and Saturday dragged a little, except that David went to Harry Phillips, the tailor and a Rotarian friend of his father's in Sandbury, to have a suit made. As an officer he was entitled to clothing coupons in the same way as a civilian and as he had not used his coupons for nearly eighteen months now he had enough for a suit. He chose a dark grey, pinhead design, top quality Huddersfield worsted, costing rather above the average at nearly twelve pounds, working on the basis he was entitled to a bit of luxury once in a while. Harry Phillip's father was a Jewish refugee from the Russian pogroms in

Poland before the Great War, and still sat cross-legged on the end of the cutting table in the workshop at the back of the small shop. His surname was so unpronounceable to the British immigration official who first admitted him that he told him, "Well I'm putting you down as Phillips", and Phillips it had remained. Harry had a lame leg and was therefore exempt from military or Home Guard service, although he did more than his share in stacking, running and serving in the Rotary Club mobile canteen, the same canteen in which David's Pat had lost her life. He told David they would pull the stops out to have the suit ready by the end of his leave, but although he made the coat, he, like all tailors, sent the trousers and waistcoat out to specialist trouser and waistcoat makers in Brick Lane E.1 – what there was left of it! – and they could sometimes be a bit slow.

"Well, do your best Harry, I would like very much to look like a civilian again, nothing else I've got fits!"

David always remembered the unfeigned, despondent reply. 'And I would so much like to look like a soldier,' from the tailor.

Saturday came and David got the early train out of Sandbury due to arrive at Dover Priory at 9.30, which it did, miracle of miracles, on time. He walked through the town to the Cliff House Hotel, one of the few hotels overlooking the harbour not requisitioned by the services, receiving and returning salutes given by passing 'other ranks, ' along with a couple of subalterns. Being a major he had discovered, particularly a major with a collection of medal ribbons, meant others considered you were entitled to a well-executed salute, an entitlement which as a lieutenant or even worse, a second lieutenant left a degree of doubt in the mind of the approaching squaddie as to whether he should bother. Added to this he wore now his red beret and his wings which together added to the aura of entitlement in the saluting stakes.

He entered the residents' lounge at the hotel, the wall clock telling him he was twenty minutes early. He settled himself where he would immediately see the entry of his darling Maria. When he had been seated a few minutes, a middle-aged waiter approached him asking if he could get him anything. David told him he was waiting for his fiancée and would order when she arrived. His stomach was turning over with the intoxicating anticipation of seeing Maria again after all these months, followed briefly by the fleeting doubt 'she might have gone off me a bit in the meantime.' When she did arrive she left no doubt whatsoever as to whether she had "gone off him a bit" – it was a full three or four minutes before she would take her arms from around him to sit on the sofa next to him, and even then she kept one arm around him, held his hand with the other free hand, every few seconds burying her head on to his shoulder and lightly kissing his cheek. Eventually she took her arms away from him.

"Let me have a look at you." She studied him intently. "You really are such a handsome, handsome man David Chandler, what have I done to deserve you?"

As this scrutiny was taking place, the waiter reappeared. "Can I get you anything Sir?"

David looked at Maria. "Have you had breakfast?"

"Yes, we eat early in the navy, or in my case the marines."

"In that case can we have some coffee and biscuits – and I suppose you couldn't find us a glass of brandy each could you – it's a long time since we last saw each other."

"Are you residents Sir?" The waiter had a marked continental accent.

"No, I'm afraid not."

"We are only allowed to serve alcohol to residents out of hours Sir."

"Oh, of course, well never mind. Some nice coffee will have to do."

The waiter returned in a few minutes with a silver coffee pot, an enormous plate of biscuits, and two balloon glasses containing substantial measures of brandy. David looked at the waiter, looked at the brandy, and looked back at the waiter with raised eyebrows.

"Sir, the brandy is with my personal compliments. I am from Lorraine. You must have given great service to my country to receive those rewards; it is my way of saying thank you."

He then added, pointing to David's Croix de Guerre won at Calais, "I too was honoured with one of those in the Great War." David sprang to his feet and shook hands with this old soldier, at the same time Maria took his other arm and kissed him on the cheek, it was a most emotional scene born out of nothing really but a tableau which would remain in each of their minds for many years to come.

Settling themselves, David asked, "Can we book for lunch?"

"We are full from week to week Sir, but I will make sure you have a table. At what time Sir?"

David looked at Maria. "Twelve-thirty?" she nodded agreement.

Having spent time drinking their coffee, making inroads into the biscuits and savouring the brandy they decided to walk for a while along the front, most of which was out of bounds to all except those who had business there. They experienced one particular irritation during this short walk which determined them to return to the confines of the Cliff House Hotel, namely having to disengage from each other every time a passing squaddy decided to go all regimental and throw up an arm in salute. After all, it would probably be frowned upon, if not be an offence with unimaginable consequences under Kings Regulations or the Army Act, to return a salute to a private soldier with one arm, and be hugging a Wren with the other. During the walk Maria had expressed to David her great sadness at the loss of his mother and how grief-stricken he must have been to receive the news so far away from home. They were silent for a while until he said, very quietly, "She will be happy to know I have found you." Maria held his arm tightly, brushing away a tear. There would never be a time when she loved David more than she did at that moment, it would have been beyond credence to have envisaged that were possible.

Arriving back at the hotel they sat in a two-seater couch in the crowded residents' lounge. David had recovered his spirits to the extent he was able to jest, "Assuming you still have a mind to marry me, when shall we name the day? As far as I can tell I shall be here in the U.K. at least until this time next year, or thereabouts."

"David, darling, could we make it the end of August? I think before then might be too soon ..." David appreciated immediately she meant 'too soon after his mothers death.'

He hugged her to him, "Beautiful, intelligent, sensitive – what a treasure you are." He took out a small pocket diary.

"I take it it will be on a Saturday?"

"I think that's best for most of the proposed guests."

"Well, we've got the 19th or the 26th."

Maria had already worked out the most convenient date for her bodily calendar!!

"The 26th would be fine."

"The 26th August it is then." As he said this the waiter arrived to say their table was ready.

"Tell me, what is your name?" asked David.

"Jean-Paul, Sir."

"Jean-Paul, you are the first to know. Maria and I are to be married on the 26th August and as you are the first to know you and your wife are invited to the wedding should you be able to honour us with your presence."

Jean-Paul was overcome at this bolt out of the blue, shaking hands enthusiastically with each in turn.

"I lost my poor wife only two years ago Sir, but I would consider it a great honour to accept your invitation."

"Right, that's settled then. Give us your address before we go so that you can receive the details in due course." Jean-Paul hesitated for a moment.

"But Sir, I ask why you invited me?"

"If I meet any other holders of the Croix de Guerre I shall invite them too." David laughingly replied.

"Then thank you Sir, and you Madame. I shall look forward to it all the summer. This way now please."

As they walked to the dining room Maria whispered, "How many people won the Croix de Guerre in the Great War?"

"About half a million."

"It could be quite crowded on the 26th August."

"I shall have eyes only for you."

"Wait till you see my bridesmaids."

"Will they include the delectable Emma Langham?"

"Yes, fancy your remembering her name."

As they sat over their lunch David asked whether Emma had kept up her correspondence with Charlie Crew, David's old Octu and Rifles comrade. Charlie was in North Africa.

"The answer is most definitely yes. In fact they seem to be getting quite close, metaphorically speaking."

"What's metaphorically?" Maria ignored the question.

"I suppose it is not unknown for two people to become attached, even loving, without actually being together. A meeting of minds I suppose. If it lasts when they actually meet is another matter. Anyway, they've swapped photos, and the letter exchange rate now appears to be weekly whereas it was monthly."

"His father and grandfather would be envious on that score. They have both told me they consider it lucky if they get three or four pages from him in any one month. Does she know he will be an earl one day?"

"No, I've said nothing and I am sure he hasn't otherwise she would have told me."

And so their conversation swayed easily from one subject to another. They had coffee in the lounge, then tea later in the afternoon. At six o'clock Maria said, "I will walk with you to the station, I can get a bus from there to Deal." David's train was scheduled for 6.40, the only one that evening stopping at Sandbury. They hugged and said goodbye reluctantly at the platform end as all lovers do. Maria promising to telephone the next evening about her leave which they had already decided would be spent half at Sandbury, half at Chingford. Her parting words with her husband to be were, "We have not decided on where we are going to honeymoon."

David's reply, since she was in on the joke was, "I believe there is a lovely little cottage in North Wales somewhere."

On Monday Fred invited David to be his guest at the lunchtime Rotary Meeting. The local hunt was kennelled at a small village near Mountfield, where the Chandlers formerly lived, named Cuddingham, and earlier that morning the hunt staff took the hounds out for exercise passing Sandbury Engineering factory where they were seen by Fred and Mrs Russell, past Chandlers Lodge where they were excitedly watched by the children, then up to the High Street past the church and back to Cuddingham. One or two cats were chased en route by hounds before being sternly spoken to by the huntsmen, otherwise it was a well behaved pack making a pretty picture on a bright spring day, using uncrowded roads where the odd vehicle on its lawful business pulled in to let the tail-wagging procession pass to the respectful touch of whip to cap by the leading whipper-in.

When Fred arrived at the saloon bar of The Angel, where the Rotarians congregated before going in to lunch, he appeared as agitated as either of them had ever seen him as he made his way to greet David, already talking to Reg Church, accountant to both of them. His face was flushed – most unusual, he was laughing his head off – again most unusual, particularly in recent months, he was wildly out of breath – again most unusual, Fred was one of those people who took his time over everything from drinking a pint of Whitbreads' Light Ale to making a decision upon which tie to wear. Others noticing these changed circumstances in one of their more sedate fellow Rotarians, turned to establish the cause thereof. Before anyone could ask, Fred blurted out.

"You'll never in a million years guess what I've just done."

The immediate conclusion in the minds of the disparate collection of representatives of Sandbury society varied, from thumping one of the local bobbies, to indecently assaulting the local, very dishy, head teacher, to winning the pools.

Fred continued, still breathless, "The hounds were out this morning. I met Canon Rosser outside the church and I said, 'Did you see the Hunt from Cuddingham this morning?' He waited for a few seconds, then he grinned at me and replied, 'Where is Huddingham, Fred?' – I'd got it the wrong way round."

At this there were roars of laughter, heard all over the pub.

"What happened then?" David asked, almost paralytic with mirth.

"Well, realising what I'd done I looked at him, and knowing he was a padre for three years in the West Kents in the last lot, knew he had heard everything there was to hear, as a result I started to almost scream with laughter, in which he joined, and there were the two of us hanging on the church railings totally incapable of intelligent speech.

But that wasn't all. Just at that moment the two Aveley sisters appeared from around the corner." (The Aveley sisters were twin spinsters, early seventies, pillars of the church.) "One said, 'that must have been an extremely amusing incident Canon Rosser, could you let us in on the joke?' I nearly exploded at that – what the hell is he going to tell them, but he thought quickly and told them that as it involved someone else he felt he couldn't. They walked on and when they had got a few yards away we heard one say to the other 'they sounded drunk, but surely they couldn't be at this time in the morning?'"

At this a fresh roar of laughter rose from the assembly, interrupted by the head waiter announcing, "Lunch is served," the fellows still chuckling as they went into the dining room, with now and then full bursts of laughter as the thought of the assault on the canon's ears at Fred's original question struck their sense of the ridiculous.

As they were seating themselves there appeared to be a bit of a 'conflict' going on at the top table between the club secretary, the president, and another fellow Rotarian who David later was told was the 'Speaker Secretary.' David saw the three heads emerge from their mini-conference one looking in the direction of Fred and himself. The third man detached himself from the group and made his way around the sprig to where they were sitting. David had a premonition he was shortly going to be involved in something he had not bargained upon when he set out to have lunch with his father. He was going to have to sing for his supper, or in this case his lunch, by the looks of things. His intuition was spot on. The 'Speaker Sec' came up to Fred and told him their proposed speaker; a fundraiser for a national charity had had to cry off, could David therefore 'fill in,' either about his recent exploits in Yugoslavia or about parachuting or any other subject of his choice. Fred's inevitable reply was, "You had better ask him."

This done and David agreeing, he had to move to the speaker's chair on the top table, but before he went Fred asked, loudly and clearly, "But since the speaker normally gets his lunch free and I've already paid for David's do I get my money back?"

There was loud applause at this from the other members, at which the sergeant-at-arms came to his feet bellowing – "All members fined sixpence for unseemly behaviour. Past president Fred fined one shilling for the instigation of the unseemly behaviour." The S at A's job was to raise small amounts of money at the lunches to be put in the community service box for the benefit of local charities. Such things as not wearing a Rotary badge would attract a fine, as would being late, dropping a spoon on the floor, or if a 'fellow' was almost always late in arriving but on one occasion was early, he would be fined for being early. It was all taken as a bit of fun, adding to the camaraderie and fellowship within the club, benefiting others at the same time.

David was seated next to the president, who told him the normal length of talk was around twenty minutes, but as he had had no opportunity to prepare his address a good dodge was to talk in general terms for a few minutes and then ask for questions. Invariably one question led to another and the twenty minutes soon passed. The meal completed, the president called the fellows to order. He said that David needed little introduction, they were all aware of his bravery at Calais where he won the Distinguished Conduct Medal, and for his gallantry won the Legion of Honour from the French Government in London. He has just returned from parachuting into Yugoslavia where he had fought with the partisans for six months. Fellow Rotarians – Major David Chandler. Loud applause greeted him as he rose to speak. His first words were "Well if you applaud like that when I finish, I shall be more than pleased!"

"Although I am a parachutist, I want to talk to you about some of the bravest people I know who operate at the other extreme. I refer to the submariners." He went on to give for ten minutes an account of, as he put it, 'His ride in a submarine,' filling them in with stories of snorkers and haricots musicalles, hot bunking, being depth charged, eventually leaving the boat smelling so pungently their driver had to wear a gas mask. Above all he told of the youth of those submariners, their fearlessness and stoicism, their pride in the section of the service to which they belonged. He then, following the president's advice, suggested the remainder of his time be devoted to answering questions, "Although without being over-dramatic, I am bound under the Official Secrets Act, so may not be able to answer on occasion." The questions came thick and fast, he managed them all, generally in a humorous vein except when he was talking of the bravery of the men, women and boys in Comrade Tito's army. He was five minutes over time when the president called a halt for one of the past presidents to propose a vote of thanks, at the end of which the applause was very considerably in excess even of the introductory plaudit.

One of the questions asked by a tall, military looking gentleman was how he and his colleague moved around over such a wide area. He replied they were on foot a great deal of the time, but for long journeys they were given horses, on one occasion covering some two hundred miles. After the meeting, when each and every Rotarian came up and shook hands with him, the military gentleman waited until the general crush subsided saying, "Do you remember where you learned to ride a horse?"

"Yes Sir, at the stables on Mountfield Road."

"I thought it was you, but you were a lot younger then. You came with young Pat Hooper as I recall. Tell me, where is she now – do you know? I've been away since the beginning of the war and have only just returned and rejoined the club."

At the height of his elation at having successfully spoken in public for the first time he was suddenly hit in the pit of his stomach. He was wordless for the moment before he could say, "Pat and I were married, but then she was killed in an air attack in November 1940."

"Oh my God, David I am so sorry to have sprung this on you. I had no idea."

"You were not to know."

"Not to know what?" Fred had joined them and heard the last remark.

"This gentleman owned a riding establishment where Pat taught me to ride."

"I still do, someone else has been running it while I was overseas. Now I'm invalided out I am back there again. David, if you want a horse, or if you want to go out with the hunt – they've roped me in as a deputy master in the last couple of weeks – please come and see me and I will fix you up. I would like to have a chat with you anyway, like you I lost my wife while I was overseas, in the London Blitz. As my name tag shows I'm Ronnie Mascall."

They shook hands, David saying, "I'll take you up on that!"

Maria telephoned that evening to say she had got her leave from the 16th for seven days only – she was entitled to 10 days but because of personnel shortages she could only have a week. "Oh, and by the way, I am now a petty officer Wren, how about that?" David was as delighted for her as he would have been if he himself had been made a general.

"So you will be here on Friday? Shall we stay here until Tuesday morning and then go over to Chingford?"

"That would be fine by me."

"Right, I'll organise a little get-together on Saturday evening." After a little more personal conversation, conducted instinctively in a different tone of voice altogether, quieter as though wishing not to be overheard, sensual in its overtones, David rang off thinking 'How can I wait till August?'

On Tuesday David decided to walk to Ronnie Mascall's, about a mile out of town on the Mountfield road. Ronnie was delighted to see him, took him around the stables which brought so many memories back of Pat and the fun they had there together in their early teens.

"Place has got a bit run down while I've been away," Ronnie remarked, "a few gallons of whitewash and a long broom for the cobwebs will soon put that right. Now, David, how about coming out with the hunt on Saturday?"

"You mean the Hunt from Cuddingham?"

"Oh my God, don't start me off on that again," but the thought of Fred's faux pas set them both off into side-splitting laughter.

"And it would have to be the canon, wouldn't it?" Ronnie guffawed, "your father will never live it down. And the problem's is that we shall all be treading on hot coals if we have to refer to it at any time in case we get it wrong." There was no doubt about it; this story was going to run and run.

"Well, now about the hunt – could you make it?"

David thought for a moment. "I have two problems. Firstly, whilst I'm a reasonably competent horseman, I've had little jumping experience for some years. Secondly, my fiancée is coming on leave on Friday and to be honest I don't know whether she has ever been on a horse, let alone ridden cross-country."

"Can you contact her?"

"She will be ringing me tonight."

"Well find out. If she likes the idea I'll fix a couple of decent horses for you. And don't worry about the jumping, you can always go round anything you don't fancy tackling, lots do."

As David made his way back into town his thoughts were assailed by the heinous whining of the air raid siren on the police station roof a couple of hundred yards ahead. There appeared to be no action taking place to cause the commotion, nevertheless David quickened his pace to reach the surface shelter adjacent to the police station forecourt. Since the beginning of the month there had been hit and run raids on Kentish towns and airfields, so far Sandbury airfield having escaped the attention of Goering's predators. However it soon became apparent that today was not going to be one of those days, as he reached the doorway to the shelter where an A.R.P. warden was standing he heard the throbbing of what he remembered only too clearly as being medium bombers, followed shortly by the scream of bombs falling on the other side of the town on to the airfield area.

"Come inside Sir, we may get a stray one over here any minute." David needed no urging, worried as he was about the family, who he knew would be in the Anderson shelter in the garden at Chandlers Lodge, it would be stupid to try and get to them while the raid was on and patently so close. After twenty minutes the 'All Clear', surprisingly, sounded.

"Another hit and run Sir, that's the third in the last week. You on leave Sir?"

"Yes, I thought you had given up inviting these people over, otherwise I would have stayed away." The warden laughed.

"Well things are quieter now than they were its true, but I don't think we've seen the last of them. By the way Sir, what did you think of Kingsley Wood's budget yesterday? Twenty fags now cost a shilling and twopence – up tuppence, and another penny a pint on beer, a pint of mild and bitter will soon cost a shilling, you see if I'm not right!"

David shook hands with the warden and walked quickly home to find everything in order, the bombs having fallen mainly on farmland and the airfield perimeter, as he established later. Maria telephoned in the evening as arranged, and with the charges reversed they had a long and intimate discourse together. David raised the question of the hunt on Saturday saying that when Ronnie Mascall had broached the subject he had to tell him he knew not whether the only horse Maria had ever been near was a clothes horse. "I will have you know David Chandler that I was riding horses from the age of six until the war started, gymkhanas, cross-country, the lot, although I would have to admit to being a bit rusty now. Although my father was a sailor he loved horses and was brought up with them on their farm in Hannover, he always wanted Cedric and I to be good on a horse."

"How can you be bad on a horse? I mean there isn't a lot of room is there? I shall have to try and puzzle that one out, could come in useful if we got separated from the rest of them."

"I'll put my thinking cap on as well."

"Well I shall have to find out what to wear, since we obviously have no hunting gear or whatever it is they call it," David thought for a moment. "I suppose you could do a Lady Godiva act."

"My hair isn't long enough."

"All the better as far as I'm concerned. On the other hand it might be a bit parky. No, reluctantly, I shall have to find out what passes for the correct attire and leave to my imagination what is underneath it."

"David Chandler you are becoming very suggestive."

"My darling, I haven't even started yet."

He telephoned Ronnie the next morning who promptly put his fears to rest regarding attire.

"We cannot to be too particular in war time," Ronnie explained. "Some visitors wear uniform, breeches and hacking jackets are OK. Everybody should wear a riding hat, although one or two military people wear peaked caps with chinstraps in place. Really, as long as you are not in spats, flannels and blazer anything goes."

Asking at what time Maria would be arriving on Friday and being told early afternoon, he suggested they came up to the stables at say four o'clock or just after and have an hour or so on the horses he had selected for them, in the paddock. The jumps there were quite small, with some bigger ones in the menage if they fancied their chances. "Not on your proverbial nelly," being David's answer.

And so they each looked forward to their leave, the thought of spending a whole week together without being parted was overshadowed by their inevitable sadness that it was only a week. Oh, when would this evil war be over so that they could be together all the time. However, this doleful thought was not to be allowed to dampen the excitement and pleasure they would enjoy in that short period together.

Chapter Fourteen

The attack on Kampong Bintang and the operation to collect the airlift supplies had left the men at Camp Six with a number of casualties. They had lost two men killed up until then, two more had died to tick typhus, another four had gone down with various serious illnesses which necessitated their being returned to their families, four were killed at Kampong Bintang, and now two more were seriously ill and would probably have to be sent home. From a force of sixty they were down to forty six. Of that forty six, due to the conditions in which they had to live, there was always a number who were unfit for duties for one reason or another. What would be an elementary matter in a temperate climate, for example a deep scratch or cut, in this damp fetid climate could become a major problem, if not treated promptly, and not allowed to become infected, could even be a matter of life or death. With so many spiky, thorny bushes and other forms of vegetation around, although they all wore long trousers, puttees and long-sleeved shirts when in the jungle some of the hazards were like needles, and just as penetrative. In addition, a common cause of infection was the bite, through the clothing by one of the hundreds of hostile insects that dwell in this environment, a bite which irritates, causes the recipient to scratch involuntarily and the damage is done. It was obvious therefore that with the dwindling numbers something had to be done to start recruiting. But who? and how? Choon Guan was of necessity to be the guiding factor in this operation.

Many of the comrades had relatives or friends who were eager to join the guerrillas, getting in touch with them and getting them to a central point to be thoroughly vetted by Choon Guan posed the main problem. Then there was the question of training them, they certainly would not be effective soldiers for some while after they were enlisted.

"Well, we can't hang around any longer," Clive decided, "or we shall dwindle down to nothing. I had hoped to do a couple of big ops during this dry season, but they will have to be put back.

Harry smiled to himself – 'Dry season? they had never enjoyed a dry twenty-four hours as far back as he could remember!'

It was agreed therefore that Choon Guan and Choong Hong would make their way to Kuala Lumpur where they would meet Chua Yong Soon, Leader of the Malayan Communists. This might take a little while as Yong Soon had of necessity to move around a great deal for safety's sake, he would, however, have a list of people, already vetted, which would save a lot of time in the long run. To cover expenses Clive gave them a good supply of sovereigns which they would be able to change into local currency with known Chinese goldsmiths, of whom there would always be a representative in every town, and many in K.L.

In the meantime, at the strategy meeting Clive had outlined three hit-and-run raids using small parties of four or five with a European leader. Sixteen miles due south of their camp, down out of the high jungle the railway ran through a small town of Bekok. Eight miles south of that it ran through another small town of Palon, and eight miles to the north, but due west of Camp Six, it ran through Labis. Each one of these stations had a signal box. It was planned that each signal box would be attacked at midnight on Saturday 17th April, the equipment destroyed and the signal boxes burnt down, the groups then retreating back into the jungle to wait for dawn and then to move back to camp. If, while they were at these objectives, they found any other target which could reasonably be dealt with – "And I mean *reasonably*," Clive had emphasised, "I don't want you chasing around looking for trouble," then they should go for them. Clive, Robbie and Harry then drew lots as to which one they would have the pleasure of gracing with their presence.

Harry drew Palon – the furthest, twenty-four miles there, twenty-four miles back, allowing for reconnaissance time – five to six days. "Oh well – the story of my life," he joked as he read the name on the paper. He would travel for half his journey with Robbie and his party, who had drawn Bekok, then continue south to his objective.

At dawn on 14th April, Harry and Robbie set off, being waved goodbye by Clive and the remainder of the force; Clive's party not having to leave until the following morning. In addition to their normal equipment they carried explosive and incendiary devices dropped to them by the Liberator the previous month. Choong Hong, who had worked for the Malayan Railways, had been able to give them sketches of the general layout of the stations, signal box and other buildings, and their relative positions in respect of their closeness to the small town of which they were a part. Judging from the sketch of Palon it was more a largish Kampong than a small town, the station being on the south side of it which meant they would have to skirt round it, or risk going through, since they were approaching it from the north.

At midday on the 15th they parted company with Robbie, wishing them well, Robbie moving south-west while Harry kept going in a southerly direction. Neither of them knew this part of the country. They had to work to compass directions, not knowing where the game trails led as they did in their hideout area. However it was all generally downhill so the going was not too hard. They hit a massive block of beluka, overgrown secondary jungle, at one stage, which slowed them down. Malayan beluka is generally agreed as being often the most impenetrable form of vegetation known to man, worse even than the Burma or Borneo forests. It took them some three hours to cover a mile, luckily Harry had allowed for such a contingency, but hacking through was, as Harry put it, bloody hard graft, as each man took it in turn to head the small column cutting his way with his machete. An hour before dark they stopped, made up their bed frames from the plentiful bamboo, lit a fire and spread the resultant ashes around the legs of their beds to prevent leeches or ants getting at them during the night, and went to bed hoping the inevitable rain during the night would not be heavy enough to wash the ash away.

At dawn they were on their way again reaching their target area in the early afternoon. Harry took Poh Chee forward with him to a bluff overlooking the railway whilst the others made a camp for the night back a little in the jungle where they could light a decent fire, make a hot meal and make a firm base to which to retreat after the attack.

Through his binoculars he could clearly see the signal box, a small siding with a turntable in it used obviously for turning an engine or guards' van round for a return journey. There was a staging, the base of which being at the height of the top of a locomotive tender, which was full of coal, and lastly there was the station, built of wood, and a small workshop where they could see men going in and out from time to time.

Turing to Poh Chee he gave him his binoculars and said. "I reckon we could destroy all that lot."

Poh Chee nodded excitedly. "Pity no Japs Sir. I like destroy Japs like Kampong Bintang." Harry grinned at him and clapped him on the shoulder.

"Me too, old son, me too."

The next morning Harry brought the others forward so that they could see the targets, then returned to their firm base and planned exactly who would do what, apportioned the explosives and incendiaries, he himself being responsible for the fuses and detonators until they reached the station. To ensure each was aware of what he had to do, they went forward again, studying the intervening territory and line of retreat until the target, the approach and the return was fully imprinted on their minds. Harry did not expect any opposition to the raid, but if there was, and the small party was split up, at least they would know what to do and how to get back to the camp.

They rested during the remainder of the day until dusk came along with the inevitable assault by hordes of stuka type mosquitoes. They covered up to combat this harassment, putting to use a mesh type face veil which had been dropped to them by their Liberator friend recently. Wrapped around the head they kept the nasty little blighters away from the neck and ears, but they found that if they covered their faces with them they soon became stiflingly hot, added to which it obviously reduced their vision.

H-hour arrived, they moved out silently, each knowing exactly what he had to do. They moved slowly and steadily towards the target initially along a game trail they had sighted from their observation point. It was at this point Harry and his men got the fright of their lives. From ahead Harry, leading the way, could hear a faint drumming sound on the ground. He put his hand up, the men behind him automatically coming to a halt and listening intently. It is to be remembered that Harry and his five men were all town dwellers. They had learnt a lot of jungle lore in the months they had been at Camp Six, but every day they learnt something new. What they had not experienced thus far was the sight or sound of the Malayan rhinoceros, an animal not as big as his African cousin, but just as bad tempered, just as short-sighted, just as fast on its feet, and just as dangerous. It was the rhinoceros, the deer, the tapir, the wild boar, the wild ox, who made the game trails, but who you rarely saw, just as you rarely saw the tiger or the leopard. Now coming at a fair rate of knots they could see in the pale moonlight at least two of these heavyweights bearing down on them. The jungle on either side of the game trail is usually very dense, needing generally the application of a sharp machete to penetrate it. It is fair to say that had they turned and ran, the last one, presumably Harry, since there was no way you could overtake anyone on a game trail, remaining at the rear, would soon have the doubtful pleasure of a ton of rhino meat helping him on his way – to say nothing of the damage the horn could do, or where it would do it!!

Harry instinctively knew there was nothing he could do. If he fired his tommy gun it probably would not stop them, and would be heard clearly in Palon only a mile away. There was no time to prime and throw a grenade or phosphorous bomb. In the seconds he had he shouted, "Get off the track." They each fought their way into the vegetation, the rhinos rushing by literally rubbing their armour-plated bodies against the legs and buttocks of the sanctuary seekers. With the panic over they came back out of the vegetation on to the trail more shaken than they would have been had they met a party of Japs.

"Everyone alright?" Harry asked in a loud whisper. One man had received a glancing blow on his thigh which was giving him pain, but he insisted he could carry on; the remainder were more scared than damaged. They would all think twice about following game trails in the future!

They arrived at the station area having had to wade through a rather smelly, unpleasant stretch of swampland which could not be seen from their observation point. It posed no great delaying factor, but each of them knew what they were probably hosting now – leeches. There was no way they could stop and look for the nasty little things, little things now, but growing rapidly into much bigger things as they feasted on the unexpected bounty which had come their way. Harry shuddered at the thought of it.

The raid itself was copybook. The signalling mechanism and the turntable were packed with explosive to which Harry fitted the fuses and detonators. This done the men took station, pardoning the pun, at the station, the signal box itself, the workshop at the rear and at the coal staging ready to loose their incendiary grenades when given the signal. Harry lit the five minute fuses and walked away – something he had learnt from Ray Osbourne in France, never run unless you have to. He gave a short, low blast on his whistle and in went the phosphorous grenades. The results from this part of the exercise were mixed to say the least. The man at the station threw his first grenade through a window; it bounced inside on the concrete floor yards from anything combustible and was therefore a dead loss. His second grenade was even more unsuccessful in that it didn't go off at all. With his third there was a burst of flame from several points at the centre dividing partition which indicated it was now well alight. The man on the signal box had better luck, both his grenades worked beautifully, the man in the coal staging lobbed his two on to the coal with predictable results, but number four struck oil, well, petrol actually. He threw his first device in one end of the shed and was welcomed by a first class conflagration, but the second one at the other end outshone all the others put together. Without knowing it he had hit a paint store, complete with cans of petrol stacked there away from the rest of the workshop, gallons of paint thinners, and five-gallon tins of cellulose paint. Seeing the first results of this little caper he took to his heels. He had covered about fifteen yards when a sheet of flame went upwards and outwards, singeing his backside as he raced round the corner of the station building. Three minutes were now up from the time of lighting the fuses. Harry blew his little whistle a second time and they all rendezvoused at a predetermined point in what would be the station approach, ready to make their way back to the base camp. As they moved off the two explosions erupted turning the whole area into a sea of flame. Quickly they made their way into the swamp out of the limelight they had produced, which was now turning the night of the quiet little town of Palon into day.

The other two attacks at exactly the same time had mixed results.

Robbie at Bekok had no problems, doing all that he had been called upon to do but without the spectacular results down the line at Palon. Clive was unlucky up the line at Labis. Since this was the area in which the guerrillas had derailed their first train a year or so ago, the Japs had positioned a small guard at the point where the railway line ran close to the main trunk road, about half a mile from the station. When the explosives went off the N.C.O. in charge of the half dozen men under his command immediately realised it was a guerrilla attack. Next he judged the raiders would retreat from the station directly east back into the jungle some mile or so away. He therefore doubled his men across country to try and cut them off, in which he was successful, the resultant fire fight in the moonlight killing two of Clive's men, before they were able to make the jungle and safety. It was overall a successful night's work, but they could not afford the loss of another two good men.

The three teams eventually arrived back at Camp Six, exhausted after the climb up into the high jungle, their overall lack of sleep and the heavy rain which had blanketed them through most of the journey, this latter particularly being the case with Harry's party. In the meantime Major General Takahashi at his headquarters in Kluang had been awakened from his post-coital exhaustion at 2am on the Sunday morning by an excited staff officer telling him of the destruction of the three stations which would effectively prevent the movement of a troop train scheduled for transit through that section of track at 4am.

"The burning down of the stations will not stop the trains running will they you idiot," was the general's immediate reply.

"At two of the stations they blew up the points and at Palon the fires have buckled the rails."

"Well, get them repaired or replaced" he screamed, "get them replaced."

"We have no means of stopping the train; the signals are out of action."

"In which case the train will stop of its own accord eventually, signals always fail-safe, you dunderhead, useless fool, everybody knows that. Get the rail gangs out and report to me every hour."

You cannot remove and relay track by manual labour, particularly if it has been subjected to an explosion, in five minutes, in the dark, and then in the torrential rain which had been the source of the considerable discomfort inflicted on the returning guerrillas. The troop train was taking combat troops north into Siam and then on to Burma, where General Wingate's chindits were causing the Japanese army staff to wonder whether they were the precursor to a more substantial attack from the 14th Army. The train was halted forty miles south of Palon at Rengam where it languished for three days until the track was put into emergency operation, but it was two weeks before the line was back into general use.

The base camp knew nothing of this added bonus of course. The whole camp was saddened at the loss of their comrades, whereas normally they would be experiencing the usual exhilaration felt after a successful strike at the hated enemy. But there was more, vastly more, misfortune to come.

Until now they had felt safe and secure in their hideaway deep in the jungle, for several reasons. Firstly it would be virtually impossible to locate from the air. The access to it on the ground was covered by only two approaches, both of which were guarded at all times. If either of those two approaches were discovered by the enemy because of the terrain, they could only attack in very small numbers and would be readily repulsed. Lastly, knowing the jungle as they did, any attackers would speedily be cut off and annihilated. There was one contingency Clive and his colleagues could not possibly have envisaged – their success could lead, indirectly to their downfall.

On Monday 19th April General Takahashi got on to his air force friend, asking him if he could make another search, as he expected General Yamashita to be tearing his balls off at any moment. He was lucky in this latter respect as this worthy was at present carrying out a tour in Java and Sumatra. His air force colleague said that he had lost his Tiger Moths for a week or so, but as soon as they were returned to him he would organise a three day sweep of the high jungle where it was suspected the guerrillas were based.

On the evening of 26th April, Terry Martin ran into the officers' mess room in a high state of indignation. "What do you think I've just heard on short wave radio from G.H.Q. India?" He held a piece of message paper in his hand from which he read, "Australian troops and Chinese guerrillas have conducted successful operations south of Kuala Lumpur."

Harry's comments are unprintable. Robbie was considerably miffed. Clive thought for a moment and said, "It may have been a Camp Four operation they are referring to that we know nothing about. There are three or four Australians there I believe. At least it shows we are not completely forgotten."

The next morning they received proof they were not completely forgotten. Twice they were flown close by the Tiger Moths, the camouflage drill being enacted again. At 10am on the 28th disaster struck. It was the practice for the cookhouse breakfast fatigue party to collect the Tilley lamps from the various huts and top them up with paraffin. Getting the paraffin to the camp was quite a sophisticated operation. Each month sympathisers from Labis would take four, five gallon cans to a drop point about five miles out of town, on their bicycles, along a track towards the fringe of the jungle. This excited no suspicion as there was a Kampong further along the track, the occupants of which all had to fill their cans in Labis and transport them to the Kampong. A working party would be sent from the camp, each fitted with a purpose made harness, to recover the cans from the hideout and take them back to Camp Six. It was a foolproof system.

On the morning of the 28th one of the men on the fatigue party short-circuited the method of filling. Instead of pouring from the five-gallon can into a jug and then into a funnel into the lamp reservoir, he decided to pour direct into the funnel from the almost full can, in doing so catching the edge of the funnel, dislodging it from the lamp which knocked the lamp off the bench where it was standing thereby spilling the paraffin already in the reservoir. At the same time, in an effort to grab the lamp he poured a considerable volume of liquid on to the bench. The bench was positioned next to the wood-burning stove, the kerosene ran in to the hot stove and onto the burning wood and in seconds the whole place was alight, made worse by the man at fault dropping the can on to the bench, where the bulk of the remainder in it flowed out while he took to his heels shouting fire – in Chinese of course! There was a strong wind blowing. In seconds the neighbouring hut caught fire, the green atap roof sending up clouds of smoke. Clive yelled for the next hut to be pulled down to make a fire break but by now the flames were licking into it. They had no fire extinguishers, they had only a few buckets to carry water from the stream, and the fire was sweeping on to the main men's barrack room, there was no way they could stop it. Once the barrack room burnt down that side of the camp would be totally destroyed and would have to be rebuilt. He ordered the men to get everything out of the barrack room on to the parade ground with the intention of leaving the fire to burn itself out. And it was then they heard the Tiger Moth.

When the stove was performing its normal function, the smoke from it drifted up into the canopy of the trees high above and became dissipated until it was unnoticeable by any observer in an aircraft. This present conflagration was a different kettle of fish altogether. The clouds of hot smoke not only themselves percolated through the canopy but in so doing raised a mist from the moisture on the leaves and branches through which it passed, which accentuated the billowing clouds. The Tiger Mother could do nothing itself, but what it could and did do was to fix the point on the ground as being so many degrees from Labis, so many degrees from Bekok, both of which he could see clearly from his elevation. The control staff at base immediately plotted the camp position from the reverse bearings, alerted a flight of light bombers from an airfield near the coast and in half an hour Camp Six was on the receiving end of an unpleasant deluge of 50 kilo bombs. They had no shelter, nor had they dug trenches. Firstly it was obvious no one could find them, secondly if you dug a trench it would be full of water in next to no time. Clive yelled for the men to disperse, an order which was totally unnecessary as they were all running like mad to get into the shelter of large trees, the trunks of which would shield them from the blast from at least one direction. Two fortunate facts were in their favour. Firstly the bomb aimers had had little practice so far in the war and in the main overshot the target; secondly the smoke had been made to drift laterally by the thickness of the canopy, emerging from a hole some hundred yards south of the camp. But that was as far as their luck went. Five were killed, two were so badly wounded they would have to be despatched, and four others became walking wounded.

The bombing finished Clive called a hurried 'O' group. "We shall have to move out before they come back. Get the men into full marching order carrying what food they can. Terry, get on the radio and inform Sunrise we will meet guides in two days at point five, repeat five. Make sure you get a firm acknowledgement then destroy the radio; it is much too heavy to carry. Harry, get a digging party of ten to bury the dead, I will attend to the two badly wounded."

He hesitated for a few moments, thinking of the ghastly duty he had to perform, until Matthew Lee told him "I have dealt with that matter Sir." He had injected the two unfortunates, one of whom being the man who started the fire, with Harry's ipoh resin. Death was instantaneous, with no pistol shots to further demoralise the men's comrades.

Quickly they dug a trench and put the seven bodies in, filled it in and piled rocks on it which had originally been removed when levelling the parade ground. In less than an hour they were ready to move off, each man heavily laden, having had to leave most of their stores and their spare clothing behind, and, saddest of all, their lovingly tended garden which had provided them with their basic tapioca diet, their spinach, bananas and much else increasingly over the months. In weeks the jungle would advance to reclaim it, and the parade ground. Gradually the remaining huts would be strangled by the vines, reoccupied by all manner of creeping, crawling and slithering creatures until they joined the surrounding rotting vegetation and became no more. There is no stopping the jungle.

Clive's force had reached a mile north when they heard the bombers fly over them followed by the sound of the explosives hitting the camp area. Matthew was marching with Harry. "I do hope they miss the grave," Harry looked at him quizzically. "I know what you are thinking Harry, they are communists, and when a communist is dead that's it – finished. I say they are all God's children, and I shall pray for the repose of their souls."

Harry squeezed his shoulder. "You're a better man than I am Gunga Din."

Chapter Fifteen

Friday came, Maria duly arriving at Sandbury station to the welcoming, rib crushing hug from David, and a kiss of salutation which lasted until they were both breathless. David had borrowed his father's Rover to come and pick Maria up, telling her that they were going to Chandlers Lodge, get her into slacks and a top, and then going back to Ronnie Mascall's for an hour. When they arrived at the stables, Ronnie had, as promised, two nicely built horses ready for them. He, having been introduced to Maria, then said he had an appointment in town and would be back about five o'clock, should they have had enough before then, Sandy (indicating one of the three stable girls nearby) would take the horses and stable them.

"If I don't see you, give me a ring or leave a message if you will be joining the hunt in the morning. Meets at the Angel at nine o'clock, so you will have to be here at 8.30 or thereabouts."

David could never have resisted it. "Do you mean the Hunt from Cuddingham?" he asked.

Ronnie turned away, his shoulders shaking with mirth, whilst David stood there with a face like a Cheshire cat, leaving Maria to wonder what the devil was going on.

They thoroughly enjoyed the next hour and a half, cantering in the paddock, taking the low jumps and the practice water jump.

"Shall we try a couple of the bigger ones in the menage?" David asked.

"Yes, I'd love to." Maria had gradually regained her old proficiency, even though it was over three years since she had last ridden. She had thought coming on the train from Dover, that horse riding was probably like riding a bike, once you had become fully competent you never lost the expertise. They both tried some medium jumps, managing them quite well.

"We shan't get any higher than those" David told her, "the landowners cut the hedges down in the places where they know the hunt will probably go."

They were still there when Ronnie returned. He was delighted when they said they would join him on the morrow. "And by the way Ronnie, we are having a few people in tomorrow evening, would you care to join us?"

Ronnie hesitated for a moment "Well the truth is old boy I have a sort of date tomorrow evening."

"Well, bring her along as well."

"No, I'm meeting a chum of mine."

"In that case bring him."

Ronnie paused noticeably, then replied, "Thank you David, I'll do that; it was most kind of you to ask us."

As they drove back to Chandlers Lodge, they were both silent for a while until Maria said, "Are you thinking what I'm thinking?"

"What are you thinking?" He was thinking exactly what she was thinking, but did not want his thinking to surface first. Neither did Maria.

"What is your definition of a chum?"

David thought for a moment. "Two of the nicest, most decent and most highly intelligent people I have ever met were chums."

"Who were they?"

"My first engineering tutor Peter Phillips and his live-in chum Reuben Isaacs. I found it out by accident, I never told anybody. They lived in fear of being discovered, of being blackmailed or even worse being prosecuted by the police. Homosexual partners do run incredible risks. Anyway, we don't know that Ronnie and his chum are in that category. If they are, that's their business. I know he was married at one time."

Maria waited a short while before replying. "Yes, you are right I suppose, but I have to say I don't understand it, and I never shall. It is supposed to go on in the Wrens, even more so in the navy, but from the Wrens' point of view I've never seen evidence of it – not that I've consciously thought about it or even had cause to think about it. I don't know whether one should feel disgust or pity." She left the latter statement in the air.

"My experience has been that when you know the individuals concerned the physical side doesn't come into it, you just take each on his own merits. They are happy together – everyone else should be happy for them." He paused for a moment, "The problem is, I am told, that because of the stresses and strains of such a relationship it rarely lasts very long, which is sad."

She turned to him as he swung the car into the drive at Chandlers Lodge. "I am so very very happy to be in love with you." Combined with operating the steering wheel, double de-clutching, engaging second gear, gently applying the accelerator, then the footbrake and finally the handbrake, they came to a halt outside the front of the house and in full view of the kitchen windows through which half a dozen or more pairs of eyes were keenly observing their progress. He encircled her with one arm, pulled her to him, and gave her a long lingering kiss at the end of which she opened her eyes to look through the car window straight at the aforementioned watchers smiling and cheering. She covered her face with her hands in mock embarrassment while David, quite oblivious to the entertainment he had provided for the spectators, ran round to open the car door for her. Only then did he see the lookers-on, realised they had seen all, promptly drew the newly alighted part-cause of the spectator enjoyment close to him, finally repeating his performance as in the car, ending in a theatrical bow to the assembled company.

That evening after dinner Maria complained to Rose that driving vehicles, although they had two or three periods of P.T. through the week, had obviously not exercised muscles she had been using on Ronnie's horses that afternoon, with the result she felt as though she could use a good massage. Ernie overheard the statement and immediately offered his services. David heard Ernie offering his services and protested it should be his job. Ernie claimed that he, as a result of all the massage he had been given, was an expert on the subject. Jack, joining the conversation, felt that his hands, as big as dinner plates as described in the past by Harry, would be more effective than either Ernie's or David's. The impasse was solved by the three deciding to take it in turns. They put the proposition to Maria. For some reason or other she turned it down. "She doesn't know what she's missing," was Jack's final word.

Fred had been out during the evening. When he returned Jack buttonholed him and led him into the breakfast room at the back of the house.

"What's all this about then?"

"Fred, I want you to be the first to know ..."

"You're having twins?"

"Bloody hell, that would be a turn up for the book." They laughed together.

"No. The government decided today to take over Shorts of Rochester who make the flying boats. They have asked me to be the chairman and managing director for six months, and then ease myself out of the M.D. bit when I have found someone suitable to take it over. This affects you in two ways. Firstly I have to resign my directorship of Sandbury Engineering as you at the moment do sub-contract work for Shorts which makes me ineligible to be a director of both, secondly I have had to resign my Home Guard commission, because knocking Shorts into shape will be taking up all my time. It follows from that, that as you are the next senior officer in the company you will, if you agree, be made up to major and take command. Any comments thus far?"

"Well, as regards Sandbury Engineering, I assume you are allowed to keep your shareholding?"

"No, I'm not, but I'm sure Reg Church can find a way to mothball that. This is only going to be a temporary affair, two or three years at the most."

"In which case, you can, when you are free again, be re-elected to the board?"

"If you'll have me." They both laughed at the thought of their not having him.

Fred continued, "The Home Guard bit is no problem, although it goes without saying we shall miss you. Can't we make you an honorary colonel or something?"

"I don't know that they have such an exalted rank in our outfit."

"Well, anyway, congratulations on the appointment, the powers that be could not have chosen more wisely in my opinion. Running an aircraft factory!! Now that really is something. Can we tell the others yet?"

"Yes, but there is one other thing I have to tell you which, as you know from your own experience, cannot go any further. They've offered me a Knighthood in the Birthday Honours List, and I've accepted."

"Congratulations again. Again you deserve it. All the hours you've spent with the ministry, without getting a farthing for it, that's the least you deserve. I hope they are paying you well for the Shorts' job?" he added laughingly.

"Oh yes, I drove a hard bargain there I can assure you."

"Sir Jack Hooper eh? Rolls off the tongue well, doesn't it? And what does the future Lady Hooper think of it all."

"Well there's the problem – again strictly between ourselves. For all the work she has done on this project she has been on she has been offered a D.B.E. – a Dame or a Lady, I don't quite know what she will call herself. I would plump for the Dame bit if it were me – she has earned that, truly earned it, all on her own, so in my opinion that gives it greater merit. Anyway, it will sort itself out I suppose."

They rejoined the family to the enquiry from David, "What have you two been cooking up? You don't retreat to the breakfast room at supper time without good cause."

"Tell 'em Jack." Jack told them and was immediately surrounded by well-wishers. He told them also about the new appointment to the hierarchy of the Sandbury Home Guard Company, at which further congratulations flowed. It was the noisiest evening at Chandlers Lodge since before Ruth had so sadly left them. It was evidence, if evidence was needed, that time heals, slowly – very slowly sometimes – but heal it does.

Saturday dawned bright and fine. David and Maria were at the stables soon after eight o'clock, their horses were got ready for them and they had a preliminary canter around the paddock three or four times to take a little of the spirit out of their mounts which sensed there was something up. Horses are pack animals instinctively looking for their leader to take them off; as a result they can be difficult to steady on occasion when first assembled, as they were here. From the stables they trooped off, picking up other individuals on the way, to the Angel, where they were met by the hunt servants, the hounds, and centre stage Sir Oliver Routledge, the master. They would be concentrating on the Downs today, fields being newly sown and orchards beginning to bloom would be out of bounds.

"But does the fox know that?" Maria asked as they sampled the stirrup cup handed up by John Tarrant and his lady assistants. At nine o'clock sharp the horns sounded and the master led the way up the High Street out of town then up on to the Downs. Hunting on the Downs is somewhat different to your average 'across the meadows' sport. Whilst you have the advantage of not having nearly so many fences and hedges to jump, the Downs are chalky, they provide sudden obstacles in the form of steep gullies, too big to jump, which a rider has to negotiate, slipping and sliding on the damp chalk into them then having to almost lie on the horses neck to scramble up the other side. They are largely tree covered which requires a constant watch for overhanging branches, on the other hand fallen trees provide good obstacles for jumping.

They drew a fox in the first hour, which proved to be a very wily customer, getting into a small stream running off the Downs and hiding in a culvert under a byroad. The hounds were running around in circles having lost the scent until one spotted him in the drain. After that he had little chance. David and Maria were not up for the first kill and not, repeat not, because David was having to slow down to wait for his beloved to keep up, quite the reverse in fact. Maria had a smaller horse than David which was however, extremely fast and nimble on its feet, whereas David had a mount of the cavalry charger variety, solid, as stable as the Queen Mary, but like the Queen Mary took a little while to change direction.

Half an hour after the first kill they drew another fox which gave them a splendid chase for over an hour, doubling backwards and forwards. By a little after midday it started clouding over as they made the second kill, thirty minutes later there was a crash of thunder and the heavens opened up. "It will probably be only an April shower," David called to Maria, both by this time thoroughly wet. But as Alexander Pope said many, many, years ago 'Hope springs eternal in the human breast,' in this case hope being dampened, literally, as a result of the April shower turning into a steady downpour, which made riding somewhat hazardous, scenting a fox even more difficult. At three o'clock they called it a day.

They rode back to the stables, where before they trudged on back to Chandlers Lodge, they helped the stable girls rub the horses down, for which they received grateful thanks from both the girls and Ronnie who came along whilst they were in the middle of the procedure. They dried out a little as a result of their exertions, only to get soaked again as they tramped on home. When they arrived, to the cheers of all the family, and of Maria's parents who had come for the evening get-together, staying overnight with Jack and Moira, they looked like a pair of drowned rats. Fortunately Chandlers Lodge, unusual for an Edwardian type house, had two bathrooms, although it must be mentioned that David suggested – during the war one was supposed only to have four inches of water in order to conserve fuel – if they shared a bath the displacement of the extra body would logically give a greater depth of water to them both, the veracity of which fact he would gladly demonstrate to her. At his proposal being voted down – very reluctantly – he consoled himself with the fact it had been worth a try.

The evening went with a swing, though underlying the jollity was, naturally, the sadness at Ruth not being there. David and Maria were more than curious to meet Ronnie's 'chum.' Ronnie, of course, having been a regular cavalryman and having fought in the Great War, would be around the fifty mark, would his chum turn out to be a young chum, a thirties chum, or a chum of his own age? As David described it to his father afterwards, "You could have knocked me down with a feather." He opened the door to the couple when he saw Ronnie's Armstrong-Siddeley sweep into the drive, to find himself being introduced to a tall, distinguished looking, very handsome in Maria's reckoning, cleric! Around the forty mark, David judged, John Husband (not a bad name for a chum David wondered?) was apparently on the archbishop's staff at Lambeth Palace, but at present was based at Canterbury Cathedral. Both he and Ronnie swiftly made themselves at home, the main image carried in most people's minds of the reverend gentleman being of his undoubted ability to punish a pint glass of Fred's Whitbreads' Light Ale with the panache of a four-ale bar regular!

Mr & Mrs Schultz soon got to know everyone and were made very welcome. Mr Schultz, when he became naturalised, had altered his Christian name from Heinrich to Henry, the 'Mr & Mrs' form of address, with the assistance of one or two tots of lubricant, speedily becoming Henry and Susan to all.

Ronnie and Canon John joined the family at church on Sunday morning. Canon Rosser had just started his sermon with a passage from the Prophet Isaiah.

"In quietness and in confidence shall be your strength."

He paused for a moment, firstly for effect, secondly so that the congregation could digest the text. All was quiet, not a cough nor a rustle, nor a dropped prayer book disturbed the peace of this ancient place of worship, when out of the blue the tranquillity of the moment was shattered by the mournful wail of the air raid siren only two hundred yards away.

"To those who wish to leave I will now give The Blessing," the canon announced. Not a soul moved. Searching the pews he continued, "Well, we had the quietness for a moment or two, we now have the confidence of you all that God will protect us. Do you know, Isaiah has proved himself as one of the greatest prophets, to us, here this morning," and he continued with a stirring sermon on the strength of the people in the times of great adversity and now when the tide of battle seemed to be swinging in our favour. One day soon our greatest test would come, when we shall need all our strength and all our confidence, when the courage of our fighting men will be tested to the full, when our prayers, our faith, our constancy will be needed to give them the fortitude to underpin their valour.

"In quietness and in confidence shall verily be our strength."

Henry and Susan Schultz went home on Sunday afternoon to prepare for the arrival of David and Maria on Tuesday. As Maria told the various members of the Chandler family – Cecely and the children, Mrs Treharne, and above all Ernie, Anni and her father were all considered family – her father would have had a fitted red carpet laid out down the garden path for David to walk on had he been able to purchase such an item. On the afternoon of their arrival at Chingford, having naturally been served tea, Henry asked if they could talk about the wedding. "Tomorrow and Thursday you will want to go out and enjoy yourselves, so it is better we get the business matters over first, no?"

The business matters mostly consisted of listing who to invite. As far as the Schultz's were concerned, Maria was their only daughter and if they wanted to hire the Albert Hall and fill it up they were more than welcome so to do. David, knowing this was going to arise had already made a list, or rather two lists, one for the immediate (and impossible to leave out!) guests, and the second for the highly desirables should the numbers be not too frightening. This problem, if it is a problem, must arise with every wedding from royalty downwards. In the midst of the euphoria of the celebration of the nuptial rites is the sincere hope that so and so is not going to feel slighted at being left out. In this case Henry Schultz showed the mettle that had brought him from being a lowly prisoner of war to becoming a businessman of considerable stature in his neck of the woods.

"When you reach a thousand let me know," he proclaimed.

They, of course, did not reach a thousand, but they did ensure that the parish church at Chigwell would be left with few vacant pews on that great day to come.

On Wednesday they had elected to go to town for the day, have lunch with Mr Stratton at the Corner House, walk in Hyde Park in the afternoon, see the Crazy Gang at the Victoria Palace in the evening, then rush to get the last underground train back to Chigwell.

"You know, if they cancel that train we shall have to go to a hotel," David announced quite casually during the interval at the bar of the Victoria Palace, then looked away pretending to study an ancient playbill on the adjacent wall.

Maria was silent for a spell.

"If it wasn't for mother and father waiting for us and wondering where we were I wouldn't need the train to be cancelled," she said in a low, tremulous voice. "I do need you so much darling David."

He slipped his arm around her. "Me too, my treasure, me too. But it won't be long now." The warning bell rang telling them to return to their seats, interrupting the most concupiscent moment of their relationship to date, which was just as well since had it occurred in another place or in other circumstances, might well have resulted in an entirely different outcome.

The 23rd April soon arrived. They said their goodbyes to Maria's parents and made their way to Charing Cross to get the train to Deal. As they parted at Deal station, not the most romantic of locations particularly with the dozens of heavily booted marines clumping around, David said, reassuringly – he hoped, "It's only four months," to which he received the reply,

"It will be longest and most agonising four months of my life."

"We'll try and wangle a weekend in the meantime."

"Oh David, please do try."

As David sat in the train on his way back to Sandbury he was suddenly struck by the fact that he and Maria were bemoaning the fact they were having to wait four months before they would be together again, when Megan and Harry, Mark and Rose, and millions of others could possibly be facing the prospect of being four years apart not four months. Many soldiers, sailors and airmen who were sent to the Far

East for example in 1941 did not return until 1945. Some captured in France spent five years in the prison camps. He was not to know these latter facts of course, but he was able to visualise they could possibly transpire. Having thought these deep thoughts, he decided it made no difference whatsoever; he was bloody browned off at having to wait four months – and that was that!

He received two letters of significance in the Monday morning post. One was from Lord Ramsford's office with his posting instructions to the Parachute Regiment depot at Clay Cross, near Chesterfield in Derbyshire, along with travel documents. The second was a bulkier package from Middle East Land Forces, containing copies of the photographs taken of Paddy and himself by Algy, the ex-A.D.C., he who had dipped his wick in diplomatic circles, or in his case, circle. They were on 'N' prints, not quite postcard size, but were clear, producing much merriment from all the family, particularly from Fred, eliciting from him the opinion they should all be enlarged and have copies sent to Brigadier Halton, the general, Doctor Carew and others.

"The sad thing is they couldn't record the pong," David exclaimed.

"How do you mean?" asked Rose.

"You would never believe how evil we smelled. We were filthy before we got on to the submarine having been sleeping in barns and hedges and Lord knows where for weeks. In the sub we absorbed all the smells of cooking, gash, sweat and the all pervading stink of diesel oil. We got off the sub in winter clothing saturated with pong, to make a hundred mile journey in a metal vehicle in a 100 degree heat, to arrive at G.H.Q. where everyone was dusted all over with California Poppy talcum powder. They had a major fumigation problem apparently after we left. Toby sent these photos – here's his letter. He says, 'we still get whiffs of your pong when we use a drawer that hasn't been opened since you were here. Powerful stuff – poor Amanda goes into hysterics every time it's mentioned.'"

Hawk-Eye – in this instance, Hawk-Ear, Rose interrupted.

"Oh, who was Amanda may we ask?"

"Well as you know, officers never talk about a lady behind her back. You had better ask Paddy."

On 28th April David made his way to Clay Cross. He had been to see Pat and his mother the day before to say au revoir – 'Not goodbye, just au revoir.' As the train pulled out of London for Chesterfield, he was again reminded of the evil of war at the sight, along the track, of all those bombed houses, each one a heartache to at least one family, and then he sat back and wondered how he was going to fit in with regimental life again after swanning around on his own for so long.

Well, I made the decision he concluded. But often decisions made in all good faith can become very unstuck – look at Ponsonby he told himself.

Chapter Sixteen

After the long and gruelling march Rosa and her fellow camp inmates had suffered before reaching the brickworks where apparently they were to be put to work, hardly any of them was fit enough to lift a single brick let alone be put to heavy labour. In the morning after their arrival, the manager of the plant came to see them in the long cobbled shed in which they had been housed the previous night, sleeping on straw on the hard uneven floor. The sight that greeted his eyes was apocalyptic. The first three forms he saw inside the door were dead. Dead women, women who had not died in the dignity of being nicely laid out, hands crossed on the breast. These women had died in the cruelly contorted posture of the final agonies of starvation, arms and legs spread out in all directions; mouths open to utter that final scream which they had been too enfeebled to emit. Inside the barn there was none alive. There were thirty or forty perhaps, living skeletons half alive, of which Rosa was one, who regarded him with the huge wide-eyed stare of the living dead. At their feet were many more cadavers, heaps of bones encased in tattered clothes, some without shoes showing bloodied feet where they had been made to march on when their footwear disintegrated. The smell was appalling. The manager rushed back outside and was violently sick.

"What the hell have you brought to me here you blasted idiot?" he stormed to the S.S. Sergeant who had commanded the guards on the march. The sergeant was in no mood to be browbeaten by a civilian, particularly in view of the fact that it was the stinkiest, foulest, rottenest job he and his men had ever been given; to say nothing of the fact that they too had been required to walk every yard the prisoners had endured, through the same snow and rain, having to despatch women who obviously could go no further – and that a regular daily occurrence. The fact they detested the duty they had been given so much had itself made each and every one of them more brutal to the women under their charge, which in turn made them hate themselves more, apart that is from the three or four sadists among them.

"I was told you were bringing me one hundred and twenty workers which I badly need, and what have you lumbered me with? – a couple of dozen corpses. By God, if I don't get you reduced to the ranks for this you bloody oaf, my name isn't Helmutt Fischer."

The sergeant took a step towards him and grabbed his coat. "Now listen to me. Nobody talks to an S.S. Sergeant like that, particularly someone like you whose mother hawked her fanny in the Reeperbahn, never knew who your father was from a hundred and more drunken sailors on stand-up grinds against the dockyard wall, produced your sister who was butch and a brother who was a pox-ridden poofter." Now in full flow he continued, "So when you talk to me you syphilitic craphead you show respect or by Christ you will end up like those concentration camp cows in there." His diatribe would have made Rabelais himself envious; the manager was white-faced and terror-stricken, the final shove which deposited him on his more than ample posterior on the cobbles being the final insult.

"Fall in, two files. Right turn. Quick march."

And with that the guards marched out of the brickworks into the road leading down to the railway station in the small town, or rather large village, of Brucksheim.

The manager levered his overweight frame – he certainly had no rationing problems – off the cobbles, Rosa and two of her more active companions approached him.

"Sir," she asked him, "can my companions be fed, we have had nothing for two days and more will die unless they receive food and attention soon."

Smarting from the indignity he had already suffered, which he blamed entirely on to this useless assembly of promised workers he replied, "You can all go to hell for all I care, the lot of you can die, but not in my factory, bugger off, the lot of you."

"Sir," Rose continued, "there are already many dead in there. Where can I get help?"

"Follow the bloody soldiers down to the town centre and see the Burgemeister, but I want you out of here by tonight. As it is I shall have to burn the place down to get rid of your filth." He stamped off.

Rosa turned to the other two. "Are you able to come with me to the village?"

They agreed so to do and moved slowly off down the road in the direction the soldiers had taken. In under half a mile they came to the pretty little village with its steep sloping roofs and gaily painted verandas and exterior woodwork. They saw the Rathaus immediately; in fact with its huge swastika flag flying at an angle from its upper floor it could hardly be missed. As they passed people they were greeted with curious stares, looking as they did like living skeletons, dressed in the black and white striped concentration camp uniforms, the like of which had never before been seen in the fair town of Bruksheim. They were filthy, dirty, with tangled, matted hair which had grown from their normal shaven condition whilst they had been on the march. But no one spoke to them. Rosa asked herself afterwards – why did no one speak to us, we were obviously in terrible trouble, why did they ignore us? But ignore them they did.

They entered the Rathaus; there was a young woman at the enquiry desk. She looked at them in horror.

"What do you want?"

Rosa, resurrecting her voice of authority developed during her medical career replied, "I must see the Burgemeister on a matter of instant and serious consequence."

The girl, struck by the autocratic tone of voice Rosa had been able to produce, was taken aback, but like all people way down the pecking order in local and government authorities, wanted to do nothing which would bring the wrath of her superiors upon her. She decided to play it safe and put the final decision of who should see who on to someone higher up the proverbial ladder.

"Wait there a minute," (no please noted Rosa). She disappeared into an adjacent office returning with a kindly looking, middle-aged lady.

"I am the Burgemeister's secretary," she announced, "how can I help you?"

Rosa quickly and concisely explained the situation at the brickworks, of the march there and the deaths en route and of the last two days. The woman's face showed shock and horror, the young receptionist, at first curious, gradually descended into tears at the horrific story.

"Come into this room," the secretary replied. She led the way to a small interview room used normally by the townspeople seeking advice or information from the local authority. To the girl who had followed them she said, "Make some coffee for these ladies and bring some biscuits." There were two immediate personal reactions from Rosa, firstly the fact they were being treated as human beings instead of slaves for the first time in a very long time which almost caused her to weep with emotion, and secondly the uncontrollable salivation induced by the fact they were being promised food and drink. She looked at the other two. One was weeping, they both were drooling. The secretary turned away, she too was on the verge of tears.

"I will see the Burgemeister."

In five minutes she returned with a large, genial looking, bewhiskered man, well past the age of retirement, obviously filling in on the job since so many men, up to even middle age at this stage, 1943, in the war, had been called into service to replace the enormous casualties being lost in Russia.

"Tell me your story again Frau...?"

"I am Frank Doktor Rosa von Hassellbek," Rosa commenced.

"What is a Doktor doing in a concentration camp for God's sake?" he asked.

"I was convicted for possessing anti-war leaflets. I received six years imprisonment."

"Six years for having a few leaflets?" he queried unbelievingly.

"My six friends, all female students at Munich were hanged for distributing them. I was lucky; at least I thought I was until I began my sentence." Rosa felt now she had said enough. She had no idea of how much of a Nazi this man was. He sat looking out of his office at a huge Nazi flag all day; he could easily be one of them.

There was a long, long, silence.

"I had no idea my country could sink to this," he said despondently.

The coffee and biscuits arrived. Rosa endeavoured her utmost not to wolf the food down, but the other two had no such inhibitions. The Burgemeister and his secretary watched as they crammed the nourishment in, leading Rosa to explain

"We have had nothing proper to eat all the time we were on the march. The last food we had, cabbage soup and bread, was two days ago. There are people in the barn who have starved to death."

"I must see this. Frau Hiller, get my car round, get a lorry up to the brickyard and meet me there. Get the youth hostel at the lake opened up, get on to the Klinick and ask them to send a doctor and nurses immediately to the hostel. And you, Ursula, find Max the maintenance man and tell him to cycle to the hostel and start the cooking fires up." They jumped to it. When the Burgemeister spoke in those tones everybody jumped to it.

In minutes the Burgemeister's car arrived at the front of the Rathaus, a number of inquisitive locals stopping in their tracks to see their civic leader getting in with the driver whilst three incredibly filthy looking women scrambled on to the rear seat.

To say he was appalled at the sight which greeted him would be a gross understatement. With all his years of experience, including the carnage of the 1914 war, nothing had shocked him as the sight of this dead, half dead and dying collection of what had probably, not long ago, been attractive female company. When the lorry arrived a few minutes later those that could no longer walk were gently carried on to it. Rosa examined the dead to ensure they had indeed succumbed, the remainder, of which there were no more than a dozen or so, climbed up on to the lorry with the help of the driver and the Burgemeister's driver.

"Drive very slowly so that you don't bump them about unnecessarily, we will follow you."

At the camp Frau Hiller, having brought three of the town hall staff with her, had unlocked the building, the blanket cupboard, and the kitchen, and with her little team were putting pairs of blankets on to the beds – simple iron framed units with cross wires and thin mattresses on top – very basic but to their new occupiers, used to sleeping on bare boards at the best of times, absolute luxury. Max had lit the wood fire in the big range and already had cauldrons of water heating up. As the lorry arrived so did the Klinik party, a woman doctor and three nurses, each of these very young, probably probationers Rosa assumed.

In a little over an hour a basic soup had been prepared.

"You will be given only small portions every two hours for the next eight hours," the Klinik doctor announced. "Who is in charge?"

By unanimous vote all the women indicated by hand or by eye that Rosa was their leader.

"I wish to talk to you as I shall have to make a report," and then as an afterthought, "but eat your soup first."

The soup, thick with vegetables, flavoured with salt and eaten with a chunk of wholemeal bread, was absolute manna from heaven to these starving prisoners. The thought that the meal, small though it was, would be repeated in two hours, and again two hours after that, induced such a feeling of elation in souls which had been starved of the slightest drop of the milk of human kindness for as long as they could remember that would have been equalled only by the decision that they were to be set free. Sadly, there was no hope of that.

After slowly eating her bread and soup, Rosa related their story to the doctor, not, she judged, a particularly sympathetic person. As she commenced they were joined by the Burgemeister and Frau Hiller. "Take this down please Frau Hiller," he asked as Rosa began her account.

"Our factory was bombed. A group of one hundred and twenty two of us were put on the road with guards to come to the brickyard, although we did not know where we were going of course, or how long it would take. The weather was bad, and people kept dropping out by the wayside. If they could not continue, they were shot by one of the guards, usually the sergeant."

The doctor interrupted. "You say, they were shot? Now be careful young woman, do not make false allegations or you will be in serious trouble."

Rosa turned to her. "Frau Doktor, forgive me, you cannot begin to know what serious trouble is as we do."

There was silence for a moment or two.

"Carry on," the Burgemeister said in a low voice, as much a

reproof to the doctor as an order to proceed. Then added,

"Who buried the bodies?"

"Any villagers or dwellers in cottages nearby were ordered to do it by the sergeant. If we were right out in the country with no one near, the body was thrown into a ditch and left there."

"Was a record kept of their names and numbers of the people who died?" the doctor asked. Each prisoner had her concentration camp number tattooed on the left arm.

"I don't know. I don't think so. I kept a mental note of the numbers."

"How can we believe you?" she asked sharply.

"The prisoner is a doctor," the Burgemeister interjected. "Doctors do not tell lies, particularly in a matter of this nature."

The Klinik doctor's attitude changed immediately. "Why did you not tell me you were a doctor? Why were you in the camp?"

Rosa repeated the story she had told the Burgemeister. The doctor sat back dumbfounded. She repeated almost the same words as had been expressed at Rosa's original account.

"Good God, don't say we have sunk to this level," she paused again, "we have thirty people here, there are, I understand, eight dead at the brickyard, that means that eighty-two people died on the march."

"You have not counted me. I made it eighty-one died before we arrived here. Most of them were shot."

The doctor broke down into tears. "I cannot believe it; I cannot believe it," she said, "My God what have we become?"

She was not to know that a little over a year later such marches became commonplace and thousands upon thousands of concentration camp victims, extermination camp victims, prisoners of war and slave labourers were put on the road as the allies advanced from the east and the west. Only a small proportion survived these terrible journeys.

There were no more fatalities. After a few days most of the inmates of the camp had recovered enough to be able to get up from their beds. The Klinik doctor emerged as being both kind and extremely efficient. Having regular meals of basic but nourishing food did more for these living skeletons than any medicines would have done.

After they had been there for a week, the Burgemeister and the doctor asked Rosa to come to the camp office. Her immediate fear was their little honeymoon was over – they would be sent back to the concentration camp, or worse, to the brickyard. The doctor put her mind at rest.

"The Burgemeister has had an interview with the State Prosecutor," she began. "He has told him – he was appalled at what has happened – that reluctantly he can do nothing since the alleged offences were carried out by the S.S., they being answerable only to Reichsminister Himmler. It was obvious he had no intention of contesting an argument with him or his subordinates. Secondly we have been in touch with your camp headquarters, who require to know the camp number of each person here, which I have given them from the list you gave me. By a process of elimination they can arrive at the names of the women who died, so that their next of kin can be informed. They do of course have the record of who was placed on the detail to be sent to the brickyard. Thirdly I have told them that the farms in this area urgently need labour and that we would like to keep the women here to work. I assured them we would see that they were most efficiently supervised. I am a senior party member from the early days, they immediately agreed to the plan because of my seniority and in their own interests since it saved them the trouble of getting you all back again and finding something else for you to do.

Finally, the Burgemeister has spoken to each farmer, told them they are to treat the prisoners fairly and correctly, or they would be answerable to him." With a smile, a very very rare luxury in which she allowed herself to indulge, she concluded "And when the Burgemeister speaks the farmers listen if they know what is good for them."

Rosa was so overcome with the turn of events her eyes misted and she took one of the doctor's hands. "Thank you, thank you both, for what you have done for us. Whatever happens to us now we shall always remember your kindness. Thirty one people will remember you for the rest of their days, however long or short they may be."

"Right, today is Saturday," the Burgemeister declared. "On Wednesday I will send the lorry to take the women to the various farms. Here is a list of numbers required at each place; the women can sort out among themselves who they would like to be with. As you can see they are mostly in threes and fours. Well, I think that is all."

"Just one thing more," the doctor added. "I shall need you at the Klinik, we are hopelessly understaffed. You will not be able to take all the decisions which, as a doctor, you would normally be empowered to make, but I don't think that should inhibit you too much. I will take you there today after you have told the prisoners what they are to do."

Rosa was unable to stop the sobs of emotion which overtook her. Softly she cried, her two companions letting her relief flow out with the tears until eventually the Burgemeister took a handkerchief from his top pocket and gave it to her. "Thank you, thank you, thank you," was all she could say.

The women looked at her with a mixture of curiosity, fear and expectation as she rejoined them. They tried to establish whether the tears which had lined her face were of joy or horror. When they heard the results of her talk with the doctor the tears cascaded to the floor, they mobbed her as if she were their saviour; not one wondering how long this good fortune would last. When death is a daily occurrence even a few days of life was a bonus. They, literally, lived for one day at a time.

Chapter Seventeen

It was May Day 1943. Before the war the children at the two elementary schools in Sandbury had always provided a display in the town centre, to include, in particular, dancing around the two maypoles decked with their coloured ribbons. Each year they had endeavoured to outdo each other with a more intricate display, in 1940 however the festival had been proscribed for the first time since the Lord Protector had in 1644,

> "Threw our altars to the ground
> And tumbled down the crosses.
> Because they hated the Common Prayer,
> The Organ and the maypole."

As this year, May Day was on a Saturday, the town council decided to renew the tradition. The Welsh Guards Battalion on the Maidstone Road was approached, gladly providing not only a choir, but also a section of their regimental band! From this, the event snowballed. Ronnie Mascall provided a 'Cavalry Cavalcade' of riders in all manner of uniforms; hunt dress, medieval clothes, even a jockey in Sir Oliver Routledge's racing colours. A football match was arranged on the town ground between R.A.F. Sandbury and the Welsh Guards, the players and spectators finally returning to the town centre for a glorious sing-song led by the finest male voice choir ever heard in this ancient town, which ended the day's festivities.

As Jack said that evening, it was a prime example of the change of spirit in the population as a whole, but being a cautious man he added they should note the subject of Canon Rosser's sermon a short while ago – we still had a long way to go, a very long way. Evidence of this had been shown by their having an air raid at the end of April, and again on the 8th of May, on both occasions bombs being dropped on the outskirts of the town causing damage and casualties.

On the 13th May Deputy Prime Minister Attlee announced in the Commons, 'No Axis forces remain in North Africa. The last remaining elements surrendered at 11.45am this morning.' The population as a whole was overjoyed. Rose, hearing the news on the wireless at six o'clock, sitting on her own in the big kitchen at Chandlers Lodge, broke down into tears of relief that her darling husband Mark and dear friend Charlie had come safely through this tremendous and long lasting battle with the Afrika Korps. When she regained her composure she clasped her hands together, looked up, closed her eyes, and whispered, "Thank you God."

At the Home Guard there was great activity. The 16th May would be the 3rd anniversary of their formation. They had grown from a motley collection of old soldiers, young would-be soldiers and all types of civilians in between, to become a highly trained force up to battalion level, throughout the country. In recognition of their services, they had been given the honour of providing the guard at Buckingham Palace for that day. Elsewhere there would be battalion parades throughout the country. It would be Jack's last parade before handing over to Fred. The Sandbury Company would march through the town to the church for a short fifteen minute service, then march to the station to join the 10.30 train, in which carriages had been reserved, to take them to Maidstone. At Maidstone they would join other companies to march through the city centre, the salute being taken by the Lord Lieutenant of the county. It was a great day, and further evidence, since their services had not thus far been required, of the growing confidence of success in the fight against the evils of Nazidom. The following Wednesday Jack's resignation appeared on the Army List, along with the promotion of one, Frederick Chandler, to the rank of major.

On Tuesday 18th May, the country heard of the raids on the Mohne, Sorpe, and Eder dams, using the incredible 'bouncing bombs' invented by Barnes Wallis which breached the retaining walls, released millions of tons of water down into the Ruhr Valley, thereby putting a great deal of war industry out of action. On the debit side, eight of the nineteen Lancasters employed in the attack were lost, and some twelve hundred people, it was later established, including several hundred Russian slave workers, were drowned. In Britain and in the occupied countries it was further evidence that Germany was losing the war.

For the next four nights, the Luftwaffe made hit-and-run raids on South-East England, causing the first major damage to Sandbury Engineering. At a little after 2am, the machine shop on the eastern side of the factory received a direct hit, putting it completely out of action, four fire watchers being killed and another dozen operators in the nearby surface shelter suffering minor injuries, concussion or bruising. Fred was telephoned and rushed to the scene where the Heavy Rescue Squad was already searching the debris for the one missing fire watcher who had not been accounted for. His badly mutilated body was at last found having fallen from his station on the roof into the workshop interior, then being buried by the cascading sandbag protection which had followed him down. For thirty-six hours without a break Fred, Ernie and Ray Osborne notified next of kin and relatives of injured persons, organised clearance units, salvaged machine tools for repair or replacement, finding to their astonishment over fifty percent of these were still in working order, organising a marquee on the hardstanding at the side of the factory to temporarily rehouse the machines, getting the maintenance people working day and night to rewire them and bed them down, all with the astounding result of having twenty-five per cent production in ten days, fifty per cent in three weeks. In six weeks the debris of the old shop had been cleared, a new, somewhat rudimentary, structure erected, the machines moved back in, replacements received as priority from the Ministry of Supply for those lost and in a little over six weeks the shop was back in full production working night and day to catch up with all that had been lost. In the meantime Fred and Ernie had the sad duty to attend the funerals of the men killed, along with those of two others who subsequently died of their injuries, it was the least they could do but their presence was much appreciated by the families concerned.

On the 2nd June the Birthday Honours List included under "Knights Bachelor" one Jack Hooper, and under D.B.E. Moira Hooper. The fact that husband and wife had received high honours at the same time being unusual; it received national coverage in the press along with a mention in the B.B.C. Home Service. As a result Sandbury Engineering was besieged by reporters wishing to interview the new 'Sir Jack,' they having been told at 'The Hollies' he was at the factory.

At the end of May the government announced that 584 people had been killed in the May air raids, 213 men, 266 women and 105 children, virtually all in the south-east. This tragic news, coming at a time when the heavy air raids had become a thing of the past, served to show the population as a whole that the war was far from over, indeed there was a great deal more suffering to come.

On the 2nd June, as Jack heard officially he was now a 'Sir,' young Oliver Coates and his pal Gordon Fotheringham also each received a letter from His Majesty, only on these occasions via the War Department, to tell them they were to report to Bovington Camp on the 9th of June to commence their training in an armoured formation.

"It says nothing about which regiment I shall be in," was Oliver's first observation.

"You will probably have to do basic training after which they will decide where to put you," was Cecely's speculation upon the subject.

The directive included a railway warrant made out in the name of Trooper Coates O., reading which gave young Oliver a momentary feeling of pride at being one of those companies of men who rode into battle for their king and country through the ages astride their chargers, except that he would be encased by solid steel and facing weaponry infinitely more destructive than a fifteen foot lance. On the other hand Cecely, noting the designation, became finally aware she would, from now on, be gradually losing her boy to others. Not entirely of course, there had always been, always would be a special bond between them, but from this day she would lose him bit by bit: a bit to the army, a bit to his comrades, a bit probably in the not-too-distant future to some young female, and then the final frightening thought, swiftly brushed aside, to his country on some foreign field.

"We shall be lonely without you."

"I will write to you regularly, I promise," continuing with, "By the way, what is Greta going to do? Is she going to stay on in the sixth form next year to go to university?"

"She will be taking her Matric next summer. We shall have to see what is to happen when we know the results of that."

"We know already. She's brilliant – you know that."

Cecely knew it quite well. She also knew her money was running out and the possibility of providing funds to send Greta to university would, by 1944, be nil. She still had heard nothing of the whereabouts of Nigel and his brother, the judge. They could both be dead, although she never ever acknowledged that possibility either to herself, her family, or her dear friends who had surrounded her with such care and comfort. Her family wealth was tied up in a country now ruled by despots, which made it valueless.

'Well, we shall see' – the answer to millions of questions to which there is no immediate answer, the answer is unpalatable, or the speaker is reluctant to give the answer. From time immemorial.

'Mummy, can we go to the seaside this year?'

'We shall see.'

It was a stock mother phrase. Oliver accepted it as such and turned away to get together the few bits and pieces he had to take with him. Should he take pyjamas? Squaddies probably don't wear pyjamas; they'll think I'm a poofter. A pair of walking out shoes? Probably won't be allowed to wear them. Wait till I come on my first forty-eight – he had heard of forty-eights and seventy-twos from David and Maria. That David's a lucky devil; if I was a bit older I would make a play for Maria. He had already had one or two fumbles with the local girls and considered himself something of a ladies' man – wait till I am in uniform he told himself – I shall be irresistible!!

Later that evening the telephone rang at the Bungalow, answered by Mrs Treharne.

"Mrs Treharne, how are you? Hugh Ramsford here. I was wondering whether young Oliver has got his recruitment papers yet?"

"I understand they came today, Lord Ramsford, can I get Cecely for you? Just hang on for a moment."

With that, she put the receiver on the hall table and hurried to the sitting room, thinking, 'any excuse is better than none,' but smiling conspiratorially as the thought went through her mind.

"Hugh Ramsford enquiring after Oliver," she announced to Cecely, followed, with a knowing smile, with, "among other things probably."

Cecely responded with a deprecatory wave, smiling nevertheless at both Mrs Treharne's innuendo, along with the anticipated pleasure of the prospect of a tête-à-tête with someone of whom she was becoming very fond.

Mrs Treharne, keeping a casual check on the length of time the telephone conversation was lasting, in other words to the nearest second, at the return of a slightly flushed Cecely in a little over thirty three minutes enquired, "Couldn't you remember whether Oliver had received his papers?"

Cecely picked up a cushion and pretended to throw it at her.

"He is going abroad for three weeks, but wants me to join him in town upon his return for the weekend of the 14th July, dinner on Friday, concert with his father on Saturday at the Albert Hall and a day of leisure on Sunday to be determined. He would install me at Berners, despite it being choc a block with Americans, whilst he would be staying nearby at his club. He repeated this last geographical exactitude on two occasions so that I did not get the wrong idea I suppose."

"Yes, but did he know whether you thought it was the wrong idea I wonder," was Mrs Treharne's machinatory reply.

"Mrs Treharne – how could you think such a thing?" said in mock horror.

In view of the exterior veil of respectability enshrouding Mrs Treharne, the reply was as totally surprising as anything Cecely could have envisaged.

"You only live once, my dear, don't waste it. These are such unusual times."

Cecely waited some little while before replying.

"But I don't know whether my darling Nigel is alive or dead."

Mrs Treharne made no reply. She could fully understand Cecely's battle with her immediate needs being in conflict with her feelings of loyalty. Cecely's raging thoughts contemplated it would be different – possibly – if she was considering just a one-night stand with someone she could dismiss the next day, or the next week or whenever. She knew however that Hugh was becoming very attached to her, and whilst she had the highest regard for him and could easily, under normal circumstances, establish a firm liaison with him, the fact remained the circumstances were not normal. If they did become normal again – the conflict raged on in her mind as to what would then happen? Boiled down to basics, she needed a man – badly – but pleasure has to be paid for as a rule, would an involvement with Hugh Ramsford result in too high a price?

The thoughts raging through her mind were brought to a halt by Mrs Treharne putting her arm around her shoulders and saying, "It will work itself out, you'll see."

On 9th June Fred took the Rover to The Bungalow to collect Cecely and Oliver and take them to the station. Greta had had to say goodbye to her brother on the previous Sunday as she had to get back to school for the end of year exams.

"You are to get a photograph taken as soon as you can so that I can swank to my form mates," was her parting shot.

"If you can swank when I am a trooper, what will you be like when I am a general?" was the inevitable reply.

Reaching the station, Fred waited outside with the car while Cecely went on to the platform to not only say goodbye to her son, but to say goodbye to a chapter of her life. When she had said goodbye to him as he left her to go to school at Sevenoaks, it had been a wrench, but then she had the weekends and end of term holidays to look forward to. Now it would be the occasional leave, followed probably by an overseas posting, and possibly... she abruptly halted her chain of thought. The train came in, whisking him away, she returned disconsolate to a waiting Fred.

"If it wasn't so early in the morning, I would whip you off to John Tarrant's for a livener" he quipped. She smiled.

"I'm only one of millions, am I not?"

"True. To know that doesn't make it any easier though does it?"

"I think I'll go straight to Country Style and get stuck into some work, that will cheer me up. I will telephone Anni and Rose to see if they can come and have lunch on me at the Angel."

When she reached the shop she telephoned Anni. No reply. She then telephoned Rose. No reply. She then had the bright idea of telephoning Nanny at The Hollies. The receiver was lifted to emit a cacophony of shrieks and yells followed by Nanny's well modulated voice, which informed her that all the junior members of the Chandler family were at The Hollies as Rose had gone with Anni in the ambulance to the hospital for the expected delivery of her second child – two weeks early! At lunch time, being Wednesday, it was early closing day, she ate a quick sandwich in the cafe along the High Street, then took herself to Sandbury Hospital maternity ward, where she at last caught up with Rose and Megan, the latter looking very professional in her blue uniform, starched white apron, immaculately laundered puff sleeves topped by an extremely fetching bonnet. Her instant thought was, it must take a week to wash, starch and iron that lot.

The baby was born a little after nine o'clock that evening. A lovely 6 pounds 8 ounces girl, to be named Ruth Rose Megan Bolton, so that all her life her names would give her instant understanding of the three people who had taken her mother into their homes and hearts, at the lowest point of her young life.

Ernie and Karl were allowed to see her for only fifteen minutes. It had not been a difficult birth; nevertheless the consultant insisted she was to have rest, as he was not entirely happy with her blood pressure. The two men therefore collected a bottle of Scotch that Karl had been saving and the bottle of Brandy Ernie had saved, it being the present brought back from Portugal for him by David, and made their way to Chandlers Lodge. The two guardsmen were there, and as they arrived so too did Jack, he too carrying a bottle of Scotch to 'wet the baby's head.' Ernie was late for work in the morning – the first time ever, Fred could hardly open his eyes to say 'good morning' to Mrs Russell, Karl had already taken the day off which was owing to him, and the two guardsmen kept well out of the way of the C.O. until lunch had revived them. Ruth Rose Megan Bolton's arrival into the world had been epically celebrated. (Is there such a word as 'epically'? – if not, there should be).

Over the next few days the undulant wail of the air raid siren sounded over the fair town of Sandbury as hit-and-run raids took place on the south-eastern corner. Only once did the airfield receive attention. They were nuisance raids, probably as much for reconnaissance to see if any troop concentrations were being made, to indicate whether and where the coming invasion would be made, as opposed to causing any serious damage. The boot was on the other foot now. Hitler knew a huge new well-equipped, well-trained army was soon to hit his Western Wall. His generals knew the war was lost, only Hitler and a coterie of sycophantic hangers-on believed otherwise. Perhaps it was a belief engendered by desperation, perhaps by ignorance, perhaps by stupidity, perhaps by fanatical arrogance, who knows. It was clearly a case of 'Fight on lads, I'm right behind you.' But fight on they did and many millions were still to die and many towns, including London and in Kent, were to suffer appalling damage and destruction.

Chapter Eighteen

It was late afternoon of 30th April. The recent occupiers of Camp Six reached rendezvous point five one mile north of the rapids on the River Muar tributary south of the huge expanse of lakes of Tasek Bera. An outlying picket had spotted them and guided them in to the temporary camp where, to their surprise, they were met and welcomed by colonel Ransomes, their Kampong Bintang friend Major Grenville, and an Australian captain, "Bowlie" Couper, Bowlie, presumably, designed to illustrate the topography of his lower limbs.

After a welcoming meal already prepared by the twenty odd members of Colonel Ransome's party, they got down to planning the next series of events. As, obviously, it would be impossible to build a new camp to accommodate the previous Camp Six personnel, and taking into account natural wastage in the other camps, it had been decided to split the Camp Six force into three and tack them on to Camps Three, Four and Five. Harry's immediate thoughts followed along the line that whoever got Camp Three had a bloody long way to go before they experienced a comfortable bed again since he guessed it would be well north of where they were now. Another thought struck him. Supposing he got Camp Four, Jack Hooper's ex wife was there; he didn't much fancy being in close quarters with her for the next year or so.

"Right," said the colonel, "I want Robbie and the two Navy chaps to go to Camp Five with a third of the men, Clive to go to Camp Four to take command there with another third, and Harry, Choon Guan and Matthew Lee to Camp Three, which is under-strength, under-trained, under-motivated, under-bloody everything since Johnny Sinclair died. Bowlie here will be taking over and the existing incumbent sent on to my H.Q. in Cameron Highlands."

Harry didn't know whether firstly he liked the idea of being subordinate to a bloody Australian, and secondly whether he much liked the look of this particular antipodean in the first place. He wasn't exactly the tall, lean, broad shouldered specimen of manhood normally envisaged of his race, nor was he loud mouthed and brash, as is the common belief held in the shires of England of their colonial cousins. He was short, wiry and bow legged, and up until now hadn't opened his mouth except to say, "G'day mate," as he shook hands.

It was to be a long trek to Camp Three – a hundred miles as the crow flies, but half as much again when diversions for topographical or other reasons were required. They would have to cross the main railway line, a couple of secondary roads and one main road to get to their destination. They had a guide, but how good he would be, in Harry's estimation, was anyone's guess. In addition they had three unfordable rivers to cross, although on the credit side, as these were coming straight out of the mountains, they would be unlikely to contain the 'nasties' which had faced Harry in his horrendous swim at Muar.

After a day's rest, they each said goodbye to old friends, the Europeans all arranging to meet at Raffles two weeks after the war was over – what the communists arranged was an entirely different matter. They took eight days to reach Camp Three to find that the colonel's description of it had, if anything, been understated. They literally walked into the camp. There were no outlying pickets, no camp guards, had they been a Jap patrol the occupants would have been annihilated, since, as it was three o'clock in the afternoon, they were all fast asleep in their beds. Choon Guan was furious. In all the time Harry had known him he had never seen him in such a demonic rage. He walked into the main dormitory and screamed at its cowering occupants for a full ten minutes, ending in seizing the camp leader and dragging him out by the hair into the compound before Bowlie and Harry and throwing him to the ground at their feet.

"I would like your permission to execute this dollop of pus, Sir," he requested of Bowlie.

"I think we must do the job according to army law," Bowlie replied. "Tie him up and we will try him in the morning."

Whilst all this mayhem was taking place the door from the European quarters opened and a bleary-eyed figure emerged, quite obviously, although it was only mid afternoon, the worse for drink. Bowlie's first words were, "Where the bloody hell does he get the liquor from?" His second words were, "Consider yourself under arrest."

"Who do you think you are talking to? I am Major Abbott, O.C. of this camp." The words were slurred; he was swaying slightly and having a positive difficulty in focussing on this diminutive captain. Bowlie handed him a sheet of paper.

"This is a letter from Colonel Ransomes relieving you of your command as from now and instructing you to report to him at Cameron Highlands. I will send an escort with you at first light. Please return to your quarters."

Whether the major was relieved at the thought of getting out of this stinking hole, even hoping for the chance of a submarine ride back to civilisation, will never be known. That night he went down with a fearsome attack of dengue fever, he apparently slept without a net, which despite the continual ministrations of Matthew, brought about his death within twenty-four hours. They gave him a military funeral, less firing over the grave, and set about turning this abomination of a force into an operational unit.

It left firstly, however, the problem of Soh Ah Yew, the previous camp leader, he whose head Choon Guan had so vigorously demanded. At a meeting later that day, Bowlie explained to Choon Guan that, in consultation with R.S.M. Chandler, who was an expert on Kings Regulations and the Army Act, which contained military law, a court of their standing was not empowered to award the death sentence. Neither was the application of corporal punishment now allowed, even under field conditions. Matthew Lee had agreed to defend the defaulter when he was brought up to trial in the morning and the question of punishment would be decided after, and if, he was proven guilty. Choon Guan, having cooled down considerably by now, acknowledged the professionalism of this decision, Bowlie having suggested that he sit with the R.S.M. and himself on the panel of judges. In his bunk later that night Harry had to admit to himself that this arrangement was a bit of political cleverness on his captain's part. Firstly it gave Choon Guan prestige in being one of the judges, secondly it made sure the Chinese, whose allegiance might well be suspect at the trial of their former leader, would know their new camp leader was part and parcel of the sentence, whatever it might be.

At six a.m. the next day Harry and Choon Guan had all the camp personnel, less those who had just arrived, on parade. They gave them forty-five minutes P.T.; followed by forty-five minutes drill, break of thirty minutes for breakfast, then another thirty minutes running around the small parade ground. The unfit, unmotivated shambles were not allowed to rest. After that, until one o'clock, they did fatigues in an endeavour to clean the place up, rest until four then more drill and fatigues until dark. Bowlie had given Matthew Lee a day to prepare the defence of Soh Ah Yew, the court martial to be the next morning at ten o'clock.

Matthew's defence of the former camp leader was well researched. He gave, through succinct questioning of the accused, a picture of the general decline in morale and proficiency in arms of the comrades as a result of the lack of leadership and alcohol dependency of the late Major Abbott. As there was no one capable of acting as prosecuting officer, the court itself took on this function – highly irregular, probably, as Bowlie had reflected, but needs must... At this point Harry asked the president "Where did he get the liquor from?" Bowlie repeated the question to the accused. "Lim Kay Tan, the medic, made it for him."

"Made it, how do you mean made it?"

"We have neap palm trees one mile from here. Kay Tan collects sap from trees, makes very strong drink."

"Do the men drink it?"

"Some of them. Lim Kay Tan drinks a lot."

"What about you?"

"Sometimes."

"Carry on Matthew."

So the trial continued, it becoming more and more obvious that the whole camp had degenerated into laxity and negligence without a strong leadership.

Matthew Lee stressed this in his summing up, using the formula that as the accused had not received specific orders relating to duties, pickets and so forth he could not be held as disobeying an order. Since also his duties had not been spelt out to him, the officer commanding not being able to give evidence to the contrary, he could not be guilty of neglect of duty. The court retired to consider its verdict. In fact the reverse actually took place. Matthew, the accused and escort were told to wait outside, whilst the court stayed where it was – which amounts to the same thing!

By the time the somewhat amateur legalities had been concluded, Choon Guan had modified his draconian views as to the punishment of the one time camp leader. They found him guilty of neglect of duty on the basis that since he was in direct command under the major, should the Major be incapacitated as a result of sickness, being wounded, or in this case alcoholism, it was his duty to see that the military structure should still function. They then came to the big stumbling block – what punishment could you exercise on a person stuck in the middle of the jungle? He, along with all the others, was permanently confined to barracks. You could not stop his pay – he was not being paid. You could conceivably build a cage and incarcerate him in it, but what purpose would that serve? Harry suggested they made him the latrine orderly for a month and that would take the smile off his face. It should be explained that, of necessity, the latrines had to be sited away from the camp, for obvious reasons. This meant they could not be used at night, again for obvious reasons. Buckets therefore were placed outside the huts, each morning at dawn, being collected and emptied into the latrines. This fatigue fell to each man once every six weeks or so. It was hated, but since it only had to be done once in a blue moon, the men took it as a necessary evil, hoping there wasn't a dysentery problem in the camp at the time of his drawing the short straw. They called the accused etc back into the court. Bowlie announced, "We find you not guilty of disobeying an order, but guilty of neglect of duty. Do you accept my award?"

This latter question gave the opportunity, under military law, for the accused to go higher up the army chain of command to have his case heard. Soh Ah Yew was not daft. He knew they could do little to punish him here whereas all sorts of things could happen to him, about which he had no knowledge whatsoever, if he was sent to Cameron Highlands. He answered, "Yes Sir."

"Have you anything to say on your own behalf before I pass sentence?"

Matthew arose with a plea of mitigation. "Soh Ah Yew has been a loyal soldier for the past eighteen months and has taken part valiantly in three operations. There is no doubt he has been influenced by the general decline in standards in the camp over the past few months. He wishes me to express his sincere regrets at his lapse in military and political standards and wishes for an opportunity soon, in action, to re-establish himself in the eyes of his officers and comrades."

"Very well. You are to be on constant fatigues for sixty days. For the first thirty days you will be latrine orderly," a look of a mixture of disgust and dejection crossed his normally impassive face. "For the second thirty days you will be on cookhouse fatigue and any other task your superiors may require you to carry out." Choon Guan stood up. "Wait for me in the barrack room – Dismiss!" An extremely disconsolate communist marched himself out.

Over the next two weeks they knocked the camp into some sort of order with tasks as far apart as clearing the undergrowth near the camp, to cleaning the insides of the buildings until they shone, to weapon training until the men's arms ached from bayonet drill. Picket posts were constructed, the approaches to the camp were not as difficult as those at Camp Six had been, and they therefore had to be secured with mantraps and thick prickly hedge defences to divert any would-be attackers into a killing ground. One advantage of this camp was they inherited a very good radio receiver and sender, dropped to it in the last airdrop! They were to find also, the drop zone, which shortly they hoped to make use of, was only about eight miles away, concealed in a long, almost treeless valley. At Camp Six it was a long, long slog carrying their goodies back up into the high jungle; here it would be much easier.

By the end of the month they received details of their first operation. On the eastern side of the main mountain range, some fifteen miles from the camp was the small town of Raub. A sleepy sort of place apparently, according to one of the Chinese who came from there, notable only for the fact that on its outskirts it boasted a gold mine. It was a surface mine, not one of your South African type deep mines. Giant excavators scooped up the surface, fed the earth into giant crushers, from which it was transferred to flotation tanks to which was then added copious quantities of water laced with cyanide. The gold particles then floated to the surface from which they were skimmed off. It was, in the main, low quality gold and the yield was, to untutored eyes, not worth all the effort, something like less than an ounce per ton of ore. However, every ounce, produced as it was mainly by prisoners of war labour, was a bonus to a conqueror who needed every dollar it could raise to continue its war effort.

There was a problem. A company of reserve class soldiers, including some Koreans and Formosans, was stationed at the mine to both guard the premises and the prisoners of war in their compound. Camp Three had only about fifty combat soldiers, not nearly enough to mount a surprise attack on a hundred or more well armed defenders without losing casualties, this therefore was to be a hit and run exercise.

"What do you think Harry?" Bowlie asked. "I haven't done one of these capers before."

It was the first time they had talked about Bowlie's past. Harry had assumed he had been with the Force since the surrender in '42. Bowlie continued, "Some blokes did an attack at Kampong Bintang where I was a P.O.W. I was one of four Aussies rescued and taken to Camp Four."

The two men had been together in close proximity for the past month. It seemed impossible that at some time during that time the subject of their individual pasts would not have arisen. Because of the initial trauma, the subsequent slave driving routine of getting the troops fit and the camp itself secure, there had been little time for personal reminiscences.

"My party was the one that sank the boat there," Harry laughingly told him.

"Bloody hell mate, nobody told me. I owe my life to you lot. None of us could have lasted another six months in that crap house of a place, eaten alive with mosquitoes and no nets, centipedes crawling over you at night, and when those bastards bite it's like a bee sting, often gets infected, your arm or leg swells up and still the bloody Japs made you work. We were infested with mice and rats and the snakes who eat the rats followed them into the barrack room at night, then those snakes that eat other snakes, kraits mainly, followed them. If you got a bite from one of them it was curtains in the condition we were in. We used to sleep on the concrete floor in everything we could put on but we still lost half a dozen Indians and one of our blokes. I tell you Harry, I shall have bloody nightmares about that place till the day I die," and then with a laugh, "if I live that long."

"Well the first thing to do is to send a couple of Choon Guan's lot to do a recce. I suppose the bloke who used to live there and one of our reliable chaps from Camp Six would be best. The equipment at a gold mine will probably be big heavy stuff, we would need a ton of explosive to do any damage to some of it, so we have got to consider what we can do the most damage to with the facilities we have, and at the same time hope to kill a few Japs."

"Right, let's get Choon Guan in."

Given the general outline of the future intention, with the admonition that nothing was to be said to the men at this stage, Choon Guan immediately suggested he should make the reconnaissance along with Philip Chai, one of Matthew Lee's men, whose father had been a merchant in Raub until the Japs came and executed him, along with others. A bonus to this arrangement, off-setting Choon Guan's natural reluctance to working with a Christian of undoubted capitalist origins, was that Philip, until the war, had been articled to a surveyor in Kuala Lumpur and was therefore more than capable of providing accurate and comprehensive sketches of the mine layout, particularly its approaches, and the uses to which the various buildings were put. As Harry said, "There's no point in blowing up a crap house unless half the Japs are in there at the time."

They were given four days to make the trip, rations for five days and strict instructions not to take any risks or contact any residents. Late on 2nd June two very tired Chinese arrived back at Camp Three, complete with over a dozen very well crafted drawings of the layout of the mine, both in plan and in perspective as seen on the line of approach from the camp. Even Choon Guan had to give grudging tributes to the excellence of the survey, including as it did, approximate distances, dimensions of buildings, degrees of slopes away from the workings to the waste land covering a hundred acres or more whence the liquid slime was drained after the flotation operation, an area where nothing, not even the jungle, would grow for another twenty years or more, such was the cyanide pollution.

Examining the sketches they decided that with their limited resources their best efforts would be rewarded by destroying the electrical substation, the motor of the giant excavator, the central building housing the office, laboratory and presumably, as Harry guessed, the gold. Looking at the sketches Harry remarked to Bowlie, "Did you see the guards' barracks are built on a slope, with brick piers at one end to give a space of a couple of feet or more beneath the floor?"

"So?"

"If we made a couple of Bangalore torpedoes out of female bamboo and set them off whilst they are asleep, it could be rather fun. The hut is close to the perimeter, it shouldn't be too difficult to get at." Bangalore torpedoes were tubes – usually steel, stuffed with explosive. These would not be as effective as steel but would still do a lot of damage.

"Harry, you're a man after my own heart – I don't see why we shouldn't get a bit of fun out of it."

They broke the operation down into four sections. Once the P.O.W.'s were put into their compound at night, Choon Guan and Philip had established the only guards left were two on the main gate and two prowlers. The prowler guard made a circuit of the perimeter of the compound every hour. "How do we get rid of them?" Bowlie asked.

Harry pointed to his blowpipe resting on four nails on the wall above his bed. "We'll get up close to the wire and see them off with that." Bowlie's eyebrows nearly disappeared into his hair line as Harry described to him how his orang asli friends had taught him how to become a one man silent executioner and how efficient it had been at Batu Anam.

There was a problem. The mine covered a large area. It was surrounded by a substantial mesh fence. The four targets ideally should be approached from different points at some distance from each other through the wire fence – problem? they only had two sets of wire cutters strong enough to do the job. They looked at the plan again.

"Everything has got to be on a time basis," Harry explained. Bowlie by now had realised that he should leave the planning to his more experienced subordinate, although of course, in reality a regimental sergeant major, although technically subordinate to a captain, would probably hold more sway in a unit that most captains.

"We will cut the wire here, and here, once I have disposed of the prowler guard. Each squad will then reach his objective, which means I'm afraid you will have further to cover, place his charges and wait for H. hour, whenever that might be. Then they will all set their fuses at the same time for the same number of minutes, after which they will scarper quickly back to the R.V. By this means all four explosions should take place simultaneously, or as near together as makes no difference."

As for the previous operations they marked out the various targets on the parade ground except that it had to be done on a quarter scale, which meant having 'cut the wire,' they then had to double backwards and forwards twice to reach their objectives. One man was a particularly slow mover, he was dropped. Soh Ah Yew, the latrine orderly, begged to take his place. Bowlie and Harry looked at Choon Guan. He somewhat reluctantly, nodded his agreement. He was placed in the central building group, which would be nearest the main entrance guardroom.

And so they practised, over and over until they could have carried it out blindfolded, well almost.

On 9th June they decided to make the approach on the following Saturday 12th, the operation to take place at 2am on Sunday 13th. "I hope it's unlucky for them and not for us," Bowlie remarked. They reached the observation point an hour before sunset, the mine was more or less deserted, the P.O.W.'s back in their compound, one or two Japs washing in buckets outside their barrack room, and a few wandering towards the main gate obviously out for an evening in Raub. As far as Bowlie and Harry could see there was nothing to interfere with the plan they had devised. Choon Guan had established the sentries were on duty for four-hour stints, changed at midnight, so would not be missed if eliminated during that time. What he didn't know was that, on their hourly circuit of the mine, they reported to the guardroom that all was well.

At midnight Harry and Bowlie approached a concealed spot where the secondary jungle was almost against the wire, and where the well-worn footpath the guards were following was only some six feet inside the perimeter. Some twenty minutes later they saw the guards approaching, chatting quietly together, rifles slung casually by their slings over their shoulders. Harry had loaded his blowpipe and had prepared two more darts ready for use in case he should miss with one. When the men were some ten yards away, one of them hesitated and turned, giving a low whistle, in response to which a large mongrel came bounding along the path to join them, jumping up on to his caller and being rewarded by the guard with a rubbing of his head and cheeks. As the dog dropped his forepaws to the ground he suddenly froze looking towards the bushes where the two men were concealed. They remained motionless. The instant thought of the two guards was that the animal had scented a snake or perhaps a deer, of which there was a number in the lower jungle. They moved towards the fence, the dog's back bristling, preparing to growl or bark. Quickly Harry put the first dart into the dog. It rolled over instantly, ipoh resin on a relatively small animal like that would act instantly. The guards, immediately judging the dog had been bitten by a snake, started to make themselves scarce. Harry hit one of them who in turn staggered a few paces and fell down. The second guard, to his credit, ran back to try and help his comrade and received Harry's third dart.

"Jesus Christ Almighty," blasphemed Bowlie Couper, "you are an absolute bloody genius. I shall remember that scene every day of my life I swear it."

"Well, let's hope there aren't any more surprises like that in store for us. You know, I don't think of bloody Japs being fond of animals."

They moved back to the R.V. point and swiftly got the four teams moving. They had particularly cautioned the party who were putting the Bangalore torpedoes under the hut to make sure they didn't knock a pile of tin buckets over or something equally stupid, in fact it might be worth a quick flash of a torch to make sure there were no obstructions. The wire was cut, the two teams made their way through each hole, each marked with a piece of white cloth so that the returning parties would not have to hunt for the way out. By 1.40 a.m. everything was in position, fuses and detonators all fixed, each group leader watching his wristwatch for 2 a.m. to come so that they could set the thing off and make their various ways back through the fence.

At this point the guard commander on the main gate suddenly realised the prowler had not reported in at 1 a.m. "I bet they are having a sleep on the office veranda," he told himself.

"I'm going to check on the prowler," he told the other sentry with him, I shan't be long." At 1.52 he was spotted by one of Choon Guan's lookouts approaching the main block. Soh Ah Yew, the long time latrine man, also spotted him. Loosening his machete he silently raced around the small building in front of which the guard would have to pass, so as to come up behind him. The moment he had passed, the latrine man sprang out, lifted his machete and with one immense blow cleaved his head down to his shoulders.

Ah Yew ran back to his group leader, who quietly whispered, "Well done."

At two o'clock they lit their fuses and were away. One of the fuses on the Bangalore torpedoes failed, but the one that exploded set the detonator off on the unexploded one with the same end result – considerable casualties inside the hut.

They got to the R.V. point – a quick roll call to ensure all present, then a speedy withdrawal up into the higher jungle. Under normal circumstances they would have waited until daybreak before they moved, but with the other half of the Jap company billeted a mile away on the other side of the mine, possibly being sent to pursue them, they could not afford to hang around savouring their successes – which indeed had been considerable as they could tell from the fires raging, clearly visible from the R.V.

They marched steadily, wading along streams for long distances in case they were tracked, until with the sun well up they called a halt, having made a wide, semi circular detour toward the camp. They arrived back during the late afternoon, the men expecting to be immediately fed and allowed to sleep. They received the same shock as had Camp Six personnel after their first operation.

"Weapon inspection in thirty minutes. Foot inspection fifteen minutes after that by Matthew Lee." Tired eyes looked at each other in dismay. Harry was most amused to see the barest semblance of a smile crossing Choon Guan's proletarian po-face that the men were now learning to be soldiers – soldiers that he would lead to throw the British out of Malaya once the British had thrown the Japanese out.

Choon Guan was to see the Japanese thrown out but was not to live to see either his grandchildren, or his proletariat.

Chapter Nineteen

David arrived at Chesterfield station in the possession of a mountain of kit which he bribed a porter to load on to a trolley to take out to a taxi. As he appeared on to the forecourt a P.U. was beginning to pull away, displaying the by now famous 'Pegasus' badge of the Airborne Forces on its front and rear divisional plates. The driver jammed on his brakes, smartly reversed the few yards to come up alongside David and cheerily called out, "You going up to the depot Sir?" He had a broad Scottish accent.

"Clay Cross?"

"Yes, that's right Sir."

"Can you give me a lift? I've an awful lot of kit."

"Hang on, and I'll throw it on Sir."

With that he jumped out, let the rear tailboard down and with David's assistance piled the luggage into the back. Once they were seated David asked, "What's your name?"

"Angus, Sir."

"That your first name or surname?"

"Oh, surname, Sir." He paused for a moment. "We don't seem to get on to Christian name terms at the depot, Sir."

"I see. Where's your home town?"

"A small town called Kingussie in Invernesshire, Sir."

"You have a long trip to go on leave then."

They arrived at the depot, previously, according to the notice board still at the entrance, a Territorial Army drill hall, and parked outside the H.Q. office.

"I'll hang on Sir until you know where your kit is to go then drop it round."

"Thank you Angus, I'm most grateful."

Angus' immediate thought was 'well at least there's one gentleman I've spoken to today.'

David was very cordially received by the depot adjutant, who apologised for the colonel not being there, he having to go to command HQ that day. However, if David would be so kind as to come to his office at 9.30 in the morning he had expressed the desire to have a general chinwag with him. In the meantime he, the adjutant, would meet David in the mess that evening and introduce him to the others. "Not that many of them, in common with most depots, are here for very long, anymore than you will be." He continued, looking out of the window, "I see Angus brought you from the station. If you will tell him you're in Room 12, he will unload your kit for you. By the way, how did you manage to arrange to be collected by Angus?"

"I didn't. He was there when I came off the train so I grabbed him, or he grabbed me, I can't remember which."

Angus drove David to the officers' block and off loaded his gear for him. When he had brought it all in he stood waiting for a moment as David parked his gas mask and beret on the side table.

"Sir."

"Yes Angus."

"Sir, have you got your batman with you?"

"No, I don't possess such an animal these days. I used to have one. God knows what they have done with him."

They both had their backs to the door as David spoke.

"Do you think I could apply to come and look after you, Sir?"

"Why would you want to do that? I shall not be here long anyway."

"Sir, I'm very good at the job I do now. I want to get to a battalion. If you're any good at your job in a depot, they won't let you go. So I'm stuck." He paused for a moment. "I'd make a bloody good job at being your batman Sir."

A voice behind then boomed.

"And I would make bloody sure you did and all."

"Paddy!!"

Private Angus was then to witness something he had never seen before and would never in his army career see again – the sight of a major and a company sergeant major hugging each other up like a couple of long lost brothers.

"You've put on weight."

"It's all muscle Sir, so it is."

"How's Mary?"

"She's a little bit pregnant Sir."

"You can't be a little bit pregnant – are you telling me I shall soon be forking out for a christening present?"

"You will that Sir."

"Well, it's a blooming miracle it didn't happen in North Wales before. Congratulations to you both. Mr and Mrs Maguire both well?"

"Both well Sir, and wished to be remembered to you.

"Right. Well. Our friend Angus here, that's his surname by the way." Looking at his would-be batman, "Which clan is Angus part of?"

"Clan Macinnes, Sir, very old clan Sir, dates from Celtic times."

"Well, our friend Angus here, for some inescapable reason, wants to come and be my batman. What do you think?" Angus butted in.

"Sir, I worked for a couple of years in the Duke of Gordon Hotel in Kingussie, so I'm well used to pressing and cleaning and so on."

"And chasing hot and cold chambermaids I've no doubt."

"Oh, we don't do things like that in Scotland Sir."

"We seem to have heard a ditty about the Ball of Kirriemuir somewhere or other, haven't we Paddy? How far is Kirriemuir from Kingussie I wonder?" The three chuckled together. David continued.

"I'll have a word with the adjutant – see what he says." Paddy thought for a moment.

"If you like Sir, I'll have a word with the R.S.M. He more or less runs this place and is an old mate of mine from India days." He turned to Angus. "But if we get you this job, you look after the major with your bloody life my son, or you'll never know what hit you – understand?"

"I understand Sir. I'm finished for the day now. Can I make a start when I've garaged the P.U.?"

Paddy looked at David who nodded assent.

"Right, you do that. Then come back and see what the major's wearing tonight and get it ready. Then find out what he will be wearing tomorrow and get that ready. Then unpack everything else, make sure there's not a crease in it anywhere, everything is put away neatly so that you know in an instant where everything is. Then find out what time the major wants his tea in the morning and his shaving water – got all that?" Not waiting for an answer he continued, "And that's only for starters – this officer always was, and always will be if I have anything to do with it, the best turned out officer in the battalion. Understand?"

"I understand Sir. I'll go and park the P.U." He saluted, turned and left.

"He looks as though he could be a likely lad Sir," was Paddy's final view on the subject.

David discovered the colonel to be a genial reserve officer, not a parachutist, but brought back out of retirement to organise the reception of would-be members of all ranks who wished to transfer to the Parachute Regiment from other units, as well as to hold those already in the regiment being transferred from one battalion to another. "It's a bit like Paddington Station," he explained, "you meet an awful lot of extremely nice and interesting people, just passing through." He explained to David that, because he and C.S.M. O'Riordan had not jumped for some months, they would be required to go on the Battle School at nearby Hardwick Hall, then on to Ringway for a refresher course of four jumps from the new Dakota aircraft which had now arrived. "I suggest," he added, "you get as much gym work and road work in as you can before you go to Hardwick – its absolute bloody purgatory over there, absolute purgatory. And you have to pass, or they will make you do it all again before they will send you to Ringway. You've got a fortnight before you go, I should make good use of it."

As it happened, a new course was starting at the Battle School, so that David and Paddy and the remainder of the new victims had not as long to wait as they had expected. In the meantime on the Saturday night, just as the May Day festivities were drawing to a close in Sandbury, the two put their civvies on to explore the fleshpots of Chesterfield. It did not take long. Apart from David commenting that the crooked spire of Chesterfield Cathedral was still crooked – the legend had it, and probably still does, that when the first virgin marries in the Church, the spire will straighten up – there seemed to be little of interest other than the pubs. The R.S.M. had told Paddy if he and the major fancied a drink, to call in at the Saloon Bar of the Golden Fleece, in the High Street. The warrant officers, senior sergeants and depot instructors had a club there which met on Friday and Saturday nights called 'The Squanderbugs Club.' It sported a largish club shield on permanent display on the wall, quartered, with a pair of ladies panties on the top left quarter, a frothing pint in the bottom right, a pair of dice in the top right and an open hand of cards in the bottom left. The club name was made out in gold surmounting the shield; beneath it was the club motto – also in gold 'SPEND IT.'

When Paddy and David arrived just before eight, the party was well under way – closing time was ten o'clock! The R.S.M., seeing them arrive came over to greet them, introduced them to the crowd in general, although both of them by now were known to a number of the resident staff. David noticed, as a pint of mild and bitter was pressed into his not unreceptive fist, that although there were a few civilians there, a couple of subalterns and a captain no one beneath the rank of Sergeant was in evidence. Later in the proceedings he was to understand why. Two lance corporals, a little after nine o'clock, a little the worse for wear, endeavoured to make their somewhat unsteady entry into the hallowed cloisters. The landlord, a very large ex-copper, made even larger since he left the force as a result of ensuring his draught beers were regularly tasted and passed fit for his customers' consumption, moved very speedily around the end of the bar, to take a non-commissioned elbow in each hand and move their owners speedily through a connecting door into the public bar, where of course the beer was a penny a pint cheaper, as befits lance corporals.

After his second pint David asked Paddy, "How do I buy a drink?" He was overheard endeavouring to ascertain how he could push the boat out by the R.S.M. himself.

"Not to worry tonight Sir – there's enough in the kitty. We all put ten bob in the box under the bar there, and the landlord takes what he wants as the R.Q.M.S. who's in charge of the ordering, orders the rounds. Anything left over stays there until next weekend." David was left wondering how trusting they were, firstly of the R.Q.M.S., and secondly of the landlord who kept the remains of the kitty. What he didn't know was that as far as the landlord went he was as sound as the Bank of England, but the R.Q.M.S. – the regimental quartermaster sergeant, the man who handles every item of clothing, food and equipment in a unit – was a different kettle of fish altogether.

It was a pleasant evening, made more entertaining by a civilian, a regular apparently, who wandered in at about 9.15 definitely exhibiting signs of close contact with spirituous materials on a number of occasions prior to his arrival at the Golden Fleece. Or to put it as the R.S.M. so succinctly expressed it, "Here's Wally, pissed again." Wally beamed myopically at the general company, finally resting his eyes on David and Paddy. With a supreme effort he commanded his brain to focus on the two newcomers, civilian newcomers as far as his befuddled brain could register, before holding out his hand and announcing

"I'm Wally, I'm on m'nishuns, are you on m'nishuns?"

David and Paddy, grinning from ear to ear, as also was the R.S.M., shook hands with this genial, bibulous inebriate.

"I'm on m'nishuns all the week, on the piss Saturday night, sleep on Sunday, sod the m'nishuns till Monday. Are you on m'nishuns? Get a load of money on m'nishuns. What m'nishuns are you on? I must get a drink." He weaved his way to the bar, was rewarded with a drop of Scotch from the landlord, which David thought remarkable since the Scotch had run out an hour ago, knocked it back, put a pound note into the Squanderbug kitty, turned and made his unsteady way out into the darkness of the High Street.

It was a stock question for ages afterwards between Paddy and David, 'are you on m'nishuns? ' raising laughter far in excess of its face value, simply because of the situation in which it was occasioned. In fact some months later when all hell was being let loose, a mud covered sergeant-major tumbled into a certain major's slit trench, his first words being 'Are you on m'nishuns?' bringing raised eyebrows from the two signallers already occupying it, indicating their belief that certain senior ranks in the company were going bomb-happy – but that will be another story.

The transition from the Golden Fleece to the hard light of 6.30 a.m. for the Monday morning road run they had set themselves, was distressing, developing as they began to realise how unfit they had become, into agonising then suffering, finally torture. The silly thing was, they had planned the run from the one-inch Ordnance Survey map. It didn't look far on the map but when you are unfit, you have not spotted two one-in-four hills, and the cross-country short cut you select is solid soaking wet clay from the previous night's downpour, better planning could have been made. As a result, they staggered back into Clay Cross Depot, past the smartly turned out sentries at the entrance, covered in mud and at their last gasp, only to find that the main boiler had broken down so that they had only cold water to wash themselves in. It was not exactly a propitious start to their self-imposed training programme!

Over the next few days, with a combination of gym work, road work and kicking a football about on the five-a-side enclosed pitch, they gradually lost their puff. On Friday 7th May they were asked to go to the adjutant's office. "The C.O. wants to see you both Sir." The automatic, unsung thought on both their parts was 'what have I done?'

They were led in by the adjutant, saluted, and said, "Good morning Sir."

"Sit down, both of you. In all my years of service, including through the Great War, I have never before had this experience." They looked at him, somewhat mystified. "I have to inform a company sergeant major he has been awarded The Military Cross." They both stared at their colonel in total astonishment. "I have known of R.S.M.s getting the M.C. but never a C.S.M., although of course it is quite plainly allowed for in Kings Regulations. You too David, have received the award" (I'm David now am I?) "which from what I have heard about the exploits of both of you in Yugoslavia is certainly no more than you deserve. The citations were made out by Brigadier Hopgood and even I, in my little backwater here at Clay Cross, have heard that he is very sparing of decorations among his coterie, so again, congratulations." He stood up and shook hands with them both.

"Does that mean we can be spared from the holiday at Hardwick Hall Sir?" David asked.

"Good Lord no. We couldn't possibly deprive you of such an uplifting and pleasurable experience, it would be very unfair, don't you agree Charles?" (to the adjutant).

"In view of the fact they are both bigger than me, Sir, I request permission to leave that question unanswered." There were grins all round.

After only ten days at Clay Cross therefore, they were removed to Hardwick, where they found themselves in separate squads for a fortnight, and where after the first gruelling day they not only were able to cope with, but even began to enjoy what they had expected to be, at the most, a doubtful pleasure, of combating their skill and strength against all manner of tasks and obstacles. Work having finished at twelve o'clock on the first Saturday, they felt fit enough to join the evening passion wagon into Chesterfield to visit their erstwhile friends of the Squanderbugs Club. They had a jolly evening, when just before nine o'clock, with the bar full of club members, the R.S.M. bellowed for quiet.

"Gentlemen," he announced, "it is not very often we have the pleasure of an announcement like this. I am very honoured to tell you that our two civilian looking guests here," pointing to David and Paddy, "are, as one or two of you will know, Major Chandler and C.S.M. O'Riordan. What you won't know is that they have each been awarded the Military Cross for gallantry in Yugoslavia." There was loud applause and cheering. He continued, "Knowing how thick most of you are, you probably haven't the faintest bloody idea where Yugoslavia is, or how you get there. Well, I have found out they jumped from a Halifax to get in, and came back in a submarine, getting depth charged on the way, after fighting Germans and Italians continuously for six months. So, congratulations gentlemen on your awards." There was again prolonged applause. Paddy looked at David, who accepted the unspoken request to reply.

"Thank you gentlemen for your very kind applause. I would like to tell you more of the incredible bravery of the Yugoslav partisans and the fact they are keeping dozens of German divisions occupied, but tonight isn't the time, and anyway we are governed by the Official Secrets Act. All I will say is that one day all will be known and you will have nothing but admiration for their bravery. I give you a toast – The Partisans."

They all raised their glasses and repeated – "The Partisans." Marshall Tito would have been very moved to know that twenty or thirty senior N.C.O.s and warrant officers – professional soldiers all – were toasting his amateur soldiers in a far away pub in Derbyshire.

As is often the case after a hullabaloo, there was a sudden silence, which coincided with the door opening and the entry of Wally, coming face to face with David and Paddy with the inevitable statement. "I'm on m'nishuns – are you on m'nishuns?" bringing about paroxysms of laughter from the assembled company, two of whom lifted him bodily by his elbows and fore-arms, carried him to the bar and presented him with the inevitable drop of Scotch which had awaited him. He lifted his glass to the assembled company, threw the Vat 69 down in one go, announced to the crowd around him, "I'm pissed again," which must be said had been obvious to all from the moment he arrived, put his pound note into the Squanderbug Kitty and made his unsteady way through the crowd, parting like the Red Sea before the Israelites, to the door and out into the High Street.

The following week completed the Battle School. Most of those who had suffered the pleasures and pains of Hardwick and were going on to Ringway would be carrying out the full parachute training course previously endured by David and Paddy. However, they themselves would be making only a short stay, assuming the weather did not interfere, just to carry out their four refresher jumps.

"We shall have to look up Amanda One Sir," Paddy suggested, "see if we can get a glimpse of that Canadian bloke she's sweet on, make sure he's good enough for her."

"I expect he is already with a battalion somewhere. I tell you what; if she's still there we'll take her out for a meal. I want to go and see Robin too while we're here, perhaps she will wangle us a lift."

"No chance of the lady from Norfolk coming over Sir, I suppose?" (with tongue firmly in cheek).

"I can't remember knowing such a lady," David replied, remembering only too well that Saturnalian night with Pamela at the Queens' Hotel in Manchester. Pamela will be married by now, he thought, by God; her husband will have to go some to keep up with her.

The journey to Ringway was made in 3 tonners. On arrival soon after midday David and Paddy were dropped off at their respective messes, with the agreement they would meet up on the morrow with the remainder of the 'refreshers,' hopefully to do their first jump from a Dakota, weather permitting. David spent the rest of the day writing letters, until at seven o'clock he booked a call to Chandlers Lodge. It was answered by Rose.

"David, the factory was bombed on Friday night. We've been trying to track you down but you have been on the move apparently."

"Is Dad alright? Was anybody hurt? Was there much damage?"

"It was the machine shop. Four people were killed and ten injured. The shop was wrecked but they are working day and night to get it working again."

"But Ernie and Dad – are they alright?"

"Yes, it was in the middle of the night, they were at home."

"Rose, I am so upset about those people who were killed and injured. Oh, this bloody, bloody war."

They talked on about family matters, about Anni's forthcoming baby, about Karl apparently having a ladyfriend, about Oliver soon to be called up.

"When do you start jumping?"

"Tomorrow if the weather holds."

"Maria will be phoning in half an hour, can I get her to telephone you?"

"Oh please do. If she just gives me the number of the call box, I can then phone her back and it will be charged to my mess bill."

"What happens if there is a delay, or there is a queue at the phone box?"

"Hadn't thought of that. In that case I shall have to rely on her having a pocketful of change." He paused for a moment. "By the way, Paddy and I have each got the M.C. for our work in Yugoslavia."

"The M.C. – Military Cross? Oh David how wonderful. And Paddy as well. I thought only officers got the M.C.?"

"No, warrant officers as well, if they're substantive that is, which of course Paddy is."

"Well, I don't know what substantive means but I now am going once again to reflect in your combined glory in front of all the family."

David waited and waited for Maria to telephone, but no call came. He began to worry, then told himself she was probably on duty or something. At ten o'clock he suddenly established the reason for his not receiving the call, either from Maria or from Rose to say why Maria had not called – he had forgotten to give Rose his number and in the excitement of the M.C. business she had forgotten to ask!!

"You bloody stupid moronic idiot," he told himself. He really could have kicked himself at being guilty of such an elementary oversight. "So pumped up with pride at your M.C. you forget everything else, you gormless prat."

It was good jumping weather the next day, Tuesday. David had a little chat with Cedric, his golliwog mascot. "Don't let me down today old son, safe landings and all that." It was the first time he had seen a Dakota. He had flown in, and jumped from, a Halifax which was much bigger and noisier than the Dakota, but the Dak had a nice friendly comfortable feeling about it. Instead of sitting in a hole, as in the Whitley, or falling through a hole as in the Halifax, you simply strolled down the fuselage and walked out of a door in the side. The chute opened almost instantaneously but without the neck wrenching propensity occasioned by the slipstream of the four engines of the Halifax. He was so pleased at the comfortable exit; the landing took him by surprise. Fortunately he had no extraneous kit to worry about as he would have on exercises, so apart from a bruised elbow, he suffered no harm. They did another jump in the afternoon. If tomorrow was fine they would probably do two more and be on their way back to Clay

Cross, at the mention of which he asked Paddy, "Are you on m'nishuns?"

He telephoned Rose as soon as he got back from Tatton Park after the second jump, very cross with himself at not giving her his number. Rose was scathing. "How shall we win the war if people at your exalted position forget the most elementary things?"

"I know. I'm an idiot. Will Maria be telephoning you this evening?"

"Definitely not."

"In that case I probably won't be able to talk to her until I get back to Clay Cross."

"Not necessarily."

"What do you mean, not necessarily?"

"It so happens she is here at my side."

David heard the laughter 'off-stage' as it were.

"What is she doing there at five o'clock in the afternoon? Don't answer that – put her on you rotter."

There was a pause as Maria took the receiver from Rose. "Good afternoon Major Chandler, M.C., D.C.M., Legion of Honour, Croix de Guere – have I forgotten anything?"

"You little rascal. What are you doing at Chandlers Lodge?"

"I had to take an admiral from Dover up to London, so I called in for a cuppa on the way back."

"You haven't told me you love me yet."

"I love you, I love you, I love you, I love you. How's that?"

"More."

"Have you jumped today?"

"Cedric and I have hurled ourselves manfully, without fear or trepidation, into the unknown on no less than two occasions."

"What's trepidation mean?"

"Haven't a clue, but it sounds heroic."

Gradually their conversation developed into that which one would expect between lovers, leaving David with a melange of feelings, happiness, sadness, longing, frustration all mixed together.

The next day a ferocious wind blew up, effectively putting the kybosh on any jumping. As he was not part of a course, David decided to try and find Amanda One, Paddy in the meantime electing to go into Manchester to do some shopping. Ringway had grown enormously since he was there, new Nissen huts of varying sizes having sprung up all over the place. After enquiring at several offices, in the main being received extremely suspiciously – after all a major trying to locate a specific corporal could only mean one thing – he came face to face with her outside the NAAFI. She saluted. He hugged her up, much to the surprise of a passer-by, as well as the knowing smirk of a clerk looking out of a window of the office he had just left.

"What are you doing here – on a refresher – how's Paddy – going to be a daddy – how's your Canadian – he's gorgeous," and so the chat rocketed back and forth. I suppose technically that should be forth and back since obviously nothing can come back until it has been somewhere, i.e. forth. No matter. Chat they did.

"Is Robin still at Wilmslow?"

"Yes, I'm taking a passenger out there in a few minutes."

"Where from – here?"

"No, I've got to pick him up at Manchester Piccadilly."

"Could I come with you? And do you think you could drop Paddy off – he's going in to buy nappies or something."

The thought of a burly sergeant major buying nappies set Amanda One into a fit of giggles.

"You haven't changed a bit," she exclaimed, "you go and tell Paddy and I will pick you both up at the sergeant's mess in ten minutes."

They dropped Paddy at Lewis's then parked at Piccadilly. The London train was running twenty minutes late so they enjoyed – well, endured – a cup of railway tea in the station buffet as they continued their chat, catching up on each other's news. Eventually the huge locomotive inched into platform four, in a large hissing cloud of steam, the carriages disgorging as varied a collection of humanity as one would be likely to see in wartime England.

"Who are we looking for?"

"Major Cheshire, Coldstream Guards. He was here before."

"I know him; we split a bottle of champagne in his room on one occasion."

"Well, he hasn't been here since then – I don't know what he had been up to, but then I wouldn't, would I?"

The immaculate figure of the major was easily distinguishable from the hoi-polloi surrounding him, as also must be said of the almost equally immaculate figure of his six foot three batman, walking behind, pushing a trolley loaded with enough kit to equip a regiment. David gave him a friendly salute, Amanda One a regimental one. "Major Chandler, how nice of you to come and meet me."

"How on earth did you remember my name?"

"My friends talk of no one else," and with that cryptic remark continued "and Corporal Amanda – two stripes now I see – how nice to see you, you haven't changed a bit, as gorgeous as ever."

The journey out to Wilmslow was a little crowded in view of the fact that the Dodge had three very bulky passengers to say nothing of the mountain of kit, leaving the slim driver of the opinion if she had been the same size as Corporal Margaret Johns – fourteen stones and lovely with it – they would have had a problem. As they drove up to the house Robin himself came out to meet them. It was the first occasion upon which David had seen Robin emerge from his diplomatic, civil-service, spymaster, aplomb. He was actually excited at the unexpected meeting with his former protégée, so much so that Major Cheshire had temporarily to wait until he too was welcomed as an old friend.

"Geoffrey, if you get yourself settled in and come down in an hour or so we'll all have lunch together."

"On one condition, dear Robin – the corporal joins us."

"I am a civilian; she can join me at any time. So if military protocol allows it, Corporal Amanda is more than welcome. What do you think David?"

"The section of the Army Act which deals with that particular aspect of service life is delightfully vague," David replied. "I seem to remember that in Section 307, subsection 3, clause 'b' it definitely states that A.T.S. corporals, provided they are going steady with members of a foreign force, can enjoy lunch with commissioned rank. It does not, however, state how payment is to be made, nor how much. I think there are other sections which deal with breakfast, dinner and supper."

"It seems to me that we must obey the implacable laws of military confusion," Robin solemnly pronounced. "Please stay to lunch Corporal Amanda."

Geoffrey looked at Amanda, Amanda looked at Geoffrey. They both tapped their respective temples with their respective forefingers.

Lunch dragged on until three o'clock, Amanda taking a full part in the conversation stakes without taking the floor in any way. David thought 'she's a highly intelligent, sociable girl, why the hell would that bloody idiot of a staff sergeant ditch her for an immediate advantage, namely the daughter of an air vice-marshall.' And then he thought 'That's probably it, an immediate advantage. If nothing comes of it to his benefit he will probably ditch her as well.'

"Wake him up Geoffrey." It was Robin trying to communicate with the ruminative David.

"A little bird tells me," Robin was saying, "that you shortly will be going to an investiture."

"How on earth did you know that?" Immediately thinking it would be a bloody miracle if he didn't know. Robin continued.

"And not on your own I understand."

"Tell us more," Geoffrey asked, "please do."

"David and Paddy O'Riordan, his C.S.M. have both been awarded the M.C."

"Congratulations old boy, congratulations, but you are not wearing any ribbon."

David took a long shot, "Neither are you."

"I shall say no more. But how does a C.S.M. get the M.C.? I thought it was only for officers."

"Well it probably is in the Guards, the area between commissioned and warrant officer rank in the real army is perhaps a little blurred, so either can be awarded it." He pondered for a moment. "I must say though I've never heard of it before."

The lunch over, Amanda One dropped David off at his mess, to find Paddy sitting on the seat outside. She got out of the Dodge, walked over to him, took his head in her hands and gave him a big kiss on each cheek.

"What the Holy Moses is that for?"

"Because you have done brave things, I don't know what and I don't know where, but I know you have done brave things."

"As a matter of fact, I have done *very* brave things, so I reckon I need a second helping." Amanda obliged.

"By the way, did you get your nappies?"

"She doesn't change Sir, does she? Now Amanda, what's the name of this foreign gentleman of yours so that we can sort him out when we get down to Bulford?"

"How do you know we are going to Bulford for God's sake?" David chimed in.

"A little nose round in the orderly room does no harm Sir. They are forming a new division down there – I reckon that's where we will be going. So, what's his name Amanda One?"

"Lieutenant Patterson, commonly known as Sandy, on account of..."

"Don't tell me, the roughness of his touch."

"Not at all, his touch is like being caressed by a piece of velvet."

David looked at Paddy, Paddy looked at David. In a very poor rendition of a transatlantic accent David said, "Now ain't that just romantic."

They said their goodbyes to Amanda, not knowing whether they would ever see her again. There were great joys in meeting such nice people as Amanda, Geoffrey and Robin, but the thought of the probability of never seeing them again gave an air of sadness difficult to describe.

The wind abated the next day, as a result they got both of their jumps in, and on Friday 28th May found themselves on the 3 tonner back to Clay Cross, to be welcomed by Angus who had now been given official recognition of his transfer to attend to the comfort, well being, and eventually, protection of one Major Chandler. On Saturday night they made their way to The Golden Fleece, where they were warmly welcomed by the resident members of the Squanderbugs Club. On Monday they were seen by the C.O. and told they would be travelling to Bulford on Wednesday to join a new battalion being formed composed mainly of ex-riflemen from City Rifles, K.R.R.'s, Royal Ulsters and Cameronians, so, he concluded, "You will be in good company, all running around at a hundred and sixty to the minute being different to everyone else." He shook hands with them both.

"Good luck," and with the afterthought – 'I think you may well need it.'

Chapter Twenty

On the 1st of June, Jack Hooper had taken over at Shorts. On the 2nd he became 'Sir Jack,' and all the letter headings had to be reprinted. On the day of his arrival he was met at the main entrance by the Minister of Aircraft Production in person, who had welcomed him warmly, introduced him to his co-directors and then promptly got back into his ministerial Humber and whistled off back up the A2 to London. The ball was now in his court. One by one he saw the various directors and departmental managers over a period of several days. He had inherited a personal secretary from the previous M.D. about whom he was in two minds – should she go or should she stay? Having been at Shorts for twenty years she knew everybody, their quirks, their failings, their dedication or lack of it. On the other hand would her previous loyalty to the ex M.D. show as resentment to the new M.D. Only one way to settle that – ask her outright. Her answer was as forthright as the question. "I want only for Short's to succeed, by that means to help win the war. Personalities do not come into it." They were on the same wavelength.

During his first week he spent a great deal of time in the factory, always making sure he contacted the departmental manager or foreman first before he walked round. By this means he rapidly instilled the belief in the various levels of authority that he was there to find out how things worked and was not trying to catch them out. With his genial presence, and his facility for remembering people's names he rapidly gained the confidence and support of the middle management, so vital in a large manufacturing concern.

He had, of course, seen the Short Sunderland flying boat. Crossing the bridge at Rochester one could often be seen taking off or landing on the Medway in front of the factory. He had, however, never seen one close-up; he was staggered at the size of it, wider, longer, and half as high again as even the mighty Lancaster, or Halifax. The fuselage had two 'decks' – the nomenclature being a relic of the old Empire flying boats from which it evolved – on both of which the crew could walk about in comparative comfort. They were designed for maritime patrol and long-range reconnaissance. Having a normal range of over 3000 miles they became the scourge of the U Boats, were nick named 'Flying Porcupines' since they were so well provided with defensive weapons, and could carry up to 2000lbs of bombs. It was a unique, beautifully crafted airplane. Jack's, sorry, Sir Jack's job was to bring the production up to schedule since these aircraft were required so urgently in both the Atlantic and Indian Oceans for anti-submarine work, and which had lagged behind so disastrously under the previous chairmanship. In addition, the profitability, or lack of it, which had caused the ministry to take the enterprise over, had to be recovered, all in all Jack told himself "You've got a bit of a job on here old son."

He now had a chauffeur and a Jaguar car which went with the job. The chauffeur was a time-served R.A.F. sergeant, a confirmed bachelor, who previously had lived in lodgings close to the former M.D.'s house at Faversham. He immediately volunteered to find suitable digs in Sandbury so that he could be available at a moments' notice, or to work unsociable hours. When Jack queried the amount of petrol which would be used in getting him to and from Rochester, a distance of some twelve miles each way, Miss Watts, his secretary stated plainly, "The whole success of this factory and of the Short Sunderland depends on you. Every time one of those aircraft runs its four engines on test it uses enough petrol to keep you going for the rest of the war." Jack considered that statement for a short while.

"Am I to assume from that remark that you have inside knowledge as to when the war is going to end?"

"You know what I mean Sir," then seeing the smile on his face, realised he was pulling her leg, gave a self-conscious smile herself, and that was the beginning of a first class working relationship.

On the 10th of June Miss Watts was a trifle worried at the appearance of her new, usually extremely sharp looking chairman. He arrived dead on time, whereas normally he was at least half an hour ahead of schedule. His eyes were red-rimmed, he had cut himself badly when he had shaved, he winced when some idiot slammed a door and his pleading to Miss Watts to find him an Alka-Seltzer was that of a person slipping slowly into the abyss. Miss Watts was worried as to which tropical fever Sir Jack was suffering a recurrence. Had it been anyone else she would have immediately diagnosed a true blue, copper bottomed, one hundred per cent hangover, but even with the admittedly short acquaintance she had enjoyed with the gentleman, she knew without doubt that could not possibly be the cause of his dire malady, he was too much of a gentleman to over-indulge.

By ten o'clock, after the Alka Seltzer and two cups of strong black coffee he began to see through the veil which had surrounded his vision since he awakened that morning. This improvement, slight though it was, was sufficient for him to tell Miss Watts, carrying out her half hourly medical observation of the brave, suffering invalid,

"We had a baby last night."

The astonishment, bewilderment, stupefaction on Miss Watts normally serene countenance was a picture to behold. Immediately following on from the tropical fever diagnosis, she suspected the brain had been damaged. She had read how little parasites burrowed in to different organs of the body in these terrible torrid climes; it looked as if this was a case in point. Her faltering reply only added to the confusion.

"Do you think I ought to call the doctor Sir?"

"We've already had the doctor – everything is alright." More confusion. Miss Watts tried another tack.

"Where did you have the baby Sir?"

"I didn't have the baby, Anni had the baby."

"Who is Anni Sir?" That stumped him for a moment.

"She's a sort of niece of mine."

Miss Watts's thought processes went into top gear. A middle-aged gent, so she was told, who took a young woman away with him for dirty weekends, always described her as his niece. Sir Jack has a 'sort of niece,' she has apparently given birth – no wonder Sir Jack was looking worried and ill. When he had first taken over Miss Watts had reached the immediate impression he was a gentleman, just shows how wrong you can be.

Gradually the fog cleared. Jack described how Anni had been saved from Nazi Germany, had married an old colleague Ernie Bolton, and had now presented him with a beautiful daughter to be named Ruth after one of his dearest friends who died only a few months ago.

"And now, can you find me another Alka Seltzer and some coffee please, or I shall never last out the day."

Miss Watts was so relieved her new boss was not a womaniser, had not got a tropical fever, and was not the father of an illegitimate child, she not only kept him supplied with Alka Seltzers but like all good secretaries, prevented anyone getting to him either in person or by telephone with the efficiency of an S.S. bodyguard. She decided he was not only a gentleman, but because of his straying from the straight and narrow, was human as well. He repaid her kindness by telling her he had a tip for the Derby, to be run on Saturday, at Newmarket, being wartime. "Back Dorothy Paget's Straight Deal" he told her. "T Carey's riding it – I've got it straight from the horses' mouth." She invested five shillings each way with the factory bookies' runner, highly illegal; everybody knew about it otherwise how could he collect the bets? It came in at eight-to-one. She was so pleased you would have thought she had pulled off the coup of the century, in fact since it was the first bet she had ever made it felt like that to her.

It took a little while for Jack to settle in. He got into the habit of taking his lunch in the staff canteen, choosing any vacant chair which happened to be available. The staff canteen did not cater just for departmental managers and the like, but draughtsmen, designers, progress chasers, estimators and a hundred and one other white collar workers, classified as 'staff' as opposed to hourly paid shop floor employees, took their meals there. By talking to them in general terms – he discouraged talking about specific complaints or criticisms; they should be addressed to their departmental committees, moving up to him if necessary through the 'proper channels.' However, he did get a feeling of the pulse of the place, and whereas previously the staff, particularly the junior staff, hardly ever got a glimpse of the chairman, now on occasion they got to have a chat with him, or if not, knew what he looked like. It could not be said that production leapt overnight as a result of this bonhomie, but it had the positive advantage of Jack noting in the back of his mind those younger people who seemed to him to be possessed of quick intelligent minds. They would be needed if and when he started to clear out some of the senior, and not so senior, people not pulling their respective weights, people who considered moving with the times was another form of anarchy. What they failed to realise, and it must be said this was only a small number, was that in war you don't have time. Just as mobility was a major principle of war on the battlefield, so it had to be in the factories which supplied the weapons to arm the people doing the fighting. No one could be allowed to drag his or her feet. Jack had a motto printed and framed. It just said:

'For the lack of a nail a shoe was lost.'

He expected everyone to know the remainder of the saying, if they didn't they would have to ask, in which case it would remain imprinted on the individual's mind. The aircraft at present being fabricated must be made on time, otherwise, like the absence of the nail, the horse, or in this case, the battle, could be lost.

Back at Sandbury, Karl had been catching his ministry bus each morning for over three months now, and his friendship with Mrs Gordon had developed to the Christian name stage.

"So when are you going home to tea?" Ernie asked. Karl's eyebrows puckered into a little frown.

"I'm afraid it is not so easy," he replied, "you see, she has the two children – you call them teenagers? She has these two children aged seventeen and fifteen. They are very close to their Grandfather Harris, Mrs Gordon's father; and have been more so since their father died. Grandfather Harris hates all Germans and has made it clear that includes me."

"Have you met the children yet?"

"No, not yet."

"If you met them away from the house somewhere they might get a fairer picture of you."

"I shall have to put on my thinking cap – that is what you say, ja?"

He didn't have to. It was done for him. The Welsh Guards Battalion out on the Maidstone road, to celebrate their six months since they arrived in Sandbury, decided to have an 'Open Day' on Saturday 26th June. There would be children's sports, rides in their Bren Gun carriers, strawberry teas – Kent is great strawberry country – and in the evening an invitation dance to those people who had gone out of their way to make them welcome. The band would be there to give a marching display and subsequently a concert, backed up of course by a magnificent male voice choir. With sideshows scattered around the perimeter of the parade ground it was going to be a first class afternoon, ending with 'Beating the Retreat,' as only the Guards can do it.

All the shops in Sandbury closed that afternoon. On the bus journeys during the week before the great event, Karl and Rosemary – I have already indicated they were on Christian name terms – plotted how they would bump into each other, accidentally of course, they being Karl, Anni and Ernie on his side and Rosemary, John and Janet on her side. In the event there was a slight hiccup, in that Grandfather Harris decided he would attend. Having been in the Royal Sussex Regiment in the 'last lot' he didn't hold much with the guards, but then those who have not had the privilege of belonging to the elite rarely do – or so they would say.

The accidental meeting took place exactly as planned, Rosemary taking the view she had nothing to lose. Robbie Burns had a somewhat downbeat view of men's plans. On this occasion he could not have been more wrong. After the first introductions were made in a totally civilised if somewhat cool manner, Ernie seized upon Grandfather Harris, who soon became Jim, and who soon was being told the sad story of Karl's wife, what a great chap he was and what was more, worth a bob or two. Anni was not surprised when Ernie announced

"Jim and I are going to have one in the beer tent – see you over by the band."

And that was how Karl and his family became accepted by Jim and his family. Later they all had strawberry teas together and bumped into Fred and Jack and the remainder of the Chandler and Hooper families. Jim was somewhat awestruck by the people among whom Karl belonged, to the extent of having 'quite a chat with Karl – seems a decent enough sort of bloke,' as he expressed to Rosemary later that evening, the beer he had enjoyed with Ernie of course, having had nothing to do with lubricating the wheels of good fellowship. As they wended their way home Karl announced, "I shall ask Rosemary and the children to come to a show with me in London, perhaps you could recommend a suitable one – a matinee of course so that we can have a tea afterwards and get home at a reasonable time."

That night, as Ernie and Anni lay in bed together they came to the mutual conclusion that they should do all they could to foster Karl's romance. "After all he has been through he deserves someone nice to be with," being the shared opinion.

In a bed a mile or so away Cecely lay awake wondering how Oliver was settling in. She had received several letters, none of which would have won a literary prize for either content or volume, nevertheless they were letters, received with pleasure, read two or three times at least to ensure nothing of import was missed, then put on one side since it seemed disloyal to throw them away. From Oliver her thoughts switched to Greta. Greta did not mention her father very often but without doubt she missed him, even after all these months, very much indeed. The thought he and Uncle Charles could even be dead was a horrifying concept with which she awoke frequently, although she rarely expressed the possibility to her mother. She had Uncle James who wrote to her occasionally from his posting in Northern Ireland, but since he apparently was romantically attached to a lady at Ballymena he rarely made the journey to Sandbury when he was on leave. That having been said he had promised to visit them in July accompanied by the lady in question.

Finally Cecely's thoughts turned, as they frequently did, to Hugh Ramsford. If Hugh asked to go to bed with her would she yield to the temptation, or as she bluntly told herself, her need. She pulled her knees up under her chin, gave a little shudder and told herself, "yes." She was not the first woman who could convince herself she could love two men at the same time, nor would she be the last. Mrs Treharne recognised her dilemma and sympathised with it. Beneath the exterior of a totally respectable upper middle class housewife, in her day she was a ferociously passionate lover, one who fortunately had never had to part from her equally sensual husband to present her with the aching predicament she recognised consuming her friend Cecely. However, she recognised also the downside. Supposing Greta suspected her mother of being unfaithful, that could, if not ruin, badly damage two lives. Greta could not be expected to know the dreadful need, her young mind being bound up with the sense of purity, duty and faithfulness which had been inculcated into her by her family, her school and her Church during the past formative years. As if the war was not enough to worry about!!

The Guards officers mess reception was a grand affair. Major F Chandler OBE, MM, had been invited as had Mrs R Laurenson, the latter at once being the focus of the eyes of the captains and subalterns who were not 'attached,' for that matter some other officers who were "attached." It was a fraction more decorous than the functions they had attended when Colonel Tim and his Canadians were in residence, Rose in particular experiencing a sudden wave of sadness as she entered, remembering the last time she was there, when she stood with Tim to give him moral support, as he had put it, in welcoming their guests. Now Tim, Jim and others she knew were either dead or prisoners of war. Their two majors, David and Dafydd, hearing their entry announced, hurried over to welcome them, Rose swiftly being whisked off on to the dance floor from which she saw little respite all the evening, except during the buffet supper, a meal reinforced with off-ration delicacies purchased at no inconsiderable expense by the officers from their regimental grocer, namely Fortnum and Mason. It was a taste of the high life few people would experience during the war, in fact for most people at any time. It did reinforce the belief, held by the proletariat in general, that if you had money you would be unlikely to starve. On the other hand who would want to live on crab vol-au-vents, smoked salmon terrine, chicken liver pate and so on? Fred's reply to the question was, "I think I could possibly manage somehow."

So the first half of 1943 ended on a high note for the Chandlers, or as high as it could get without the presence of Ruth, Harry, David and Mark.

July was to be a different matter. On the 10th the BBC nine o'clock news announced that the Allies had invaded Sicily. Rose automatically assumed Mark and Charlie would be part of the invasion force – she had heard nothing from her husband for nearly two weeks which had caused her to wonder what could have interrupted his usual letter writing, always weekly, often twice weekly or more. To allay her concern Fred put forward the view that, in view of the invasion, the powers that be had put a block on the mail to U.K. for security reasons. In point of fact he was only half right. It was for security reasons that mail had been held up, but not because of the invasion, but because Mark's armoured division was being returned to England to prepare for the forthcoming assault on the continent. It was logical really. The desert was tank country, Sicily and Italy far less so. Therefore fewer armoured divisions would be required, whereas the assault on France, or Belgium or Holland, wherever it was going to be, would require every tank we could lay our hands on. So Rose's misery would, in a week or two, turn to joy at the thought of seeing her husband again. She would not be the only one looking forward to a romantic encounter. Charlie Crew's correspondence with Maria's friend Emma had progressed apace. Would the actual meeting live up to his hopes and expectations? They had swapped photographs, several in fact, the receipt of which had far from reduced the warmth of the penmanship. He had a good ally in Maria – she would have put a good word in for him that was for sure, on the other hand she must meet dozens of good looking young naval and marine officers – 'and they are there and I am here.' Soon, he would not be 'here,' he would be 'there,' then it would be down to him. One thing he was not going to do was to tell her he was an 'Hon,' until he was sure she liked him enough to 'go steady.' Then he had second thoughts. Suppose she considered his not telling her meant he thought that that would make any difference? That she might be a social climber? His final thought – 'go to sleep you silly sod.'

Chapter Twenty One

A week after the successful raid on the gold mine, Camp Three received another airdrop. In addition to the necessary ammunition and food there was a large bundle of mail for R.S.M. Chandler and a smaller bundle for Captain Couper. It had been determined back in Sandbury that Harry would appreciate lots of photos, particularly of all the children, and especially, of course, his own. They could not have imagined how much it did for Harry's morale to receive these. Without consciously realising it, the long absence, the unpleasant conditions in which they lived, the constant apprehension they would be discovered, to say nothing of the lack of the bodily comfort of his wife, were causing him to suffer depression from time to time. Harry was not a natural depressive, but living constantly in a Turkish bath atmosphere, with being the incessant target of all sorts of tiny creatures that bite, sting or just irritate, when your skin comes away under your finger nails when you scratch, all combine to make a man down in the mouth, or in the local vernacular-'chocker'. Even the Chinese had incorporated 'chocker' into the dialect in which they conversed. It meant generally that you were bloody fed up but on the other hand you were not going to let it interfere with, in their case, their political resolution, nor with their object of killing Japanese monkeys.

To get back to Harry. The pictures lifted him right out of the doldrums into which he was descending. One photograph in particular of all the family, and that of course included Anni, Cecely, Mrs Treharne, and all the others, taken on the front lawn of Chandlers Lodge with the house clearly shown in the background provoked considerable interest, not only at the size of the 'family,' but also the imposing proportions of the family residence. Up until that time Harry had never thought of Chandlers Lodge as being anything greatly out of the ordinary, he now, thousands of miles away, fostered considerable pride in what his mother and father had achieved in owning such an impressive home, but above all in making it the centre of a united family and the meeting point of an enormously wide and varied circle of friends who considered themselves family and would be welcomed as family.

A further morale boosting ingredient was a bundle of copies of the Times of India showing the positive advances being made by the allies against the Wehrmacht, against the U-boat menace in the Atlantic, and the defeat of the Japanese in the Solomons. The war was not over by any stretch of the imagination, but the aura of defeat enveloping all those in Malaya in 1941 and 1942 was now, to the few who were able to receive the information, gradually beginning to be dissipated.

The rest of June 1943 and July was spent in improving fitness, tactics and in sport. Some genius at H.Q. had thought to put a couple of footballs in their drop; in fact he must have been a genius since he also included a substantial pack of repair patches. Either he knew there was such stuff as prickly bamboo and sundry other needle like hazards which could surround a jungle pitch or they happened to be lying around so he threw them in. The space available allowed only five-a-side games, nevertheless it did a great deal to keeping the morale high was well as adding to the physical fitness of the participants.

Another element of their supply drop was a substantial quantity of the new plastic explosive; along with detonators so well cushioned they could have been dropped without a parachute and would have come to no harm. Accompanied by a manual of suggestions as to placing, quantity required for a specific purpose and so on, it opened up possibilities of further action against the enemy. Bowlie handed the booklet over to Harry with, "This is your department I believe."

"Do I get danger money?" Bowlie grinned, replying,

"The point is, now we've got it, what do we do with it?"

"As the bishop said to the actress?" Harry added, and continued, "Well I suppose it is a gentle hint from the powers that be to cause alarm and consternation somewhere. Let's have a look at the map."

About thirty miles to the west the map showed the main north-south railway bridging the River Bernan at the small town of Slim River, that same river where in January 1942 the Argylls fought desperately to hold the Japanese advance, but, without anti-tank weapons, they were ruthlessly overcome.

"If we could hit that," Bowlie suggested, "it would shake them up."

"A big, important bridge like that would probably be well guarded," Harry replied. "Not only that, even with the amount of explosive we have you can't just dump it on the bridge and run for it, it has to be secured at different strategic points. That takes time and for safety's sake should be done in daylight. Amateurs like us can't muck about with detonators in the dark; we would end up blowing each other up. No, I think our best bet would be to do a reconnaissance patrol, establish where the guard is positioned and how many there are and go from there. If we haven't enough explosive to seriously damage the bridge we shall have to devise a means of derailing a train on the bridge and hope that does the trick for us."

It was decided that Harry would take three men, including Choong Hong, the 'Railway Man,' one of Harry's original Camp Six fighters who had worked for the F.M.S. Railways and who had been an invaluable asset in their first operation at Labis. However, fate determined otherwise. On 23rd July, the day before the patrol was to set off, Harry was stung by a scorpion as he walked from the home-made shower rigged up by diverting water from the nearby mountain stream through tubes of female bamboo joined together. Malayan scorpions are not as venomous as those his brother-in-law Mark and Charlie Crew experienced in North Africa, nevertheless their sting is extremely painful, leaving a skin laceration which needed to be treated by Matthew Lee, who immediately told him that under no circumstances could he make a five day jungle patrol for at least another fortnight.

"There is no way you could avoid getting the puncture infected, the leg poisoned and yourself R.I.P. unless you kept that clean for a fortnight, and you can't do that in the jungle."

"In which case I will take the patrol," Bowlie decided.

Harry chose not to argue the point. He had first-hand experience of what happened to people with the slightest wounds incurred under the conditions in which they lived. Bowlie had been present in the pre-op briefing so was completely aware of the plan, method of operation, and information to be obtained. There was no reason why he couldn't make as good a job of it as it was expected Harry would succeed in doing.

Soon after dawn on Friday 24th the patrol set off.

"See you on Wednesday or Thursday," Bowlie estimated, "depending on how long we need to stay at the target." They shook hands.

As the small party disappeared into the jungle Bowlie turned and gave a little wave, Harry made his painful, swollen-legged way back to his room.

The patrol did not reappear on the following Wednesday, Harry not being particularly concerned. When it did not turn up on the Thursday, he became concerned. When it was still missing on Friday and then Saturday the alarm bells really rang. At soon after ten o'clock on Saturday morning August 1st, one of the extra pickets posted by Harry as part of the stand-to procedure, signalled, by pulling on a length of nylon cord salvaged from the parachute drop, that something was moving in front of his post. Immediately Harry put the full stand-to silently in motion, and made his way to the picket post to see what was up. It could be an animal – false alarms were not uncommon – but the sentry said it sounded like a human being coughing, then moaning.

"Keep me covered." Slowly he crept forward using every scrap of cover he could find. He had moved some thirty yards, in that jungle it felt like three hundred, when he distinctly heard the moan again a little to his right. Very, very carefully he moved inch by inch, his heart thumping, until he almost fell over the unconscious body of Choong Hong, the Railway Man. Picking him up and putting him across his shoulder he staggered back to the picket post, and then on back to the camp hospital.

Matthew Lee worked miracles that day. Choong Hong had been shot in the side, the bullet emerging from his back missing his spinal column by a fraction of an inch. He had lost a lot of blood, suffered numerous punctures of his skin from one or another of the spiky thickets dispersed throughout the jungle, and at one point on his left leg showed clear evidence of having been bitten by, probably, a wild boar.

Harry continued the stand-to all day. Until, and if, Choong Hong came to and told them what had happened, it was possible that somewhere Bowlie and the other two Chinese were being interrogated. If one of them cracked, the Japs could well be organising an attack at this very moment. Harry was not concerned at Bowlie having a map. It was a standing order, religiously followed, that no maps would be marked in any way, thereby giving away either the base, or the objective.

The hours dragged by. Choong Hong came too briefly in the late afternoon but lapsed into unconsciousness again. It was nine o'clock, with the frogs and cicadas making a tumultuous racket outside, he came to again, but only long enough to tell Harry

"Patrol all dead," and then started to weep until Harry held his shoulders, softly telling him,

"No more now Choong Hong. You are a very brave man, you get to sleep now – we will talk tomorrow."

With the knowledge that the patrol could not be compromising the safety of the camp and its fifty or so occupants Harry breathed a sigh of relief, to be immediately followed by the overwhelming sadness of losing Bowlie and his two men. This was followed by the realisation that the viciousness of a jungle scorpion could possibly be the cause of his not being the one struck down at this moment. He then reasoned, that would have been unlikely, however the patrol ran into trouble it wouldn't necessarily mean he would have been in the same place at the same time for the catastrophe to happen to him and his men.

He stood the men down but put the camp on full alert, double sentries, going back on to 'stand-to' before dawn for an hour.

During the day Choong Hong came to and was able to tell what happened. They arrived at the objective mid afternoon, keeping it under observation until dark. At midnight they moved out of the beluka to get a closer look at the bridge structure having already established no guards were posted on the bridge itself, but to get to the bridge from their vantage point meant they had to cross the main trunk road from K.L. up to Ipoh, along which there had been a steady flow of military traffic. At midnight this had more or less ceased, crossing the road into the paddy approaching the bridge therefore caused no problems. They stayed for some fifteen minutes on the bridge, Bowlie taking notes in the pale moonlight which he would be able to amplify later. As they were about to leave they heard a train approaching from the south, there would not have been time to get off the bridge and across the open paddy before the train arrived, Bowlie therefore, presuming it was just an ordinary goods train of which type they had seen numerous examples during their watch, told the three men to hide behind the upright girders. It was, however, no ordinary train, which became apparent to Bowlie immediately he saw it. There were two flatbeds at the front, then an open topped tender with a searchlight and a machine gun mounted on it, followed by a pair of engines and a dozen or more coaches filled with troops. The flatbeds at the front were there to take the blast of any mine laid on the track, or would bear the brunt of an attempt at derailment, the two engines having the power to reverse out of trouble even on adverse gradients. At the rear of the train there was another tender complete with searchlight and machine gun.

There had been no trouble on this section of the line so far, the guards therefore were not being overly watchful. However, as they approached the bridge the operator on the forward tender thought he would give the people at Slim River station about a mile ahead, advance warning of their approach, flashed his searchlight half a dozen times, during which one of Bowlie's men overbalanced, showing himself clearly to be armed. The searchlight operator shouted a warning, the machine gun crew cocked their weapon and started to spray the track in front of them, Bowlie jumped out from behind his steel upright in an attempt to put the searchlight out and was cut down immediately. Choong Hong was hit and fell on to the lower structure; the other two were killed where they stood.

The commander of the train immediately ordered the driver to accelerate out of the danger. There would be no way, since they had no idea of the size of the force they were dealing with, that the train could be halted to deal with the incident. It would be reported at Slim River and the garrison there left to deal with it.

Although he had been hit and felt somewhat battered by falling on to the lower steelwork, Choong Hong climbed back up on to the track, established that his three comrades were all dead, pushed their bodies off the track into the river so that the Japanese would not be able to immediately identify the attackers. Hopefully the river, and its inhabitants, would ensure their complete disappearance over the next few hours.

Before rolling the bodies into their watery grave below, he had the forethought to take Bowlie's revolver, compass and map, along with the field dressings carried by each of his comrades. It was the latter items which saved his life; in that being able to replace the pads tightly over his wounds when the original ones became soiled prevented excess loss of blood and the inevitable fly-borne infection. As it was, he barely made the camp; only the watchfulness of the outlying picket saved his life.

The conclusion of this story is somewhat bizarre, completely unknown of course to Harry. The small garrison turned out at Slim River making their extremely cautious way along the railway line to the bridge. It had started to pour with as heavy a deluge as even Malaya can produce. Reaching the bridge, they could find none of the bodies which according to the Japanese officer were lying there in their dozens, there was no sign of pools of blood where these bodies would have been – the rain had seen to that. They had no desire to stand out there and be shot at if there really had been guerrillas on the bridge; the N.C.O. in charge therefore swiftly gave the order to get back to the shelter of the guardhouse. They were after all, Formosans; they had no intention of getting killed on behalf of the bloody Japanese Emperor.

Harry sent a coded message off to Sunrise. 'Captain C two men k.i.a. Will assume command. C.' A reply arrived that evening. 'Message received and understood. Out.'

The Slim River project obviously had to be aborted; on the other hand Harry did not intend that they should be unsettled by having received casualties. In section strength – ten to twelve men – he led ambush parties south hitting Japanese traffic on the Frasers Hill Road, north bringing down power lines in the undulating jungle beyond Batu Talam, and to the west where they did, what Harry called, 'our standard Mark One Signal Box Job' at Trolak. On the 29th of August they received a message from Sunrise to expect him at any time, which Harry assumed would mean he would be bringing a new camp commander. It would not be practical to run the operation from this camp for any length of time with only one European officer – even with two of them it had been a bit difficult at times.

Later that evening Harry went out on to the clear parade ground with Matthew Lee, having calculated it would be early afternoon in England. They each raised a small tot of rum in the general direction of England, studied the stars which would be shining unseen on the congregation at Chigwell and toasted, "The bride and groom," to which

Matthew added, "God Bless and keep them both."

A few days later Sunrise arrived, bringing with him, or rather being led by, Bam and Boo, Harry's great orang asli friends, his mentors in the manufacture and application of his sudden death machine with which he had done such sterling work. He hugged them both, again to the astonishment of those Chinese who had not seen them before.

"Mr Chandler, this is Tommy Isaacs and this is Reuben Ault." Harry shook hands with the newcomers. There could not have been two dissimilar looking people in the whole of Malaya. Tommy Isaacs was slightly built, had a bright intelligent open face and was as black as any Tamil Harry had ever seen. With a name like that he was obviously Eurasian, with, equally obviously, less than one per cent of the European in him. He had been an inspector in the Malay police and was a great friend apparently of Robbie Stewart, he who had introduced Harry to this way of life. Reuben on the other hand was a giant. Six feet three and built like a barn door with features as impassive as the Sphinx and almost as badly bashed about. As Harry was to find out his thought processes operated at approximately the same speed as his Egyptian doppelganger, but once started it would take a Churchill tank to stop him. A regular officer, he scraped through Sandhurst in 1938 because the war was coming and the army had no intention of failing anybody on intellectual grounds, least of all if they looked like 'Man Mountain Dean' of comic fame.

"Mr Chandler, as from today you are promoted to captain and will continue to command this camp with these two officers, both lieutenants, to assist you. Secondly I have been officially informed that you have been awarded the Military Cross for your action specifically at Kampong Bintang, along with sundry other exhibitions of gallantry at other engagements. It will doubtless give you great pleasure to know that your family will have been notified of this decoration. May I add my personal congratulations and the thanks of all in Force 136 for the leadership you have given in sustaining the battle against our Japanese adversaries."

There was a tremendous round of applause from the whole camp. As Sunrise recounted to his staff when he got back to Cameron Highlands, "Even the communists applauded like mad, and by God it takes some doing to get any emotion out of those blighters."

"Captain Harry Chandler," he mused as he lay under his mosquito net that night. As David had said a while back, 'not bad for a farm boy,' and then gave an involuntary sob – he would so much rather be plain Harry Chandler with the seductive warmth of his Megan beside him.

Chapter Twenty Two

It was a tedious journey to Bulford. The small convoy of four three tonners got lost on two occasions. Having left at eight o'clock it eventually rolled on to the parade ground at Aliwal Barracks at ten past six, where David and Paddy, clambering stiffly down from the front compartments of their respective vehicles were greeted with the biggest surprise of even their not uneventful lives. Standing there, as immaculate as ever, and with a salute to David as militarily perfect as a salute could possibly be was none other than R.S.M. Forster – his mentor from Winchester in days gone by, the person who had pulled strings to get Paddy the job of looking after him and who, with his wife, had become firm friends of the Chandler family.

David returned the salute properly then held out his hand to shake hands warmly.

"What the hell are you doing here?"

"I got a little bored with knocking sense into fluffy-arsed second lieutenants at the depot so when I heard they were forming a Rifles battalion in the paras I applied for the R.S.M.s job and got it, did my jumps and here I am."

"But aren't you..."

"A bit old in the tooth for this lark? I'm a year younger than the C.O. and the same age as the second in command."

"And what does Marianne think of all this, and how is she – as lovely as ever?"

"Yes, she's here in the married quarters. She thinks I'm stark raving bloody mad, but then we all are aren't we – or we wouldn't be here?"

"What is it our transatlantic cousins say? I'll plead the fifth amendment on that one!"

The chaos of the arrival of thirty odd paratroopers of different ranks was soon sorted out, the assistant adjutant, a lieutenant having been assigned to take David to his room, and the R.S.M. showing Paddy his quarters in the sergeant's mess.

"Dinner is at seven thirty Sir," began the young lieutenant (young? he was only two years younger than David).

"What's your name?"

"Rafferty Sir."

"Christian name?"

"Miles Sir."

"Well Miles Rafferty, except on parade, you can cut out all this bloody Sir business. I am David and you are Miles – right?"

"Yes, David, thank you very much."

"Now, what's the griff on "R" Battalion the Parachute Regiment?"

"Well, it's only at about twenty five per cent strength yet." Miles continued to give him the low down on the people already there, the C.O., second in command and the only other major. David got the impression, although he could not exactly put his finger on what gave him cause for this feeling, that Miles Rafferty was not exactly enamoured of Colonel Stockbridge, the C.O. I'll see what R.S.M. Forster thinks about him he told himself, then corrected himself immediately. R.S.M. Forster would not say a word out of place about his C.O.

"...So we don't dress for dinner at the moment, the 2 I.C. says we will wait until we get a few more here, then posh ourselves up."

"The 2 I.C. seems a reasonable bloke."

"Good sort Sir. I mean David. Twenty years in the Scottish Rifles, but he keeps up jolly well."

"And the other major?"

"Mid-thirties, ex terrier from Queen Vic's. Was wounded at Calais. Neville Long, quiet sort of chap, haven't seen much of him as he has only been here a few days."

So, thought David, a fellow Calais man. His mind went back to those terrible days in 1940 when his brother-in-law and best friend Jeremy was killed and where he buried most of the platoon he was in. The Queen Vic's – proper name Queen Victoria Rifles, a territorial battalion of the King's Royal Rifle Corps – covered themselves in glory at Calais.

They were interrupted by Angus arriving with a trolley load of kit, asking the usual question, "What will you be wearing tonight Sir?"

"I'm going as I am Angus; I don't think I pong too much, so I'll leave you to get sorted out. Right Miles, lead on to the bar."

The next morning David had his first meeting with the C.O. It did not start off too propitiously.

"I understand you have never commanded a company before."

"No Sir."

"What makes you think you can do it now? Medals don't command companies, only experience commands companies."

Lieutenant Colonel Horace Stockbridge was in the Territorial Army for twelve years before the war, and now for nearly four years during the war, but as yet had not seen a shot fired in anger. His reference to the 'medals' was as malicious as it was envious. Apart from that David had to admit in all honesty that his experience as a company commander was woefully lacking, just as thousands of officers like

Stockbridge, forming initially the anti-invasion army, were now forming the invasion army – it was not their fault they had as yet seen no action.

"All I can say in answer to that Sir, is that I shall not hesitate to ask questions when I am stuck and I've no doubt I shall be stuck a few times at first."

"Right, I'm giving you B Company with O'Riordan as your C.S.M. I suggest you get off to your spider and start getting yourself organised."

"Thank you Sir." David saluted and marched out. He was hoping he would get Paddy what he didn't know was that R.S.M. Forster had paved the way, few people realise how much sway an R.S.M. has in a battalion of around six hundred men.

The 'spider' was a compact block of single storey buildings with three main barrack rooms each holding a platoon, a small barrack room housing company headquarters staff, additional smaller rooms for the sergeants, a company office and the company commanders' office. All the rooms were interconnected with covered in passageways, making the complete company of around 120 men a self-contained unit. When David reached his office he was not surprised to find Paddy already there.

"Good morning sergeant major."

"Good morning Sir."

"Shall we have a wander round?"

David surveyed his fiefdom.

"Plenty of space but no bodies."

"The C.Q.M.S. is here Sir, good solid bloke."

The company quartermaster sergeant supervises pay, issue of equipment and the general office routine; the C.S.M. is responsible for discipline and issue of ammunition. An efficient company demands these two to be of the best; it looked as though David was starting off on the right foot with those two.

As they returned from walking around the spider, they bumped into Miles Rafferty.

"Hello Miles, what are you doing here?"

"I've had a word with the adjutant and asked him if I can take over one of your platoons when it's formed. I told him I was not cut out at shuffling paperwork and I think, as a result of one or two minor cock-ups I have made, he was inclined to agree. Will you take me on Sir?"

David looked enquiringly at Paddy.

"With a name like Rafferty Sir, I shouldn't think we could go wrong."

"OK Miles. Four Platoon, you have a platoon sergeant and two men at the moment, don't let that feeling of power over the masses go to your head will you?"

And so through the rest of the month they built up their company. The other two platoon commanders both new second lieutenants were a bit like Charlie Crew, likeable lads but wet behind the ears.

"Never mind Sir, I reckon we've got a year to knock them into shape." Paddy was almost exactly dead right in his guestimate.

At the end of the month two things happened. Firstly David, who still had built up no rapport whatsoever with his C.O. but had at least managed to stay out of his hair, asked the adjutant if he would arrange leave for him on 24th August or thereabouts as he was getting married on the 26th. He was, in fact, due for ten days a couple of weeks before that but arrangements for the wedding having been made for the 29th he was quite happy to delay his entitlement.

"Hang on; I'll have a word with the C.O."

When he returned – "The C.O. wants to see you."

David presented himself to the colonel, saluted and waited for him to speak. There was a pause.

"Well?"

"I'm sorry Sir; I presumed the adjutant had informed you of my request."

"You have made arrangements, as I understand it, without ensuring there will be no operational exigencies on that date?"

David felt his hackles rising. If it had not been for the training to ensure his self-control given him by Lord Ramsford's professionals he might well have given Lieutenant Colonel bloody Horace Stockbridge a piece of his mind. Instead he replied

"Sir, I am asking well in advance. The arrangements are, of course, being made by the bride's family. Should we be called to take part in an operation or to combat an emergency my duty would come first."

"Very well, with that proviso I will allow it."

'Allow it?' David thought, 'allow it? I'm bloody well entitled to it.'

"Thank you Sir." With that he saluted, turned about and marched out past the adjutant's desk who raised his eyebrows in sympathy with him as he passed, noting his extremely rubicund expression.

The second incident which again did nothing to enamour the feeling between the C.O. and the major was that on the 25th of the month the announcement was made of the creation of the first two campaign medals of the war, namely the 1939-43 Star and the Africa Star. Both David and Paddy were entitled to both of these medals,

David for Calais and Yugoslavia, Paddy for Yugoslavia, the pair of them for 'service' in Africa. They were both proud of their 1939 Star, but equally both discomfited at wearing the Africa Star when all they had done was to be in Cairo for a few weeks.

"I shall be very embarrassed facing Mark and Charlie wearing an Africa Star knowing they had to fight like the devil to win their medals," David deliberated.

"Well Sir, we don't make the rules."

However, two more medal ribbons on David's already well furnished chest did nothing to endear him to his C.O., to the extent that David began to wonder whether he should put in for a transfer to another battalion before he ended up in a court martial for marmalising his superior officer.

The situation resolved itself. The two companies which made up the battalion at the moment, took off from Netheravon airfield for practise jumps on to Salisbury Plain. No equipment, routine stuff, into the Dakota, ten minute flight, red light on, green light on – GO – and out they went, except that on this occasion the C.O. who had elected to go last, instead of his usual first, was slow in getting out and ended up in some trees beyond the drop zone, breaking his leg in the process. The second in command, Major Hamish Gillespie, late of the Cameronians, assumed command of the battalion although as he told David and Neville Long, he understood they were sending a new C.O. who had been wounded with the 1st Airborne in North Africa, and was now returning to duty.

Over the next two weeks, in addition to a further draft of men, the officers' mess increased with the addition of several newcomers including a somewhat diminutive padre of whom we shall hear more shortly, a tall, gangly medical officer and a captain quartermaster who must surely have been the oldest man to have jumped out of an aeroplane, since he had had thirty years service in every rank from Boy Drummer in the Royal Sussex through to a commission. They were certainly a mixed bunch, but quickly got to know each other, although as is the way in an officer's mess, the different ranks tend to fraternise more with each other than with their seniors or juniors. David had received a captain to be his company second in command. He was ten years older than David and was obviously taken aback when first introduced to find his new O.C. to be much his junior age-wise. Nevertheless rank is rank; he accepted the situation and proved to be solid and reliable in the running of 'B' company's affairs as delegated to him.

Padre Roberts swiftly gave an indication that his mess bill was going to be in the top sector of 'R' Battalion's officers' mess. To put it plainly, he liked a drink and divorced from his parish, he failed to see why he should not indulge himself. Now in an officer's mess if a subaltern or even a captain appears to be lifting his elbow too much the mess president has a word in his ear. If he takes no notice, and he would be utterly stupid not to, then the C.O. steps in. However, the padre is rather a different kettle of fish. Technically he doesn't belong to the battalion; he is only attached from the army chaplain's department. The second difficulty was that the mess president at the moment was one Major Hamish Gillespie, and his mess bill outstripped even the padre's by a considerable amount. Hamish decided therefore to let sleeping dogs lie. He could, of course, say 'don't do as I do, do as I say,' but that would look a bit silly. "When the new C.O. arrives" he told himself, "I'll chuck the mess president's job and somebody else can sort it out!"

In the meantime padre Roberts went to Upavon for a practice jump. He went out of the Dakota at number seven but his parachute malfunctioned. The static line, secured inside the plane, unfurls to its length of about thirty feet, then snaps open the parachute pack pulling out the chute which is then inflated by the slipstream from the aircraft. The malfunction in this case was with the static line which failed to unfurl properly causing the parachute to be pulled out of its pack in the doorway. The Dakota has a rear landing wheel. The padre's parachute was pulled out of its pack and snagged itself around this rear wheel leaving the padre swinging around in the slipstream thirty odd feet behind the aircraft. In the meantime the remainder of the stick had jumped successfully.

After the first moments of bewilderment, quickly followed by an appreciation of the situation, to put it in military terms, then a moment or two of blind panic, Padre Robert's brain started to look for a way of escape from this predicament. Very swiftly his not inconsiderable intellect told him there was none over which he had any control. He was being buffeted around by the slipstream to such an extent he wondered how long he would remain conscious, he wondered how long it would be before the chute tore away from the landing wheel, how damaged it would be, whether it would 'candle,' that is not open properly, whether it would be so rent as to be almost useless. He was distinctly unhappy to say the least.

In the meantime the pilot had been told from the Upavon control tower of the situation since from within the plane the crew could not see their reluctant passenger. As a result he slowed down to almost stalling point to reduce the beating the padre was receiving, whilst he, the navigator and the R.A.F. jumpmaster, who dispatches the paras when they jump, swiftly conferred as to what could be done if anything. They were facing some hair-raising decisions which would need to be made very shortly indeed if the padre was to survive. Obviously they would not want to land with the padre still attached, although they might have to face up to that eventuality. Secondly if he tried to manoeuvre the clumsy old Dakota in an endeavour to shake the padre free, the chute could become so badly damaged as to be useless. British paratroops of course have no reserve chute.

The jumpmaster looking sightlessly at first down the fuselage from where he sat against the cockpit bulkhead, focussed on a kit bag lying at the tail end.

"Hang on, I've got an idea."

Despite the gravity of the situation the navigator could not help but reply. "That's unusual for a P.T. wallah." The sergeant hurried down the fuselage and collected the kit bag.

"If we stuff this kit bag with static lines from the stick that jumped, then pay it out to the padre using more static lines secured inside the aircraft, maybe he will be able to grab it and we can pull him back in."

The other two thought for a moment, the pilot commenting, "Well, if there ever was a solution born from desperation this must be number one – let's give it a try." They stuffed the kit bag, normally used by paratroops to carry down bulky items or heavy equipment which would be dangerous to land with on the person, and which were suspended from the soldier's waist belt. They worked rapidly, joining static lines together until they had a long enough span to reach their target. They secured it inside the fuselage.

"Now the point is, is he compos mentis enough to know what we are trying to do?" the navigator wondered. "He's been knocked about out there for nearly half an hour and what's more, if he does realise what we are up to will he have the strength to hang on?"

"Well, let's pay it out slowly. Here goes. Shit or bust. I just hope the kit bag doesn't get caught up in the bloody rigging lines."

"I just hope if he does grab it we've got enough strength to pull him in." The pilot obviously could not leave the controls to be of any help, the rescue, if indeed there was to be one, would be down to the navigator and the sergeant, they not only had to pull the weight of the padre, which fortunately was far from being too burdensome, they also had to pull against the slipstream blowing into the partially opened chute.

"And what happens if we take the weight off wherever the bloody chute is snagged and it snatches him away?" asked the sergeant.

"We will just have to pray."

"I reckon he's already working overtime on that, seeing that's his job."

Little by little the kit bag was paid out, the slipstream playing absolute havoc sending it round and round in circles at some considerable speed which would make it not only difficult to get hold of, but if it thumped the poor old padre it would be like stopping one from Joe Louis.

By some miracle, although his whole being was racked with fear, padre Roberts still retained his mental faculties. Because of the angle at which he was suspended, that is almost at the horizontal, it was a little while before he spotted the kit bag bobbing about. Seeing it, he registered immediately what they were trying to do to rescue him, decided he would not try and grab the kit bag itself, but let it go past him, grab the static line and then give it a couple of tugs to indicate to the people on the other end he had made contact. He would then let them pull on the line until the kit bag came close to him so that he could sit on the top of it. He was sure that there was no way he would have the strength to be pulled in by just holding on to the strapping. He prayed:

"Oh Lord, blessed is the man whose strength is in thee, in whose heart are thy ways. Strengthen my weak hands so that I may survive this dreadful ordeal and continue with thy work, for the sake of Jesus Christ our Saviour. Amen."

The rescuers started to pull him in. As the kit bag came up to him he sat on the top of it as he had planned, wrapping his legs around it as best he could, again twisting one arm round the strap, holding on with the other, and all the time with fear in his very vitals as he watched to see whether the chute would whip away from the rear wheel and take him with it to his death.

"How are we going to get him over the cill?" the sergeant asked "and what's going to happen to the chute when we take the harness off him?"

As they gradually inched their man to the doorway they realised the most difficult part was yet to come. Pulling an almost helpless body into an aircraft meant putting oneself in a position where you could easily be the one falling out – R.I.P. Having secured the static line round one of the seating supports they wedged themselves in, one on either side of the door, to grab the shoulder strap of the parachute pack.

"On my count of three," the navigator called. "One, two, three, heave."

With a superhuman effort they bodily lifted padre Emlyn Roberts out of deaths' jaws on to the hard corrugated floor of the Dakota, swiftly unbuckled his harness but before they could make it secure it disappeared out of the open doorway having been drawn out by the slipstream.

"That solves that problem," the sergeant joked.

"As long as it doesn't wrap itself around the tail plane or none of us will see tomorrow," was the uncompromising view of the navigator.

The padre lay on the floor, face down, gasping for breath, tears streaming down his face, blackened by the plane's exhaust. Slowly he raised himself on to one elbow, holding his hand out to shake the hands of his two rescuers.

"I thought I'd had it there," he told them "thank you for my life and God bless you both."

As soon as they landed he was taken to the station medical room. The resident R.A.F. medical officer was a Harley Street man in civilian life. All the Harley Street wallahs seemed to end up in the R.A.F. it seemed, like professional footballers and boxers. Anyway the M.O. pronounced him remarkably unharmed considering the battering he had received, though what mental traumas might result he was unable to say.

That night there was the biggest party in the mess the fledgling battalion had yet experienced, it was a real mother and father of all celebrations. The padre made it clear that one does not come back from being a few yards from the 'Pearly Gates' without marking the event with a monumental binge. The M.O. poured him into bed after midnight, not to be seen for thirty-six hours, but the story went round the paras and will continue to do so, until paras are no more.

Chapter Twenty Three

Rosa soon settled into her work at the Klinik in Brucksheim. Her main involvement was with the 'Auslander' – the foreign workers, prisoners of war and Russian slave workers – of whom there were substantial numbers working on the farms, in the forests, and in a number of medium sized shadow factories scattered around the district. From time to time she was called in to assist in the maternity ward. It was to be expected that in a district where British and French P.O.W.'s were working on the farms, repairing roads and so on, living almost cheek by jowl with Russian, Polish and other female slave workers, the inevitable would happen. The procedure therefore was strictly adhered to. The expectant mother would be brought into the Klinik a week or so before the baby was due, tests for V.D. or any abnormalities would be carried out, the woman would go into labour and the baby removed immediately for adoption by a family in another town to be brought up as their own. The mother never saw her baby.

It was pointed out to Rosa, who at first was horrified at the apparent callousness of this policy, there was no alternative. How would the woman look after the baby? What likelihood would there be of the baby surviving? Above all consider the amount of lost labour to the Reich if thousands of women were having to spend time looking after children. Finally, how great a benefit it was for the baby to be brought up in a caring German home as a German citizen.

Rosa's unspoken question was 'Yes, but what about the feelings now and for the future, of the poor mother.'

But then, slaves are not entitled to feelings.

There was another aspect to this sad state of affairs. On rare occasions a child would be born deformed in some way. The child, in common with a similar child born to a German family, would just be put to sleep and pronounced 'still-born.' The Reich only wanted, and intended only to have, facially pure, physically perfect, mentally flawless subjects to maintain its master-race philosophy.

It was a strange existence for Rosa. During the day, or when she was on night duty, she worked on her two wards, partly as a nurse, partly as a doctor, partly as a ward orderly. The staff shortage was so great with all the really experienced nurses and doctors having been transferred to the big city hospitals to take care of the wounded from Russia and the increasing numbers of air raid casualties now that the American daylight bombing was beginning to take effect, adding to the constant and increasing assault of the R.A.F. at night. She had established that Brucksheim was about thirty miles south of Hannover, not in itself a big enough place to invite the attention of bombers but near enough to Hannover to receive attention from time to time.

She received no pay of course. She had been warned by Fran Doktor Schlenker under no circumstances was she to attempt to contact her own, or her husband's family, as this could not only jeopardise her own job but also cause trouble for Doktor Schlenker. She was, therefore, on the horns of a monstrous dilemma. Her mother, her husband and her husband's family were without doubt worried sick about her, whilst their fears could be set at rest with a simple letter or phone call.

June had been a warm and pleasant month. She was not allowed to go out into the small town – Doktor Schlenker was being very strict in adhering to the terms Ravensbruk had laid down regarding her incarceration at the Klinik – but next to the small hospital there was a park which was shared by ambulant patients with a small number of local residents who wandered in from time to time. Rosa had taken to sitting on a bench here during her breaks, enjoying the sunshine and listening to the doves cooing at the nearby dovecot. She wore her white doctors uniform, three sets of which, along with some underwear, Doktor Schlenker had given her. She had no clothes. The iniquitous concentration camp number tattooed on her left wrist she kept covered with a leather-buckled strap to give the impression of being possessed of a strained wrist. Whilst the food at the Klinik was neither plentiful nor cordon bleu, it was a thousand times better than the pigswill she had received at Ravensbruk. When she thought of all those thousands – she had no way of knowing there were millions! – of people in the camps and dying day by day, she sobbed in despair, and remained fearful every day that something might happen to get her sent back.

One afternoon in late June, sitting on her favourite seat in the semi-shade, a well-dressed man passed her, politely raising his hat as he did so. He walked with the unmistakeable gait of an amputee, raising his right shoulder as he swung his artificial leg. He was, Rosa judged, in his early forties. In feeling desperately sorry for a man to be so cruelly impaired, she smiled back at him in reply. Two days later but during lunchtime break; she was seated on the same bench when he passed again. This time he not only raised his hat, but also wished Rosa good morning and commented on the glorious weather.

It was nearly a week later when she saw him approaching again. He came up to where she was seated.

"May I sit down?"

"Please do."

He lowered himself on to the bench, then fiddled with some sort of mechanism at his knee to enable him to bend his artificial leg.

"Fiddly things these. But then I presume you are well acquainted with mechanical limbs. Allow me to introduce myself. I am Friedrich Strobel, one time major in the Panzer Grenadiers, now I'm afraid rusting on the sidelines, and I said rusting, not resting." He smiled as he made the poor but well-intentioned joke.

"May I ask where you received your wound?"

"In France in 1940. We were pressing on to Abbeville when the British tanks attacked our flank out of the blue. They cut our column in two and then for some mysterious reason withdrew leaving a good number of us brewed up. Their medical people in the meantime had followed up, collected such wounded as they could, including me, and took us to a field hospital where they had no option but to amputate above the knee. Three days later they retreated towards Dunkirk leaving hospital attendants to look after us, who were themselves then taken prisoner. The strange thing was they were all volunteer pacifists – Quakers – people who had they lived in this country, would have ended up in Dachau or have been shot." He looked out across the park saying, "I often wonder what they did to those people. Their expert attention at that time saved my life."

"Now" he continued, "you haven't told me your name."

"Rosa."

"Just Rosa? are you not blessed with a family name?"

"Just Rosa, please."

"How intriguing, I can sense a story here but being the gentleman I am, just Rosa it shall be. My wife always used to say I always wanted to know too much, it was another more polite way of saying I was a nosey devil, which I have to admit to being. What is it the mass says? Mea culpa, mea culpa, mea maxima culpa." They laughed together at his genteel witticism, thereafter sitting in silence for a while.

"You said your wife 'always used to say.'" Rosa resumed hesitantly.

"Yes, I'm afraid I was a year in hospital because one operation after another went wrong and they had to start again. In the meantime she had met an S.S. man, pretty high up in the pecking order I believe, and went off to Hamburg to be near him. The British came over about six months ago and they were killed in the bombing. He got a full military funeral. I had to reclaim my wife's body from among over five hundred others and have her buried. Had things been normal I would have called him out, but one-legged people find it extremely difficult to duel and in any event an S.S. thug would probably not know one end of a sabre from the other."

There was a long silence, then...

"I must be getting back."

"Would you care to come and have another chat tomorrow?"

"My hours are extremely irregular. I never know when I can take my break."

"That's no problem. I am living in that apartment over there." He indicated the corner flat at the third floor. "Provided the confounded lift is working I can see you arrive and be here in a little over five minutes. I have in fact, as befits a military man, made a thorough reconnaissance as to time. If, on the other hand, the confounded lift is not working it will add a little over six minutes in which to conquer the stairs." With that he actuated his tin leg, hoisted himself up, shook hands, raised his hat and made his way to the park exit, while Rosa walked back to the Klinik buildings.

They had brief meetings twice during the following week. On the weekend of the 4th July they met again.

"I shall not be seeing you again for two or three weeks Rosa."

"Oh I am sorry, are you going on holiday?"

"Well, combining duty with pleasure I suppose. I have to go to Munich for my annual medical board. That takes three days as a rule. I thought then I would visit, on the bus or train, Oberammergau, Innsbruck and Salzburg and get a bit of culture back into my life."

The sound of the name Munich reached physically with Rosa. The thought that this gentleman would be visiting her home town, could even be passing her front door, made tears come to her eyes which she could not contain.

"Rosa, are you alright, have I said something to distress you?" She shook her head.

"Rosa, I have not probed into what you are or who you are, I have been quite content to have the pleasure of your company. But I can sense that you are a highly intelligent professional woman, and that behind that usually serene exterior you have problems."

Rosa turned towards him, holding her wrist-strap out. Slowly she unfastened the two buckles, as the cover came off it showed the obscene dark blue concentration camp number tattooed into her skin. He looked at it aghast.

"I have never seen one of those before – is it what I believe it to be?"

Rosa nodded.

"Rosa, I swear to you on my honour as an officer and a gentleman if you want to tell me your story it will never be repeated without your fully sanctioning it."

Rosa told him how and why she was sent to Ravensbruk, of the executions of the other six students, the march to the brickworks and how she was rescued by the Burgemeister and Doktor Schlenker. The major listened in horror to the low, coherent account of this dreadful chronicle of events. When she wound up her story he just said, repeating exactly the words the Burgemeister had used when he had been told of the affair, "I had no idea the German nation could sink to this." There was a silence between them broken by Rosa saying

"My people must not know I am here for two reasons. Firstly Doktor Schlenker obtained my services as a result of her influence as a senior and very early party member. I am afraid if anything was to happen for the situation to be made public, that is a concentration camp inmate acting as a doctor, she could get into trouble and I would be sent back to Ravensbruk or worse. Secondly my husband is a major in the Panzer Grenadiers in Russia. Having it generally known he has a criminal for a wife could cause him problems."

Major Friedrich Strobel thought, 'if he's a Major in the Panzer Grenadiers in Russia he's up to his neck in trouble anyway,' but did not comment. He thought for a moment.

"What I can do, with your acquiescence is this. I can visit your parents."

Rosa interrupted. "There is only my mother, my father was badly wounded in the last war and died a few years ago."

"Then I can visit your mother, tell her I have met with you, that you are well and so on, but tell her it is not advisable at present because of the risk to you and to others for her, to visit you. And to trust me. I could get her to contact your husband's parents to tell them, but under no circumstances for either of them to write to your husband with the news. With censorship the way it is nothing is confidential any more." He thought again for a few moments. "When I come back I will write to your husband, a long, long boring letter from an old comrade, towards the end of which I can say I met that doctor friend of his he knew at – wherever it was you spent your honeymoon. By the time the censor has read seven or eight pages of old comrade nonsense he won't even notice the bit about the doctor friend being fit and well and so on, and it wouldn't register as anything important anyway."

He took a small notebook complete with pencil from his pocket.

"Now, would you like to give me your mothers' name and address? I promise you I shall be the absolute soul of discretion."

Rosa was ten minutes late getting back into the Klinik and as luck would have it bumped into Doktor Schlenker. She looked enquiringly at the clock, in answer to which Rosa apologised.

"I'm sorry Frau Doktor; I sat in the sun and dozed off. I was up half the night with that Czech woman."

"Time is time Doktor, you know that," and with that mild rebuke passed on down the passageway to her office.

On Monday 6th July the major set off for Munich. His first appointment on the 8th was a routine medical check, the next day an interview with the pensions board at which he was told they would not need to see him again for two years, and that was that. On the Friday morning therefore he telephoned Rosa's mother.

"Frau Reuter, I am Major Friedrich Strobel, a friend of your son-in-law. I am in Munich for a day or two and wondered if I could call and see you."

"Yes, of course, when would it be convenient?"

"Would this afternoon suit you?"

"Yes indeed, let's say two o'clock."

Promptly at two o'clock Friedrich's taxi drew up at Rosa's front door. Frau Reuter, watching from the front room, saw a tall, rather handsome man, in civilian clothes, alight from the front seat of the cab, swinging one leg out which he had to adjust from bent to straight before he could stand up. She hurried to the door.

"Frau Reuter? I'm delighted to meet you."

They shook hands warmly; he then followed her into the sitting room.

"As you can see, I am no longer on active service," this said with a smile to indicate he was far from feeling sorry for himself.

Being comfortably seated in a high armchair thoughtfully indicated by Frau Reuter, she drawing up another opposite him, he said

"Frau Reuter, I have to tell you I have introduced myself to you under false pretences."

The welcoming smile on Frau Reuter's face left her quickly. She had suffered so much at the loss of her daughter that she was fearful of every knock on the door, every ringing of the telephone, even of people looking at her with any degree of intensity when she was shopping. What did this man want? Who really was he?"

"Please Frau Reuter, do not be disturbed. I am who I say I am, but I am not a friend of Dieter. I am a friend of Rosa. I could not tell you that over the telephone for reasons we shall go into."

The excitement on Frau Reuter's face was palpable, and as he began his story as to why he was here, how he had met Rosa, her present circumstances and so on she listened to him with an agony of intensity. Tears ran down her face, tears of relief that her daughter was still alive, tears of sorrow she could not be with her, tears of gratitude that this kind man could befriend her daughter and then come to set her mind at rest from the turmoil of not knowing whether her darling Rosa was alive, half alive or dead.

"So you see, she is still in all respects incarcerated, in that she is on her honour not to leave the premises. She would be most unwise to break this trust, as it would result in her being returned to the camp. The general public knows little or nothing of the workings of these camps. Rosa has enlightened me as to the bestiality which exists there. It would be a tragedy if she was returned for any reason."

Having waited a while for Frau Reuter to regain her composure he continued "Frau Reuter..."

"Please major, do call me Gita – Frau Reuter seems so formal when you have just performed the greatest kindness to me that one person could do for another. The fact that I know my daughter is alive and, if not fine, at least has a degree of freedom; that she is physically sound and performing the work she loves; not being brutally treated. The knowledge of all these factors combines to make the greatest gift I have ever received." She took his hand and kissed it. The major smiled.

"Just to think, I saw a young woman sitting by herself looking sad. I made polite conversation with her, as a result a short while later my hand is being kissed by her very attractive mother four hundred kilometres away, and I have done so little to deserve it!"

Gita released his hand. "I will make some coffee," at the same time apologising in her mind in advance for the noxious brew which passed for coffee in Germany in 1943. When she returned she had carried out some running repairs to her appearance so ravaged by the tensions of the past hour. Their conversation turned to her asking, if it did not upset him to talk about it, about his wound, how he passed his time now, studiously avoiding whether he was married or not!! What his immediate plans were and so on. When the large grandfather clock in the hallway struck five o'clock Gita said, "My word, how the time has flown by," not probably the most original statement of the age, but intended to subtly inform her guest that if he had further appointments she would not think ill of him should he wish to depart.

To her surprise he said, "Gita, would you consider accompanying a somewhat battered old war horse to dinner this evening, either to a restaurant of your choice or to the officers' club here in Munich, which I am told looks after kaput people like me rather well."

Gita came close to tears again at the simple fact of being asked out to dinner. Like most widows, and particularly in wartime Germany where there was not only a surfeit of widows from the 1914 war, but also increasing numbers from the current conflict, not to mention the grass widows of those serving in the Wehrmacht, like most widows she was rarely asked out. Added to that many of her friends had discretely vanished into the shadows after the arrest of her daughter. In Germany, just to know a person in a camp was in itself almost a crime, one kept one's nose clean.

"I shall be delighted to have dinner with you – the officers' club sounds intriguing," followed by the inevitable "but what shall I wear?"

"What's wrong with what you have on?"

"It's not very eveningy."

"Well, find something eveningy – people do not dress up too much these days though – or so I am told. I'm no expert on the subject.

Gita found a neat green linen dress, light enough in weight to cater for the warm weather, but firm enough to look classical and not get easily creased. When she reappeared, Friedrich – they were both on Christian name terms now – Friedrich stood back and stated, "It is most obvious from whom your Rosa inherits her elegant looks and appearance."

Gita, totally unused to flattery, in this instance quite sincerely articulated, blushed for the first time in many years, giving a deprecatory wave of the hand saying "Oh, away with you."

When Fritz ('all my best friends call me Fritz' he had told her) dropped Gita off at her home later that evening, he took her hand and kissed it. "You know, we haven't stopped talking all the evening," he told her, "and I've so much more to tell you. If I cut short my Salzburg visit to spend a little more time here, can we see each other again?"

"There is nothing I should like more." She put her arm up around his neck, pulled his head down gently and kissed him lightly on the lips.

"Thank you, thank you a million times for bringing my Rosa back to me." She turned and went into the house giving him a little wave from the doorway as he was driven off. The next day a large bunch of roses arrived with just 'Thank you for a lovely evening' written on the front of the card, and on the reverse 'Until Soon – F.'

Chapter Twenty Four

On Wednesday 10th July no fewer than four people had highly exciting letters. Rose Laurenson ran to the door as the postman came into the driveway on his bike at Chandlers Lodge and met him on the doorstep, to immediately spot, among a handful of mail for her father, the envelope for which she had been aching for over the past three weeks. She ran in, suddenly realising to her horror she had not said 'thank you' to Eric the postman, put Fred's letters on to the hall table and continued her precipitate progress to the large deal table in the kitchen upon which she knew lay a sharp pointed knife with which to open this long awaited, much valued epistle. In the eight pages of mainly luvvy duvvy, as Harry would have described it, was the phrase 'By the way, Aunt Margaret asked me to give you her love and will be seeing you soon.' She let out a shriek of excitement, quite startling Mrs Stokes, the cleaning lady and general factotum since Ruth died, who had just come in the back door.

"What's the matter Mrs Laurenson?" she asked. Rose jumped up, grabbed the astonished Mrs Stokes and proceeded to dance around the kitchen with her.

"My husband is coming home. I don't know when, but he's coming home."

In her excitement she had totally forgotten Mrs Stokes's husband was serving in Palestine, he would not be coming home, until the good lady replied, "I am very, very happy for you Mrs Laurenson, I really am."

It was then that Rose realised she was not the only one who had to suffer the agony, physical and mental, of being parted from her loved one.

"Oh, Mrs Stokes, I was so excited, I forgot you too were suffering like me."

"Well, one day Miss, they'll all be home and all this will have been a bad dream. Now, anything special today?"

The second person to receive a letter was Leading Wren Emma Langham from one Lieutenant Charlie Crew in which he had boldly stated at the risk of its being censored, "I think it highly probable that we shall be visiting The Troc in the not too distant future." He was relying on the possibility the censor would not know what 'The Troc' was, or who the 'we' was to be. His intuitions were correct and the message passed. Emma seeing Maria standing out in the vehicle park ran out at a speed which would not have disgraced an Olympic hopeful.

"Maria, Maria, look at this," she called waving the letter.

"You want me to read one of your innumerable love letters? Is it that original? Come to that; am I not too young and innocent for such salacity?"

"Shouldn't that be salaciousness?"

"I think it could be either, anyway, what's all the fuss about?"

"Charlie's coming home."

"How exciting! I suppose that means Mark will be coming as well. I wonder if they will be here in time for the wedding. Oh!! I do hope so, then when I throw you my bouquet it will give Charlie the opportunity to pop the question to you."

"Oh don't be a nutter, we only know each other through writing to one another. He will probably take one look at me and run when we first meet."

"If he did he would be different to any one of the six hundred odd lusty males at this depot, given half a chance."

"You flatter me, at least a dozen of them are married already anyway."

"Anyway, what does this all-important letter say?"

Emma read out the passage of substance.

"I'll phone Rose this evening and see if she has heard anything – she will be dancing on air if she has."

The third letter arrived for Cecely at The Bungalow. She at once recognised her brother-in-law James's artistic scrawl. Receiving a letter from James was an event to be chalked up on the wall she had repeatedly told Mrs Treharne. If her husband had been away from home for more than a couple of days he would always drop her a few lines. James could be away a couple of months before you might get a postcard. She eagerly opened the unexpected epistle.

'My dear Cecely,

I am coming on leave for seven days arriving Sunday 23rd, leaving on Sunday 30th.

I shall be accompanied by a friend of mine Claire Armstrong who I would very much like you to welcome, as I know you will.

Could you book us in at The Angel, and before your mind starts working overtime, SINGLE ROOMS, on a bed and breakfast basis as we shall want to be out in the evenings. If your mind did start off working overtime I can give you a hint that the next time we see you, if my plans work out as I intend, we could well require double roomed accommodation – but I have a few hurdles to overcome before that happy day (or night) which I shall tell you about when we meet.

With love to Greta and Oliver and my very best wishes to the gorgeous Mrs Treharne.'

Yours ever
James

Mrs Treharne looked at her enquiringly.

"He thinks you're gorgeous."

A peal of laughter from the recipient of the tribute.

"And he is coming on leave with a lady friend in a couple of weeks, staying at the Angel if I can get them in." Registering Mrs Treharne's raised eyebrows – "and SINGLE ROOMS, I have been instructed."

Mrs Treharne turned away to the kitchen with the throw away line fully intended for Cecely to hear – "I wonder which room they will use first."

"They are not all like you, you know."

"I think most of them are, especially in wartime."

They both chuckled, as much about the pleasure of their camaraderie as the actual content of the conversation.

The fourth letter dropped on to the doormat of the Bolton's residence, addressed to Mr Karl Reisner and embossed with the Home Office seal on the reverse.

It stated simply and plainly:

Mr Karl Reisner.

In view of special circumstances the government of the United Kingdom had been pleased to grant the above full naturalisation as a British subject as from the above date. You will be required to attend the Maidstone District Court at 10 a.m. on Wednesday 19th July 1943 to take the Oath of Allegiance to His Majesty King George V.

Signed
H. Grigg.

A separate sheet of paper indicated how he should obtain his identity card as a British subject, national insurance card and so on. Unfortunately the letter lay on the doormat for nearly an hour before Anni got up and spotted it there, she living like a cat on hot bricks until her father returned from Fort Malstead later that afternoon.

Karl opened the letter, pulled a long face of disappointment and handed the communication over to a despondent Anni who had been watching his face for signs of expression. Having quickly read its content she screamed, "Oh you terrible man, teasing me like that." Her excitement then went into volcanic eruption mode, when she came down to earth her first words were:

"I must telephone Ernie."

"He will be here in a few hours."

"He can't wait that long."

"Since he does not know what is going on, what difference will it make?"

By this time in the course of the argument, she had got through to Sandbury Engineering only to find Ernie was on a job in the factory and would not be back in the office for about an hour. Waving the paper she said:

"We must have a party."

"Where?"

Now that really did bring her down to earth. Their home, small and comfortable, was certainly not built to house the sort of shindig already forming itself in her mind.

"If we bear all the expenses, perhaps Uncle Fred will let us use Chandlers Lodge."

"Have a word with Ernie first, then we'll have a talk together. We could always book John Tarrant's function room – that might be the best idea – nein?"

"Nein is not English."

"Do you think I should go to what you call them – electrocution classes?"

"Elocution."

"Elocution – ja."

"Ja is not English" – she then realised he was teasing her again.

By dint of non-stop telephoning, a fair proportion of the Chandler family and immediate friends received the good news in the next hour, resulting in a continuous fusillade of congratulatory calls from far and wide.

The next morning as he and Rosemary awaited the government bus he showed her the letter. To his surprise she threw her arms around him and gave him a long kiss, a sight the bus driver and front seat passengers were singularly unused to witnessing at eight o'clock in the morning in the Market Square of the fair town of Sandbury as they drove up to collect their presumably amorous, passengers.

On Friday 14th July Cecely, dressed in her extremely fetching barathea suit caught the 10.30 out of Sandbury for Victoria. She was a little concerned at the weight of her suitcase. As Mrs Treharne had succinctly put it, "You've left out the kitchen sink." The point is one never knows what sort of weather one is going to enjoy – or otherwise – or whether one might get invited to somewhere where one needs a long frock. Mrs Treharne's reply to that was, "Well, leave the nightie out, you probably won't need that." To summarise, it was a bit on the heavy side, and although Berners Hotel was not far enough from Victoria to demand a taxi, it would be a bit far to carry, what appeared to be, a hundredweight of mostly unnecessary clothing, including the nightie. It is odd to think that, as she rode through the gorgeous Kent countryside into the long tunnel under The Downs, she was more concerned with the weight of her suitcase rather than whether she would be sleeping on her own that night. But then women do worry over trivialities, as all males will testify.

As she stepped out of the First Class compartment on to Victoria Station's platform three, she came face to face with none other than Hugh Ramsford. He raised his hat – he was in civilian clothes – took her hand, kissed her lightly on the cheek, indicated her suitcase to an attendant porter, put her arm in his and proceeded to the exit. She looked at him in astonishment.

"How did you know I would be on that train? And which carriage I would be in?"

"Well there you see, my dear Cecely, the military strategist at work. He firstly telephones his forward observation post, namely Mrs Treharne, as to what time you left. From Bradshaw's he then finds out the time of the train from Sandbury. He then telephones Sandbury Station to ask which part of the train an extremely fashionable-looking lady had boarded carrying a black suitcase and wearing a green suit – details of which he had obtained from the aforesaid observation post. Since all eyes, Sandbury Station staff eyes that is, were observing the breathtaking elegance of this person; they were able to state carriage two. Have I answered your question?"

She looked up at him, smiling, "Thank you very much for meeting me, you really are very very kind and thoughtful."

Reaching the hotel, ensuring she was booked in, he took his leave saying he had meetings that afternoon but would be back to collect her for a drink at say six o'clock and then dinner at his club, The Army and Navy. "And don't get chatted up by one of these millionaire Americans in the meantime please!"

"I won't even look at a multi-millionaire I promise – by the way, how do you tell the difference?"

He gave her a little hug, a lad took her suitcase, escorted her to the lift and to her bedroom.

In the afternoon she took a walk to see the bomb-damaged Buckingham Palace, sat in the sun for a little while, was conscious of the blatant obtrusive regard of a number of the American forces who seemed to have taken over the district, to many of whom she would be old enough to be their mother. Why is it, she wondered, that perfectly civil, decently brought up lads can change just because they have put on a uniform? Oh, I do hope Oliver isn't like that.

After their six o'clock drink at the rather plush bar of the Berners Hotel – again they wondered, as David had in other bars in other places, how very sleek, well fed and prosperous some of their fellow imbibers looked – but then, they are probably saying the same about us, being Cecely's view.

"Would you describe me as sleek and well fed?"

"No.o.o... chunky and well fed I think."

They decided, since it was less than a mile away, to walk down the Mall to Hugh's club. With him at her side, she was at least spared the aspersions and suggestions she had experienced during her afternoon stroll.

"I've never seen you in uniform."

"Well, I suppose being in an anonymous sort of job I tend to capture the atmosphere to remain anonymous. Added to which, moving around in London in uniform, particularly as a brigadier, means that half the population is waving an arm at one – can get very tiring replying to all those salutes." He thought for a moment. "Do you know, I was in uniform in Piccadilly one day, just going into the Burlington Arcade when I noticed something that interested me in a shop window. As I looked away a young private soldier in a well known county regiment must have saluted me without my noticing. The next minute there was a tap on my shoulder and I heard an East Anglian voice saying quite forcefully 'I just saluted you Sir.'"

"What did you do?"

"I was so taken aback I said, 'Oh I'm frightfully sorry I missed you,' and saluted him back. It came home to me afterwards that some of these chaps don't salute you because they have to, but because it is part and parcel of the giving, taking and returning of a courtesy from one comrade to another, no matter how far they are apart in rank. I always return salutes properly, none of this general waving of the hand to cap, or waggling of swagger stick some officers tend to indulge in. Have you ever noticed on newsreels how Monty always salutes properly? He may dress a little unconventionally but when he is saluted he is punctilious in his reply." He was silent for a few moments.

"Got me off on a very boring hobby horse there for a moment or two, did you not?"

Cecely squeezed his arm, "I loved every word of it."

They arrived at the Army and Navy Club around seven o'clock and were seated in the guest's dining room. The menu was plain but extremely well cooked and presented, the wine was of a high standard and the surroundings were, to say the least, impressive.

"What a lovely room."

"Well, this was built in the days when army officers all, as my son Charlie would say, had a bob or two. We certainly couldn't afford to build it these days; not taking into account the fact it could get knocked down again at any minute.

"Charlie is coming home soon then?"

Hugh sat up, visibly surprised.

"How did you know that? I didn't think even Charlie's lot knew it yet."

"Which means that you knew it."

"I hear all sorts of things."

Cecely put her hand on his on the table.

"Do you also hear that he has an extremely charming young Wren named Emma Langham he will be introducing to you in due course?"

"You are not serious?"

"Cross my heart."

"He's never told me a word about this, the young blighter."

"Well, he probably wants to make sure of her before he introduces her to you and his grandfather. I understand from Maria that she is, as yet, unaware of, what shall we say, his aristocratic connections."

"At least, if anything comes of this it looks as though we shan't have to troll through Debrett to find him a wife, like they did for me. Look where it landed me, someone with whom after a few months I found I had nothing in common and who went off with an American to Kenya."

"Were you shattered?"

"My ego took a beating I suppose. I had realised we were a poor match, but I would have stuck it out, one did in those days, they frowned on divorce in the Guards anyway. Since I was the innocent party I survived, but only just." She took his hand and squeezed it in sympathy, only to be interrupted as this warmth of expression was being put into effect by a cheery voice from over her shoulder saying,

"Hugh, how nice to see you."

"You would not have bothered to even nod to me if I had been on my own."

"You are quite right of course, but how else could I shake hands with this beautiful companion of yours and ignore you at the same time?"

"Cecely, this is Monty FitzRoy, one time friend of mine when we were subalterns together, now a major general only because he hasn't been found out yet."

They shook hands.

"And are you an army person Cecely – I may call you Cecely may

241

I not, since in his usual bumbling way Hugh has forgotten to tell me your surname or title?"

"To answer your question General, by all means call me Cecely. Secondly, I am not an army person, my husband being a banker. Thirdly I am Cecely Coates, an unfortunate refugee from Malaya, enjoying the cordial hospitality of my dear friend Hugh and his father over the weekend."

"Hugh and I have been friends for a long time Cecely despite the fact he owes me a tenner from back in '37. I must say however, among the thousand and one ladies with whom I have seen him from time to time, none approaches you in the classical elegance you enjoy. Should you tire of him you will remember me won't you?" With that he shook hands again and moved reasonably steadily to a table where a stern looking lady and three late-teenagers, two girls and a young man, a second lieutenant in the Irish Guards, obviously his family, were seated.

They were silent for a few moments, both smiling at the repartee.

"Why do men always say insulting things to each other when they are obviously firm friends?"

"I don't know. It's a way of life in the mess. Perhaps it's a way of showing your regard for someone of your own sex. I mean after all, you can't go up and hold hands with another fella now can you?"

"Some do I believe," she replied mischievously.

"Oh, but that's only in the navy. I think probably it's the fact that you can be modestly rude and insulting without the recipient taking umbrage, which shows you are true comrades. However," he took her hands, looked intently in her eyes, "I would much rather talk about you. Shall we walk back when we have had our coffee so that I can talk to you?"

"Yes of course," her mind racing as to what he might, or might not, want to talk about.

They walked back into the Mall, arm in arm, at ten o'clock, double summer time, it was just getting dusk.

"Cecely, dear Cecely," (this is it she thought, not knowing whether to keep her fingers crossed or not. Not knowing for that matter for which reason she would be crossing her fingers. Faithfulness in marriage was ingrained in her, was the basic tenet of her upbringing, sheer physical need was her very present overpowering desideratum, so would she be crossing her fingers for the former or the latter? What a quandary!).

"Cecely, dear Cecely, I have never before professed my love for another man's wife, but I have to tell you that I loved you from first moment we met in Sandbury. Sounds wildly impossible I know but it is true. I was brought up on the basic principle from the Book of Exodus that thou shalt not covet, and in particular, thy neighbour's wife. Secondly our family motto, translated is 'Honour is Sacrosanct.' So you see whilst in modern times all that seems old fashioned mumbo-jumbo, that you should take what's going and enjoy yourself, it is so ingrained in me that I cannot ignore it."

They walked in silence for a while. He continued

"I have no idea of course how you feel about me, other than I can tell you have some regard for me." Cecely accepted this as an invitation to be frank and honest, as he had been. She laid her head against his shoulder.

"If it is possible to be in love with two people, I am in love with you. I too am torn apart with my duty to my husband and..." she hesitated for some little while "... and my desire for you. If we were to have a relationship, it would endanger my marriage, the feelings of my children towards me, and the opinion of the dear friends who have taken me into their homes. Although I would have you, it would ruin my life and all those dear to me. That in turn would probably affect our feelings for each other for all I know."

They walked slowly on.

"You are quite right of course. The only thing I can do is to stay your very dear friend, happy in the knowledge that you know I love you and that if circumstances were different we could be together." She looked up to kiss him on the cheek, but having anticipated the movement he bent his head and kissed her fully on the lips for long, long moments.

When they reached the hotel he saw her to the reception desk to get her key, walked her to the lift, held her close and said, "Goodnight my darling," she kissed him lightly and was whisked up to her room, where she swiftly undressed, creamed her face, fell into bed and cried and cried.

Chapter Twenty Five

The new colonel arrived at 'R' Battalion on Thursday 20th July with the news that a Brigadier had been appointed to command the three battalions gradually now reaching full strength, the other two battalions being "L" Battalion, a light infantry lot and "C" Battalion, a Canadian crowd. The officers were all gathered in the anteroom at the mess that evening when the adjutant entered with the colonel. Asking for their attention he announced, "Gentlemen, I would like to introduce our new colonel, straight from Africa via hospitals in Algiers and Marlborough I understand, and decorated with a D.S.O. awarded last week for his service with the 1st Division. Gentlemen, Lieutenant Colonel Jeffrey Hislop."

There was applause, while David studied his new commanding officer. He had, David considered, the physique and appearance of a scholar rather than a warrior, but you can't judge a book by its cover – look at Monty!

"Thank you Tommy." Captain Atkins was the adjutant, with a name like that, therefore, automatically being nick-named 'Tommy' even though his Christian name was, of all things, Hilary, hardly a befitting name for a paratrooper anyway!

"Gentlemen, I shall see you all in my office at some time during tomorrow – I run a fixed system of no shop in the mess, and that applies to company commanders and their underlings as well I hasten to add." There was general laughter at this, some company commanders had a habit of pinning down young platoon officers after dinner as if they were still on parade.

He sent for David at 9.30 the next morning. David entered his office, gave an impeccable salute.

"Sit down David, please."

Bit different to bloody Stockbridge was David's immediate assessment.

Looking through his papers the colonel said, "You've been around a bit I see. Calais, then a blank for three months, back to Ringway etc, then another blank for several months, then Africa and Yugoslavia, then back to Clay Cross. Are you able to fill in the blanks?"

"Not really Sir, I was working for Brigadier Lord Ramsford in Europe."

"God, I'd dearly like to know about that – wouldn't you Hamish?"
"Yes, Sir, I've tried pumping him but his lips are as sealed as..."

He was about to end with an extremely lewd, extremely soldierly comparison when the colonel interrupted, "Now then Hamish, mustn't pervert the youngest major in the regiment." They all grinned. This is going to be a good battalion was David's further assessment.

"And I understand you are going to be married next month."

"Yes Sir, God and the war willing. I lost my first wife in an air attack on our local airfield where she was doing canteen work. My wife-to-be is the sister of a comrade of mine killed at Calais."

"David, it says here you were born in 1919, which makes you twenty-four years old if my mental arithmetic isn't sadly at fault. Yet you fought at Calais, have taken part in two extensive covert operations in Europe, fought with the partisans for six months, lost your wife through enemy action, and now you are preparing to drop back into Europe again, which is where we all know we are heading. And you are still only twenty four!"

"I don't seem to have had much to do with it Sir – it just seems to have happened."

"Well, all I can ask you is make 'B' Company the best in the brigade, and if you need any help regarding company matters ask Hamish here, what he doesn't know isn't worth knowing, I've already found that out."

Taking that as a polite form of dismissal David stood up, put his beret on, saluted again and marched out.

Back at company H.Q., Paddy was awaiting him.

"OK Sir?" – a wealth of meaning in that simple question.

"I reckon we've got a bloody good colonel and a gem of a 2 I.C." David replied, "and what with there being a first class R.S.M. to back them up, the only problem I seem to have is my blooming company sergeant major – still, he'll learn when he gets some service in. Anyway the C.O. has asked me, asked me mind, to make B Company the best in the brigade. Now, putting on one side he's said that to the other three company commanders so that it can be put in the bullshit file, I am now saying WE are going to make B Company the best in the brigade – bar none. That includes drill, rifle shooting, P.T., football – even darning socks – that is Standing Order No.1 for B Company 'R' Battalion The Parachute Regiment – agreed?"

"Definitely agreed, Sir."

"Right, get the platoon sergeants in and we'll make a start."

Later that day a runner came from Battalion H.Q. with a directive from the C.O. that as from today, Friday, work will continue all through the weekend, the following weekend passes would be issued from 1600 hours Friday until midnight Sunday. The system, work through one weekend, free the next weekend meant that those who lived in London or regions adjacent, or at a reasonable distance from Bulford could get home, if only briefly, every other weekend. It was a tremendous morale booster. Even those from the Midlands, the North and even further distant regions, headed for London, provided they had the money for a couple of nights lodging.

By the middle of August 'B' Company was really beginning to take shape. They had had half a dozen who had overstayed their weekend leave and been given fourteen days confined to barracks (commonly known as 'jankers') by David, along with two future passes disallowed. The word soon got around, 'Play the game or you will muck it up for everybody.'

By the weekend of the 18th August there was no doubt that David's mind was considerably more focussed on domestic rather than on military matters. On Friday they were to carry out a company 'night-op,' leading Paddy to suggest that by the time the major returned from leave he would be an expert on 'night-ops' and would possibly like to give lectures to the company on the subject.

"If anyone can be classified as an expert on that subject I would refer to the Baron of Bangor. By the way, you never did give me that address."

The night-op and the subsequent weekend forced marches went well, the company returning on Sunday evening ready only for weapon and foot inspection, meal and bed. The company, David felt, was really coming together.

It had finally been arranged that David would go on leave on Wednesday evening. On Tuesday evening there was a larger than usual gathering in the mess, called to order by the mess president, newly delegated with a sigh of relief by Hamish Gillespie.

"Gentlemen, as you know David is taking the plunge on Saturday. I would like to present him with this present from us all and wish him and Maria a long, happy and fruitful marriage." With that he produced from a box a magnificent silver salver, engraved with the regimental crest and the legend 'To David and Maria 26 August 1943 from his fellow officers.'

Afterwards David could not remember a single word of the speech of thanks he had given in reply. The gift was quite unexpected. They had, after all, only known each other a few short weeks. What it did present was further evidence that slowly but surely a comradeship was being formed between individuals of all ranks, which would eventually gel into loyalty to each other, loyalty to the battalion, and ultimately a fighting force to bring further distinction to that already founded in North Africa and Sicily by 1st Airborne. Not for nothing had the German Wehrmacht there called them 'Rote Teufel' – the Red Devils, in a years time they would have good cause to remember that sobriquet, as this battalion dropped in on them.

When David telephoned home that evening he was astonished to have his call answered by none other than Mark Laurenson

"Mark, what the devil are you doing there?"

"Landed yesterday afternoon. Travelled all night to Winchester. Arrived here an hour ago. Waiting for a call to my parents. That's why I am answering the telephone. Does that answer your question major?"

"Yes major," David continued,

"Does that mean you can be my best man on Saturday?"

"If I am asked and the money's OK."

"I am asking and you don't need to pay me."

"I'd be delighted, dear old sport, as Charlie would say."

"How is dear old Charlie?" And so the conversation went on, two friends delighted to be in contact with each other again after what seemed to be such a long time, during which they had both enjoyed, if that is the correct word, experiences of which they would have never dreamt at their last meeting.

The next morning David had another surprise. Walking from the mess, having had breakfast, he reached the parade ground in front of his spider to find the company drawn up as for a drill parade. He thought this rather odd, since so far the men had been drilled only in platoons, company drill being rather more intricate. As he approached, C.S.M. O'Riordan brought them to attention and saluted the officer. David returned the salute, mystified as to what was going on. Immediately following the salute, the youngest soldier in the company, a little over eighteen years of age, broke ranks, marched forward, saluted, announced an obviously well-rehearsed address in a strong Ulster accent.

"The men of the company have collected to present this to you Sir, on the occasion of your wedding to Miss Schultz. We wish you long life and happiness."

With that burden successfully fulfilled, he gave David a wrapped box, took a pace back, saluted, turned about and marched back into the comfort of his peers.

They were all waiting, obviously, for him to say something.

"As I once heard my brother say, 'My flabber has never been so ghasted.' I shall not open this yet but will wait until my future wife and I can open it together. I want to thank you from both of us most sincerely for both the present and for your good wishes, I really am most touched." He paused for a moment, "If I could give you all the rest of the week off I would," this sally bringing a chuckle all round.

"Over to you sergeant major."

Paddy saluted, faced the parade, "Parade dismiss."

Afterwards in the office David asked Paddy if he had organised it.

"Not at all Sir, not at all. That young McGlusky who presented it saw the C.Q.M.S. and asked if he could be allowed to organise it, and then to come with him to Salisbury when he'd got the money. I had nothing to do with it at all, nothing."

"Well I think it's bloody marvellous. I haven't gone out of my way to be nice to everybody, quite the opposite at times, so why they should dream up something like this I don't know."

"I think I do Sir. 'B' Company is the only company with a hero as its commander; they all think it's a privilege to be here. You see, it's not the M.C., it's the D.C.M. They know you got the Distinguished Conduct Medal before you were an officer, so at some time you've been like them. They know you've had to rough it, so the chances are you will understand them much more than someone straight out of Sandhurst. What's more, they know the powers that be don't dish out D.C.M.'s with the rations, you have to do something bloody well worthwhile to get one of them."

David thought for a moment.

"A hero? Well, when we go into action don't, for Christ's sake, tell them about my brown leak-proof underwear will you?"

"Not a word Sir, not a word."

After the morning parades were over and David had handed over to his second in command, he went to the mess for lunch. He checked with Angus that all his kit was ready, he was to travel in his best battle dress, keeping his immaculately pressed service dress neatly put away ready for the great day, and then wandered into the dining room. As he arrived, a mess steward called to him, "There's a phone call for you Sir, number two booth." He lifted the receiver.

"Chandler speaking."

"I'm sorry to have dragged you out of the jolly old bar your excellency, your worship, or whatever it is they call buckshee majors in your lot."

"Charlie, you blighter. Where are you?"

"In London old sport, centre of the universe, or so they tell me."

"You're coming to the wedding?"

"You don't think I would turn up the prospect of a free meal and booze-up do you? That would be against a long-standing family tradition. So the answer is yes, and so are Father and Grandfather, and as far as I know Grandfather hasn't been to a wedding in years."

"And how is the delectable Emma?"

Charlie's voice sobered a little. "That's why I am in London. I am meeting her tonight. You see I am going to have to tell her about the jolly old family tree since she will be meeting Pater and Grandfather on Saturday. She's got seven days leave. I understand Maria has fourteen days, though I should think after fourteen days with you she'll be glad to get back to the Wrens."

"She'll be more likely to go absent."

"I'm coming to your stag party tomorrow night, John Tarrant's putting me up as your house and The Hollies will be chock-a-block, so I'll see you then. Take care."

"Cheerio." He walked into the dining room, grinning. Just to hear Charlie speak made him grin; there was always something in the timbre of his voice indicating cheerfulness and bonhomie which was quite infectious.

The journey home passed without incident except that on the train from Salisbury he was seated in a first class compartment with a full colonel opposite him; a middle-aged, very elegantly dressed and coiffured lady seated next to him, emitting an extremely subtle and expensive fragrance; two lieutenants from the Gunners next to the colonel; and another officer in the corner on the other side of the only lady. The two lieutenants had been talking quietly together, David engaged in looking out of the window meditating on what the next few days would bring. He was brought out of his reverie by one of the lieutenants addressing him.

"Sir, Tubby here and I were saying how unusual it was for an officer to have the Distinguished Conduct Medal. We felt there was an interesting story attached to it and we wondered if we could pump you about it."

He has all the innocence of another Charlie Crew, was David's first reaction.

The colonel chimed in. A frightfully, frightfully staff college voice pronounced, "It's damned bad form to ask a fellow officer about his decorations, damned bad form."

The innocent waited for a moment, looked at the lady keenly following the conversation, and asked

"Would you think it bad form madam?"

"No, I wouldn't think so, provided it was asked in a polite and courteous manner. After all, he is your superior officer so could quite well tell you to go and jump in the lake if he wanted to."

The colonel took up the cudgels. "With the greatest respect Ma'am, this is a military matter about which one assumes civilians, especially female civilians, know little."

"Ah, but then colonel, having followed the drum all over the world for over thirty years I do know a little of military matters. I am Lady

Ironside. You may possibly have heard of my husband."

General Sir William Ironside was, at one time, chief of the Imperial general staff.

"My apologies, your ladyship." The colonel sank back into his corner and said no more.

"Well, carry on major," Lady Ironside indicated, "I, too, am anxious to know how a major got the D.C.M."

David told the story of when he was a corporal in The Rifles at Calais, how a tank, hulled down in front of them and blasting his platoon position, could not be seen by their only two pounder anti-tank gun. He climbed on top of it, lifted its access lid, dropped a grenade in and destroyed it. He concluded the story by saying that many other people did things of more merit than that at Calais; it just so happened his C.O. witnessed the event.

"You are Major...?"

"Chandler, Ma'am."

"I thought all the Rifles were killed or captured."

"Six of us managed to steal a boat and row back to England."

One of the gunners exploded, "Holy bloody mackerel – oh I do beg your pardon Ma'am."

"I've heard worse than that in many places and from far more senior officers than you in my time I can assure you young man."

The young man grinned.

The conversation becoming general, they at last reached Waterloo, all, including the colonel, shaking hands with David as they left.

The future bridegroom arrived home to a welcome which totally exhausted him. There were so many people there – even the children had been allowed to stay up until seven o'clock to see him. The person he would have most liked to have been there to welcome him was sadly, so very sadly, missing. In the morning he arose early and went to the churchyard to see his Pat and his mother. It was so difficult to reconcile the deep sadness of losing these two lovely people with the excitement, pleasure, jollification and union with another which he was to experience over the next few days. As he stood there deep in thought, Canon Rosser, clad only in slippers, slacks and a chunky pullover broke his reverie.

"Saw you from the study window as I drew the blackout curtains David old son."

He paused a moment. "Can I help?"

"No, I don't think so padre, no more than the sound of your voice always seems to help."

"In which case, fancy a cup of coffee?"

"I'll take you up on that, thank you very much."

The David Chandler stag party that night at The Angel was memorable, except that the following morning was equally as memorable in that few who were present could actually remember anything about it!! During the early part of the proceedings, having given Charlie a bear-hug which almost broke his ribs, David asked, "How did you get on with Emma?"

"David, dear old mucker, she is doubly gorgeous, compared to her photograph, doubly intelligent compared to her letters, and they were more doubly intelligent than any others I've ever received, she has the figure of a goddess, the wit of a farceur..."

"What's a farceur?"

"Someone who writes farces of course – I would have thought all majors would have known that."

"Well alright, so I've got the general idea. But what happened about the aristocracy lark?"

"Well there, dear old boy, I was a bit windy. In fact I kept leaving it and leaving it until it was almost time for me to see her off to Buckhurst Hill. Then I said, "Look Emma, I've something I've got to tell you. She looked at me, put her hands on my face, gave me a big kiss and said, 'I know already, your father is Lord Ramsford.' I was totally dumbstruck."

"I wouldn't have thought that word existed in your vocabulary."

"I was, as the thriller writers say, rooted to the ground. Well yes, I said, that was what I was going to tell you. You see, he and my Grandfather will be at the wedding and I would like you to meet them."

"What did she say to that?"

"She said, 'I wouldn't care if your father was the King of Bohemia or in chokey for fraud, if I fancied you that would be that. And do you know what she then said? 'Having met you after all that letter writing I really fancy you, and she gave me another big kiss. So, how about that?'"

"You're a jammy bugger aren't you?"

"Yes, and I owe it all to you, you got Maria to put us in touch with each other. And I'll tell you something, my battle hardened friend, you will know what it's like to sit in a fly infested slit trench in the middle of nowhere and get a lovely letter from a lovely person. She made my day time and time again."

"But how did she know about your father and the Earl?"

"Well, her parents have got to know the Schultzs, and they told Emma's father that he and Mrs Langham would be seated with Pater and Grandfather. Of course, they asked what the devil they were doing there and, I understand, were a trifle surprised to find they belonged to me, and I, sort of, belonged to Emma. They told Emma, Emma threatened to do me bodily harm for not telling her when we did at last meet and that was that."

On Friday, once they had surfaced and their eyes had opened sufficiently to peer through the mists enveloping them, the three warriors settled in a corner of the saloon bar at The Angel for a livener, and swapped stories of their escapades since they last met. In particular of the time when Charlie had manned a six pounder anti-tank gun on his own when the crew had all been killed, and had knocked out three Mark IV panzers at almost point blank range, loading, aiming and firing whilst all the time being plastered by the Jerries.

"I put him in for an M.C.," Mark said, "but so many did valiant things that day they could have decorated half the battalion, the half that wasn't already dead or wounded that is."

David sat back, saying to the world in general, "Who would have thought on that first day at Worcester Octu you would one day be one of the heroes of Alam Halfa, which made Alamein possible."

"Well, dear old sport, we've got more things to do in the not too distant future."

Mark concluded the exchange with, "We most certainly have," and they made their way back to Chandlers Lodge for lunch"

Chapter Twenty Six

On the flat plateau some twenty miles north-east of Camp Three, Harry's reconnaissance patrols had been watching P.O.W.'s building a landing strip near Kuala Lipis. In point of fact it was an extension to an original R.A.F. fighter drome, which had housed, like the remainder of the British air stations in Malaya, aircraft which were no match for the Japanese zero fighters and were wiped out in days at the start of the war. Since the strip was being extended and a concrete runway laid, it was obvious that the intention was to have heavy aircraft either stationed there, or at least landing there from time to time. Harry could see no strategic reason for this activity, on the other hand Kuala Lipis was sited in almost the exact centre of the Malay Peninsula, therefore if a central control point was established to operate against Allied landings on either the east or west coasts this might be as good a place as any. One of the two main rail links between Singapore and Siam ran close to the airfield, supplies therefore flown in could swiftly be transferred on to the rail system for despatch north or south as required.

This information was coded and the progress notified to Force 136 HQ in the Cameron Highlands and from there transmitted to Colombo. Harry kept regular four-day observation patrols of the progress of the work every three weeks, by this means giving his force some action to offset the boredom of camp life and training. At the end of September he decided to lead one of the patrols himself, taking Reuben Ault with him and leaving Tommy Isaacs in charge at Camp Three. As soon as he heard about this Matthew Lee asked if he could join them – he so rarely had an opportunity to get out of the camp 'for some fresh air' as he put it. As a result Harry, nine of his communist force, Reuben and Matthew started on their way north to make a big right handed sweep to reach some high ground in fairly close jungle overlooking the airfield site. Camping back in the jungle a mile or so from the observation point they brewed up and made up their beds and 'bivvies.' It was not a pleasant spot. They were only a couple of miles from the paddy at the side of the Jelai River, the home of a special breed of mosquito, which seemed, when you swatted one which had landed on you, just shook its head and flew off to plague someone else.

After two days of meticulous observation, working in pairs in three-hour shifts, they bedded down for the third night, preparatory to moving off back to camp the next morning. At first light, after a quick brew, they moved out, carefully checking no item of rubbish had been left behind and their tracks covered as best they could. The rain would do the rest.

Some ten miles from their camp they became particularly watchful. They had to cross a tributary of the River Lipis. It was easily fordable but at the ford a track from the north and one from the west met, to join up, cross the river, and head for Raub to the east, the same Raub where Harry and Bowlie had seriously damaged a gold mining installation back in June. The tracks were little used, but one had always to be careful.

Having forded the river without incident they followed a game trail which meandered in the general direction of camp three. After half an hour or so the two scouts ahead of the small column suddenly came to a halt indicating to those behind to be still. Harry moved forward quietly.

"What's up?"

"I heard noises around that corner."

About twenty yards ahead the game trail with thick undergrowth on each side, made a right hand turn. Harry crept forward to the bend, inching his way on until he could get a view of what was going on. Suddenly the rest of the patrol behind him heard him give a yell – something which normally would never happen in the jungle where you rarely, if ever, spoke above a whisper. With the yell he disappeared at a gallop round the bend into a small clearing, followed by Matthew and the other Chinese, who were astonished to see two wild pigs of ferocious size, and very dangerous, standing beside a seemingly dead leopardess, one pig holding a newly born cub in its mouth, the other about to grab another just being born. The mother, however, was not quite dead. As the pig made to seize the new baby, the mother used her remaining strength to claw the pig across its eyes and snout, totally blinding it and leaving it screaming with pain, running around in circles in the clearing. Harry quickly took a dart from his quiver, dipped it in his ipoh resin flask, and in seconds despatched the pig with his blowpipe. He always carried his blowpipe, in an emergency such as this it was silent, efficient and to those who had not witnessed its efficacy up until now, very impressive.

They approached the leopard slowly to ensure it was as dead as it looked. It had got a very bad bite mark on its spinal column near the tail, what from and whether this had caused its death, or whether it had died in giving birth, they had no means of knowing. Lying against the mother the new cub was wriggling around obviously trying to find something upon which to feed. Harry picked it up and laid it against one of its mother's paps, in the hope the infant would get at least one meal before the mother's body ceased to function. Greedily the little one suckled, the guerrillas looking on fascinated at a scene which they would never witness again in their lives, not, but for the exception of Matthew and one or two others, that their lives would be particularly long, most of them were to die in that jungle during the 'Emergency' after the war ended.

The bloated, tan-coloured, little bundle of fur eventually had enough and rolled over against its mother to sleep. Harry picked it up and slipped it into his bush jacket pocket.

"Let's go," he ordered, and they moved on past the dead pig to a comment from Matthew, "Pity we can't carry that, I could really fancy some roast pork."

And that is how Camp Three came to have a leopard as its mascot.

When they got back to camp Harry took his tiny passenger out of his pocket, who by now was searching again for food, endeavouring in the first instance to gain sustenance from Harry's little finger as he was removed from his sanctuary, but with no success.

"What do we feed him on?" Harry asked.

"All we've got is exasperated milk," Matthew replied, using one of Harry's standing jokes. "I think that might be a bit strong, so I suggest we water it down a bit."

"Righto, my post-natal expert, having decided that, *how* do we feed him?"

"How do you know it's a him?"

"At the moment sex doesn't come into it. I've got an idea – those French letters they dropped to us. If we get a piece of hollow bamboo, put the French letter on it, burn a little hole in the teat, we've got a feeding bottle."

The inclusion of the French letters in with their last air drop – not indented for whatsoever – had caused a mild hysteria among the Chinese, most of whom, as has already been recorded, Matthew believed to be a miserable lot of sods. Speculation ranged from: one, H.Q. believed we have comfort girls with us; or two, in the next air drop they would provide parachuting comfort girls; or three, we have trained up some compliant pigs or goats. Since back in Kandy, or Colombo, or wherever the loads were packed, the organisers listed these items at the head of their own personal shopping requirements they had in fact automatically included them in the loads, on the basis of their omission from their clients list being entirely accidental. As a matter of interest the items in question were undoubtedly manufactured by a maker of cycle inner-tubes, probably as a side line. They had the same appearance, were of the same thickness of material and the same tensile strength, these latter properties being of advantage when used to feed a baby leopard but doubtless rather off-putting to an amorous male bereft of shall we say, finer feelings (in the physical sense).

The news went quickly through the camp of the acquisition of a mascot, resulting in a steady stream of visitors wishing to see the little bundle of fur, completely helpless in its little padded box, and in particular to be much amused by the patent feeding mechanism, which had, in fact, to be operated every two to three hours. By the middle of October its eyelids opened to show a pair of vivid blue eyes which quickly began to take in its surroundings. It really was a quaint, loveable little animal, still possessed of a tiny body with outsize paws and a head totally out of proportion to the rest of her – it had been established she was a female by Matthew, now designated Chief Sexer. It was obvious she was to have a name, but what?

"She's got pretty blue eyes – what's that in Malay Tommy?" Harry asked.

Tommy Isaacs replied, "Pretty blue eyes would be 'Chantek biru mata,' but that's a bit of a mouthful for a name don't you think?"

"Well, if chantek means 'pretty' then we'll call her 'Chantek' – how does that sound?"

Tommy laughed, "As good as any I suppose." So 'Chantek' she became, to grow eventually into the most beautiful, most elegant mascot any unit has ever possessed – or at least that was Camp Three's opinion – but that was to be in the future. Camp Three had other things to do in the meantime, but until the next operation Chantek would sleep in her box or be carried around in Harry's bush jacket pocket without his being aware of the fact that the little animal was bonding to him to the extent that it was unhappy when she had to be left behind.

In early October, Sunrise had visited them and asked Harry if he could carry out a three pronged simultaneous op on three railway stations in a similar manner to those which had been done by Camp Six earlier in the year further south. They would be at Trolak, Sungkai and Bider, all stations being on the main west coast line to Siam and then Burma, and each one immediately adjacent to the main trunk road. He would like it carried out by the end of the year, now that the south western monsoon was more or less over.

Harry decided to set up a firm base some thirty miles north-west of Camp Three on the slopes of the jungle covered mountains overlooking, and some ten miles from, Sungkai. They would then patrol north and south to reconnoitre the other two objectives. Having made the two day journey to the firm base, they set up a small bivvy camp hidden away at the junction of two streams which eventually made its way from the mountain slopes down through flat, swampy jungle to the sea.

Choong Hong, the Railway Man now recovered from his wounds, had family in Trolak, where one of his uncles was a dentist. He suggested to Harry that if he and Chee Hong made their way to his uncle's house and lay up overnight they could make their way to the station at a reasonable time before the first north bound train arrived, in that time making mental notes of layout etc, which they would then immediately transfer on to paper in the confines of the station lavatory. They would then travel to the next stop, Sungkai, get off the train and go into the town for an hour, come back to the station and repeat the operation. Finally they would travel on to Bidor and complete the reconnaissance. It could all be done in a day having made an early start. No one would suspect two Chinese walking up and down the platform chattering away – Chinese did that all the time! Furthermore, with Choong Hong's previous knowledge of railway installations he would know exactly what to look for, as well as any peculiar or unexpected hazards which would have to be overcome.

Harry thought for a few moments. He was essentially a 'hands on' type of leader. He could, however, see that detailed, close-up information about each site would definitely be more advantageous than distant observation through field glasses. On the other hand there was always the fear that the two men might be stopped for some reason. With their carrying paperwork covered with sketches of key installations like railway stations the Kempetai would slowly but surely extract all sorts of information from them before they eventually killed them. Well, he decided, they mustn't get caught.

"Alright Choong Hong, we'll do it your way. I think you are very brave men, but you must abort everything if you think you have caused anyone to be suspicious of you. Is that clearly understood?"

Choong Hong looked steadily at Harry.

"Sir, would it be possible for each of us to carry one of your darts in case we are caught?"

Harry looked at the impassive face, a face so devoid of expression it could well have just asked him what time of the day it was. His stomach turned over at the thought of two people, of whom he had the highest regard technically, and as individuals, could end their days as a result of his developing his lethal plaything.

Choong Hong could read his thoughts.

"Sir, it would be better than being at the hands of the Kempetai."

"Alright. We will make up bamboo tubes to carry them in, you will have to fix them somehow in your waist belts." He paused a while. "I am beginning to think this is not such a good idea after all."

"Don't worry Sir, no one will suspect us, and we can do in a day, two at the most, what you would take a week to carry out."

Harry's usual sunny outlook returned momentarily.

"Well, don't get caught up with any beautiful women whose husbands don't understand them. I shall expect you back here in three days at the outside."

"Yes, Sir."

Harry, thinking about it later told himself, "And they actually smiled for once when Choong Hong said that," though whether it was at that which he had said, or whether they had got a couple of prospects lined up he could not guess.

"Well good luck to you my sons if you have," was his ultimate thought on the subject, "dirty rotten lucky devils."

During the three days the two comrades were away Harry was like a cat on hot bricks. He was essentially an action man, leading from the front. "I would never be any good as a general," he told himself. Generals had to plan sometimes weeks ahead, re-planning as circumstances changed before the day of the operation or the attack. They then had to go to bed and leave the whole shebang in the hands of others. General Montgomery, on the eve of the great battle of Alamein later wrote, 'In the evening I read a book and went to bed early. At 9.40pm the barrage of over 1000 guns opened. At that moment I was asleep in my caravan – there was nothing more I could do.'

You need a strange kind of heroism to function in that manner.

Harry was no Monty. He farted around like an old woman until just before darkness fell on the third day and his two man reconnaissance patrol returned, each to his total astonishment carrying a roll of close mesh galvanised chicken wire.

"What the hell have you got there?"

"We thought these be very useful to make house for Chantek Sir, she need one soon."

"Well, if this doesn't beat bloody cockfighting. You go off on a mission which could end up with you being cut up in little bits by the Kempetai and all you think about is a blooming leopard cub thirty miles away."

"That wasn't all we thought about Sir." With that Choong Hong pulled a flat rubberised waterproof container from inside his shirt, literally bulging with sketches. "We also brought these back Sir," he added, as the pair handed back their bamboo tubes containing their self-destruct darts.

Harry put his arms round their shoulders. "You'll never know how proud I am of you two," he told them. The strange thing was that the two communists could not decide whether to be pleased with the approbation and esteem of this officer-class white man who nevertheless had proved himself time and again in battle, or whether to shrug off the praise as capitalist flattery designed to produce even greater output from the rank and file.

Soon after dawn the next day they set off back to the camp, arriving just after midday on the 24th, to the news from Tommy Isaacs that 'Chantek has been racing around in her box for the last hour. She knew you were coming.' Harry picked her up and she nuzzled into the cloth of his bush shirt, her claws opening and closing in sheer delight.

"Haven't you grown while I've been away?" he asked her, "and have you been a good girl?"

Reuben and Tommy looked at each other, eyebrows raised, with Tommy saying, "He's got jungle fever at last." As he cuddled her up she started making a sort of coughing noise.

"Bit like wood being sawn," was Reuben's opinion. Harry was immediately concerned.

"She's got a cough," he said, stating the obvious. "Where's Matthew?"

Tommy grinned. "All leopards make that noise" he said, "they don't purr like pussy cats or roar like tigers, they have this throaty noise when they're pleased."

"Thank God for that. I was a bit worried for the moment."

"You know, you've soon got to wean her off your exasperated milk," (everyone in the camp gave it this name now – one of those silly things which catch on in an enclosed community, with little else to laugh at).

"What do they eat normally?"

Tommy thought for a moment. "They are carnivores of course. I would think if you could wing a bird and throw it to her she might play with it, and eventually take to eating it. With a bit of bully in between she should do well."

Harry was a great bird lover; he hated the idea of winging one with his blowpipe – not using a poisoned dart of course. But he couldn't get chickens, which would have been the best bet, so he decided he would concentrate on wild ducks of which there was a small colony on a lake some half-hour away.

"You are going to go for an hour to the lake and back, just to get a meal for your pet?" Reuben asked incredulously.

"It will be good exercise," was Harry's ludicrous reply. The Chinese thought he was mad, several of them volunteering to go with him!!

After having a shower he went to bed for a couple of hours

awaking at around 5.30 for a preliminary look through Choong Hong's sketches. They were first class. Besides the usual station buildings Trolak had a large water tower – a hole blown in that, or better still, one of the legs blown off, would cause problems to the F.M.S. Railway, or whatever they called it now.

At Sungkai there was a main postal station and telegraph office and at Bidar both of these alongside a large rubber godown. All very tempting. There was a lot of detailed planning to do, a lot of work on the ground with each team rehearsing the role given it, finally a scheduled date for the attacks. Harry decided it would be the weekend of 24th of November. On that same weekend Berlin would become the most bombed city of the war with 2300 tons on the Wednesday, 1000 on Friday, another 1000 on Saturday and another on Sunday. It was announced that over 10,000 were killed in the raids – the Reich really was reaping the whirlwind as Jack Hooper had forecast to David at the time of the Blitz on London.

Chapter Twenty Seven

When Major Fritz Strobel returned to Munich at the end of July, having cut short his proposed tour by not going on to Salzburg from Innsbruck, he telephoned Rosa's mother again. They spent four days together. On the first day Fritz called for Gita at a little after 10 o'clock and they spent the day in Munich 'acting like tourists,' as Fritz put it, except there were precious few tourists these days, their main overseas visitors before the war being from Britain. During lunch he suggested that Gita might like to contact Dieter's parents and arrange to meet them at the half way point at Augsburg station, a journey for both of them of roughly one and half hours each way.

Gita telephoned her sister – Dieter's mother – Rosa was Dieter's cousin – who suggested that she and the major may like to come on to Ulm and stay for a couple of days or for as long as they would like. The next day she gave Fritz this information who immediately fell in with the arrangement. They would travel on the morrow, Wednesday, and stay until the weekend; he would then get the Hannover train after seeing Gita off on the Munich one. Gita telephoned these arrangements to Elizabeth, whose final word on the subject was, "By the way, do I prepare a double room or two single?"

"We are not at that stage." A dramatic pause. "Yet."

They both laughed.

Doctor von Hassellbek and Elizabeth warmly welcomed their two visitors when they arrived at Ulm station. They drove out to the house in a four-seater barouche, the house sited close to the River Danube, so loved by David after his visits there to stay with Dieter before the war. However the two elderly servants who had so painstakingly looked after David during his visits were no longer there. Both had died during the previous year and it was no longer possible to get staff. As Frau von Hassellbek said, "You will have to put up with my cooking, though I do have a lady who comes in each day to help with the cleaning."

They enjoyed their stay. They spent a morning visiting the cathedral, a magnificent building dating back to 1377 possessing, as the citizens of Ulm were proud to claim, the tallest spire in the world. They walked the city walls, visited the beautiful Wiblingen Monastery where they saw the Rococco Library, truly one of the most magnificent rooms in the world with its magnificent woodwork, painted ceilings and exquisite statuary. In a years' time two thirds of this beautiful town would be reduced to rubble by allied bombing -- but then – who started it? The most bizarre aspect of Ulm's claim to international fame was the fact that its most famous son, Albert Einstein, was a JEW.

On Monday 7th August the couple were driven back to the city station, Gita's train due to leave for Munich at 1106, Fritz to Hannover at 1136. As Gita's train was sighted entering the station Fritz took her in his arms and kissed her long and tenderly.

"I will write to you and come and see you again soon if I may. I feel a new and very happy part of my life has begun in meeting you."

"Please do, as soon as you can. Tell Rosa from me how very much meeting you has changed my life. She will be happy for both of us."

In the tedious two hundred and fifty mile journey back to Hannover, intercepted on no less than three occasions by anti-aircraft fire attempting to bring down American Eighth Air Force Flying Fortresses taking advantage of the clear August sunshine to precisely attack enemy targets, Fritz thought with great warmth of his feelings for Gita. "You are not some love struck adolescent," he told himself, then dismissed that thought with, "No, you are an extremely love-struck forty-four year old, and at that age you cannot afford to waste time." He thereupon decided he would telephone Gita that evening when he arrived at his flat, provided he could get through – the long distance telephone system was a lottery as a result of the heavy and varied British night bombing of industrial centres. He would tell her that on his long journey home he had weighed in his mind every minute of his time with her and knew that he loved her very much. That was all. Did not expect a reciprocal answer in the same vein – no, leave that bit out, give her a chance to reply, see how she feels, might easily say ridiculous, perhaps it's not a good idea after all, yes it is, nothing ventured nothing gained, she certainly kissed me back with plenty of feeling, I'll phone her as soon as I get in, bloody bombing, doesn't give you a chance.

He did telephone her and was through in less than ten minutes. Her answer was clear and unequivocal.

"I had no idea I would ever love anyone again, but from that first day we met I knew there was something special between us."

"There is one thing we have not talked about at all."

"What is that darling Fritz."

"Suppose my gammy leg puts you off."

"If your gammy leg did put me off I would not be worth knowing in the first place."

"You are an angel, that was really worrying me. Goodnight dear, dear Gita."

The next day he watched from his window but there was no sign of Rosa. Nor the next. The next day it rained horrendously, she obviously would not appear to sit in the park in that weather. On Friday the weather improved but still no sign of Rosa. He began to really worry – suppose she had been sent back to the camp, suppose she was ill – she could easily catch something from one of her patients – Saturday was a blank. On Saturday evening Gita telephoned and he had to tell her that as yet he had not been able to meet Rosa. Immediately Gita assumed he was not well. He had to admit he was in good health; the problem was that Rosa had not ventured into the park. He went on quickly to reassure Gita that this was not unusual, she could easily be on night duty for instance. He knew perfectly well that Rosa was on call twenty-four hours a day, having an emergency at night would not preclude her having to be on duty during the day.

It was therefore with little hope he watched from his corner window on Sunday when he saw a white coated figure emerge from the rear door of the Klinik, walk towards the bench, and before being seated gave a stealthy look up towards his window. He leapt to his feet – well, he hung on to the solid mahogany table and pulled himself up at twice the speed at which he normally assumed the vertical – and made his way to the lift. Out of order again! He expressed an opinion about lifts in general and this one in particular at which his new love Gita might have been a trifle surprised in respect of the adjectives used, and descended the stairs in five minutes instead of the usual six.

As he approached Rosa he raised his hat, made a very visible request to be allowed to join her on the park bench, and then sat some three or four feet away in an endeavour to positively show the casualness of their meeting. Quickly Rosa told him she had been unable to get out for the past week. They had had an inspection by the party health officials, one of whom as a particularly obnoxious little man – "I'm sure he wears his swastika on his pyjamas," was her firm view of him – as a result Frau Doktor Schlenker had told her not to leave the building under any circumstances, the officials being aware that she was on loan from a camp.

"That didn't stop the nasty little pig asking me to go to his hotel with him on the night before they left. I told him I was on duty. He pinched my bosom and said 'what a pity – you don't know what you are missing.' I wonder why he is not in the Wehrmacht?"

"He probably knows somebody who will pronounce him unfit. There are senior doctors who will do that for people who can do them a good turn, at a substantial fee of course. However, in case we are disturbed I need to tell you quickly what has happened."

Looking away from time to time, smiling occasionally using his hands to illustrate some mythical point, all for the benefit of anyone, most improbably, but you never know, who might be watching them, he gave her an account of his visit to Munich and Ulm.

"What is the time?"

He looked at his wristwatch.

"Two o'clock."

"I must run. Tell me the rest tomorrow."

She ran back to the rear door, regaining her small room without having the misfortune to bump into the Frau Doktor. That evening Fritz sat down to commence the long, boring epistle to Dieter. After pages of 'do you remember all that fun we had shooting up the Polaks and then racing... Do you hear from... I believe his wife ran off... I lost touch with you... I hear you've got your Oak Leaves...' and so on and so on until even his inventive prose ran out and he gave up until the following evening.

At one o'clock the next day he again saw a white coated figure emerge, but – horror upon horror – accompanied by another white-coated lady, presumably the Klinik director Frau Doktor Schlenker. They sat in the sun talking, without once Rosa glancing in his direction, which he intelligently accepted as a warning to stay away. After half an hour or so they both got up and walked back to the clinic. He went back to add a little more padding to his already infinitely boring epistle, with the firm hope that by reading thus far Dieter would not have run out of patience and dumped it in the fire.

Considering his padding had now sent any censor off to sleep he continued:– "I had to go to Munich for my medical last week and I bumped into an old friend of your family – Gita. She's about to same age as me; we got on like a house on fire.

Her husband died a few years back as you may remember. Oh, and that girl you knew up at Obersdorf, I see her quite often. She is in good health and asked me to give you her kindest regards. I reminded her you were an old married man, to which she replied she was an old married woman, but still to give you her kindest regards.

Well, that's about all for now, my dear old comrade. Send a few Ivan's to their great Soviet in the sky for me.

Yours ever

Fritz

He had headed the letter 'Major Friedrich Strobel' in the hope that just that inclusion would automatically re-assure the censor that there was nothing for him to be concerned about. As it happened he could have headed it 'Winston Churchill,' it would have made no difference, it went through without being opened.

Dieter received the letter when he was in reserve, waiting for replacements for all the Tigers he had lost in the great battle of Kursk back in July. Kursk was the greatest tank battle the world had ever known, or would ever know for that matter. Some 3000 tanks were involved; operating in clouds of dust raised from the bone-dry steppes to the extent you rarely saw your target until you were on top of it. The German Tigers and the massive new Ferdinand tank destroyers blew the Russian T.34s out of the ground, but for every one of these killers there were four T.34s. The battle lasted five days, during which time the losses on both sides were so astronomical they found they had fought each other to a standstill. As a result Hitler, for the first time, gave the order to withdraw and set up a defensive line. Some five hundred tanks had been lost by the Wehrmacht, double that number by the Russians. Dieter had, time and again, led his regiment until they literally clashed head on with the enemy, until the time when his ever decreasing numbers were operating almost as individuals. Their recall to harbour and then retreat was logical, but they had lost the battle of Kursk. They would now begin the long retreat back to the Fatherland from whence they came.

He read the letter twice, at one stage almost tearing it up, thinking it was from some crank he had never met in his life. It was before he reached the Munich page he thought again – someone must have given him my unit and address. Only my parents and Rosa's mother would know that, and Inge of course, but she would be unlikely to know this chap. Then came the reference to Munich, which led him to believe there was something of significance somewhere between the lines he had not as yet spotted. Then he read about the girl at Obersdorf, and he immediately understood the reason for all the previous rubbish. He had met Rosa! It was at Obersdorf they had spent their honeymoon. Having read the letter a second time he hurried over to his colonel's tent. His colonel was of the old school, fervently anti-nazi but even more fervently anti-communism and Russia in particular.

"Sir, have you got a minute?"

"Certainly Dieter. What is it?"

"I wondered if you would mind reading this letter and giving me your opinion of its contents."

"Is it as salacious as all that? I haven't had a read like that in years."

Dieter handed him the envelope. Reading the name of the sender on the back he commented, "Strobel is an old army family, how have you got to know them?"

"I've never met the man in my life."

The colonel looked at him, slightly perplexed, but made no further comment until he had slowly and methodically read the ten pages of closely written waffle.

"This man's clever. Somehow he has met your wife – I presume the reference to Obersdorf makes that certain?" He looked up at Dieter.

"Yes Sir, we had our honeymoon there."

"Who is Gita?"

"She is my mother-in-law. But what is all that nonsense before that?"

"Cleverly designed to bore any censor to tears – a letter from a bone-headed old soldier to another equally bone-headed comrade. Very clever. The main thing is he is telling you your wife is well and must be in a state of some freedom if he has been able to talk to her at regular intervals. Now, if you write back to him, as I am sure you are dying so to do, you have got to be equally careful, more so probably, since your letters will most definitely be censored. Anyway, this is jolly good news, I am very happy for you."

Dieter was silent for a moment or two.

"Do you realise Sir, today is the day four years ago we moved into Poland?"

"Yes I do. Four years of war and where has it got us?"

The answer to that was left unsaid, each thinking of the hundreds of their men they had left in unmarked graves in the monotonous steppes of Russia. Multiply that by the hundreds from each of all the other regiments and you have a million. Add to that the Russian dead, vastly in excess of their fascist foes and you have say three million. Add to that the civilians!! God, where do you stop? Mostly thrown into shell holes and quickly covered by shovels or a bulldozer and you have the greatest necropolis man has ever created, without a single headstone to indicate where somebody's loved one lies. "And it isn't over yet by any means," Dieter thought.

He went back to his tent to plan out the reply to his 'friend' Fritz. 'Plenty of bullshit to start with,' he thought, so he gave a couple of pages about how their magnificent Tigers had blown the T.34s off the face of the map. He failed to mention the 250 mile retreat afterwards of course. Did he remember old Werner, the one who couldn't keep his hands off anything in skirts, 14 or 40, they were all fair game to him? The last he'd heard, the licentious blighter was going to marry a widow who owned a big hotel – and so on and so on. Having expressed the view that it would be great for Gita to have a friend like him, 'like many she has suffered so much,' he ended by mentioning the girl from Obersdorf. 'I can't remember her name. Was it Anna? or Ingrid? or perhaps Monika? oh, it doesn't matter. I know you are an expert on Shakespeare – or you were. With your thick head you have probably forgotten it all by now. Anyway didn't he say something about a rose by any other name would smell as sweet?' Whatever her name is therefore doesn't matter – I shall go to bed tonight thinking of her, even if I can't remember her name. Thank you for writing, please write again.

Yours

Dieter

Pleased with his literary work he sealed it and instead of giving it to his servant to take to the regimental post, he decided to take it himself to the unter-offizier in charge.

"You are just in time Sir; I am just off to Divisional H.Q."

Dieter therefore had the satisfaction of seeing his letter disappear into the mail sack, and the post corporal disappear, in turn, in his kuppelwagen, the thirty miles back to the Division H.Q.

He strolled back to his tent, a sense of euphoria engaging him at the thought that his darling Rosa was alive, well and had a friend who would keep him informed, if only superficially of her well-being. He had been living a life of constant fear, since her incarceration, that one day he would receive that dreadful notification, by one means or another, that she had died in the camp. How could his nation create such evil? Even more, how could his own sister be a part of it? The strange thing was, despite his hatred of the Nazi system, brought to head by their treatment of his dear Rosa, he still felt that fight against the Russians to be just and necessary, no way did it reduce his determination to destroy this vile communist system which would enslave the world. There were so many intelligent Germans who failed to see the wood from the trees, maybe because they were in an impossible situation to start with.

The letter took two weeks to get to Fritz. Having read it thoroughly he booked a call to Gita. There was a three hour delay, which in fact stretched into over four hours. Just before three o'clock in the afternoon Gita was about to leave the house to chance her luck at the shops when she was stopped in her tracks by the insistent shrilling of the hall telephone.

"I have received a letter from Dieter. He obviously has fallen in with our little ruse; so he now knows Rosa is fit and well. I shall show Rosa the letter today, assuming she can get away."

"Oh darling Fritz, oh, you are a wonderful, wonderful man. The mere fact that they each know the other is alive and well will mean everything to them, and it is all thanks to you. None of us, Dieter's parents as well, will ever be able to repay you." She cried a little, he did not interrupt.

After a short while he said, "But you have already more than repaid me by bringing fresh hope and love into my life. You just cannot imagine how low I felt at being deserted when I most needed help, and then having to face life as, at the very least, an encumbrance to others. Now that I have met you I have decided to do something with my life. Financially I do not have to work, what with my inheritance and my pension, but because of you I have made up my mind to do something useful. However, I shall not do anything yet all the time Rosa is here, we must make her the first priority."

"Thank you darling, please come and see me again soon," and then hurriedly, "I have plenty of spare room."

He hesitated a moment. "It's funny you should say that, I was just wondering how I could ask whether you had any spare room."

Her reply sent a shiver of anticipation down his spine.

"I don't somehow think we need a lot of spare room, do we? I certainly don't"

"I'll telephone you again tomorrow about Rosa, then we can arrange my visit. Goodbye darling Gita."

Rosa not having appeared that day, although he had sat glued to the window in case she had been delayed from her customary one o'clock routine until the telephone call to Gita tore him away, he went to bed that night, impatient at the fact Dieter's letter was being delayed from serving the purpose for which it was written. That was not the only thought going through his mind as may well be imagined. It was more than two years since he had slept with a woman. He had no fear his masculinity would be a problem, but would being limbless make him clumsy? Would his unsightly stump be repugnant at a time when everything should be idyllic? The frown on his forehead remained there until at last he fell asleep.

The next day was a Saturday, a fine, warm, September day, when many people were in the park either sitting or strolling in the sun or watching their children at play. At one o'clock Rosa appeared and walked towards her usual bench to find it occupied by a family of, she guessed, a grandmother, mother, and three quite small children. As she made to walk on the grandmother said to two of the children, "Now, stand up and let the Frau Doktor sit down." They guessed, presumably, that Rosa was a doctor as a result of her having her stethoscope tucked into her waist pocket, an item she normally never took outside the confines of the clinic.

They were very, very nice people. The children friendly and lively. They engaged her in conversation, offered her some beautiful home-made cake, there was no way without appearing rude she could get up and walk away. Fritz immediately appreciated her dilemma from his monitoring point and kept looking at his watch, calculating that if the circumstances did not alter in the next few minutes Rosa would have to return to the clinic anyway – another day wasted! His fears were obviously well grounded in that some ten minutes later the Frau Doktor took her leave of her new found friends, shaking hands with each, even the children, as is the custom. Fritz threw his hat, which he had been carrying throughout his surveillance; on to the sofa with a loud curse he would not have liked his Gita to hear. Another twenty-four hours!!

On Sunday he had better luck. Although a little later than usual, she walked to the bench, looking up continuously towards his window. He quickly took up his hat, still upside down on the sofa where he had slung it yesterday, hurried to the lift which today was not only working but was actually at his floor, and in five minutes was raising the aforementioned headgear to a smiling Rosa. He passed the letter to her, which she took with trembling fingers. As she read the script she had seen so many times before, written by the hand of her darling Dieter, she had difficulty in restraining her tears. Giving it a little kiss, and having read it through twice she handed it back.

"Thank you, thank you dear major." There was silence between them for a short while.

"Rosa, there are three things I wish to raise with you. Firstly, you do not wear your wedding ring. Why is that?"

"The S.S. in Ravensbruk took all our rings and jewellery, even our crosses, and threw them in a bucket. They said you will not need those any more."

"Are you saying these people STOLE your wedding ring?"

"They took everything. Clothes, watches, earrings, everything. We were stripped naked and had to stand there with the S.S. men watching until they gave us the striped prison clothes. We stood there, naked, for an hour while these lecherous louts made lewd remarks about the thin ones, the fat ones, the big breasted ones and so on. But that was nothing compared to what we had to put up with from the trustees. Half of those were lesbian perverts, the other half sadists, all chosen because of their predilection for other females. Anyone who was at all attractive, including myself, was repeatedly groped, assaulted, or at the very least propositioned. I had no conception there was such evil in the world. But enough of that, you said you had three things to raise with me."

"My stomach feels as sick as it has ever felt at what you have just told me. To think we, as a nation, have sunk to this level." He shook his head, fighting hard not to release tears trying to force their way out.

"Rosa, dear, I am so sorry."

"I've put that behind me now. What was point two?"

"I wondered if I wrote to Dieter and suggested he wrote to say

Monika Becker at my address. My address, because Monika lives with her parents while her husband is serving in Norway, and she would hardly want letters from her paramour to their address. You could then write back from there. Obviously you would both have to be very circumspect about what you say, but at least you would be in touch, however tenuously. I could give you paper to write on, and you could do it at night so that Frau Doktor Schlenker did not know of it. What do you think?"

"A marvellous idea. Oh you are wonderful. But I must go. Quickly, what is the third point?"

"Would you have any objections to becoming my step-daughter?"

Rosa, puzzled for a moment, cottoned on to the meaning behind the question. The penny, or in this instance, the pfenig, having dropped, she excitedly said, "No, no, no, a thousand times no. No objection at all, it would be simply wonderful. Have you asked my mother?"

"No, but I am going to Munich next week and I intend to. We have become very close over the recent weeks and we both need a loving partner."

"I must rush. I must never be late. It might spoil everything. Goodbye dear Fritz, or should I say step-father?"

She rushed off, smiling more widely than she had at any time since her arrest, nevertheless, losing the smile the minute she approached the Klinik. When you have been in a camp you quickly learn how to control your appearance and feelings so as to contain your anonymity. Being anonymous in a camp was often the difference between life and death.

Chapter Twenty Eight

It was the 25th of August 1943. Despite the monumental hangovers deeply seated in the crapulous craniums of most of the male members of the Chandler clan, along with their innumerable friends from far and wide, love was positively in the air in the fair town of Sandbury. At his court appearance on 19th July Karl had been accompanied not only by all the Chandlers, but Rosemary Gordon was very much in close and very welcome attendance. Elsewhere Rose and Mark were hardly ever apart for more than five minutes; Emma and Charlie were no sooner apart than they were on the telephone to each other. Cecely and Hugh, though more toned down than the others, were no less impassioned in their feelings for each other. Which leaves David and Maria looking forward to the great day with a mixture of feelings, all wonderful, that all young couples have on the eve of their wedding day. That afternoon the whole Chandler family moved off to a large hotel on the outskirts of Chingford looking out over Epping Forest, which Mr Schultz had, by dint of early booking, combined with the fact the owner was a very good friend of his and his family, combined also with the fact the owner and his wife had been invited to the wedding, had reserved en bloc from Thursday night until Monday morning. This arrangement gave an early indication of the lavishness he intended to demonstrate in respect of the wedding of his only daughter to the only man who could have raised him and his wife from the depths of despair into which they had sunk at the loss of their only son. The clan gradually gathered. The Lloyds from Carmarthen, the Cartwrights from Romsey, the Earl from Worcester, Paddy, Mary and the Maguires from Aylesbury, Charlie and his father, with whom he had been staying so as to be near Emma, and then all the Schultz family guests who lived at any distance from Chingford. Since all knew they were there for the same purpose they speedily got to know each other, as a result Friday evening became a pre-nuptial party. Hugh Ramsford quickly snapped up Cecely and Mrs Treharne and presented them to his father. They all dined together, along with Charlie, Emma of course being at home at nearby Buckhurst Hill to prepare herself for her duties as bridesmaid the next day, duties to be shared with a cousin of Maria's from Bury St Edmunds. It was noticeable that the Earl appeared quite taken with Mrs Treharne. He was normally a retiring sort of man, preferring his own company. This, in part, was due to the fact that, like most members of long standing aristocratic families, he was always conscious of people seeking to know him for their own benefit. He was always unfailingly polite to everyone, a quality instilled in him by his father in the days when egalitarianism was an unknown word, but rarely made deep friendships. He had done so with David's first wife Pat, with Rose, and particularly Ruth Chandler, being terribly upset at her death. Now he was here to see David's second marriage, to Charlie's surprise, who had certainly thought it unlikely he would travel up from Worcester for the occasion. And now, here he was, chatting away to Mrs Treharne as if he had known her all his life. Well why not, Charlie had always considered Mrs Treharne to be, what he called, an immaculate lady. No matter what clothes she wore she always looked as though she had stepped out of a bandbox – even, he had noted on one occasion, when she was gardening at The Bungalow. Her conversation too was bright and intelligent, with a mischievous touch from time to time illustrating a well-developed sense of humour. She had travelled widely, and unlike some people who go all around the world and see nothing, was able to converse in a well-informed manner without monopolising a conversation. Gradually she drew the Earl out until he found he was telling her of parts of his life about which he had totally forgotten. With his father and Cecely talking head to head, Charlie felt a bit out of it over dinner, nevertheless very happy that these two people who meant so much to him had found company with whom they could relax and share colloquy, not that he would have had the faintest idea of what colloquy was.

Paddy and Mary, Mary a little bit more pregnant of course, were listening to Eamonn Maguire telling Jack and Moira and several others the hilarious story of their 'transportation of the priest' after the wedding party at Aylesbury. Each time it had been told, and it had been told many times, Eamonn with his inherent Irish ability to tell a good tale, embellished it further, until now it was approaching the designation of odyssey.

Saturday dawned fine and dry. Maria's mother went into her daughter's room with a cup of tea at eight o'clock.

"Did you sleep alright dear?"

"I took a little while to get off, but then slept like the proverbial log."

Mrs Schultz drew the curtains back and lifted the blackout blind.

"It's a lovely sunny day. You've been blessed with a lovely husband and a lovely day to start your married life. Your father and I are so happy for you."

Maria wiped away a tear.

"I'm so sad that Cedric will not be here."

"His spirit is watching over you. It was through him you met your loved one. He too admired David and thought the world of him, as indeed David frequently told us he did of Cedric. When this evil war is over we shall all go to wherever Cedric has been laid to rest. He will never be forgotten."

Maria smiled, pressed her mother's hand, sat up and took the cup of tea. As we have noted before, tea is a peculiar substance, bringing solace to the downcast, energy to the listless, in this instance became a vehicle over which to think of the hours ahead before her union with her darling David – yet it was only the chopped up leaves of an evergreen shrub grown on a hill in India. I wonder if anyone has ever thought of chopping up privet hedges, there are plenty of those about!

The wedding was scheduled for 2.30. Maria, attended by the proudest father in the world who had ever given his daughter away to another man, arrived at the church seven minutes late, which according to the vicar chatting to David and his best man Mark, his brother-in-law, was par for the course – a keen golfer was the vicar. Now when I say seven minutes late, that was seven minutes late at the point in the road where the bride descends from the Rolls Royce which carried her from her home, to walk through the beautifully-kept churchyard along the path to the west door of the magnificent pale, elegant, chequer-board walled church of Chingford's Saint Peter and Saint Paul. Attended by her bridesmaids, who had been awaiting her at the lych-gate, they moved in a stately manner, watched from the road by a number of people who knew them not, but loved to see a good wedding. However, since this took a further three minutes, they were now ten minutes late. Entering the west door and turning right into the nave, Maria almost took fright. The magnificent nave seemed to stretch for ever it was so long. In the distance she could see the vicar dressed in his long white alb with a black stole hanging down from his shoulders, along with the backs of her husband to be and his brother-in-law, both in service dress uniform and Sam Brownes polished so that you could see to shave in them, – if you were a fella that is. On either side of the aisle, faces turned to the oncoming bride, a sea of smiles and the sorts of hats seen only at a wedding or, before the war, at Ascot. Beyond the priest, the choir looking expectantly down the nave from the chancel, trying to determine who would win the sweep, organised in the vestry, of the exact number of minutes late the bride would be at the finishing point – i.e. next to her husband to be.

As she turned into the nave, the beautiful tones of the Norman and Beard organ thundered out Wagner's wedding march drowning the soft undertones of whispered conversations of some three hundred people patiently waiting. In the beauty of the church, the occasion to which it was being lent, the care the congregation had directed to ensuring their clothing, uniforms and personal appearance matched the elegance of the occasion – one harsh touch of reality was in evidence. During the London Blitz a stick of bombs was dropped across Chingford Green. One fell in the churchyard, disturbing the dead who had the right to remain undisturbed, and at the same time demolishing the St Elizabeth Chapel alongside the nave. It seemed that nowhere in London, and in many other British cities were you far away from the evidence of war, war which in this case meant the draping of ugly tarpaulins to cover the damaged chapel until long after the war ended and the reconstruction could be effected. This beautiful church was probably unique in that it had been built and paid for – £5000 – in 1844 by the incumbent at that time. As Harry would have undoubtedly said had he been fortunate enough to be in attendance instead of raising his mug with Matthew Lee to toast the happy pair in a fetid jungle thousands of miles away – "That bloke must have been worth a bob or two."

Maria, on the arm of her, oh so proud, father, supported by two extraordinarily pretty bridesmaids, made her measured, almost regal way to the side of her husband – very shortly – to be. They smiled at each other through her veil, watched by the benevolent looking rector, his stole proudly bearing the campaign ribbons indicating he had been a services padre in the Great War, along with the debonair best man, he too wearing his ribbons from the Africa campaign.

The service was very beautiful, the mellifluous quality of the choir augmented by the substantial input from Megan's Welsh contingent, a reinforcement out of all proportion to the numbers involved. At last they were man and wife and had retreated to the vestry with seemingly an enormous number of people joining them to view the signing and witnessing of the register. At last all was complete and the signal given to the organist the grand procession back to the western end was to begin. Mendelsohn's Wedding March thundered out as a smiling Major and Mrs David Chandler led the procession out of the church into the churchyard for the inevitable photographs to be taken, as always by a fussy little photographer making sure that every detail was correct before diving under the shroud enveloping him and most of the camera. At last he gave the all clear and the final long procession through the churchyard to the entrance took place. As the newlyweds reached the lych-gate, Maria turned and tossed her bouquet to Emma, holding her train a couple of yards away. As it happened, Charlie too was close behind and as the flowers sailed upwards toward them he deftly moved in front of Emma, caught the bouquet in mid-air, and with a little bow handed it to her amid great applause from all, but especially from the Earl and Mrs Treharne.

The reception was held in a large marquee covering two hard tennis courts, with nets and fixtures removed of course, in the grounds of the hotel where many of the guests were staying, the general view expressed by Paddy, Eamonn and many others being they would not have far to stagger to get to bed. There was a long 'top-table,' seating all the important family people, the remainder of the guests being seated at round tables of eight or ten. The Earl, Lord Ramsford, Mrs Treharne and Cecely were on a table of eight, to be accompanied by Charlie of course and Mr and Mrs Langham, Emma's parents. When planning the seating Maria's parents considered this to be a shrewd move, they were very fond of Emma and considered it would do no harm for her parents to get to know Charlie's father and grandfather at a function of this nature.

Although no children were included in the occasion a table had been set aside for eight teenagers who had been invited, Mr Schultz reasoning that the young ones would be happier together rather than stuffed in with boring grown-ups. Greta was one of this number: sadly Oliver could not get leave. She was facing this part of the proceedings with a little trepidation in view of the fact she did not know the others. Greta was now fifteen years and five months. She was a very pretty, well-developed girl, with the social graces one would expect of a young lady from Benenden. Looking for her table card she found herself seated next to one of Emma's cousins, a tall blonde haired, very good looking young man, 'eighteen next month' she subsequently discovered. He was a little on the shy side. Emma soon established he had another year to do at Stowe, then to university medical school. His card read P. Langham.

"What's the "P" for?"

"Peter – Peter James Edgar."

"You're greedy – three names!"

"Actually my parents went mad. I've got four – they included the family name from my mother's side."

"What was that?"

"If you promise faithfully you will not breathe a word about it to anyone else I will tell you."

"Cross my heart."

"Ramsbottom."

"Truly?"

"Truly. It's a highly respected name up in the frozen north I understand."

"Well I doubt if many other people have such an assemblage of names – makes you sound frightfully posh."

And with that highly unsophisticated opening conversation was forged Greta's first real crush and the subsequent plethora of letters and telephone calls from one to the other. These things tend to happen at wedding receptions.

The reception being well organised by a professional toastmaster engaged by Mr Schultz – again one from his seemingly endless coterie of friends – the proceedings proceeded, the speakers spoke, the guests ate, and quaffed liberal quantities of the juice of the grape. It seemed impossible that only a week ago Maria had, on several occasions, driven from Deal to Dover through shellfire from across the English Channel. Already the East Kent Omnibus Company operating from Folkestone along the coast road to Margate had suffered fifteen drivers, conductors and conductresses killed and forty-five injured by the shelling, to the extent that the route was beginning to be named 'The Busman's Malta.' That south-east corner of Kent would not only be the target of continual shell fire, but in turn would be a major recipient of the noisome buzz-bombs – but that's another story.

After the guests had been thoroughly wined and dined, they were invited to take their leisure for an hour in the hotel grounds whilst the staff cleared the tables and made ready for the evenings' entertainment. During this time Maria and David would circulate among them. It was at this stage that the Earl stated that he really was too old to join in the fun of the evening, he couldn't dance to save his life, and that he had thought he would be better off in his room listening to the wireless. This plan was immediately, thoroughly and successfully scotched by both Mrs Treharne and Charlie literally grabbing an arm each and saying:–

Mrs T– "Oh you really can't go, I was so looking forward to a slow foxtrot with you."

Charlie – "You can't go grandfather, if you do we shall only talk about you."

The Earl looked at the smiling faces. He had not been in a position of almost being forcefully detained by two people who really desired his company for as long as he could remember.

"Well, I really couldn't be so curmudgeonly as to rebuff you now, can I? I shall consider it a privilege to join you all."

They had a super evening. At eight o'clock the newlyweds were scheduled to leave. They were seen off by a cheering crowd of well wishers who then, in the main, returned to the marquee where a small band and a first class young lady singer kept the party going. The Earl's professing he could not dance to save his life was somewhat exaggerated. Once he got into his stride, with considerable help by Mrs Treharne in her ability to change step when his dance pattern went a little haywire, he not only did very well, but as a result was tempted to repeat the enterprise on a number of occasions – to Charlie's total surprise who had never seen his grandfather let his hair down like this in all his life.

During the evening, while the band was having a breather, Charlie brought R.S.M. Forster and his wife along with Paddy O'Riordan and his wife to meet his father and grandfather. Lord Ramsford of course already knew Paddy. However when he shook hands with Mary he said, "I understand we shall be losing you soon."

"Yes Sir, as Paddy keeps saying, I'm a little bit pregnant." The company laughed at the quip, Paddy in turn thinking 'How the hell would he get to know a thing like that about one of his very junior staff in Sussex,' but then Paddy did not know that Lord Ramsford knew, and made it a point to know, everything about everybody in his firm.

"And you Mr Forster, along with Mr O'Riordan, here sporting these wings." The Earl pointed to the parachutists' wings on the right arms of the immaculate green and black pre-war service dresses worn by the pair. "I would have thought you two more than any others would have had infinitely more sagacity than to go jumping out of aeroplanes – the very thought of it gives me the willies."

R.S.M. Forster answered this pleasantry with a serious reply. "Well Sir, I sat at my desk in Winchester after Mr Crew and the others had left. I wondered what was going to happen to them, and I felt that other people were doing my dirty work for me. I spoke about it to Marianne, telling her there was a vacancy in the new division for an R.S.M. she said she would be proud for me to take it, so I did. My colonel, Lord Gravely, gave me a good recommendation and that was that."

"Lord Gravely? His father was my colonel in South Africa. Well I'm blessed. We used to call him Old Gravy Face – behind his back of course."

"And do you know what Sir? That's what they call this colonel at Winchester now."

"Oh, I say, talk about father to son! Has he any family do you know?"

"I understand Sir, that the younger son joined the R.A.F. and was lost over Germany. There seems to be what you might call a lack of knowledge of his heir."

Hugh Ramsford gave a quick glance and slight nod to his father indicating he knew what the situation was.

The band, having returned for the final session of the evening, the Earl said, "Well it's lovely meeting you both and your charming wives," shaking hands warmly with each in turn. After their departure, to the remainder of the assembled company he pronounced, "Do you know, with people of that calibre we couldn't possibly lose a war."

To which Charlie added, "Grandfather, you never spoke a truer word."

His grandfather turned to him, put his hand on his shoulder and said, "Yes, and people like you as well. Mark Laurenson has told me of your action at Alam Halfa, we are all very proud of you." Mr and Mrs Langham, joined by Emma as soon as Maria and David left, looked at the Earl, evidently not aware of the significance of his remarks.

"You hadn't heard about it?" queried the Earl.

"Not a word."

"Tell 'em Charlie, no false modesty, and none of that other material the army seems to dislike so much."

Charlie hesitantly told the story of his manning the six-pounder on his own when its crew had been killed, knocking out three panzers. He failed to include the fact he was being sprayed with machine gun bullets from the lap gunners on the tanks the whole time but ended up by saying, "Lots of people did more than I did on that day."

"I doubt it," was the Earl's definite judgement. Emma's eyes were brimming with tears as she held Charlie's arm tightly. Mr Langham, a Royal Navy veteran from the Great War, had until now thought Charlie a nice lad, but perhaps a bit immature. Any doubts on that score vanished on the spot, there's a lot more to this lad than meets the eye being his conclusion.

As the evening ended the Earl turned to Mrs Treharne. "Do you know I've been calling your Mrs Treharne all the evening. How ridiculously formal! Would you mind telling me your Christian name?"

She smiled at him, "Provided that you tell me yours."

"That's easily done. It's Christopher, known to my friends as Christopher – I hate being called 'Chris.' Since I count you as a very, very good friend, my expert dancing partner, my number one in the conversation stakes, I insist you use no other name. Now, am I to know the name of the lady who has been so kind as to provide me with the most enjoyable evening I have had for years?"

"Gloria."

"Gloria. What a beautiful name. And how apt. If my Latin does not escape me I believe it can mean a number of things, in particular 'resplendent beauty.' By jove, your parents were enormously far-sighted when they chose that name. Gloria! How marvellous."

"What's marvellous, Grandfather?"

Charlie had returned to find out what was delaying the Earl.

"Mrs Treharne's name is Gloria – don't you think it's a wonderful name and just suits her?"

Charlie had no idea of the significance of the connection between the lady and her name. He knew Mrs Treharne as being a gentle lady, sweet smelling and always impeccably turned out. But what that had to do with her name being Gloria escaped him. He reacted quickly.

"Yes, absolutely, absolutely." The Earl nodded. Mrs T knew he hadn't a clue as to what his grandfather was talking about.

As they walked along the garden path to the rear entrance of the hotel, the Earl having offered Gloria his arm, "Can't have you tripping over in the dark can we? Would you care to join me for breakfast in the morning?" he asked.

"At what time?"

"Say 8.30?"

"I shall look forward to it."

"I'll show you to your room."

As they parted he took her hand and lightly kissed her on the cheek. She responded by holding on to his hand, and kissing him lightly on the lips. It was the beginning of a really beautiful friendship between two older people who had thought that romance, however gentle or spiritual, had not deserted them.

These things tend to happen at wedding receptions.

David and Maria spent the first night of their honeymoon in London – making sure that nobody – but nobody – knew where. He had this peculiar idea that Charlie and Mark, not to forget Paddy and Eamonn, or for that matter Ernie and Jack, might dream up some jolly whizz-o prank to interrupt their nuptials. They had intended originally to spend the remainder of their time together, before the inevitable return to service life, at Bournemouth. David had booked the bridal suite at The Metropole, but on checking that all was confirmed in the middle of June was re-directed to another number, where a polite and solicitous young woman told him that The Metropole had been destroyed by enemy bombing at the end of May. As all the records had been lost they had been unable to notify forward bookings. She apologised profusely, at which David reassured her she was in no way to blame and how desperately sorry he and his fiancée were at their loss.

The Metropole, the Central Hotel and the huge department store, Bobby's, were all destroyed on that hit and run raid, by twenty-two Focke Wolfe 190 medium bombers who flew in on the Sunday lunchtime of 23rd May. Seventy-seven civilians and twenty-four service personnel, mainly Commonwealth R.A.F. flyers, were killed in The

Metropole. The numbers could have been vastly greater had it been a weekday when Bobby's would have been full of shoppers. Five of the attackers were shot down, but one wonders what military objective the Luftwaffe hoped to gain from pinpointing the centre of Bournemouth to attack?

A further problem arose at the beginning of July when the government declared from the Humber to Penzance and ten miles inland a regulated area. In other words you had to have a permit to enter it, or a pass if you lived in it. The reason was stated as being 'for offensive action.'

Left with the problem of 'where to go' – Maria had suggested a tent in Epping Forest if necessary.

David said, "They say Scarborough's very nice."

Maria had told him quite emphatically, "I don't care where it is as long as it has a large, comfortable double bed. You can be sure we shall see very little of its surroundings if I have anything to do with it."

"You are a wanton woman."

"Wanton and wanting as you will find out."

So Scarborough it was. The honeymoon was everything a honeymoon ought to be. They did see a little of the surroundings of the Royal Hotel at which they were based – a little – not a lot – before they reluctantly made their way back on the following Sunday. It was the third of September 1943. David had now been at war for four years. He had served in France, Switzerland, Germany, Egypt and the Balkans. Where would he be on the third of September 1944 – would it all be over then?

Chapter Twenty Nine

Oliver Coates who had been told to report along with his friend Gordon Fotheringham, to Bovington on the 9th June, completed his basic training in early September, arriving home for seven days leave proudly wearing the black beret of a tank man. Despite the fact that he was well built, good-looking, well educated, smartly turned out, and above all a tank man, he had so far been singularly unlucky in, or incapable of, pulling a bird, which was apparently the vernacular of his immediate and close cohorts. It had to be admitted that in a place like Bovington where there were probably fifty lusty squaddies to every unattached bird, you would find yourself on extremely competitive ground at the best of times. As a result he was eagerly awaiting his imminent descent on the killing ground of the fair town of Sandbury. Having arrived at The Bungalow he swiftly noticed his sister was actually receiving telephone calls. It was apparent that not only was he bird-less, but his younger sister on the other hand was starry-eyed man-struck by some twit she had met at David's wedding. For some unaccountable reason he thought this incredibly unfair in that while he was away fighting for his country, well, learning how to fight for his country, his sister should, behind his back, land on her feet. Not that he was jealous you understand, well not very, but as the elder of the two siblings it was his indisputable right to be the first of the two to score – (more of the Bovington vernacular). His initial research resulted in his discovering there was a dance in the church hall that evening. He asked his sister whether she would like to accompany him, hoping she would decline the invitation so as to give him more scope in the killing field. No such luck. She accepted.

"But wouldn't that be being unfaithful to your Fred or Bill or Joe or whoever he is?"

"His name is Peter. And anyway we're going to a church hall dance not to an orgy."

"You wouldn't have the faintest idea what an orgy is."

"When you are in the Upper Fifth at Benenden there are, my lad, few things you don't know, even if the knowledge is second-hand."

Oliver was beginning to get a very different view of his little sister to that which he had previously held. Greta asked her mother whether she could go to the dance with Oliver, her mother readily gave her permission on the understanding that she came straight home afterwards with Oliver. Oliver, overhearing this used further Bovington vernacular in saying to himself "That's buggered that up." He was firmly convinced that by the end of the evening he would be on a snogging exercise, now he was detailed to nanny his sister.

At the dance Oliver suffered further humiliations. Since there were some six hundred Welsh guardsmen a couple of miles down the road, and even more R.A.F. wallahs on the local airfield, a fair proportion of each station having decided they should investigate the same Sandbury killing field, he failed to stand out in his tank man's uniform as he had anticipated he would. In fact, quite the reverse, since as a buckshee trooper surrounded by guards sergeants, R.A.F. in collars and ties, even the odd pilot, navigator and so on, he became relegated to the sidelines. Another problem was, on arriving at his first dance, he realised he did not know how to dance properly. He could shuffle around the floor with a compliant amateur partner, but here it would appear all the girls were budding Ginger Rogers and the men, if not Fred Astaires were certainly attempting to be. To cap it all, since there were at least two men for every female, Greta was seized upon for every dance and showed a degree of competence in the quick-quick-slow stakes as proficiently as any of the other girls.

"Where did you learn to dance?"

"We had a thorough grounding at Benenden. Girls have to be comprehensively equipped socially before they leave to go out into society. That includes knowing how to dance. Didn't they do that at Sevenoaks?"

"No, we just had to be good at rugger."

"Well, I'll teach you the basics tomorrow. Mrs Treharne has got a gramophone, though whether she will have any dance records I don't know. If not we will have to buy one."

Oliver's ego was marginally saved from total disaster by his passable attempts at the waltz, as a result he was not the complete wallflower he might have been, but it was a salutary lesson – never count your chickens etc etc.

While the two youngsters were at the dance, the telephone at The Bungalow rang, being duly answered by Mrs Treharne. It was Hugh Ramsford.

"Good evening Mrs Treharne, how are you?" followed by the usual pleasantries involving the state of the weather, no problems with air raids? – there had been activity at Sandbury the previous week – "Have you spoken to my father recently? If so you probably know he has just gone up to Scotland for a few days."

Mrs Treharne failed to mention that Christopher, as she now thought of him, had asked her if she would care to join him but she had had to decline the invitation as she had a hospital appointment which she felt bound to keep.

"Do you know," she had told the Earl "you now have to wait a whole month to get another appointment with a consultant – a whole month!" Answering Hugh she replied,

"Yes, we spoke only a few days ago. Now, I expect you will want a few words with Cecely," thinking 'and that's the understatement of the age!'

"Thank you Mrs Treharne, good evening to you." Mrs Treharne went into the sitting room where Cecely was listening to the wireless.

"Your paramour is on the line."

"Oh, I thought it was yours!" Mrs Treharne's leg had been pulled since the wedding not only by Cecely, but also by Fred and Jack quite mercilessly.

"Do we address you as 'Your Grace' yet, may I ask" – from Fred.

"Have you ordered your coronet Mrs Treharne?" – from Jack.

Cecely took the receiver.

"Cecely, I have some quite disappointing news for you. As you know the Japanese agreed back in January to open a postal service via Switzerland, from the U.K. to civilian internees. They also promised the Red Cross a list of names of all civilians held in the camps in Malaya and elsewhere. They have, I am very sad to tell you, reneged on both of those promises. I have been to the Foreign Office today to see if I could find out more but there is a complete blanket on any information about civilian internees, and for that matter P.O.W.'s as well, as to where they are and what they are being required to do. I'm very sorry my dear, terribly sorry."

Cecely was silent for a little while, Hugh not interrupting the silence, but allowing her time to compose herself.

"Thank you, dear Hugh, you are a very thoughtful man, I do appreciate your concern."

They talked on for a few minutes, Cecely then returning, to the enquiring look from Mrs Treharne.

"Bad news dear?"

"No, not really, just no news. They say no news is good news. That's all very well I suppose, but my 'no news' means I don't know whether Nigel and his brother are alive or dead. How can those evil swine not let us know what is happening to our loved ones. They have been incarcerated now for nearly two years. I do hope that when we finally defeat the nasty little yellow pigs we make them suffer as much as we have suffered."

But they did no such thing, the Americans saw to that. They built Japan up as a bulwark against communist China, just as they did the Germans against communist Russia. Justice did not come into it.

The two ladies sat reading for a while until Mrs Treharne put her book aside, Cecely following suit surmising her friend was about to address her.

"I was wondering whether we could have my grandchildren home for good. I know we would be rather crowded when Oliver is on leave, but I'm sure we could manage."

Mrs Treharne's grandchildren, Patricia and Eric, were orphaned when their parents, Mrs Treharne's daughter and doctor husband, were killed in an air raid on their home in Hampstead. She went on.

"I know they are well settled in Wales where they were evacuated before the bombing, but Mrs Davies, who took them in and has been very kind to them, is not so well, and unlikely to get better. It would be a wrench for her to lose them and for them to have to leave, but it is beginning to look inevitable."

"How old are they?"

"Patricia is nearly eleven, Eric is nine. They have been there for two years now."

"Look, Greta goes back to school on the 20th, why don't we take a few days in the following week and go and see them. If we can drop a line and ask Mrs Davies to make a reverse charge call to us, perhaps we can ask her to get us put up at a local pub for a few days. If they are coming to stay here it would be good for them to have some time with us, the parting from Mrs Davies will be pretty dreadful for them."

Tens of thousands of children all over Britain were facing this parting at this time. Now the major bombing raids would appear to be over, gradually the drift from the country back home to the cities began. The whole gamut of exchange of circumstances would be experienced. Children evacuated to wealthy homes having to return to squalid slums, from brutal domineering households back to happy-go-lucky homes, from farms where mud was an every day factor to homes where a speck of dust was alien, and in many cases returned to homes where mother and a strange 'uncle' lived together while their father was serving overseas. It was a terribly traumatic time for many, many children from which a number never ever really recovered.

Mrs Treharne agreed wholeheartedly with the plan, wrote a note that very evening and got Greta to pop it up to the G.P.O. first thing on Monday morning. On Wednesday evening, the 20th, the day upon which Greta had returned reluctantly to Benenden, Mrs Davies telephoned. She was quite upset at the fact of losing the two children. They had got on so well with her two; it really was one big happy family. But her 'problem' – she never did tell them even when they were with her what her 'problem' was – meant she was 'slowing down' as she put it, so that even looking after her two, with her husband away in Africa, was as much as she could manage. When asked about being put up in the local pub she said she would arrange that with Mr Williams the landlord. It was decided therefore, that the visit would be made the following week arriving on Tuesday and leaving on Saturday, taking the children with them.

"And that," concluded Cecely, "is not going to be easy."

That evening Fred called in to see all was well – he usually called in on one or two evenings each week on his way home from the factory.

"I'll take you to the station" he told them.

"How shall all three of us get on your bicycle?" queried Mrs Treharne. In these petrol exiguous times Fred's main method of motivation was pedal power, in common with most others, except those of course who had contacts with the black market.

"I shall bring the Rover and you shall go in style. By the way, whilst you are in Wales shall you be calling at your future country seat?" He and Cecely grinned at each other.

"The Earl is away in Scotland."

"Yes, but if he knows you are going to be within a stone's throw of Ramsford Grange he will without doubt hire a special train to bring him back – don't you think so Cecely?"

"Indubitably."

"That's a posh word for not half," Fred added, as he recovered his bicycle from where it leaned against the porch, and peddled away.

"He's a lovely man," said Mrs Treharne.

"Which one, Fred or Christopher?"

Mrs Treharne pondered for a moment. "When I think of it, they are both among the nicest people I have ever met. Oh, what a shame, what a terrible shame that our dear Ruth is not with us, I so often think of her and how Fred and Rose must miss her. When I think of all the help she gave to me, to you, to Anni, to Karl and dozens of others I feel so sad."

They walked back into the bungalow. As they passed the telephone in the small hallway it shrilled out, literally making Mrs Treharne jump.

"Sandbury 306."

"There is a call for you from Scotland." There were some weird clickings and buzzings for a few seconds before a very welcome voice asked,

"Is that you Gloria?"

"It is I," she answered, adding mischievously, "you notice I use the correct grammar when talking to a peer of the realm?"

"I'm so ignorant, I would hardly know the difference. Now, how are you and what are you up to that you can tell me about without compromising yourself."

They chatted awhile, Cecely having made herself scarce, until Gloria told him that she and Cecely were going to New Radnor on the following Tuesday to see her grandchildren and then bring them back to Sandbury for good.

"Now look, have you bought your tickets yet?"

"No – we are going up to the station on Friday or Saturday."

"Right then, I am coming home on this Saturday. How about your booking to Worcester and I will pick you up on Tuesday and drive you to Radnor, it's only an hour or so away. Then when you come back – you say on Saturday week – I will pick you up, you can visit here for a night or two, and then I'll put you all on the train at Worcester again on say Monday afternoon and arrange for Hugh to meet you at Paddington to transport you to Victoria. How does that sound? You are bound to have a few bits of luggage the children have collected in the last couple of years so you will probably need a hand."

"Christopher, you are an angel."

"Many things I may be my dear, but I can positively assure you an angel is not one of them."

"I shall confirm it with Cecely. I am sure she will be able to fit in the extra couple of days. I shall look forward so much to seeing Ramsford Grange; our dear Pat told me so much about it. Are the kingfishers still at the lake?"

"Yes, they are still there – fancy your remembering that."

"Pat said seeing them in the half light was one of the most beautiful moments of her life."

"Isn't it sad? Well, I will ring you when I get back to the Grange. Goodnight my dear, goodnight."

"Goodnight dear Christopher."

She went into the sitting room, excitedly telling Cecely the news and asking whether she could manage the extra days.

"I think you should go on your own, I've heard about those four-poster beds they have at Ramsford Grange."

"Away with you. Can you manage the extra days?"

"Yes of course. I have had no holidays yet and we are not busy at the moment. Mrs Draper will be able to cope with the help of the new junior sales we engaged."

"What about Susie?"

"I'll ask Rose if she could pop in night and morning to feed her. She has the cat flap on the door so that she can get in and out – the cat that is, not Rose."

So it was arranged. The two ladies duly arrived at Worcester only half an hour late, surrounded by hundreds of American troops being disgorged from the carriages, the private soldiers each seemingly carrying as much kit as a four star British general would encumber himself with, so much so that the figure of the Earl was not to be seen at first, until the stentorian voice of a porter called out, "Here my Lord, here they are." At this, a number of the G.I.'s turned to stare at their first sighting of a real live English Lord, finding him to be very ordinary looking but definitely something to write to the folks back home about.

"Welcome to Worcester." He took each one's hand in turn and kissed their cheeks, again to the considerable interest of the watching men, one of whom was heard cheerfully to call out,

"Give 'em a proper hug buddy."

The Earl smiled in the general direction of the would-be advocate, the porter picked up their bags and they moved slowly through the throng, through the mountain of luggage to the estate car waiting in the forecourt where they were introduced to the Earl's agent, Captain Morgan. It was a most pleasant drive to New Radnor through Bromyard and Leominster. They arrived at Mrs Davies's cottage just after four o'clock, and were greeted by two excited youngsters running out to meet their granny. Mrs Davies followed more slowly. The Earl had whispered to Gloria, "Introduce me as Mr Crew – it saves a lot of confusion."

"Mrs Davies, how lovely to see you, this is our friend Mr Crew, who kindly collected us at Worcester." The introductions being made, Mrs Davies asked them to come in for tea, but the Earl excused himself and Captain Morgan on the basis they had to get back to Worcester. 'Not only that,' he thought, 'she probably hasn't catered for two extra anyway.'

"Now where can we drop your cases off?" he asked.

Mrs Davies answered, "At the Rising Sun, Mr Williams is expecting you."

"Very well, we shall do that, and wish you goodbye Mrs Davies. Now Gloria, we shall collect you and the children on Saturday as arranged. Goodbye ladies."

He and Captain Morgan raised their hats, got back into the car and were waved away by the little assembly.

Over the next three days they walked the four children to and from school each day, which entailed their getting an early, and enormous, breakfast from Mr Williams, and which combined with the gargantuan evening meal he provided left them with no desire to eat in between. On

Friday the children were having to say goodbye to their friends of the past two years. Gloria and Cecely realised this was going to be the first of their agonising partings, so they had arranged they would have a special treat for their tea at Mrs Williams's that evening. During the day they caught the bus into Llandridnod Wells and bought a large cake with icing on, with the names of the four children piped on it in red. When they returned to collect their charges the whole school of twenty-four pupils, less Gloria's grandchildren, tumbled out into the playground, were lined up in two files at the gate to receive their departing friends. Patricia and Eric, led to the door by the head teacher, (as there were only two teachers at the school presumably the other one would have been the deputy head?) threaded their way between the two lines to loud cheers, much back slapping, and not a few tears from a number who had become close companions. As they emerged from the school gate they waved back to the cheering crowd, took the hands of their grandmother and walked away crying. It is true that Eric manfully tried not to cry but even he had to surrender to his tears for a while

The next morning at ten o'clock the station wagon appeared again, containing only Captain Morgan. This time everyone, with the possible, only just possible, exception of Captain Morgan, descended into tears. With three, perhaps three and a half, adults and four children indulging in a degree of lamentation not seen in New Radnor since Wales lost to England at rugby in the year before the war, it was relief to all when at last a grim-faced captain had stowed the luggage and headed out towards Leominster. A little over an hour later, the ladies in the meantime having as surreptitiously as it is possible to be surreptitious in the confines of a station wagon, repaired the damage caused to their respective images, they drove up the long drive to the beautiful, imposing Ramsford Grange. The Earl had obviously been watching for them since by the time they swept up to the front door he was already waiting at the top of the steps.

The two ladies were awe-struck, but not as awestruck as the two children. Eric blurted out, "Do you live here all on your own Sir?"

The Earl said, "Well yes, with a couple of people to look after me."

"Don't you get lonely Sir?"

The Earl's smile left him for a moment.

"Do you know Eric – it is Eric isn't it? – I do at times. I think you are a very clever young man to think of that. Do you think I ought to have someone else to be with me here so that I am not lonely?"

"I think that would be a jolly good idea Sir."

"Perhaps I should put an ad in the paper."

"Oh, I don't know Sir, you might get anybody then."

"Eric, you are wise beyond your years. Now come on in all of you, come on in, lovely to see you. What a lovely day it is to be sure." The tears of the morning had been left behind. Children are very resilient, which does not mean they forgot Mrs Davies's two offspring, in fact they talked fondly of them often in the following days and months.

On Sunday, it was the 1st of October; they decided they would attend matins at the ancient church of St John in the village. "Although as I remember saying to dear Pat, our pews do not see us very often these days," the Earl remarked. It being a crisp, cool but dry day, they elected to walk the mile or so, hurrying their pace a little when they heard the first bell. When they arrived, the Earl being greeted most civilly by others who nevertheless would be wondering who the two elegant ladies were along with the children. They would not, of course, have to wait too long to find out, the two elderly man servants who had waited on them at dinner the previous evening and at breakfast this morning would be having their Sunday pints in the Ramsford Arms in an hour or so. News travels fast in small villages.

Outside the church they had noticed an American forces jeep, but took little notice. However, on entering the porch, they were greeted by the senior churchwarden to be conducted to their private pews, only to find to the churchwarden's embarrassment they had been occupied by two clean-cut young army officers.

"I'm sorry, my Lord, perhaps I can ask them to move?"

The senior American overhearing firstly 'my Lord' and then 'to move,' immediately rightly concluded they were in someone's seats, and the someone was a Lord no less. He nudged his companion to get up. Quickly the Earl checked him.

"Please, please don't move, there is ample room for all of us."

The service pursued its gentle, harmonious way through the psalms, hymns and gospels, to the sermon, during which a specific welcome was given to 'our American friends, here to join us in the great adventure we all know lies ahead,' to the final hymn and the parting handshake at the porch doorway – "How is Lord Ramsford, my Lord, and young Charlie?" the Americans following close behind eager not to miss a word of what was going on. When they reached the clear space beyond the west door the senior of the two approached the Earl.

"I am Captain Radzicki Sir, this is Lieutenant Tremain. We would like to thank you for letting us join you today. We were just driving by when we heard the church bell and decided we would like to spend an hour here."

"You are most welcome. Allow me to introduce us. I am the Earl of Otbourne, these are my friends Mrs Treharne and Mrs Coates, this is Patricia and this is Eric, grandchildren of Mrs Treharne."

They shook hands in turn.

"Lieutenant Tremain – you must come from Cornwall," Gloria suggested, "It is a very well known name there. We Cornish people are very special, lots of names beginning with TRE down there."

"Is that so ma'am," the younger man replied. "I am afraid I know little of my family tree, my parents were killed in a rail crash when I was three, so I was brought up by foster parents, very kind Christian people they are, but know nothing of my family."

"Well now," the Earl suggested, "would you care to join us for lunch. Being Sunday it will only be cold platter with some soup and cheese but you are most welcome if you have no other plans."

The pair answered in the affirmative in unison! The thought they would be writing home having had lunch with a real live Earl was something they had never contemplated in their wildest dreams since they landed at Liverpool six months ago.

"We will be too many for the jeep Sir – by the way how do we address you Sir?"

"Sir, will do fine."

"We will be too many for the jeep Sir, would you and the ladies like to jump in and I will walk with the youngsters?"

The Earl glanced at the ladies, they shook their heads slightly – the last thing they would want would be to have their hair blown about in an open jeep.

"No, you give the children a ride around the park, we shall enjoy the walk. You will see the entrance just a couple of hundred yards along on the left."

"Right. Jump in kids. Ever been in a jeep before?"

"No, never," they chorused excitedly.

Off they went, waving furiously, the congregation of St John, Ramsford, having the unusual experience of seeing their liege Lord waving back equally as excitedly until they disappeared into the Grange.

The lunch was a convivial affair, supplemented by a trio of bottles of wine brought up in honour of the occasion. "We have no scotch left I'm afraid, and it's difficult to get."

"Sir, I would have thought there would have been little difficulty for what I believe is known as a peer of the realm?"

"The war makes equals of us all, captain. You can get stuff on the black market I am told, we would not countenance that."

"No Sir, of course not."

As they spoke the door from the main entrance hall opened and who should walk in but Lord Ramsford, in uniform, showing his decorations and parachute wings. Immediately the two Americans sprang to attention.

"Please, please carry on, don't let me interrupt."

Cecely likewise had stood up and moved towards him. "Hugh, what are you doing here, how lovely to see you." He took her elbows and kissed her on both cheeks, moving to Gloria and repeating the operation.

"Hugh, let me introduce you. We met these two gentlemen at church of all places. Captain Radzicki and Lieutenant Tremain." Hugh shook hands with the two men. The Earl continued, "This is my son, Lord Ramsford."

Holy smoke, Radzicki thought, we're getting two Lords for the price of one – no one will believe us.

"And these young people are Mrs Treharne's grandchildren, Patricia and Eric. They are going home to stay at Sandbury. Now, have you had lunch?" The brigadier shook his head. "Right, Thomas," to one of the two man servants waiting on them," another place please," quickly provided by Thomas who had anticipated the probable need and was half way towards satisfying it.

"Right now, what are you doing here?"

The brigadier told them he had spent Friday and Saturday at Ringway, was on his way to Bristol to meet some American colleagues "who I understand have taken over the best hotel in the city."

The inevitable comment from the Lieutenant, "That figures Sir, that figures."

Hugh gave one of his rare smiles at the observation and continued, "Since I had been informed you had highly prized guests here I extremely fortuitously lost my way, or at least my driver did acting on my instructions, as a result I found myself by the gates of Ramsford Grange."

"And if you believe that you will believe anything," laughed the Earl, "particularly since," he added, addressing the Americans, "he has hunted every square yard of the country around here for miles and miles before the war, and knows it like the back of his hand."

"Well that's my story and I'm sticking to it."

The Americans were astonished at the conviviality they were enjoying with their host. The ladies added to the repartee; even the children, unused as they were to 'grown-up' conversations, sat in wonder at all these very important people talking to each other, and to them. Like most Americans, these two had been led to believe, and on occasion experienced, the aloofness of the British upper middle and higher classes before they had been properly introduced. Technically, the United States was a classless society, or so they all vouchsafed, a man could call any other man 'Hey, buddy,' without offence. It would be unknown for a British working man to address a gentleman wearing a bowler hat and carrying an umbrella with 'Hi, mate!!' On the other hand there is a lot more to class than freedom of address, you can be poor in Britain and have class, in America to have 'class' you have to be rich.

The lunch over, the Americans made their farewells, the children going with them to the front steps and running after their jeep for a few yards as they drove away.

"I'm going in to listen to the wireless, would you care to join me Gloria?"

"Yes, I could do with putting my feet up for a while after those walks to the church and back this morning."

"I thought I might take the children down to the lake," Hugh said "would you care to join us Cecely?"

"Very much, perhaps we shall see the famous kingfishers."

And so the afternoon passed as pleasantly as any Sunday afternoon could pass, with Christopher and Gloria sitting close together on one of the luxurious sofas in the wireless room, although strangely the wireless did not appear to be emitting any form of broadcast, with the children racing around, occasionally holding a hand of either Hugh or Cecely as they excitedly made comments or asked questions, Hugh and Cecely themselves walking arm in arm until they were out of sight of the buildings, when Hugh slipped his arm around his companion's waist as she snuggled up to him.

Very early the next morning an American jeep appeared at the tradesmen's entrance to the Grange with a small, wrapped parcel, addressed to the Earl. It was placed on the side table in the breakfast room. When the Earl opened it, it contained a bottle of Jim Beam whiskey and a bottle of Southern Comfort, along with a little note.

"Sir, sorry even we can't get any scotch at the moment. Thank you for yesterday. Radzicki and Tremain."

There is a sad end to this episode. Captain Ray Radzicki was killed in the water on the edge of Omaha Beach some eight months later, Lieutenant Cyrus Tremain at the Battle of the Bulge in the Ardennes the following Christmas.

Chapter Thirty

David returned to Bulford on Thursday 5th September on a day that produced nothing but pouring rain all day long. Angus met him at Andover with a P.U. and all the gossip from the battalion, which included the fact that a couple of Canadian lieutenants had been posted to them.

"You wouldn't know their names I suppose?"

"There's a Mister McLeod and Mister Patterson Sir. They seem very nice, quiet sorts of officers, but then they would, wouldn't they, both being descended from Scottish families."

"I would have thought the opposite might have applied, judging by some of the hell-raising jocks I've met in my time."

Having reached his quarters mid-afternoon he decided to stroll over to his company office, bumping into Paddy on the way, receiving as military a salute as any officer anywhere had ever received, along with the observation, "Your shoulders seem a bit more rounded then they were, so they do, Sir, but we'll soon cure that."

"Cheeky bugger. Now have you met this Mr Patterson?"

"He's been posted to us Sir, the young second lieutenant we had has been grabbed as assistant adjutant, something to do with the fact he was a trainee solicitor."

"Have you said anything to him about Amanda One?"

"Not a word Sir, not a word."

"Right, we'll have a bit of fun with him. Where is he now?"

"In his platoon hut, Sir, we couldn't do much outside in this weather."

"True, on the other hand we've fought in weather worse than this."

"And will again Sir, I expect."

"Well, send a runner and ask Mr Patterson to come to the company office."

David made his way to his office while Paddy organised a runner. Well it wasn't so much a case of organising anything, it was a case of grabbing the first private soldier who chanced to be passing at the time to go to Five Platoon hut and tell Mr Patterson to report to company office straight away. Lieutenant Patterson duly arrived, stood in front of David's desk, saluted, remained at attention. David got up, came round the desk past a straight faced sergeant major, did a complete circuit of the somewhat puzzled Lieutenant Patterson and returned to his chair.

"Tell me Mr Patterson, how old are you?"

"Twenty-three Sir."

"Are you sound in wind and limb?"

An even more mystified lieutenant answered, "Well yes Sir, I would have to be to be here Sir, wouldn't I?"

"I see. And tell me, are you sober and industrious?" Paddy nearly blew a gasket.

"Well, yes Sir, I think so."

"Finally, do you spend your money on licentious living?"

"No Sir, of course not. There's not a lot of scope for that on Salisbury Plain."

"Ah, so you have already found that out?"

"No Sir, I mean, I haven't had the opportunity to find it out. I mean, even if I wanted to which I don't."

David looked at Paddy, "Do you think he's passed?"

"A.1. Sir, I would say."

The look of baffled bewilderment on Lieutenant Patterson's face was comical to behold.

"Right Sandy – it is Sandy isn't it?"

('How the hell does he know that?')

"Yes Sir."

"You may now like to have a pew, and we will tell you what this is all about."

Sandy sat himself on the only other spare chair in the office, thinking to himself, the pair of them are right round the bend.

"You see, Sandy, we happen to have a sort of ward whose interests we, Mr O'Riordan and I, are pledged to look after. This ward is very pretty, very intelligent, extremely vivacious, therefore cannot be allowed to consort with any Tom, Dick or Sandy who happens to cross her path. In this case you happen to be the one who has crossed our Amanda's path, so we determined we would establish you were a suitable candidate for her affections."

"You know Amanda Sir?"

"Now the next thing you need to know is my name is David, except of course on parade – right?"

"Right Sir, I mean yes David. So you know Amanda."

"We, the sergeant major and I, have known Amanda for a long time. She even has a number two Amanda out in Cairo, but that's another story. Amanda One at Ringway is the absolute tops. I shall write and tell her you have passed the acid test. I have to say even if you had not passed, it would have made no difference, she is obviously, as you transatlantic people say, nuts about you, and we are very pleased for her – oh and you are a lucky sod, as my brother would doubtless describe you."

Sandy laughed, "So you have been having me on?"

"Not at all. If we had found you objectionable in any way we would have got you posted to Italy or somewhere. We would do anything to protect our Amanda."

Sandy still did not know whether David was pulling his leg or not – he had a very strong suspicion that beneath the jocularity there was a very firm intention to look after Amanda's interests – and he was grateful for it.

When David returned to the mess that afternoon the talk was buzzing that Italy had surrendered, although the German army in Italy fought on of course. A complete Italian division, the Bergamo Division, in the Balkans, surrendered to the partisans to form the Garibaldi Brigade to carry the fight against the Wehrmacht. Daily reports were arriving of heavy Balkan fighting, where it was stated openly British officers were now involved. The German divisions being employed against the partisans, and to a lesser extent against Greek irregulars in the south, were contributing considerably to the shortfall of troops required on the Eastern front, a shortfall being met by employing Rumanian, Slovakian, Bulgarian forces, and others, generally of inferior ability and certainly of inferior fighting spirit. One of the main reasons for the fall of Stalingrad had been the collapse of such divisions north of the salient, thus allowing the Soviet army to encircle Von Paulus and his 6th Army.

"And soon," Hamish was saying, "we shall be hitting the bastards from this side. Surely they must now see they cannot possibly win. Why lose another million men for no good reason, to say nothing of the million the Russians, Americans and ourselves could possibly lose in the meantime."

There was no answer to that unusual example of profundity on the part of Major Hamish Gillespie, once Scottish Rifles.

The following weekend David found himself with the standard weekend free, except that as he had had the previous two weekends off he was detailed as field officer of the day on Saturday and Sunday. There was little for him to do except to act as commanding officer in the event of a sudden emergency during the absence of the colonel. Had he not been on duty it would have been doubtful whether he would have been able to see Maria as she too had been saddled with weekend work to make up for the time she had 'been away enjoying herself.'

"Who said I was enjoying myself?" said Maria

"Well, you did, didn't you?" Emma asked.

"I just lay back and thought of England."

"You were already in England."

"This was an old flame – Freddie England."

With time to think David wondered, and worried deeply, about brother Harry. Wondered how anyone could manage to live month after month in that environment, with the same companions, some of whom would undoubtedly get on your nerves at the very least. But then he thought of his erstwhile friend Rusty Gates of His Majesty's Submarine Thunderer, they were all living cheek by jowl in that oversized sardine can but seemed to get on. What he did not know was that Thunderer had been sunk with all hands only two days ago. He would have been sick to the bottom of his stomach had he known.

The men came back off weekend leave to face a gruelling four day exercise after having been dropped in Wales, and so the training went on, all through September into October. Londoners in the battalion, and there was a fair number from the City Rifles and K.R.R.s who came from the Smoke and the Home Counties, were involved on Saturday night, 7th October, with an air raid, reported by the Germans as a revival of the Blitz, but dismissed by the Ministry of Information as 'devoid of any significance.' It was a small raid, only 60 aircraft, but 60 bombers can still make a considerable mess of a capital city badly knocked about to start with. The next night there was a smaller raid largely on the Kentish towns. David had been staying in Dover at the Cliff House Hotel over the Friday and Saturday nights, Maria having obtained a sleeping out pass, but was already back in London for the Bulford train leaving Waterloo at 9 p.m. full to the brim with sober, semi sober and three parts sloshed paratroopers making more noise than all the rest of the station, trains included, put together. A handful didn't make it back for one reason or another. If there were compassionate reasons the company commander would judge their absence in as reasonable a manner as he could and the Army Act and Kings Regulations allowed him, otherwise the miscreant would be sent to the commanding officer to receive, according to the length of the absence and frequency of the crime, anything from fourteen days confined to barracks to twenty-eight days in a military prison – the glasshouse – where life was very uncomfortable indeed. If he was absent for twenty-eight days he became a deserter and the police and military police would be after him.

When Gloria and Cecely arrived back at Sandbury, Gloria's first task was to get the children into the local school. The financial affairs of the tragic parents, with the considerable help of Jack Hooper and Reg Church, had now been sorted out; as a result there were sufficient funds to be able to send them to private schools. Neither of them wanted to be boarders. Patricia was bright but not overly so, Eric had yet to show whether he was going to develop any particular talents. The two ladies talked it over and decided their charges should stay at the town school for at least the remainder of the September term. In the meantime they would approach Brasted House Girls School, situated about a mile from The Bungalow to which Patricia could cycle each day, secondly to contact Doctor Carew at Cantelbury College, David's old school at Mountfield some four miles away with regard to Eric.

Both the children were the source of some ribbing when they first joined the town school. Having been living in deepest Wales for over three years, they possessed strong Welsh accents, accents indeed which they never totally lost. They soon settled in however, making new friends as children so speedily do. In the meantime Gloria visited Brasted House and found it to be well equipped and the staff to be better qualified than in many other private schools she had heard about. It was arranged therefore that Patricia would join in January, when she would be assessed as to which form she would be placed. There were no problems with Cantelbury. Doctor Carew agreed that Eric should join at the September term 1944, and be placed in the 'B' form until they had established his ability.

At Sandbury Engineering, Fred was sitting in his office when through the window he saw Megan cycling across the hard standing. He was immediately very concerned. Megan led an extremely busy life as a hospital sister, and mother of three children she constantly had to ferry to Nanny at The Hollies, so much so that a visit to Sandbury Engineering to see her father-in-law must be as a result of some sort of disaster. Fred's thoughts obviously were centred on the possibility that something awful had happened to Harry. Then he quickly thought, if that was the case, the last thing that Megan would be doing, level headed though she was, would be to be pushing a bike around to Sandbury Engineering – she would use the phone. He hurried out past Miss Russell's desk to meet her.

"What's up love?"

"I have had this letter from the War Office."

"Not bad news?"

"I don't even know if it is meant for me."

"Come in the office. Would you like some coffee?"

"Oh yes please. I feel I could do with a double brandy."

"Well, Sandbury Engineering doesn't run to that I'm afraid, so coffee it will have to be."

Miss Russell, hearing this repartee as they passed through her office, smiled a welcome to Megan, who she admired enormously, and envied considerably – she had always had a soft spot for Harry – and made her way into the little kitchen.

"Right, let's have the letter." It was addressed to Mrs M Chandler."
Re: Captain H Chandler M.C.

Dear Madam

Will you kindly return your pay and allowances book to this office. As from 26 August 1943 you will be paid by cheque monthly from this office.

The letter then went on to give a calculation of the weekly allowances she had already drawn, deducted from the money she should have received at the new rate on August 31st and September 30th, which left her with a credit balance of seven pounds and eight shillings, a cheque for which was enclosed. It concluded,

We remain madame,

John Tighe, Major

Paymaster

"Well, it looks, my lovely Megan, that your husband has been commissioned in the field, made straight away up to captain, I imagine so that he can be put in command of a unit, and has been awarded the Military Cross for some sort of gallant action or other. Now. First things first. I can telephone the paymaster and find out what he knows – he's bound to have a record of the promotion dates, and then I will get on to the War Office, find out who knows where to trace citations, and see if I can get a copy. Now what is Harry's number?"

"He was 66774, but on here he has a new number," she pointed to the letter, "it's 320012."

Megan finished her coffee, said her goodbyes to Fred and Miss Russell, remounted her bicycle and pedalled off home. Fred immediately put a call through to the paymaster, which took only fifteen minutes, establishing his judgement regarding Harry's promotion to be correct, along with the date and the authorisation. However, the paymaster could give no help in respect of the 'M.C.' he said. "The authorisation arrived with that on; it must therefore have been awarded prior to his promotion to commissioned rank." So, Fred concluded, he must have won it as an R.S.M. He had no luck whatsoever regarding the citation. He finally got through to 'The Times,' they told him that an 'R.S.M. H Chandler' had been included some weeks ago in their list of awards, but that no citations for awards other than V.C.s and G.C.s were issued in war time.

So they had to be satisfied with that. "We'll find out one day," being Fred's final report on the subject.

When Oliver returned to Bovington after his leave, he and his friend Gordon found themselves on a series of courses, wireless, gunnery and driving of mainly Cromwell tanks, during which they applied to their squadron commander to become officers. Having been told to wait for a decision until the outcome of their various courses was known; they sweated blood to make sure they got good results. In the middle of October, therefore, they were presented to the regimental commander, who agreed they should go to the selection board, who would decide whether they were suitable material to be sent on to O.C.T.U., the armoured corps cadet unit being at the pre-war home of officer cadets – Sandhurst. But it would be the beginning of December before they were ordered to the selection board at Barton Stacey. "God, we shall miss the war altogether at this rate," was Oliver's view, "a month to decide. If we pass, three months at Sandhurst. Then settle in to a unit, it will be six months before we command anything worth commanding, by then it will be all over." It wasn't of course, and they got eventually a good deal more than they had bargained for – as we shall probably eventually find out.

There had been a number of hit-and-run raids on Kentish coastal towns and airfields during October. In addition, the periodic shelling of the coast road between Folkestone and Deal was causing concern. Both Folkestone and Dover towns found themselves being targeted. The shells themselves, whilst individually not causing as much damage as, say, a 500-pound bomb, gave little or no warning. The screaming whoosh as they impacted however began to have distressing effects on the townspeople. In a bombing raid you would have warning and could probably find shelter. Shelling was a different kettle of fish altogether.

Maria was driving back to the barracks at Deal, having collected a Commodore at Folkestone. The weather was clear, if a little on the blustery side. Ahead, a quarter of a mile or so, just before the turn off for Kingsdown there was a queue of stationary vehicles, mainly army lorries. As there was no traffic coming towards them Maria assumed some kind of accident was blocking the road, so she decided to pull up to await events for a short while, and if necessary to go back towards Dover then cut off on a circle through Eastry and back into Deal that way.

"What's happening?" asked a somewhat plummy voice from the back.

"I think there must have been an accident, Sir, the road appears to be blocked. I'll give it a few minutes and if nothing moves I'll detour through Eastry."

"Well, don't take too long, I want an early dinner this evening."

What Maria replied to that remark, under her breath of course, might well have surprised most people who knew her. You do not, however, spend a couple of years in the Wrens and not increase your vocabulary, no matter how nice a girl you are.

They waited two or three minutes, with the commodore – not an ocean-going sailor incidentally – getting frustrated at the possibility of his having a late dinner, when there was an awful rushing noise followed immediately by an enormous explosion, that followed by the car being hammered by stones and lumps of chalk and rocked over on to its near side wheels, coming back on to its four wheels again with an almighty thump. Maria, who had instinctively hung on to the steering wheel, looked over her shoulder to see her passenger flat out on the floor of the rear compartment shaking like a jelly.

"What the hell was that?" he asked fatuously.

Maria for years afterwards felt so proud of her reply.

"Just a shellburst, Sir, we often get them along here."

"Well bloody well get us out of here."

"Yes, Sir, of course Sir. But I shall have to clean the windscreen and rear window up first." With that she took a cloth from beneath the dashboard, climbed out, hanging on to the roof of the car so that her passenger should not see her wobbly legs, and as nonchalantly as she could, cleaned the soil off the windows so that she could see to drive. In climbing out she could see where the shell had struck. It was only some fifteen or twenty yards away. Only the high bank on the side of the road between them had saved them from getting more than a fair share of the blast, as it was, a large flint, found so commonly in the chalk, was imbedded in her door panel, several others in the bonnet and wheel arches. This vehicle is going to require a considerable amount of panel beating or replacement she judged – more paper work, court of enquiry etc. Then she realised how near she had been to death, and looked upward, put her hands together and whispered, "Thank you God."

"Come on driver, don't be all night."

One word, in the plural, was muttered under her breath as she climbed back in, singularly different in tone and texture to her previous prayer. She made her way back to the St Margaret's turn off, up to Eastry and then back into Deal, her charge getting out at the officers' mess without a word of thanks or enquiring whether she was alright. Maria's final thought regarding this apology of an officer was, "I suppose he will apply for a Distinguished Service Cross for that act of gallantry."

Back at Sandbury, Reg Church had arrived late for the Rotary lunch meeting, as a result the sergeant-at-arms fined him one shilling for tardiness. As a consequence of suggesting that if the sergeant-at-arms could spell the word he would pay the shilling, if he could not do so he should be let off, he was fined another shilling for audacity. You cannot win against the sergeant-at-arms. However whilst he was on his feet he did ask the president if, after the lunch and business affairs had been completed, he could recount to the assembly the extraordinary circumstance, which had brought about his alleged tardiness. He was promptly fined another shilling for suggesting the sergeant-at-arms could have been incorrect in his fining Past President Reg on the basis of an allegation. The service box, into which all the fines end up was swelling nicely. However, since there obviously was a story to tell, his request was granted.

At the end of the meal therefore Reg got to his feet again. "Mr President, Fellow Rotarians," he began "today I had to go to the assizes in Maidstone."

"They've caught up with him at last," interjected Fred, followed by general laughter and 'hear, hears.'

"As I was saying until I was rudely interrupted, I had to go, as a witness, I hasten to add, to give evidence in a fraud case. In the event the case was put back because of the fact the accused had attempted suicide that morning and had been rushed to hospital. As a result, the next case on the list was brought forward. It concerned a smallholder from out on the wilds of Sheppey marshes who had been charged with gross indecency with an animal. I thought this sounds interesting so I stayed on in the public gallery, which as you can guess was choc-a-bloc, people even queuing outside. Briefly, a neighbour on a small holding some three or four hundred yards away, at ten o'clock one night saw lights, and heard squealing coming from the accused's pig pen. There had been some rustling of animals locally a little while back, he thought that thieves were about so he phoned the local bobby. The bobby then gave evidence. He was large, corpulent and way beyond retirement age, obviously having his service extended because of the war. Anyway he got on his bike, leaned it against a fence on the accused's property, and crept forward to look into the pig pen through a gap in the slats."

"And what did you see," asked the prosecuting counsel.

"Horatio..."

"You mean the accused?"

"Yes, Sir, Horatio Cowper the accused," he answered in his broad Kentish accent.

"Well, what did you see?"

"The accused was kneeling down with his trousers round his knees. He had got a young pig into the corner of the pen and was trying to get hold of it."

"I see and did he say anything?"

"Yes, Sir, he was saying 'Now come here my little beauty, you been tant-er-lising me long enough'."

At this, the Rotarians roared with laughter, as indeed had all the people in the court, even the judge was seen to draw his handkerchief and pay more than casual attention to a supposed runny nose.

Reg continued, "But that wasn't all." His audience looked at him intently not wishing to miss a word of this bucolic saga. "The judge broke in, in an effort I would guess to get some gravity back into the proceedings. 'Now constable' he said ' you say this was a pig. Was this a male or a female pig?' The constable looked straight at him and replied, 'Oh it was a female pig, my Lord, I've known Horatio Cowper for twenty years and there's nothing queer about Horatio Cowper.'

Reg's audience collapsed in hysterics, the worst affected of the thirty-odd people there being the congregational minister, the Reverend Andrew Carstairs, who was heard to say "My wife will never believe this." None of his fellow members thought it odd that he, a man of the cloth, would be the only one who would dream of telling the story to his wife!!

Chapter Thirty One

Harry studied Choong Hong the Railway Man's sketches of the three targets the two scouts had reconnoitred so effectively, and by the end of October 1943 had worked out plans for the operation as a whole and for each individual assault. There would be three groups of eight, one led by himself, one by Tommy and the third by Reuben. As before, he marked out on the parade ground the layout of each target, scaled down of course, drawn from the excellent sketches and estimated distances the two men had brought back. It was decided they would move out on Thursday 23rd November to a firm base in the mountainous jungle about ten miles equidistant from the three towns. Each raiding party would then move on Friday to a bivvy area in the secondary jungle four or five miles from its target, carry out what reconnaissance they could ready for the attack on Saturday night. Tape would be laid to their respective bivvy areas to which they would return after the raid, to hole up until dawn and then return to the firm base, be checked in, and move back to camp. Altogether it would be a four to five day operation for which they had not only to carry their weapons, demolition materials, a number of tools of various kinds and a blanket each, but also food for four days – if the job ran for five days they could go hungry for a day.

They rehearsed and rehearsed – Harry had proved before that if time spent in reconnaissance is seldom wasted, time spent in rehearsing until you can do the job in your sleep is absolutely invaluable.

Harry's target area was Bidor where there was a larger rubber godown. This was the most likely objective to have guards posted, although Choong Hong had not been able to establish whether this was in fact the case whilst they were there – he had a suspicion that a station official was watching them rather too closely for comfort. Harry therefore worked on the assumption there would be guards.

As the moving out day drew near you could feel the men getting keyed up. They talked a little more, even laughed a little more, which was not difficult to achieve, since their Marxist lecturers harangued them to such an extent there was very little for them to laugh at in the first place.

But the best laid plans of mice etc etc.

On Monday night 20th November, Harry started to run a fever. By Tuesday midday he could hardly stand, so Matthew immediately ordered him to bed, Tommy Isaacs as the senior officer taking command. In the early hours of Wednesday morning his temperature was at a point that 'if he goes another degree he's had it,' being Matthew's opinion to the other two officers and Choon Guan. They had an immediate conference, or 'O' group as it was known. They had to decide whether to abort the operation, or if not, who would be in charge of Harry's section of the attack. They decided the operation would go ahead and Choon Guan would lead the Bidor section.

Harry was delirious all Tuesday night and most of Wednesday, Matthew nursing him, dosing him with quinine, constantly changing his sheets and pillows, getting very little sleep himself for forty eight hours. On Wednesday evening the thermometer had gone back to 104 degrees indicating Harry was far from being out of the woods but at least was showing marginal improvement. Matthew had almost to fight with him to get him to drink the volume of water he knew his patient had to take to stay alive. As he became more conscious a further problem arose with the appalling stomach cramps which often accompany this type of fever, to be followed by even more painful muscle cramps in the arms and legs, to the extent his cries, half conscious as he was, were loud and persistent. Around midnight he quietened and went into a sleep of total exhaustion. Matthew instructed one of his small medical squad to sit with him while he, Matthew, got four hours sleep. At 4am the young assistant took Harry's temperature, it had gone back to 102, he decided to give Matthew an extra hour knowing how exhausted he had been, and at five o'clock on Thursday morning got a resounding telling off from the camp doctor for not strictly obeying his instructions.

At 5.30 the men moved out on their mission, Tommy, Reuben and Choon Guan all first coming in to see how Harry was before they moved off, but finding him completely dead to the world. It was midday before he awoke long enough to be fed a little mashed rice, before going back to sleep, his temperature now having gone back to 100 degrees.

All the time he had been ill little Chantek had been clearly upset, making that distinctive coughing sound, at times showing her displeasure at the world in general by growling and hissing at people who approached her in her big, covered, chicken wire compound. The enclosure had been so constructed that a wire tunnel had been made to connect with a swinging door in the wall of Harry's room, large enough for her to pass through when she became much bigger than she was at present – even now she appeared to be growing every day! This access flap could be bolted on the room side so that at night Harry could put her in the tunnel and bolt the door on her. Having said that, it was not uncommon for her to make a peculiar mewing sort of noise when he went to put her out which clearly indicated she would prefer to stay; when allowed to do so she would snuggle up against his back and sleep soundly – except that from time to time she would express her appreciation by putting her claws into his back! Now she was being denied this intimacy and she was very much down in the dumps about it!

She was now two months old. The little brown blind bundle of fur Harry had rescued now bounced around on its short legs and outsized feet. It had started playing games with Harry, hiding when in his room and suddenly pouncing on him as he passed. Under normal circumstances the little cub would have spent most of its time snuggled up against her mother in a well-hidden den. If they had had to move for any reason her mother would have picked her up by the scruff of her neck and carried her. Chantek had had no mother, all of her closeness had been with Harry, wherever she had travelled she had been carried, in the large pocket of Harry's bush-jacket. Harry's smell was now recognised by her as her protector, if she felt threatened, particularly by the noise of approaching thunder, it was to Harry she ran, climbing up on him to safety, nuzzling into his tunic and licking his neck with her strong, rough tongue. To a lesser extent she bonded with Matthew, as he frequently fed her, and acted in locum parentis should Harry be out of the camp for any reason.

The French letter feeding bottle had worked well. At two months Tommy had suggested they ought to start weaning her off the exasperated milk. As a result Matthew had been hand feeding her little bits of bully which at first she ignored, then played with, and at the third attempt actually chewed and ate. Harry had decided that early in December, after the railway operation, he would make his first foray in the 'duck lake,' by which name it became known since on their map it was too small to be named. He would bag a small duck, bring it back, throw the carcass into Chantek's pen and see what she made of it.

"You could of course bring back a couple of birds for us," Tommy had hinted, which idea unfortunately had to be scotched. It would not do for the communist rank and file to know the bourgeois officer class were living at a higher level than they were.

Harry eventually came to on the Saturday. He was as weak as little Chantek had been when he had rescued her from the foraging pigs. He ate a little porridge, then sank back to sleep again for an hour. Gradually during the day his waking periods increased until just before the tropical night swiftly set in he asked Matthew, firstly which day it was, secondly had they aborted the mission, thirdly where was Chantek – was she alright? and lastly could he sit up. The questions answered, and his having been sat up he asked Matthew to let Chantek in. The bundle of excitement must have been listening on the other side of the trap door since the second Matthew drew the bolt the door flew open and a mottled streak of lightning ran at the bed, scrambled up on to the thin mattress and hurled himself at Harry's chest, pushing her nose into his, by now, bearded chin, rasping his ear with her coarse tongue, all the while emitting that coughing note of pleasure. It was ten minutes before she settled down. Matthew pulled the mosquito net down with the comment from Harry "If a mosquito takes any blood from me tonight it will be committing suicide." He talked to Matthew through the net.

"I wonder how the lads are doing."

"They practised and practised, each knows what he has to do."

"That's all very well, but something or other always turns up to bugger up the planning." Having said that he instantly regretted swearing in conversation with Matthew. Matthew was a deeply religious young man. Even the communists, who were, or were supposed to be, atheist, respected Matthew's beliefs and were circumspect in his company.

"All I know is that the next three days are going to be the longest days of my life."

"We will get you out of bed tomorrow and walk you up and down a little. You could do with a shave too. By tomorrow the attacks will have been made so you won't have to worry, unless you consider that without you they may get lost on the way back. Now, come on Chantek, back you go to your den."

"Leave her with me, she will be alright."

"Well alright, but you shout if you want me to remove her."

They both slept the sleep of exhaustion. Harry exhausted by his fever, Chantek exhausted by hours of sitting by that hatch door knowing that something was wrong with her guardian and protector. She was, after all, a cat, and cats are the wisest and most intuitive of creatures. Once during the night distant thunder woke her. She burrowed into the covering sheet as close to Harry as she could get. The faint rumble stopped, she considered the unknown danger had passed, she went back to sleep again. She was safe.

The next morning Harry took more porridge. His temperature stood at 99. Matthew washed him with warm water obtained from the cookhouse stove. There was no lack of water, cleverly diverted from the nearby mountain stream, in which to have a shower, but it was not only cold, but first thing in the morning it was bloody cold, straight out of the high mountain. Harry had expressed the view, ad nauseam, that when they eventually got out of this blasted God-forsaken place his first pleasure would be to spend a day in a warm bath. On being asked what his second pleasure would be he refused to answer.

The all-over wash having been completed they let Chantek in

again, accompanied by a similar demonstration of excitement and energy as had been previously demonstrated, which gradually subsided as Harry was seated on the camp chair ready to be shaved. Matthew produced the only mirror in the camp of any size. It was roughly a twelve inch square piece of stainless steel. There was no glass in the camp, with the exception of a number of medicine bottles in Matthew's care. No windows, no glasses only mugs, no mirrors. No bottles – they had lived without glass for nearly two years. At Sandbury they would have thought that was impossible.

Harry looked at himself in the mirror and was plainly shocked. "God Almighty, is that me?" he asked.

"God Almighty would know you anywhere," was Matthew's cryptic reply. Harry grinned at him.

"Well I can tell you, Matthew old son, if my lovely Megan was to walk in here now she wouldn't recognise me, and when she realised it was me would run a mile."

"Well let's get you shaved, you'll look all pretty again then."

When he had been shaved – he himself could not have done it, his hands and arms were still atremble from the fever – he looked again in the mirror and was quite shocked. His face, never fleshy, was thin, bony and lined, his eyes stared and his hair, which had gradually been getting greyer over the past two years, he was of course now thirty three, was almost white.

"Bloody hell – what a mess," was his only comment.

Matthew called one of his assistants to come and lend a hand. Harry stood up, swaying all over the place. The two medics positioned themselves one either side, and under the continuous and watchful gaze of the brilliant blue eyes of a tiny panthera pardus – leopard to you – they slowly walked him up and down his room. He could not believe how weak he had become in just a few days. By the time he had traversed the twelve feet, three or four times, he was exhausted and ready to go back on to his bed, to the eminent delight of one, Chantek, who immediately snuggled up to him again, not however as enamoured of his new soapy aroma as she had been of his former smelly self. But as she said to herself: beggars can't be choosers, or whatever it is baby leopards do say to console themselves.

The next day dragged. Harry got up and was able to take a short walk around the camp before returning to his bed, sleeping soundly although it was only eleven in the morning. The old adage that sleep, like time, is a great healer is very true. However, that night he slept fitfully, concerned at what news his men would bring on the morrow. During the night there was a tremendous thunderstorm, so common in

Malaya and the East Indies generally. The rain lashed down on to the atap roof, but fortunately was kept out by the lining of parachute nylon recovered from their air drops. Chantek was terrified, burrowing into the thin blanket covering Harry, he, knowing what it was like out in the jungle with only flimsy protection, or none at all, felt so sorry for his men hopefully making their way back to camp. Although the thunder and lightning relented before dawn, the rain continued to bucket down. The parade ground was awash, everything in what one might call 'the dry' was dank and clammy. On the plains, and there are not many of those in Malaya, the sun dries the land out quickly; in the jungle, it turns the whole stinking mess into one huge Turkish bath. When the sun did break through after breakfast that is exactly what happened. It was virtually impossible to see across the parade ground for the steam arising from the sodden soil. It had, however, been such a common sight over the past two years that no notice was taken of the phenomenon whatsoever.

Just after midday the troops straggled in. The camp guards, medics and cooks left behind started counting, knowing how many had left the camp, willing them all to return. They took nearly half an hour before they were all in, the last two being almost carried by the comrades, one having been wounded and another having had a fall in the dark. The two injured men were swiftly taken into the hospital hut, the remainder inflicted with the routine weapon and foot inspection before being allowed to dry off and get the food already prepared for them. This having been completed, the three commanders went to Harry's hut to make their reports.

Choon Guan, who had taken over Harry's target at Bidor reported first. Everything had gone according to plan except that there were, as had been feared, a couple of sentries on the godown. He and Choong Hong had dealt with them with their machetes, but as they were throwing phosphorous grenades into the rubber the guard commander arrived with two sentry reliefs. They had a short gun battle, killing all three, one of Choon Guan's men being hit in the thigh in the process. He detailed two men to help the wounded man back to the tape point and thus back to the bivvy area while he and the other five men blew up the telegraph office and set fire to the postal station.

Reuben Ault, in his lugubrious manner told of his attack on Sungkai. Everything went according to plan, the result he affirmed of them practising over and over again before they left.

Tommy Isaacs had attacked Trolak. Great success with the station and the telegraph office but the detonator failed to work on the plastic explosive attached to the leg of the huge water tower used to re-supply the trains. He gave it a few minutes leeway, then decided to fix a second detonator on it, at which Harry interjected.

"Silly sod."

"I agree," Tommy replied smiling, "I had got within twenty yards of it when the bloody thing went off. The blast took me off my feet and I landed against a wire mesh fence, which was damned lucky, had it been a brick wall I would have had it. Anyway I was more frightened than hurt, then I saw the tower toppling in my direction and I took to my heels as a tidal wave chased me. It caught up with me, I got bowled over and soaked from top to bottom but fortunately by then the power of the flood had lessened so I just got a few bruises. Anyway, all the targets were successfully dealt with."

"Well, this will make a nice report for our Sunrise, I understand he will be visiting us before Christmas."

"In a Father Christmas outfit?"

"Probably with another job for us on Christmas Day," Harry replied.

At 3am on the night of the return of the men from the raids, Matthew Lee came in and shook Harry. Instantly awake Harry whispered, "What's up?"

"It's the wounded man, it looks as though gangrene is setting in."

Harry was quickly out of bed, dressed and shod, particularly shod – he had no desire for contact with another scorpion – and hurried with Matthew to the tiny adjacent hospital. Matthew's two assistants were already there. Harry examined the wound, Matthew pointing out the infections, whilst the injured man lay looking at them both with fear in his eyes. Harry led Matthew away.

"What can you do?"

"Unless the leg is removed he will die."

"Can you remove the leg?"

"I have no anaesthetic."

"Can it be done without anaesthetic?"

"I have never carried out an amputation before, although I have seen it done on several occasions. Without anaesthetic the shock could kill him anyway."

"So he dies if you don't and he may die if you do – is that it?"

"Yes, except that it would not be 'may' die, it would be 'probably' die."

"Have you got the tools to do it with?"

"They have them in the kitchen. A heavy knife and a meat saw." Harry's stomach turned over at hearing that.

"Well, it's your decision Matthew, if you want my view we ought to try."

"In that case I will practise on one of the men, not removing his leg of course, so that my two men and Mr Ault, Mr Isaacs and yourself know what to do. This will have to be done in less than five minutes or he will die from the shock." They called Choon Guan to act as the unfortunate patient, putting him on a table in the kitchen. Matthew took charge. "Right Mr Ault, you hold his shoulders down firmly. Mr Isaacs you hold his good leg at both hip and knee, hold it out towards you to give me more room. Captain, you hold the wounded leg at the knee and ankle, and whip it away quickly once it is severed. I will wrap the thigh firmly with my left arm while I cut the flesh down to the bone. John" (one of the Chinese medics) "you will immediately seize the artery and tie it securely. James will be holding the saw and will immediately take the knife and hand me the saw. All the time if he is still conscious the patient will need to be firmly held down. Now we need to grind down M and B tablets from the dispensary to make a powder. Has anyone got a talcum powder puffer?" All three officers had one.

"Mine is empty. I'll go and get it," said Tommy.

"As soon as the cut is made Andrew will start puffing on to the flesh." They practised the forthcoming operation half a dozen times until Matthew felt reasonably sure they each knew what to do and when to do it. "Of course, we can have no idea of the degree of reaction by the patient, so we have to be prepared for anything. Before we had anaesthetics, it had to be done this way always of course. Trafalgar, the Peninsular War, the American Civil War, an amputee who survived was the exception. This patient is young and fit, he stands a good chance if we all do our job properly."

The three medics prepared the man for the operation, disinfecting the table as far as they could upon which they were to work. The kitchen knife had been honed to its limit, boiled with the saw to sterilise it, the fetid atmosphere in which they were to work was as big a hazard as the operation itself, but at least the instruments would be bacteria free.

Three Tilley lamps had been suspended over the table as the 'surgical team' took their positions. Matthew paused for a moment.

"O Lord God, please bring success to our labours for the sake of your son, our saviour, Jesus Christ."

They all murmured, "Amen."

With that he wrapped his arm firmly around the patients thigh, the operation went smoothly and entirely to plan, except that no plan could have anticipated the awful screams emanating from the poor unfortunate sufferer before he lapsed into unconsciousness. The leg removed the medics swiftly pushed all the muscle and flesh upwards into the thigh, swathing it in bandages made secure around the stump. The patient had survived the operation, but would he survive the aftermath?

Harry's final words after all the tidying up had been done were "Matthew you are a miracle man." He paused. "I think we all need a large measure of our medicinal rum," to which sentiment all agreed.

Whilst there can of course be no happy ending for this grim tale, Matthew's constant care and attention, and perhaps the prayers of he and his two fellow Christians, resulted in the survival of his patient, his fighting days now behind him. They made him a pair of crutches from bamboo. Bamboo is light in weight and very strong, yet it is not classified as a tree, it is in fact a grass!! As a famous personality was to remark some years later – not a lot of people know that!

Over the next two weeks three things happened. Firstly they had notice of an air drop, weather permitting on the night of 5/6th December.

"That will be our Christmas puddings," was Tommy's guess.

Secondly, Sunrise would be arriving on or about 12th December.

"He'll be bringing more Christmas puddings," Tommy predicted.

Thirdly, they had an unwelcome visit over a period of three days of Tiger Moths flying about over them. They had obviously stirred up a hornet's nest in making three attacks in one night, and in particular having killed five Japanese soldiers. The Japs had reasoned there must be a sizeable force to carry out an operation of that diversity, therefore they must be holed up in a substantial camp, therefore they should be visible to low-flying aircraft. The local commander, who had knowledge of the finding of Camp Six and its destruction, contacted the air unit commander of The Tiger Moths, arranging to 'borrow' them for three or four days whereupon the three aircraft were despatched from their base near Kluang to an airstrip at Tapah, a few miles north of Bidor. They methodically searched the high jungle to the east of a line Tapah down to Trolak, but again the camp was so well hidden they found nothing, on this occasion Harry making sure that no idiot was in a position to set the place on fire!

The night the air drop was due was fine and clear. Although Harry was much improved he was still not strong enough to make the journey to the drop zone, much less to carry a load back! The general expectation was that, being Christmas, there would be a little extra something in the loads somewhere, although as Harry had joked to Choon Guan who had expressed this view to him, "But you don't believe in Christmas, so you won't want to share in it, should something be there." Choon Guan had made the only joke Harry could remember his making.

"I could probably have a temporary conversion for a few hours."

Harry, recounting this to Tommy and Reuben later that day told them, "And he smiled, he actually smiled – I don't think I've seen the bugger smile before in nearly two years."

The air drop was on time. The men, experienced by now in recovering the supplies, speedily broke down the pallets, rolled up the parachutes, secured loads on each other on the back packs they had made from previously dropped parachute harness and canvas covers, and started the long trek back to camp. Two men with light loads led the way as scouts – they still had to move as a patrol should move – followed by Tommy and a runner, then the crocodile of carriers, with Reuben at the rear. They would be going back a different way to the outward route to avoid some steep gradients which being downward had presented no problems on the way out. This involved a detour of some three or four miles through lightly wooded country on the edge of the valley drop zone. As they breasted a slight rise the two scouts stopped, froze, then moved slowly back. Tommy and his runner moved forward carefully.

"What's wrong?" he whispered.

"Airplane crashed," the first scout replied.

Tommy crouching low, inched forward. His binoculars around his neck, they were indispensable on these drop operations for watching where out of the way loads had landed, he crept to the slight ridge and from behind a bush studied the crashed aircraft. It was one of the Tiger Moths. He could see no sign of the pilot, or the body of a pilot, reasoning therefore:

1) The pilot lay dead somewhere nearby in which case, since it was three or four days since the search was on, the local carnivores would have made a meal of him.

2) He was injured but had tried to make his way back to civilisation. If he succeeded all well and good; if not, possibility one would apply.

3) Hang on a minute, the Tiger Moth carried two people, perhaps one was injured and the other uninjured.

Tommy came to the conclusion that whatever had happened, had happened three days ago, they would be unlikely to still be here at the crash. Nevertheless he called the men forward telling them to fan out and approach the aircraft with care, which they did and finding nothing continued back to camp.

When they told Harry the news he was a little concerned. The crash was only about seven or eight miles away. If they – the Japs – had not yet spotted it, they might well send foot patrols in. On the other hand, the fact that no further aircraft had been observed searching for the missing plane would surely indicate the occupant, or occupants had survived, made their way westwards where they knew they would hit the main north to south railway line and trunk road, and hitched a lift to their base. The Japs would not bother to try and salvage the aircraft; it would just not be worth the trouble, particularly since they did not have to pay for the blasted thing in the first place! Nevertheless, Harry doubled the guards at the picket posts for the next three days as a precaution.

In the meantime they unpacked the goodies. Harry left the sorting of the various loads in the capable hands of Tommy Isaacs, having feverishly scanned each load to establish which contained the mail. There was a large cardboard box for him, posted in Sandbury in July, along with a bundle of letters tied with string which an educated guess from Matthew put at one from not only every member of his family, but also from every other family in Sandbury. Strangely enough Reuben also had a largish bundle, which Matthew holding up to his nose proclaimed were obviously not from just one admirer but, according to the different perfumes emanating from different colour envelopes in the package suggested two, if not three, different females having put pen to paper to the gallant lieutenant. Harry continued with the leg-pull.

"Now Reuben, this is something we have not been told about. We know you are not married but we had no idea you were a Lothario. Come on, tell us the secret of your success."

Reuben made reply with probably the subtlest pronouncement he had issued to his comrade to date.

"Sex appeal my lads, sex appeal. Some of us have it, some of us don't. You would be incapable of recognising it, the ladies feel it straight away."

"Are you telling us," Tommy asked, "that you let them feel 'it' straight away?"

"I have to fight to keep them off," countered Reuben, "either that or I ask them to line up in an orderly manner while I book them in." He took his bundle of letters from Matthew and walked off to his room using the package conspicuously as a nosegay as he went.

Harry took his batch off and sorted them into piles, the largest naturally being from Megan. He was so grateful to be receiving this mail and felt so sad that he could only so rarely reply. He wrote, and kept, a few pages each week on airmail paper the lads who occasionally left the camp for one reason or another, like Choon Hong, brought back for him from a Chinese shop. His recent jottings had been largely about Chantek, Megan and the family would be astonished to know he had a real live leopard who never left him without a fight! He was only sorry he had no camera that he could capture her growing up. When Sunrise came he would ask him if he could get one dropped on the next airlift, then realised that he would not be able to get the film developed. One of the Chinese was an illustrator for a weekly journal in Singapore in real life; he was already making drawings, really clever drawings of the little animal, with a tremendous amount of movement and affection showing in them. His efforts however were being somewhat frowned upon by the commissar who thought it was a frivolous use of time, so how long the endeavour would continue was anyone's guess.

"Matthew!!" A loud and singularly unusual shout from Harry had Matthew running into his room.

"What is croup?"

"Croup? Croup is an inflammation of the larynx and trachea of children. Throat downwards to you. It usually is accompanied by a hard cough and difficulty in breathing. I should think its unlikely you have got it if that is what you are worried about."

"No, you nutter. Baby Ceri has it."

"Baby Ceri? She is nearly two years old."

"Well then two years old Ceri has had it. Is it dangerous?"

"What date was that letter?"

"Fourth of August."

"Then she will have been over it by the 11th at the latest, and totally forgotten it by now. And anyway Mrs Chandler is a nurse and knows exactly what to do, so you have nothing to worry about."

Harry was left with the realisation he still thought of Ceri as a baby when she would now be running around. The excitement of receiving all this mail was temporarily diminished by the knowledge he was missing the growing up of his children, stuck as he was in this place of no escape, and worse of all, no hope of escape for a long while to come as far as he could see. The Allies were going to win the war in Europe before they finally mopped up the Japs in the Far East.

Included in his post were the photographs of Maria and David's wedding, his comments aloud including 'She's much too good for him' and such other witticisms. A sad letter from Cecely saying she still had no news of either Nigel or the judge and how the Japs had reneged on their promise to the Swiss Red Cross to hand over the names of all their civilian internees.

All the letters read he turned to the parcel, a light but strong cardboard box which he opened with some difficulty, and then only with the use of a large knife borrowed from the cookhouse. It was not until he had succeeded in despatching the cardboard exterior that he realised it was the same knife as had sliced so rapidly and cleanly round the amputee's leg. He shuddered. Inside the box was an envelope with a note in it. 'Merry Christmas and much love from all at Sandbury,' and beneath that a round stainless steel tin some twelve inches in diameter. He removed the lid to find the inside sealed with a further sheet of very light gauge stainless steel. Both the tin and the enclosing sheet were obviously hand made as opposed to being a straightforward tin, tin as one might say, which indicated to Harry it had been made at Sandbury Engineering. He got a tin opener from the cookhouse and carefully cut the lid off. Inside there was the fruitiest of fruit cakes he had ever seen and from the aroma which came from it was literally soaked in brandy. His mouth watered beyond belief as he quickly put the lid back on so as not to lose a single droplet of that vapour. He was then faced with one of the greatest dilemmas of his life – was he to tell the others about it or keep it to himself? In the end he did a Sydney Carton utterance.

"It is a far, far better thing that I do now that I have ever done" and gave his two fellow officers and Matthew a slice – not a big slice, he was not entirely in the heroic mould of Sydney Carton when it came to giving away brandy soaked cake.

Chapter Thirty Two

On the 20th September Fritz Strobel took the train to Munich. In his waistcoat pocket he carried a small plush lined box containing a gold ring with a single, rather beautiful, solitaire diamond set on it, in claws studded with tiny diamond chips. How did he know it would be the right size? Fritz had not been a career officer in the German Army without learning a thing or two. He had known from the time he first met Gita that he would marry her if she would be mad enough to have a crippled old war horse like him. As a result, when they were at Ulm, she had offered to mix some pastry for her sister Elizabeth, and in doing so took her rings off, other than her wedding ring, and putting them on a small ornamental sweetmeats plate on the sitting room table joked to Fritz, "You can guard the family jewels." Having disappeared in to the kitchen Fritz took out his small pocket book, placed the sapphire ring Elizabeth wore on her third finger on to one of the pages, quickly traced the inside circumference with the little pencil such books carry, telling himself 'This is what is known as forward planning.' It was a simple matter therefore for the jeweller to establish the correct size to suit the purchase of the solitaire.

Sitting in his first class compartment as the train rumbled on, his satisfaction at the thought of his ingenuity in getting the size of the ring right, began to be tempered by the doubts he had already expressed to Gita, and worried considerably about inside himself, as to whether his hideous stump, as he thought of it, would distress her. He was, suddenly, rudely shaken from his reverie as the train screeched, it seemed interminably, to a juddering halt, in doing so dislodging several pieces of baggage from the rack above, one of which had obviously contained glass bottles, the contents of which were now seeping out on to the floor emitting a pungent odour of cognac. The owner of the parcel, a Luftwaffe officer, swore volubly. "I've carried that bloody parcel all the way from bloody Calais for a comrade of mine to give to his parents – now look at it." His bad luck however was not as great as a lady seated beside him who was leaning forward at the time and had a small piece of luggage give her, not only a nasty blow on the back of the head, but caused total ruination to a rather fetching hat she was wearing. Those minor incidents aside, Fritz came off worst. His own suitcase, fairly heavy, as he had intended to stay several days, toppled over and landed with the forward edge on the knee mechanism of his artificial limb, thence on to the floor. He attempted to operate the appliance so that he could stand up but it was jammed solid. Two civilian men and an army officer sitting opposite him immediately offered to raise him to his feet, an offer he declined saying he had better look at what damage had been done, and if possible, at least straighten the leg out so that he could eventually get off the train.

"So if you will excuse me madam," he said to the lady in the once, fetching hat, he commenced rolling up his trouser leg to examine the damage.

In the meantime the Luftwaffe officer, who had made his way into the corridor to throw the ruined parcel away, came back in saying, "We've only hit a bloody cow. A cow on the line, how the hell could that happen? And why did the idiot have to brake like that if he was going to hit the blasted thing anyway?"

As no one could give him a sensible answer, nobody did, but turned their combined attention to the damaged mechanism to see if they could get the impaired veteran back on the road, or to be precise, on to the railway. One of the civilians, a man of about forty, was an engineer with B.M.W. in Munich, as his card, which he handed to Fritz, stated.

"What has happened, as far as I can tell, is that this piece of the mechanism here which took the point of the suitcase has stretched, thereby impeding the interlocking of the adjacent pieces."

He looked at Fritz as if he were giving a lecture on some advanced technicality in respect of one of their latest internal combustion engines. Fritz started to grin, then to laugh, then to almost split his sides, whilst the others, who up until now had considered a major tragedy had taken place before their very eyes, decided he could possibly be suffering some derangement due to his obvious war service.

"I'll go along to the guards' compartment to see if he has any tools – a screwdriver or something to try and bend it back," said the Luftwaffe man, disappearing up the corridor and returning in a few minutes with the guard, at the sight of which everyone in the compartment was paralysed with laughter. He arrived carrying a hammer, not your ordinary domestic hammer, but the type of long handled implement customarily used for tapping the wheels, complete with a hammer-head which must have weighed at least a couple of kilos. In his other hand he had a large screwdriver which would have been eminently suitable for prising open carriage doors stuck for some reason, but little else.

"I'll go into the second class carriage and see if there is an artisan in there with some tools," again volunteered the Luftwaffe man. In under ten minutes he was back with a stocky little middle-aged man carrying a small leather holdall.

"This good fellow is a telegraph engineer," Luftwaffe man

announced.

The telegraph engineer examined the damage.

"Bending that back will do no good now it has been stretched," was his immediate diagnosis, "it will just foul the mechanism on the other side. What I can do is to take that piece out, drill here and here, plait some thin wire up and attach it to the two holes. That will enable you to straighten and bend it and not cause further damage if you tread carefully."

"Herr engineer, you are a genius," Fritz told him, "an absolute genius. As long as it will hold until I can get to the orthopaedic people in the hospital at Munich tomorrow I shall be eternally grateful."

The engineer set to work. Removing the offending strip causing all the trouble was not difficult. Drilling the two new holes was a little more difficult. The small hand drill seemed to make little headway on the hardened steel strip, thin though it was, but with persistence and a continued look of grim determination on the face of the telegraph man the desired result was eventually obtained. He then took a reel of fine wire from his holdall, cutting three short lengths each a little longer than the length finally required. Clipping one end he asked Fritz to hold the clip for him whilst he patiently plaited the three wires so that he obtained a single very strong strand. This completed he fed the ends through the respective holes he had drilled and then secured them with small brass grummets fitted with tiny screws, which obviously played some part in his normal everyday life as a telegraph man.

"Right, try that."

Fritz operated his straightening mechanism which worked straight away. There was a burst of applause from the other passengers in the carriage, who had all been watching with keen interest. After all, you don't see an artificial limb every day; although God knows there were enough of them about in Germany at that time. Certainly you don't see a 'field operation' on one; it was going to be a topic of conversation for all of them for a long time to come. Fritz shook hands with his Good Samaritan.

"Will you please let me reward you in some way," he delicately put it.

"Sir, you rewarded me when you lost that limb in the service of our country, I need no further reward."

With that he bundled his tools back in to the holdall, shook hands with each occupant, and made his way back to his compartment with the good wishes of them all following him. When they reached the Hauptbahnhof at Munich each occupant shook hands with him as if they had known him all their lives, the Luftwaffe man insisting on carrying his case off the train, Fritz gingerly trying out his repaired leg.

"You alright now, Sir?"

"Yes, thank you very much; I'm most grateful for your help."

With that the young flyer gave a typically lazy Luftwaffe salute, leaving Fritz on the platform to take those steps towards committing himself to a different existence for the rest of his days – or so he confidently aspired.

To his surprise Gita was waiting for him at the platform end. He hugged her close.

"This is a lovely surprise," then he thought of the delay, altogether over an hour and a half. "You must have been waiting for hours – we had a hold-up for nearly an hour and the train was already late when it left Hannover."

He hugged her again.

"And I have had to have an operation on my leg."

Startled, she pulled away and looked at him.

"Oh darling, no darling, you haven't travelled immediately after an operation?"

"No, I had it on the train."

"How could you have an operation on the train? Oh Fritz, you are joking with me, how could you possibly have an operation on the train?"

"I did, and I will show it to you later."

She looked at his smiling face, shook her head saying, "I have a barouche waiting," and led him off to the forecourt.

Reaching Gita's apartment she made coffee, which along with some small cakes she had made that morning they ate sitting together on the sofa. When they had finished, and Gita had cleared the crockery, Fritz took her hand, kissed her lightly and without further delay asked,

"Frau Gita Reuter, will you marry me?"

The monosyllabic answer came without hesitation.

"Yes."

They laughed together. He took the small plush-lined box from his waistcoat pocket, opened it and placed the ring on her finger. It was a perfect fit.

"It really is beautiful," she said "Oh Fritz you have made me so happy."

"Can we register at the City Hall tomorrow?"

"Yes of course," she replied.

"How long then before we can be married?"

"Only three days in wartime."

"Then in three days it will be, now, can I talk about other things?"

"Yes of course, but as far as I am concerned there is little else of consequence to talk about."

"Rosa."

Gita came to earth with a bump. "Rosa is alright isn't she? Oh please tell me she is alright."

"Yes, she is fine. I thought that as soon as we are married we could go back to Brucksheim and you could see her – even meet her if you were very careful."

"How do you mean, careful?"

"Well, if you could steel yourself to sit on the park bench as I do and just talk."

Gita paused for a long while before answering.

"Yes, I could do that, but oh how difficult it will be, and Fritz, darling Fritz, why does it have to be like this?"

He held her to him and comforted her as best he could. "It can't last for ever my darling, it can't last for ever. Nothing does."

They had a simple meal that evening, listened to the news on the radio, and soon after ten o'clock Gita said "I have only made one bed up; I thought we would be more comfortable that way."

It was probably the most fatuous reason she could have invented. As far as Fritz was concerned it was the most brilliant. It should further be recorded they each awoke with a smile to the world in general, and to each other in particular.

They went to the City Hall a few minutes after it had opened, filled in the necessary forms, it was all so simple. From there they took a horse cab to the military hospital which again provided evidence of the superb efficiency of the German Army in that they placed Fritz on a bed in a cubicle, sat his 'wife,' which is what they automatically assumed her to be, in a chair beside him, removed the damaged limb, commentated very favourably on the running repairs it had received, took it away and almost exactly an hour later brought it back and strapped it back on. With handshakes all round, they left the building, went back to Frau Reuter's home to telephone Ulm to invite them to the civil ceremony in Munich on Monday 25th at 3pm. Here they encountered their first hitch. Only Elizabeth could come, her husband had to be at the Gymnasium on that day to welcome important visitors from Berlin.

"Not the Austrian corporal I suppose?" Fritz remarked to her. It was the first overtly political statement he had made to her, leaving her in no doubt as to his feelings about the National Socialists.

"Right, over the weekend, in addition to getting to know you better," he continued. Gita interrupted.

"How precisely do you intend to achieve that?"

"I have a list of ways in my note book here," he took the little book out of his waistcoat pocket and waved it in front of her. "It is only a small book, but the list is endless I can assure you."

"Well, just remember you have to be able to walk up all those stairs at the City Hall on Monday."

"I shall continue. In addition to getting to know you better over the weekend we shall, between us, contrive a letter to Dieter telling him about Monika Kemper who would like to hear from him. She hears very little from her husband in Norway and knowing him as she does believes he has, without doubt, found himself another mistress. Send his reply care of my address as she lives with a virago of a mother-in-law, and that's about it, except for all the padding, including the fact that his friend from Munich is now my wife and that we are blissfully happy together."

The wedding ceremony conducted in the full gaze of the Fuhrer from a gigantic portrait on the wall behind the registrar, flanked on both sides by large swastika bedecked flags, left no doubt in the minds of romantic young, and not so young, couples that they belonged to the Third Reich, the Thousand Year Reich as Hitler had named it. Those same couples had been required to sign a declaration that they possessed no Jewish blood and would bring up their children to be loyal National Socialists. Elizabeth and another lady, waiting to attend a later wedding, signed the register as witnesses, the registrar handed the marriage certificate over to Gita, faced Fritz and raising his right arm proclaimed, "Heil Hitler".

To this Fritz, caught turning to kiss the bride half turned back and said, "Oh yes, indeed, Heil Hitler," vaguely waving his right arm upwards, then proceeded with the more important part of the ceremony.

They put Elizabeth back on the train soon after six o'clock, having told her of their plans with regard to Gita meeting Rosa, the Monika plan, as they had named it, and their removal for the time being to Brucksheim.

"Do be very very careful my dears. Don't do anything to risk Rosa's present position. This terrible war will not last for ever. The longer she is kept at Brucksheim the greater chance she has of returning to us."

"We shall be very careful," they replied as the train started to move away, with Elizabeth waving from the window until it curved at the end of the platform, when she was lost to sight.

They went back to Brucksheim on Wednesday, having spent Tuesday tidying up, leaving dust sheets over the furniture, and packing clothes into two large suitcases. It was a long and tedious journey, made worse by a daylight raid by American Fortresses on Kassel as they approached the city. As a result they were extremely travel weary by the time they arrived at Fritz's apartment, however there was just enough daylight left for Fritz to show from the window his new wife the bench in the park where they would meet her beloved Rosa.

"Tomorrow" he said, "should she appear. I will go down and prepare her. If you will stand at the window she will see you, if only vaguely, but it will help her to steel herself for the meeting when you come down on Friday."

She turned to Fritz and held him tight.

"I'm so frightened," she whispered.

"Why frightened my love?"

"She may not appear, she may have been sent away."

"She will appear, you mark my words," but he said this with hope in his heart more than any degree of certainty. The assertion gave Gita confidence, however, so achieved its purpose.

Thursday the 28th September 1943 was a day which would be remembered for all the days in the lives of three people. Fritz and Gita Strobel and Rosa von Hasselbek. It was a bright autumn morning when Rosa slipped out of the Klinik into the park, looking up at Fritz's window as she made her way to her bench. Standing there she could clearly see was not only the tall figure of this wonderful man who had befriended her, but beside him a slim fair haired lady who, even at this distance, she could recognise as her mother. She hurried to the bench, sat down, and burst into tears. It was at this point that things began to go not entirely according to plan. A middle-aged lady, walking a friendly black and tan dog of somewhat indefinite lineage, approaching from the opposite direction, saw the distress the young woman was experiencing and stopped to speak to her, whilst the dog rubbed against her ending up by putting his head on her lap, looking into her face with his big brown eyes, obviously as solicitous as his mistress.

"Are you alright my dear? Can I help in any way?"

"No, thank you, it's very kind of you," she rubbed the dog's head, who responded with a furious wagging of his tail. "I had some sad news earlier today, and it caught up with me again as I came to sit out here for a little while. I am really alright now." She smiled at the lady and again made a fuss of the dog.

"Well, if you are sure you are alright I will get on. My husband will be home for his lunch soon and I must be on time for that."

"Thank you very much for stopping. And thank you too," she said, addressing the dog. "He's a friendly chap, what is his name?"

"We call him Dieter, after my son who was killed in Russia."

Whether Rosa's emotions had been sent topsy-turvey already at the brief sight of her mother, or whether this poor woman's dead son bore the same name as her husband, who too was fighting in Russia, or whether she was so sorry this kind lady had lost her son in this evil war, or perhaps a combination of all, plus her own present insecure hold on life, again brought a flood of tears, through which she was able to say "My husband too is Dieter, he is in the panzers in Russia."

The lady sat down beside her and put her arm around her shoulder.

"Have you had bad news of him?"

"No, no, he is alright. The bad news I had was to do with a patient of mine." She added this last fib, wiped her eyes, turned to the lady and added, "I really am alright now. Thank you so much for helping me, and thank you too Dieter," for which remark she was rewarded with a slobbery tongue licking her hand.

"Then I will go, perhaps I shall see you again here one day. Goodbye now." With that she shook hands and moved purposefully away to present her spouse with his midday meal. Rosa would have been surprised to know that the lady was none other than the wife of the very kind Burgemeister who had befriended her when she first arrived at Brucksheim back in May, a living skeleton, more dead than alive.

Whilst this tableau was being enacted Fritz had descended the stairs, 'the bloody lift out of order again.' Actually it was not out of order, the electricity supply had been temporarily cut off to enable bomb damage repairs to take place, as a result there was no power to operate it. He reached the bend in the path, saw Rosa had reached the bench, was sitting with her head in her hands, and being spoken to by a passer-by. He stopped at another seat where he could observe what was happening, while Gita anxiously watched from the apartment window. At length the passer-by resumed her walk; Fritz gave her a few minutes to get clear then slowly walked towards the bench. The usual charade took place of his raising his hat and sitting a yard or so away.

"What happened?"

"I saw mummy with you at the window – it was her wasn't it?"

"Yes, she is there now." Rosa looked up for a long long minute, smiling through the last of her tears.

"I thought it best not to bring her down without talking to you first. Oh, by the way, you are talking to your new step-father."

"Oh I am so happy for you both. Now, what do I call you?"

"Fritz – just Fritz."

"Fritz, I wish I could hug you. I will one day; you have been so good to me." She was almost crying again.

Fritz looked at his watch. "You must get back. If I bring your mother down tomorrow will you be alright?"

"Yes, I promise. Frau Doktor Schlenker is going to Berlin for a long weekend to a family wedding tomorrow. I shall be able to take a little longer away from the Klinik, barring accidents of course!" she added with a little laugh.

And accidents, as we all know, do frequently happen.

Chapter Thirty Three

Chandlers Lodge seemed strangely empty on Monday 16th October 1943. The two Welsh Guards officers who had been billeted on them since January had been posted elsewhere during the previous week; as a result their two servants no longer were in and out of the house at all hours. They had been a cheerful pair, extremely deferential where Rose was concerned – after all, her husband was a major, with an M.C. to boot, not in the Guards it was true, but in the next best thing, the Rifles. It is strange really where the Guards in general get these funny ideas.

Monday 16th was however to start a week of being in and out of the shelter. Apart from a small raid on London at the beginning of the month, things had been very quiet, now the siren was howling away two or three times each day. Usually there was only a small cluster of aircraft, the general opinion of those who professed to understand such things, as had been expressed before, was that they were coming over to see what was going on rather than to do any real damage. However, having made the trip presumably they could hardly go back home without leaving their calling cards. It was the receipt of a nearby five hundred kilo example hitting the soft earth of Kent that again blew half the windows in and shattered the quiet of Chandlers Lodge as well as Jack Hoopers' 'The Hollies' some quarter of a mile away. It was a frightening thought that had the bomb aimer up in that Heinkel pushed his button a second before or a second after, one or other of these houses could have been turned into rubble.

Fred was in the factory shelter when they clearly heard the bomb screeching down. From the rough direction of the subsequent explosion he and the others with him judged it had landed in the direction of Chandlers Lodge where Rose and little Jeremy were hopefully in the shelter, or where Nanny Hooper and young John were similarly taking cover. He made for the exit, closely followed by Ernie.

"We'll go on the Ernie-bike."

Ernie was one of the few staff at Sandbury Engineering who got a special allowance of petrol for his motorcycle combination in view of his disabilities. They got to the Hollies first, but there was nobody there. They raced on to Chandlers Lodge as the 'all clear' sounded, to find Rose, Jeremy, Nanny and Mrs Stokes, the daily, climbing out of the Anderson.

"Where's young John?" Fred called.

"I took him to school as usual, he will be in their shelter," Nanny answered, "then I called in on Rose on the way back to scrounge a cup of coffee, and this is the sort of reception I get."

There was glass everywhere.

"We could just do with the loan of those blooming batmen now," Fred reflected, "blooming Guards are never there when you need them. I will get on to the glaziers who do work for us at the factory and get them down to secure the place and The Hollies. One thing about it, we don't have the looting problem they have in the cities, although having said that there's a first time for everything I suppose, so we had better get cracking."

This was the only bomb that fell on Sandbury during that particular alert. Rose wondered why only one bomb was dropped. After discussion they concluded that it must have got stuck in the bomb bay when originally released over a target – it had come from the general direction of Biggin Hill, so they probably had been the recipients of the other five – and by some means freed itself later. That happened on many occasions to both the Luftwaffe, the R.A.F. and the American 8th Air Force. It was not unknown for an aircraft to have to land with a bomb stuck underneath despite the efforts of the crew to dislodge it. Decidedly off-putting to say the least.

Fred and Ernie returned to the factory leaving Rose and Mrs Stokes to start clearing up, Rose having first parked young Jeremy in a room at the back free of broken glass, leaving him with some toys to play with.

"How can one window produce so much broken glass?" Rose queried in exasperation as they walked into the sitting room. Pieces were imbedded in the carpet, the upholstery, the walls – everywhere. Fortunately the room they used most, the kitchen, had relatively small windows, was towards the rear of the building and, apart from some plaster coming down, had escaped damage. The hallway and stairs had small amounts but Fred's bedroom, being at the front was absolutely unusable.

"He will have to go into one of the guest rooms until we can clear it all up," Rose told Mrs Stokes. "We shall have to keep a close watch on Jeremy in the meantime," Jeremy normally had the run of the house, "these little slivers embedded in the woodwork could do a lot of damage."

They had been working for about an hour when a glazier arrived with his young helper. "I've sent my other pair round to Sir Jack's at The Hollies, Mrs Laurenson, all we can do for the minute is measure up and board up, then come back and fix the new glass in the next couple of days. You were unlucky here, on the other hand if it had dropped in the town, say a quarter of a mile away, it would have done a devil of a lot of damage."

"That is, I suppose, a small consolation," Rose agreed, then continued "that being the case, in view of their deliverance from disaster, do you think they would all come and give us a hand to clear this confounded mess up?"

The glazier grinned, "Somehow I don't think people are quite that public spirited."

As he spoke they saw the young glazier's mate, who had been sent to The Hollies, running up the gravel drive. They hurried to the door.

"What's the matter Joe?" his boss asked him.

Breathless, the young lad gasped out, "When we got to The Hollies, we found the lady there had been hit on the head and was lying bleeding on the stairs. I tried to dial 999 but the phone had been ripped out. Mr Smith is staying with her."

Rose turned back into the hall and immediately dialled for the police and an ambulance. She then put in a call to Jack at his factory at Rochester, and was through almost straight away. "Uncle Jack, your house has been bomb-damaged and Nanny has been attacked by a looter. Can you come home? We will collect young John from school and keep him here for the time being." Jack answered he was on his way. Rose then telephoned Cecely at the shop and asked her if she could collect young John – the school was only two or three hundred yards away – and bring him to Chandlers Lodge.

Mrs Stokes said she would wait here until Mrs Coates arrived, then she would go on home. Her two youngsters would not be worrying if she was late, she often did a bit of shopping on the way home. They would clear the rest of the mess up tomorrow. With that decision made Rose got her bike out and peddled off to see to Nanny. When she arrived she found the ambulance already coming down the main road from the town. Nanny had a bad gash on the side of her head, her face on that side already swollen and bruised. The ambulance men, actually one was a woman, gave immediate first aid, and whilst doing this a police sergeant with a plain clothes man in tow came in.

"Can you tell me what happened Lady Hooper?" asked the detective. The sergeant corrected him, straight away. "That's not Lady Hooper, that's Miss Cavendish, the Nanny."

"I'm sorry Miss Cavendish, now can you tell me what happened?" His tone of voice had now changed slightly so that a keen observer of the niceties of class distinction, had there been one present, could have clearly noted he was no longer talking to a 'Lady', but was now addressing a lady. Very respectful nevertheless on two counts. One, she was a lady employed by a 'Lady', secondly with a name like Cavendish; she must be a bit posh anyway. What's in a name? The answer to that of course is would you rather be Mr Fortescue or Mr Bloggs?

Nanny, in considerable pain from the blow just answered, "I can tell you little except the door was open – I thought it had been blown open by the blast – and as I picked my way in through the glass a man came out of the drawing room door with a poker in his hand which he swung at me. It glanced my head. He then hit me in the face and ran."

"What did he look like?"

The ambulance man butted in, "Look, we've got to get her to hospital to have this wound cleaned and stitched up."

The detective persisted: "Can you tell me what he looked like?"

"He was roughly dressed, had a cap on, very dirty hands and nails, unshaven, grey corduroy trousers, shabby black overcoat. I can't remember anymore."

"Miss Cavendish, you are an absolute pearl, I wish all witnesses were like you. I will come and see you later."

With that they whisked Nanny away. The detective asked they did not touch anything until Sir Jack had checked what, if anything, was missing, particularly if they found the poker not to touch it. "We will drive around for half an hour or so until it's dark to see if we can find anyone fitting that description."

They did, and they didn't. That is they drove around but had no luck in spotting anyone. The detective, who was new to the district, asked the sergeant, who had been at Sandbury for twenty-five years, whether he thought it could be a local. "I know three or four it might have been although the most likely one is in Maidstone gaol already."

"Right, we'll go and shake them up first."

Jack arrived just after the police left and was given the news by Rose. His chauffeur, an ex-R.A.F. sergeant, who came with his job at the aircraft factory, and who had relocated to Sandbury, immediately suggested Sir Jack took the Jaguar to the hospital to check Nanny was alright, whilst he started clearing up the mess.

"The police said not to touch anything," Rose said, "they told us they would be back soon. I don't suppose that means the glass can't be swept up. It's mainly at the back of the house, whereas Nanny was assaulted here by the front door."

"Look Harold, you stay here then" Jack said, "and when the glaziers have boarded up you can hang on for the police to come back, and for me to return. My wife is away for two days, we'll have to get it all straightened out before she comes home."

And so the big clear-up began. Ernie took an early evening and he and Anni, Karl and Cecely all came to Chandlers Lodge to assist in the tricky business of finding and removing tiny barbs of razor-sharp potential hazards, after an hour or so all moving to The Hollies to assist Jack and chauffeur Harold perform a similar task. These were elementary clean-up jobs. With every bomb that was dropped, in addition to the demolition of whatever property it hit, for up to half a mile radius depending on the size of the bomb, the glass would suffer in this way. Putting sticky paper crosses on each pane helped, but only marginally. Buses and underground train windows were covered in a thick protective linen mesh which totally prevented passengers from looking out to see if they were near their bus stop or tube station. As a result efforts had frequently been made by travellers to scrape a peephole in the material to prevent their overrunning their destination. In an effort to persuade people not to do this, little notices were put on each window in the form of a rhyme.

> *'Pardon me for my correction*
> *This stuff's put here for your protection.'*

On at least one underground train a wag had written in indelible pencil underneath such a spy hole

> *'Thank you for your information*
> *But I would have missed my f------ station.'*

A prime example of the spirit of the people during the Blitz and in the many raids afterwards.

Nevertheless, the knock-on effect of a bomb, or an 'incident' as the local authorities bizarrely termed it, often affected hundreds of homes beyond the poor souls who had lost everything they had built up over many years.

When all was more or less shipshape Jack suggested they all adjourned to John Tarrant's for some supper on him. Rose said she would go back to Chandlers Lodge to make sure Mrs Treharne was all right – she had elected to look after the children while the others were at The Hollies.

A dishevelled party presented itself to the saloon bar for a much needed drink. Being Monday night the restaurant was closed so they all had soup and sandwiches, having brushed off the fact they had been bombed as if it was included in the standard pattern of life, like Market Day on Tuesdays. It really is quite amazing what the human constitution can accept as the norm.

The next morning Jack telephoned Rose to tell her Nanny was making good progress after a sound night's sleep. He had to go up to town on the train, so he had asked Harold the chauffeur to buy some flowers and take them in. It was way before visiting hours, nevertheless because she was in a side ward the sister in charge allowed him in. "Ten minutes, not a minute more. I've already had the police here this morning while they should have been out catching the villain that did this," she stated firmly.

"Sir Jack asked me to bring these from him." Although he was a time-served R.A.F. sergeant he was an extremely reserved man, even a little shy at being at a lady's bedside. He continued, "And I brought these from me. I wish I could get my hands on the brute who did that to you Miss Cavendish."

"Thank you, thank you very much, but please, my name is Eleanor – after all, I only know you as Harold."

They chatted on about the police visit – they had not yet caught anyone – until sister poked her head round the door. "Off you go, visiting hours are 2-4, 6-8."

"Could I come and see you again?"

"Yes, please do."

"With the irregular hours my job causes me it could be anywhen."

"Then anywhen it will be," she said with the effort of a smile which her damaged face found difficult to produce, nevertheless, the eyes smiled.

As has happened so many times before in these chronicles of The Chandlers, the stone in the pond paradigm resulted in Harold returning to visit Eleanor on three occasions, finally suggesting to Sir Jack that he collect her from hospital when she was discharged, as she was to stay at her aunt's for a week or so at Tankerton some twenty miles away. Sir Jack readily agreed, as a result Eleanor Cavendish arrived at her aunt's rather lovely house in some style, being helped from the beautifully polished Jaguar by a well set-up man who manifestly was extremely solicitous of his passenger, indicating to the observant aunt he was definitely more than just her chauffeur.

So began the friendship between Harold the confirmed bachelor and Nanny Cavendish who had been firmly of the opinion that at the age of thirty-seven love had passed her by. Not that true love ever runs smooth – each had a skeleton in his or her respective closet which would have to be laid to rest first – but that is another story.

The hit-and-run raids continued right up until the end of October, then petered out. No further damage was done to Sandbury however, the windows gradually got re-glazed, the comment from Fred being "Pilkington's must be making a blooming fortune."

To which Jack had replied, "we don't seem to be doing too badly either do we?"

And it was true; largely because they only took on jobs they knew they could do and do well, and were seldom, if ever, late on a contract. On the one or two occasions upon which this had occurred, it was solely due to components not arriving on time through enemy action. The Hamilcar project was going well under the watchful eye of Ray Osborne. It was always an exciting moment when the huge R.A.F. trailers arrived to take one of these gigantic gliders away. The giant body, capable of carrying a seven ton tank went on one transporter, the two enormous wings, overall over a hundred feet long on a second, whilst the tremendously high rudder assembly, and the tail planes went in a third.

"How the hell does it get off the ground?" Ray asked.

"I'm told a Halifax usually tows it" Fred replied. "You know how big a Halifax is – the wing span on the Hamilcar is six feet wider than the Halifax itself. I tell you what, I'll ask the ministry wallahs if we can't go and see a flight – after all we make the blooming things, or at least some of them, so that's the least they can do for us."

The M.A.P. – Ministry of Aircraft Production, through the usual Sandbury Engineering contacts willingly arranged a visit. As a result, on a cold frosty morning at the beginning of November a black Humber arrived to take Fred, Ray and Ernie up to an airfield in Cambridgeshire where they saw one of their very own products take to the air, circle the airfield, cast itself off and land back again, as precisely as if it had been under power, down the centre of the runway.

"Would you like to go up?" they were asked.

The fact that each was too windy to admit to the others he would rather stay on terra-firma, resulted in a unanimous, "Yes, please."

Followed by Ernie asking "Where do we draw our parachutes?" In reply the squadron leader conducting them laughed heartily.

"I wasn't joking," Ernie continued, "don't we have parachutes?"

"Good Lord no. The glider pilot doesn't have a parachute, his co-pilot has no parachute and the people travelling in the glider definitely do not have parachutes."

"What happens if they get hit?"

"We try not to think about that."

These three men, seeing day after day the construction of these giant, powerless carriers, had not at any time envisaged the fact that the men who fly them, and the tank crews, gun crews, and others who fly in them were encased in thin plywood in the main, totally reliant on the skills of firstly the towing aircraft crew, and secondly, and most importantly on the glider pilot and his co-pilot. These two men had no power to assist them in their manoeuvrability, no means of calling on extra power if required, no means of going round a second time should they overshoot their target, along with the constant need to keep their craft at the correct height above their tow at all times. They were to see at first hand what that entailed, the skill it required and the constant stress it produced, in a few minutes time.

"I'm beginning to wish I hadn't come," Ernie said jokingly. He was in fact looking forward to this unique experience very much indeed.

The huge glider on its comparatively tiny landing wheels having been towed back down to the start point on the runway, the three passengers were driven down in the back of a fifteen hundred weight truck to be introduced to the pilot and his co-pilot.

"Hamilcar people are hand-picked from glider pilots with experience on Horsas and Hotspurs, small troop carrying units, but then you probably make those as well I suppose?" their guide asked them.

"No, we just make the Hamilcar," Fred replied, adding, "I trust you are not a German agent pumping me for information?"

"One has to have a second string to the bow to make ends meet, doesn't one?" came the reply.

Reaching the aircraft they were introduced to the pilot and co-pilot. Looking at them both Fred felt absolutely antediluvian. The pilot, a staff sergeant, was no more than twenty or twenty-one, whilst the co-pilot was a lieutenant of the same age if not a bit younger. Fred wondered why it was that the 'boss' pilot was junior in rank to his understudy, later being told it was fairly common in the Glider Pilot Regiment, where seniority in the air depended on experience and ability more than pips or stripes. These aircraft, and other gliders, were all flown by soldiers, of course, not airmen. As soon as a glider landed the pilot became, like the people he had carried, a fighting infantry soldier, he was far from being a glorified bus driver.

The pilot gave them details of the flight plan. They would be towed by a Halifax which was in fact taxiing toward them already. The flight was for thirty minutes. For the take off they would sit in the body of the aircraft and after five minutes or so the co-pilot would vacate his seat for each of them in turn to have five minutes 'up top.' The Hamilcar was entirely different to other gliders in that the pilots sat in a little Perspex enclosure on top of the aircraft instead of in the nose. Apart from some small windows in the sides of the main body, this was the only place from which anything outside could be seen. It was reached by a stairway from inside the cavernous body – well not a stairway as such, more like a ladder, and when reached, instead of the usual side by side arrangement of pilot and co-pilot, the co-pilot sat behind the pilot.

When they had first seen the drawings for the aircraft Ernie had said, "it seemed a daft idea." Now they were to experience it in operation.

The ground crew having connected the tow rope to the glider and the tug, the co-pilot carried out his first duty – walking the rope! The main purpose of this exercise was to ensure the darned thing was properly attached at each end! The secondary duty to inspect the telephone wire which ran from pilot to pilot, along the tow rope, so that they could keep in touch during the tow, and in particular when the moment of separation arrived. It was essential the glider pilot released his end of the tow rope first otherwise he could fly into it with possible disastrous results. In the first glider operations, in Sicily, a number of poorly trained American pilots, meeting anti-aircraft fire for the first time, detached their ends, sending their tows down into the sea. It was not appreciated.

"Prepare for take off," bellowed the pilot. The passengers strapped themselves with seat belts on to a bench on the side. They could hear the roar of the Halifax increase as its four mighty engines built up the power required not only to get itself into the air but also to tow this massive glider which when fully laden would weigh nearly fifteen tons. The tug moved off, the tow rope, laid in zigzag fashion on the runway, gradually straightening out until with a perceptible jerk the Hamilcar, now to be called the tow, moved forward.

Ernie was heard to exclaim, "And God bless all who fly in her."

It is at this point the glider pilot would be a little apprehensive about his telephone line to the tug pilot. The telephone wire was not as elastic as the nylon tow rope. If the take up was too sudden it was not unknown for the wire to snap with the consequential loss of communication between the two aircraft. He would check as soon as they were in level flight.

They had a bumpy ride down the runway until two or three larger bumps heralded smooth flight – they were airborne, although the tug itself was still belting along on the runway. Eventually the tug took to the skies, the tow riding above the slipstream until they levelled off at about three thousand feet. Gradually then the glider pilot lowered his aircraft, through the slipstream , getting a bit of a battering as he went, until he had positioned himself in what they described as 'low trim,' that is, the slipstream was passing over their head. They held steady at three thousand, as the co-pilot joined them.

"Right, who's first?" he bellowed.

"Off you go Ernie," Fred suggested.

Ernie was away up the stairway although he still could not navigate stairs as rapidly as most people, a result of the polio he had suffered as a child. Afterwards he told everyone who would listen that it was the second most thrilling experience in his life, sitting there looking out over the enormous body and wings of this contraption that he had been involved in constructing, looking forward to the twin rudders and tailplane of the Halifax, its four engine exhausts leaving trails of dark blue smoke, the odd vehicle below, the tiny houses, it was a world he could never have dreamt about a few years ago. After five minutes he tapped the pilot on the shoulder, said, "Thank you," descended the ladder and was replaced by Ray. He too thoroughly enjoyed his five minutes during which time the Halifax started to make a 180° turn to head back to the airfield. Fred took his seat. He too marvelled at the fact that only a little over ten years ago he was working on a farm, now here he was being treated as a V.I.P. and riding in an aircraft whose manufacturing supervision was his responsibility. Fred was not a particularly religious man, nevertheless he felt obliged to admit that God does move in a mysterious way at times. He rejoined the others.

"I shall go up top now," the co-pilot told them. "You will know when we have released the tow because it will go all quiet. We then descend at about a thousand feet a minute until we hit the deck." The 'thousand feet per minute' did not really register at this moment with the passengers, as the young lieutenant re-took his place behind his skipper. It would do shortly!

They put their seat belts back on and waited. Up above them the pilot, after a brief chat with the tow pilot, pulled a lever which was fitted with a large red knob, red presumably so that it could not be mistaken for any other purpose, and the tow rope fell away for the tug to jettison on the runway after the glider had landed. In the meantime the glider banked over to the left and started to fall, the roar from the Halifax motors being replaced by the whistling of the wind past the fuselage and through the aerilons, a strange silence compared to the previous clamour. It was at this point as the nose went down in a steep dive, their stomachs, or at least the contents of their stomachs, seemed to exert a strange desire to elevate themselves up through their respective oesophagi. This lasted only some two minutes but it was a long, long two minutes for the intrepid flyers until the aircraft levelled off, hit the ground with a bump which proved its solid construction, and eventually rolled to a halt. Comment from Fred – "Bloody hell."

The three were entertained to lunch in the R.A.F. officer's mess, after which they were driven back to Sandbury, arriving in the blackout of another frosty night, fearful that Sandbury Engineering had ground to a halt in their absence. As it was, the place, as usual for 6.30pm on a Wednesday evening, was going full blast, proving Ernie's point that 'they don't really need us.' Without either of them suggesting it, they walked over to the Hamilcar bay, stood and looked at the next one being fabricated and marvelled that this cumbersome object, this most ugly duckling of aircraft could fly so sweetly, turn so responsively, descend so swiftly and land so positively in the hands of a young man only a year or two out of school. It was quite unbelievable, but they had now experienced it for themselves, as indeed would a Tetrarch tank crew and a medical jeep party, in Normandy, in this very aircraft, in only a few months time.

"Let's call it a day," Fred suggested, "I don't think I'm up to getting myself organised after a day like this. By the way Ray, how are you getting on in your lodgings?"

When Ray had come out of hospital and joined Sandbury Engineering he had rented a room from a friend of John Tarrant, the landlord at The Angel.

"To be honest Fred, it is not working out too well. I have my own little kitchen and a shower room, but John's friend Bertie and his wife keep themselves very much to themselves so I have no company. I thought of moving into that guest house in Chatham Street, at least I would have a bit of company at times, a lot of commercial travellers stay there."

"Well, why don't you give it a try? Either that or buy a house of your own and take in lady lodgers, the odd Land Army girl, or whatever. Better still, get yourself married."

"Buying a place had occurred to me, but getting married?" He paused a moment, "Who would want a maimed person like me?"

Ernie, seeing that Ray was serious and not just looking for sympathy put his arm round his shoulders, saying, "That's how I used to think a few years ago Ray, but someone did want me. I thought it was a bloody miracle that someone could be attracted to me, my not having the use of my legs, yet a wonderful girl saw beyond what she thought was secondary, and the rest you know."

"You're right. Sorry about that bit of self-pity. I shall go wife hunting without delay."

And he did, but he made little headway for a while until ... but that is another story.

Chapter Thirty Four

David literally staggered into his quarters at Bulford at 3am on Thursday 19th October, soaked to the skin, unshaven for three days, and desperately tired. For the past hour he had been visiting his three platoons in their company spider, where, under the vigilant eyes of their platoon commanders the men were having rifle and foot inspections after completing the first of their major exercises. It was not unknown for some company commanders at the end of a long and arduous exercise to slope off and get into a bath, leaving the tidying up to their junior officers. David made it a point to be the last to seek the comfort of his room, not to appear heroic, but simply and solely to show his one hundred and twenty or so men and their officers they were all part of the same team, the same duty, the same discomforts, the same setbacks, and the same triumphs.

When he arrived, Angus had got a coal fire going, had run a bath and although he too had been soaking wet, cold and miserable, he had swiftly changed into dry clothes and set about looking after his officer. Many in the battalion thought a batman's life was a 'cushy number.' So it probably was at a depot or at an H.Q., but in a field unit it was a different kettle of fish entirely.

Their exercise had commenced early on Monday morning when they had been bussed to an airfield near Reading. That night they had been dropped on a featureless Salisbury Plain in pouring rain and almost pitch darkness. A series of exercises had then taken place on Tuesday and Wednesday during which time it rained, nearly all the time, they had been required to cover forty miles in the two days, carrying out a full scale attack on a defended ridge, sleeping in cat naps when they could and eating from what they could carry. It was hard, a few didn't make it. Running into an attack across a muddy field carrying sixty pounds of equipment was not for the inadequate, but this is what they would be called upon to do in a few months time, with the added unpleasantness of having nasty Germans trying to stop them by firing MG42 machine guns at them at a thousand rounds a minute. All in all David was very satisfied with his company, particularly his three platoon commanders. Paddy was an absolute tower of strength seeming to be everywhere, chivvying here, joking there, encouraging the slower ones, blasting the idle ones. It was a very tough three days, but it proved they were a tough, well led force which would be difficult to reckon with.

David lay back in his bath. In thirty-four hours time, he calculated, he would be getting on that train for the forty-eight-hour pass they were scheduled on completion of the exercise. Maria likewise had a forty-eight-hour entitlement so they had arranged to meet at Waterloo and then spend the weekend at Chingford. All went according to plan – for a change, David remarked – as he hugged her up on the Waterloo forecourt, to remarks from men of his company being disgorged from platform 16 such as, "Has he told his wife Miss?" and, "You're prettier than his ATS girl at Bulford." Maria smiled and waved, there was no doubt she was an extraordinarily attractive young woman in her immaculate Wren uniform. They made a strikingly handsome couple.

David had travelled up with Sandy Patterson, his Canadian platoon commander, who was waiting patiently to be introduced. He was going on to Blackheath in South London to stay the weekend with Amanda One and her parents, Amanda being already on a seven day leave. Duly presented, they went their separate ways.

The red carpet was well and truly out when they arrived at Chingford. They spent the evening swapping stories, listened to the nine o'clock news, heard the loathsome wail of the air raid siren at 9.30, decided to ignore it and at ten minutes to ten the 'All Clear' sounded, followed by Mrs Schultz saying, "Well, Heinrich, we must be off to bed, it's getting late." Mr Schultz was, at first, a little puzzled at this since they rarely went to bed until eleven or thereabouts, but quickly cottoned on. "Lie in as long as you like in the morning," were Mrs Schultz's last words to the newly married couple, "I shall be down at the shops and your father will be at the works."

When they had gone David commented,

"Now that's what I call a really accommodating lady."

"It runs in the family, I am an extremely accommodating wife as I shall yet again prove in a few minutes."

"As I have said before, you are wanton."

"Yes, and as I replied, and wanting!"

If the meaning of wanton is to include a feeling of uninhibited abandonment, a state in which prudence, caution and planning take no part, then there is no doubt such a state existed that night in the fair town of Chingford, and for that matter the following morning as well, resulting eventually in – well, we shall have to see, shall we not?

The weekend went all too quickly before they found themselves back at Waterloo, David first seeing Maria off on the Dover line, then crossing over to Waterloo terminus in the company of seemingly thousands of red-bereted paratroopers, some a little the worse for wear, but strangely enough not being reprimanded by the various pairs of military police – the Redcaps – who, faced with the already widely postulated pugnacity of the airborne troops, judiciously kept their distance. They were, after all, outnumbered by at least twenty to one!

Once on the train – a special, straight in to Bulford – the hullabaloo so in evidence at Waterloo gradually subsided, as those with a skinful, or for that matter half a skinful, gradually dozed off. Others less inebriated sat quietly mulling over the pleasures of the past weekend to the musical clickety-clack of the train's wheels; others sat and wondered how many months they would get for desertion, followed by grinning to themselves at the thought. A few chatted by the dark blue light which was all the illumination provided in the third class compartments of troop trains. In the first class – officers and warrant officers only – a white light was provided, just strong enough to read by, as blinds were fitted to the windows. By the time Bulford sidings were reached it was close to midnight as weary and subdued troops of all ranks made their way to their various billets. That blasted bugle would be blowing in six hours time in an endeavour to rouse some six hundred men from a stupor brought about, in many cases, from two days and nights of over indulgence in one form of entertainment or another, or in a fair proportion, a miscellany of such activities.

To show that leave was a privilege, David had called for a five mile road run at 0700 hours – before breakfast!! the men only discovering this when they returned to their billets that night. It was barely light when they paraded in their P.T. kit plus pullovers, the air being turned blue with the somewhat forthright comments, opinions, threats, theories regarding the major's parentage, the platoon commanders' mental states, and above all that bloody Irish git of a Sergeant Major yelling them into wakefulness. To make matters worse there was a very keen northerly wind blowing, nevertheless despite the stiff climb out of the camp on to the Andover road, they were back well within the hour, ready for breakfast, with the surfeit of overindulgence occasioned by their weekend away having been sweated out of them despite the temperature.

As they had doubled across the parade ground the colonel pulled back the blinds to his living room – the colonel was the only one with a living room and a bedroom.

"Who's that?" he enquired of his batman.

"That's B Company Sir, mad as March hares."

The colonel was quiet for a moment.

"Mad they may be, but they're the best of the lot." He paused, "You didn't hear that!"

"No Sir, of course not."

The C.O.'s batman saw, heard, and overheard all sorts of things of which other people, even officers, knew nothing. The C.O.'s batman had the tightest lips in the battalion, it was part and parcel of the make-up of the breed, and when they were in action, with the colonel moving backwards and forwards into the various trouble spots being contested by his companies, the batman became his bodyguard, changing from shoe polisher to shield. It was an odd sort of job.

The routine of training carried on for the next two weeks. On the weekend of the 4th November, the battalion went off for its usual 36 hour pass, David having to stay at Bulford doing his turn as field officer. He had a long talk with Maria on the telephone after dinner on the Saturday evening, noticing at times she was a little, well a little, how can I describe it he was saying to himself, well, a little vague.

"Darling," he at last interrupted, "is something worrying you, have you had more shelling?"

"No, why do you ask?"

"Well, I seem to sense that something is not quite right. You're not unwell are you?"

"No, I'm as fit as the proverbial."

"Oh well, it must be my imagination."

There was a definite pause while he waited for her to continue.

"There is one small thing."

"You're not in any trouble or anything?" He was beginning to get really concerned.

"I probably would be if it was not that I am an old married lady." He still failed to follow her, and then the penny dropped.

"You don't mean..." he almost bellowed into the telephone.

"I mean that I am a week overdue. That does not necessarily mean what you are obviously thinking, but bearing in mind the constant ravishing I received a couple of weeks ago, at the hands of a sex-starved warrior it has to be considered."

"But, but," he was all of a fluster," but when will you know?"

"By Christmas or the new year sometime I imagine – I shan't forget to let you know."

"Maria Chandler, if you don't start talking sense to me, I will go absent and come and, and,"

"Come and what? Now there's a thought – did you mean you might make sure? In which case..."

"Darling, please tell me. I don't know about these things."

"Well I will give it another week, then go to our M.O. here. If I am in this delicate condition I take it you would like me to retire to my country estate?"

"Yes indeed. But will the Wrens allow you to retire?"

"I imagine that a petty officer Wren in what I believe you uncouth soldiery call the pudding club, would not be of much use dodging shot and shell on the coast road from Dover?"

"I worry and worry about that already."

"It has been a bit quieter lately."

"Thank God for that. Now, how long before you know? and what happens if it is what we hope it is?"

She re-commenced her teasing.

"And what do you hope it is? It could just be wind!"

"Be serious. I was not fitted with a bicycle pump. What happens?"

"Darling, I don't know. Wrens can leave the service at any time since they are all volunteers, so there are no discharge problems. I imagine that when it's confirmed I just get an honourable discharge and that's that!"

"Do you want to leave?"

"There is nothing more I want than to have lots and lots of your babies."

"Darling, I am going to the bar. I shall be the only one there I expect, and I am going to have a very, very large whisky. Goodnight my love."

"Goodnight dearest David – but not a word to anyone until I am sure – alright?"

"Cross my heart."

But he could not keep such news to himself. When he met Paddy in the company office on Monday morning he asked, "How is Mary?"

"She's fine Sir, she's quite big, she's afraid it might be twins."

David paused, noticeably. Paddy turned, sensing he wanted to say something.

"I think we might be a little bit pregnant too – although Maria has told me to keep my big gob shut until it's certain. Now I've let the cat out of the bag."

"Oh, I know the feeling Sir, you want to tell everybody. Well, I'll not repeat it so you're OK there. You'll know for certain soon I wouldn't be surprised."

The days dragged until the next free weekend when, since Maria would not be able to get away, he had planned to go to Dover. He should have known. There is a special unit tucked away in the War Office which by some devious devilry finds out about soldiers' plans, soldiers of all ranks I would add, and plots to bugger them up. Upon this occasion the battalion H.Q. runner arrived at B Coy spider on Thursday afternoon asking that Major Chandler please report to Colonel Hislop, the C.O.

"David, sorry to muck up your weekend but I've been instructed to go to Western Command tomorrow for a three day sand table exercise. What all the rush is I don't know unless they have us down for an urgent op. I'd like you to come with me."

"What's the dress Sir?"

"Oh, battledress, but take your service dress in case there is a dinner night." He paused a moment. "So that we look a bit more professional I think we will wear our Denison smocks over the battledress. I don't know who else is to be there but it won't do any harm to look a bit different to the county and corps wallahs will it?"

David grinned. "No Sir, definitely not," thinking as he said it, 'so even colonels like a bit of bullshit occasionally.'

When Maria telephoned that evening she was more disappointed than she could have believed.

"It's like a child having its lollipop snatched away from it," she told her David.

"Are you comparing me or part of me to a lollipop?" he demanded to know. "Now when are you seeing that M.O.?"

"On Monday."

"We shall be back on Tuesday – can you telephone me on Tuesday evening?"

"Yes, of course darling. David – you are not going on an operation or a raid or anything?"

"I can categorically tell you the only thing I shall be raiding will be Western Command's bar, so don't worry your pretty, correction, beautiful head about that."

Angus, having got his travel gear ready, the C.O.'s Humber staff car came round to his quarters after lunch on Friday just as the other officers were getting themselves tarted up in preparation for their visits to the fleshpots of London or wherever. Angus went with them to look after both of them as he had intended to stay at Bulford anyway for the weekend.

The eighty mile journey to Exeter was covered in a little over two hours, arriving in time to be shown to their quarters for the weekend and to have afternoon tea. Whether Western Command were pushing the boat out a bit or whether, as David noted, they always lived on the fat of the land like this, an almost pre-war display was spread out before them in the form of thinly cut sandwiches and a large selection of battenberg and other small iced cakes, clearly bought from Fortnum and Mason, or made by a chef originally with that illustrious firm before being called up and snaffled by command H.Q.

"Shows us up a bit, David."

"They are just showing off, Sir, they will probably present us with a bill before we leave."

As far as David could see he was probably the most junior officer present. As the room filled, other colonels, a couple of brigadiers, a clutch of majors, the same rank as David, but mainly in their early thirties, all crammed in, some acknowledging old friends, one or two standing on their own, and a number scoffing away as if there was no tomorrow. As he watched the assembly a firm hand clutched his shoulder. Turning he found himself facing none other than his brother-in-law Mark Laurenson, accompanied by his first commanding officer Lieutenant Colonel Brindlesby-Gore. Giving Mark a bear hug, he introduced the pair to his colonel.

"How is your brother Sir?" David asked Brindlesby-Gore. David and B-G's brother had been cadets together.

"For an ex-lawyer he's a bit stingy on the correspondence caper. He telephoned a couple of weeks back saying he had been made up to captain, second in command H.Q. company. I think he's probably angling to get the adjutants' job in the 3rd Battalion, that would suit him down to the ground."

Mark chimed in. "Do you know if there is one job in a battalion I would hate it would be the adjutant's. He's never off-duty, always getting court martial papers ready and other rigmarole, it must be like being a town clerk in civvy street."

"Except that town clerks get paid rather more bountifully," commented Colonel Hislop. "As a one time adjutant I can attest to that."

A gong sounded. "Gentlemen, may I have your attention please." It was a somewhat rotund major with a clutch of Great War medal ribbons on his ample, if not exactly muscular chest. "Gentlemen, if you will be in the anteroom this evening at seven o'clock the general will circulate among you. Dinner will be at seven thirty, ordinary battle-dress tonight, service dress Saturday and Sunday. Parade in the main theatre room tomorrow morning nine o'clock. Thank you gentlemen."

"So we still haven't a clue as to what it's all about," observed Colonel Hislop.

"I wonder if they know themselves," came the answer from B-G, Mark and David each raising their eyebrows at each other.

They found out the next morning when they presented themselves to the main theatre room. In the centre of the room was a long table, measuring some 25 feet by 10 feet. On the table an Intelligence Corps unit had constructed in coloured sands a foreshore along one long side, topped with defence positions, beyond them mine fields and entrenchments, and even further back on the other long side of the table some fields with small villages and woods at intervals. A great deal of work had been done in moulding the sand to give a clear picture of the topography of a classic beach landing assault. A full colonel commenced by saying:–

"Gentlemen, this beach could be anywhere. Norway, Northern Germany, Holland, Belgium or France, even Mediterranean France, so it is no use your trying to second guess where the second front will be from this layout, but this layout is the first step towards our assault on the Atlantic Wall. It is designed to ensure that everybody, down to the youngest private soldier knows exactly what the plan is so as not to repeat previous mistakes."

David's thoughts immediately flew to the abortionate planning of the Dieppe fiasco. He whispered to Mark, "They had better keep Mountbatten out of it then."

The colonel continued by explaining that this representation was of a stretch of beach in West Wales, and that all units taking part in the forthcoming invasion would practise their particular objectives on it, mostly in brigade units, by day and by night, since we do not know at what hour the first assaults will take place. Parachute units, glider units, underwater obstacle removal units, indeed all specialist units will practise over and over again. Armoured units, headed by special mine exploding tanks of the 79th Armoured Division will clear paths through coastal mine fields to allow other armoured formations through and fan out into the countryside beyond.

The outline of the plan was gradually unfolded. It being Armistice Day, they broke at 10.45 for a short service, followed by the two minutes' silence at eleven o'clock. They then were served coffee, and after a break for lunch resumed until four thirty. Although David had hardly moved from his chair on the banked seating positioned on either side of the table, he felt quite drained. A combination of excitement at being in at the beginning of this great enterprise, of concentration on the plans being presented, of perhaps a little presentiment of the fearsome fighting that would result in invading a well defended position against an enemy who knew you were coming even if he didn't know exactly where, left him as exhausted as a five mile run would have done.

"Let's get some tea," Mark suggested.

As they settled into comfortable armchairs in the command mess, all the normal residents presumably being away for the weekend, Mark remarked, "They seem to do themselves alright here don't they?"

"Well, it must be an extremely exhausting business pushing all these papers around, that end up on our desks, they obviously need the comfort."

"David." Something in his tone alerted David straight away.

"David, we think you may soon be an uncle again. I've been told under pain of death itself not to say anything to anybody yet but I can't keep it to myself any longer."

David sat absolutely motionless, whilst Mark searched his face for any reaction.

"Mark, we think you may soon be an uncle again. I've been told under pain of death itself not to say anything to anybody ..." He got no further; Mark gave him an almighty thump in the ribs.

"By God, is that true? That calls for a very large drink."

"The bar's not open."

"We shall be first in the queue when it does."

"In the queue for what may I ask?"

David's colonel and B-G had joined them.

"Well Sir," explained Mark "it appears that David and I have performed what I suppose can be loosely described as synchronised procreation."

"In other words Sir, as my Sergeant Major O'Riordan would say, our wives are both a little bit pregnant."

"Tho', mum's the word for the present," added Mark, at which they all looked at each other and roared with laughter.

"Mum's the word, oh how apt," Colonel Hislop exclaimed. "This calls for a drink."

"Bar's shut Sir, that's why we were going to be first in the queue."

They did wet the two, as yet unconfirmed babies' heads that evening, not too wet you understand, not under the eagle eyes of their respective colonels, who had they known it would have welcomed the chance of a good booze-up away from their respective messes, and the eagle eyes of their juniors.

All day Sunday, and Monday morning, was spent in small groups studying the sand table from the angle of their own specific tasks, that is, underwater clearances, mine clearances, armoured attacks and so on, as they would take place on the ground in Wales over the next three months.

"So we're not going on the real thing before spring then," concluded Mark.

The G.O.C. Western Command gave a final talk before they all departed after lunch on Monday saying a further meeting would be called for all commanding officers early in the new year for a presentation by the Royal Navy and R.A.F. on inter-service co-operation. In the meantime all troops must be brought to a peak of perfection – and kept there until the great day.

"Or night," David whispered.

After lunch the brothers-in-law bade farewell to each other with the words 'See you at Christmas' said as much as a statement of hope as of certainty, both aware of the historic great event in which they had just taken part – the first step in a long hard slog to final victory in Europe.

David arrived back at Bulford late on Monday evening, the colonel having called in at his home at Marlborough on the way, introducing him to his very charming wife and twelve-year-old daughter. He took them to The Castle and Ball in the High Street for an early dinner, where David and young Sandra got on like a house on fire, she, obviously having heard about him from her father, pumped him about life with the Partisans, about which he was most surprised to know they had been discussing at school.

"Do you have any family?" Mrs Hislop asked. David and the colonel looked at each other and started to laugh. Quickly the colonel took his wife's hand.

"Sorry darling, not laughing at you I assure you. You see, mum's the word." He and David chortled again.

Mrs Hislop looked at her equally mystified daughter.

"I think they may have caught something down at Exeter, don't you dear?"

"As David's Irish sergeant major would say my dear, we think that David's wife is a little bit pregnant."

"Oh how lovely. Is your wife at home David?" asked Mrs Hislop.

"No, at present she is a Wren stationed down at Deal."

"Ah, a Royal Marine Wren."

"Yes – you know about these things?"

"I have a friend there – just an ordinary Wren, she loves it, except the shelling."

"Yes, I'm very worried about that. Maria suffered a near miss only a short while ago. There has been a number of fatalities all along that coast road I am told." Sandra took his hand.

"How did you meet, David?"

"Sandra is an incurable romantic David, really Sandra you shouldn't ask such things," her mother chided.

"Well, it's quite a romantic story, although like lots of stories it is both sad and happy. I was in a battle called Calais of which you may have heard. I met a man there called Cedric who used to bring our food up to our position every night no matter how heavy the shelling was, and at times it was very heavy. Every night we got a hot meal no matter what. Then one night as he drove back he was hit and lost his life. One day when I had got back to England I went into a Corner House for a spot of lunch and started talking to a very sweet looking girl and without going into more detail it emerged she was Cedric's sister. Now, how does that rate as the wildest chance of all time? We fell in love, and now hopefully a little Chandler is on the way."

Sandra wrapped her arms around his arm excitedly saying to her smiling mother and father, "Wasn't that a lovely story? And when your baby comes you will bring them both down to see us, won't you David? I would like that so much."

"I'll make sure he does," her father assured her.

As David lay in bed that night wondering how Maria had fared, the incident of the Dover shelling flooded back into his mind. He would have to persuade Maria to get away from that danger area. He knew what she would say. One, would you run away? Two, wherever you go, particularly in south-east England, there is always the danger of bombing. Nevertheless, the latter was less dangerous than the former – until the flying bombs, the V.I.s began to fall in a few months time, but of that, of course, they knew nothing.

Chapter Thirty Five

Ray Osbourne, M.C. and bar, had made up his mind. He was seriously going to look for a soulmate. Having made the decision, the mild euphoria this resolution had engendered in his manly breast evaporated somewhat when the next stage in the campaign came to be considered, namely, how and where? Go to dances? He wasn't much of a dancer. Go to church? Probably find the choice a trifle thin on the ground. Join a choir or opera club? Sang like a corncrake. Canvas previous girlfriends back home? All married by now – he was, after all, thirty-three years of age. So how the hell do I start? he asked himself, getting more and more despondent as the various avenues blocked themselves in his mind. He did have one stroke of luck. Before the war Fred and Jack had formed a property company to build some rather up-market flats on the site of a factory they had taken over only a couple of hundred yards from Ray's present lodgings. One of these was falling vacant due to the present elderly tenant going to live with her daughter and her family. Unlike the situation in later years when married children were more likely to push parents into 'homes for the elderly,' it was not uncommon for three, or even four, generations of a family to be living together, often overcrowded but never unwanted.

But back to Ray.

It being established that the flat was to be vacated, Fred asked Ray if he would be interested in taking it on. Ray went to view it a couple of weeks before the present tenant was to move out, found that it had been very nicely kept, and immediately decided that this was stage one of his quest for a wife settled. Next problem – furniture and furnishings. Furniture at that time was, like most other things, (including wives it seemed to Ray), rationed. If you were setting up home you could get enough furniture coupons to buy a dining room suite, or a bedroom suite, which by an uncomplicated piece of logic meant you either ate on the floor, or you slept on the floor. There was furniture to be had very occasionally, off-coupons, known as 'non-utility,' the rationed variety being 'utility.' Utility furniture was of the plain, no nonsense variety, but very well made. Many people who bought utility furniture kept it for thirty or forty years after the war ended. Finally there was always 'second-hand,' usually obtained via the small ads in the Sandbury Gazette or the Kent Messenger.

It was at this point Ray had his second piece of luck. The good lady had insisted to her daughter she took her bed to her new home, the rest she would arrange for a dealer to come and collect.

"Not that I shall get much for it, they are all a lot of crooks," being her forthright and, most would agree, entirely accurate description of the trade in general.

"Can I make you an offer for it all as it stands, less what you wish to take with you?"

"Well yes, thank you very much. I was told a dealer would probably offer about thirty to forty pounds."

"Well, if I say seventy five would that be acceptable?"

The dear lady burst into tears. "Oh yes, that would be very acceptable, thank you very much."

The next thing to happen could only happen in a novel. Having said that, happen it did. A knock came at the front door which the good lady answered, returning to the sitting room, where Ray waited, accompanied by a well dressed, attractive woman in her mid-twenties. Coming into the light of the room – blackout was in force in the small hallway – the newcomer noticed her grandmother, for that was who she was, had been crying. Before the grandmother could say a word of introduction the young lady exclaimed, "Granny, you've been crying," then turning to face Ray demanded, "What have you been saying to my grandmother to make her cry?"

Ray was, to say the least, a little taken aback, but before he could reply she turned again to her grandmother, who by now was beginning to smile.

"It's alright dear, Mr Osbourne has made me a very generous offer for my furniture and so on, and I was upset that someone could be so kind to me – isn't that silly? Now, dear, say hello to Mr Osbourne – this is my granddaughter June Morris."

The introductions made, a somewhat shamefaced young lady held out her hand to Ray – her right hand of course. He returned the gesture by offering his left hand, neither of the two ladies until that time having noticed that his right hand wore its customary leather glove. June was momentarily taken aback, as most people are who meet this situation, but swiftly took the hand offered.

"May I ask what happened to you?" she asked.

"I was removing a fuse from an unexploded bomb and it went off." He hesitated for a moment. "The fuse that is, not the bomb. The bomb would have presented a different result altogether had that gone off." The two ladies were silent until June suddenly realised she was still holding Ray's good hand. Somewhat flustered she let the hand go, looked into Ray's eyes, saw he was smiling and smiled back.

"So you are a civilian now?"

"Yes, I work at Sandbury Engineering."

"Where they make that big glider?"

"How do you know about that – it's supposed to be the war's number one top secret," Ray joked.

"Since when one of them leaves the factory on those lattice work trailers the R.A.F. brings in, everybody in Sandbury sees it, it could hardly be a secret could it?"

"Well, put that way, I suppose you are right, but if you were to see the forms we have to fill in to enable a visitor in to see one being fabricated, when they could stand out on the road at the right time and see the complete article, you would come to the opinion that the secrecy lark was even dafter than you had previously believed."

"But surely something as big and heavy as that can't get off the ground, let alone fly?"

"We had a flight in one a couple of weeks ago. It flies like a bird."

Mrs Wilson, the grandmother, stood listening to these two young people talking together hoping against hope two things. One, that Mr Osbourne was not married, he was such an engaging young man, two, that perhaps her June could overcome the heartbreak she had suffered for the past two years since her young pilot husband had been shot down and killed on a raid on Duisburg. She heard Ray continuing his story.

"Mind you, when the pilot, not more than twenty years old I swear, brought her down to land it was like going down in a lift at ten times the normal speed. Frightened the life out of me."

They were both laughing, he at the recollection, she at the ridiculous thought that this obviously brave man could be frightened, though quite how she would justify that belief she would have found difficult to explain.

"And is your husband in the services?" Ray asked, noticing her wedding ring. Her smile left her, Mrs Wilson held her breath.

"He was in the R.A.F. and killed over Germany two years ago."

"Oh, I'm sorry to have asked you that question."

"You were not to know." Ray hastened to change the subject.

"Mrs Wilson, since you are taking your bed I shall have to buy one. Please do take anything else you may need, I will give you a cheque now at the price we agreed."

"Thank you Mr Osbourne, oh, I am so glad that is all over. I was so dreading having a dealer coming in and haggling with me. But, Mr Osbourne, won't your wife want to see the flat?"

"I regret to tell you Mrs Wilson that there is, as yet, no Mrs Osbourne."

June broke in. "Mr Osbourne..."

"Oh, Ray, please."

"Ray, I work at Chiesman's, the department store in Maidstone. I am the manager in the Counting House."

"That's where all those little packages winging around at high speed on wires end up isn't it?"

"Well yes, that is part of it. We take care of the bought ledger, staff wages and so on."

"A very responsible job."

"Well yes. I have graduated to it rapidly as a result of the men having been called up. Anyway, I was going to suggest you come in to us and I will introduce you to the manager of the bedding section. A man of course – the Mr Chiesman who started the business always insisted that only men were to be employed in beds and bedding – he considered it was not seemly that ladies should sell beds."

They all laughed heartily at this patriarchal whim.

"I shall telephone you before I leave so that you can arrange a meeting place."

They shook hands.

He telephoned her the following Saturday morning. He asked her to have lunch with him, after which she could introduce him to the 'Beds and Bedding' man. She agreed, and that is how Ray's romance started.

The view has been previously put forward that the sequence of events related above could only occur in a novel. I think we have now shown, indubitably, that not to be the case – have we not?

The next day, Sunday, he had been invited to Sunday lunch at Chandlers Lodge. Rose had taken on the mantle previously worn by her mother, in that although the bulk of the housework was very efficiently done by Mrs Stokes, Rose did the cooking for her father, herself and little Jeremy, as well as for the occasional visitor. Visitors were not as numerous as they were in days gone by. Rationing now was beginning to hurt. Even if one could afford to eat out, the meals, since the restaurant owner could only charge five shillings (25p) for the whole meal, contained no extravagant portions nor cordon-bleu contents. Nevertheless most people managed.

When the three were about to settle at the dinner table, the telephone rang. Rose hurried to answer it.

"Rose, Otbourne here. Am I interrupting your meal or anything?"

"Lord Otbourne, how nice to hear from you. No, we have not sat down yet. How are you?"

The pleasantries concluded, the Earl continued.

"I am thinking of having a party here for Christmas. Christmas Day is on the Monday. I thought if people arrive on the Saturday and stay through until Wednesday it would make a nice break for everyone. I wondered if you and Mark, and your father, would care to come. I understand Mark will be on leave. I shall also ask David and Maria, Mrs Coates and Mrs Treharne and of course Sir Jack and Lady Hooper – plus the children of course. Oh, and if anyone has made any arrangements with anyone else they can come as well, we have plenty of room and it's about time this old house was livened up – and that includes me as well!"

"It sounds a marvellous idea. But what about the food?" This was the first problem raised in everybody's mind as soon as visitors, whether two, or twenty-two, were envisaged.

"Well there we are lucky. We have been saving a few non-laying hens on Home Farm, we have two large turkeys, and my cousin in Scotland will send a box of grouse. Add to that rabbits and hares and some venison off the estate and we shall not starve, even if you do not get legs of lamb or joints of beef with every meal. I shall get a whole host of non rationed goodies sent down from Fortnum's and again non rationed fish, smoked haddock etcetera from our suppliers in Aberystwyth, so we shall not be down to eating acorn sandwiches!"

"You say Mark will be getting Christmas off? He hasn't told me, the blighter."

"Oh, I've got it on the grapevine, Charlie's grapevine, though how he found out I can't tell. Probably bribed someone in the orderly room I suspect. Anyway, he will be here along with that nice girl of his. Her parents are unable to come. They have two horses running on Boxing Day at Market Rasen and must, of course, go and back up their trainer. I telephoned Buffy but they are going to friends in Cirencester, and then I believe coming to you for the new year."

"Lord Otbourne, we do have one problem. Captain Osbourne, who now works at Sandbury Engineering was to spend the Christmas with us, he has no family..."

"No problem, bring him as well."

"In that case, can I discuss it with father and Ray and telephone you this afternoon?"

"Yes, of course my dear. By the way, tell them to bring some boots, we shall be having a shoot on Boxing Day."

They discussed it over lunch. Arranging Christmas is, for many families, the biggest headache of the year. In this instance it was working out very well. Rose had qualms about Ernie and Anni being left out, but a further telephone call that afternoon put her mind at rest, Anni putting it to her gently that they, that is Ernie, her father, and herself had been invited to Rosemary Gordon's for Christmas, did they mind? Maria's parents were hosting some relatives, but would be at Chandlers Lodge for the new year, Megan had already told them she was having ten days at Carmarthen with the children but would be back the day after Boxing Day.

So it all worked itself out. But before the great expedition was to take place, Herr Goering decided he had not finished with the people of Kent. On the Friday following the telephone call to Rose he sent his bombers over both during the day and at night. They hit the airfield during the daylight raid, causing some damage and several WAAF casualties who were caught out in a truck on the perimeter, and at night, deluged the south side of the town with a shower of incendiaries. One house was burnt out along with a number of garden sheds on an allotment, otherwise little damage was done. Having said that, the unfortunate family which found itself homeless that night, facing a bleak Christmas until relatives rallied round to help, would hardly have shrugged their shoulders and said it could have been worse. As it was, that was exactly what they did do – it could have been a five hundred pound bomb instead of two incendiaries that hit them! It is amazing how the human psyche can console itself in times of great trouble.

The next night, Saturday/Sunday, another fifteen hundred tons of bombs were dropped on Berlin. However, some were beginning to wonder whether it was worth the losses we were beginning to experience. That night we lost forty-one Lancasters. Not just the aircraft of course, but forty-one crews between three and four hundred trained airmen. In two weeks' time we were to lose another thirty when another fifteen hundred tons were dropped, but there was to be no let-up, the German people had to be shown they could not win the war, Russia to be shown that even if we were unable to mount a second front yet we could still play our part.

On Sunday 10th December Rose was getting Jeremy ready to take him with her to church when the front door received a relatively gentle application of its lion-headed knocker, a knocker incidentally which would make the house itself tremble when fully assailed. On opening it she confronted a smiling Alec Fraser and a somewhat bulky Rebecca.

"Come in; come in, how lovely to see you."

"I'm on leave which means I shall miss Christmas at Mountfield, but beggars can't be choosers." Alec was his old ebullient self they all knew and loved from when he was billeted on them when the Canadians first arrived in Britain three years ago. Now he was married to Ernie Bolton's gorgeous sister, and she soon would be presenting him with their firstborn. Alec continued, "You have your coat on, were you going out?"

"No, I was just going to have a bath."

"You see, Rebecca, as cheeky as ever."

Jeremy poked his head round the corner.

"Hey, Jeremy, come and give your Uncle Alec a big kiss." Jeremy ran as fast as his nearly three year old legs would carry him and threw himself at Alec, to be picked up and whirled around with great glee.

"We were just going to church."

"Shall we join them dear?"

"I'd love to, and I've no doubt you could do with a little spiritual cleansing after being three months incarcerated with the licentious soldiery in the wilds of Wales."

"Licentious they might be, able to indulge their licentiousness was a very different matter. That's why those Welsh hill farmers wear Wellingtons."

"Alec, stop it, you are just going to church."

Rose pulled at his sleeve. "Come on Alec, why do they wear Wellingtons?"

"Well, apparently they stick the back legs of the sheep in them so that they can't run away." He paused for a moment as Rose split her sides with laughter. "We wondered why the men kept asking for an issue of Wellington boots, then we found out why. Mind you, there would have been plenty of sheep to go round when you come to think of it. Still as we had no Wellingtons the matter didn't arise."

"I think you are disgraceful Alec Fraser, don't you Rose?"

"Absolutely disgusting, he will have to put twice as much in the collection plate than he normally does, to atone for all that."

"You mean two pence instead of his usual one penny?" asked Rebecca.

Alec hugged Jeremy tight. "And how is my little godson? Do they give you enough food? And what about sweets like this?" With that he pulled a large bar of chocolate from his pocket. "All the way from Canada for Jeremy Cartwright."

Jeremy's eyes lit up in wonder. He had never seen a bar of chocolate as large as this – ever.

"Now thank Uncle Alec, and let me put that on the sideboard until you come back from church."

"Thank you Uncle Alec ... Mummy, how long does church last?"

"Don't worry; it will still be there when you come back."

That wasn't what I asked thought Jeremy, grown-ups never seem to answer questions properly. You say, "Mummy I'm hungry when will tea be ready? and they say, boys are always hungry. What sort of answer is that?"

They walked the quarter mile up to the church, waited at the side of the road, opposite, while a detachment of Welsh Guards marched up, as only guards can march, for their church parade. The Guards filed in, followed by Alec and his companions. A couple of paces in front of Alec was a guardsman having completely forgotten to remove his headdress. A sergeant stationed in the porch, presumably there to ensure no reluctant worshipper should skive off, spotted this delinquent and in a stage whisper called out, "Take your bleeding 'at orf in the 'ouse of Gawd, guardsman." Alec, shaking with mirth turned to the others.

"What's the matter?"

"I'll tell you later."

And with that they had to remain mystified until they were walking home again, when Alec, having recounted the story, added the comment, "How did a cockney sergeant get in the Welsh Guards?"

On the following Wednesday, it being early closing day, an excited Cecely arrived at Chandlers Lodge for lunch with Rose, with the news that Oliver had passed his selection board tests and was to go to Sandhurst on January 8th. That was the good news. The bad news was that as he had been away for the selection board, and would be leaving the training regiment anyway, he had been detailed for guard and other duties over the Christmas. He would not therefore be coming to Ramsford Grange.

"Well, as David always says, you can't win them all," Rose observed.

"How did your father get on with the booking of the seats?"

"He left it to Miss Russell. Having done so, and being told the cost, apparently, according to Ernie, who was there at the time, the colour drained completely from his face, his lips twitched and he had to sit down. You see, you can only book first class, so booking twelve seats on a return basis in two first class compartments, with fares and booking fees, amounted, or so he said, to enough money to start another business. Miss Russell then reminded him that they were, he must remember, going to stay with an Earl, under no circumstances could they travel third class. Suppose the Earl came to see them off when they returned, how would he feel being seen scrambling into third class compartments."

Fred apparently replied, "Well, when I can't pay your salary next month you will know why."

"Well at least Charlie and Emma, David and Maria and Mark are making their own ways there, so you won't have them to pay for."

On Saturday, therefore, 23rd December, they made an early start from Sandbury station. They had difficulty in getting cabs at Victoria, and as a result had to rush to get the train from Paddington. It was extremely fortunate they had reserved the two compartments: the train was packed to the gunnels, every corridor was overflowing with bodies, suitcases, kitbags and packages – presumably Christmas presents – of every shape and size. The whole world was seemingly on the move.

They arrived at Worcester three quarters of an hour late, due almost entirely to the extra length of time the train had taken to disgorge its passengers at its various stopping points. Just as people, plus accoutrements, had had to fight their ways on, so they also had to fight their ways off, people with children having an extra burden. The mass had thinned somewhat by the time they reached their destination, where they found, as Miss Russell had confidently expected, the Earl with Captain Morgan waiting for them with a large luggage trolley, the Earl himself pushing it into position for them to load their luggage on to it. Out on the forecourt there were two hire cars, plus the estate's shooting brake into which Captain Morgan loaded all the luggage.

Waiting at Ramsford Grange were Lord Ramsford, Mark, David and Charlie. There was much hugging, kissing and general excitement when they were delivered to the steps of the beautiful old Grange. Captain Morgan had organised extra help from the village, mainly active pensioners who knew the house inside out. As they all gathered in the lofty entrance hall, the Earl, standing on the stairway called out, "Could I have your attention please ladies and gentlemen." There was instant hush.

"Captain Morgan will tell you which room you are in. One of the staff will then take you to it. I have to tell you that the west wing is out of bounds as it is currently in use by very hush-hush military people." Looking straight at Eric, and John Hooper, standing side by side he added, "Any inquisitive people found there are locked in the dungeons." This had the wholly to be expected effect of the two lads looking at each other, without a word putting the exploration of the west wing at the top of their operational agenda for the following day.

It would take another book to tell you what a great time they all had from dinner that evening until they landed back at Worcester station on the following Wednesday. An enormous Christmas tree from the estate had been erected and decorated before their arrival and placed in a barrel, embellished with some lengths of burgundy coloured velvet cloth, which had obviously served as curtains at some time or other. The presents they had brought were all placed around the tree, although the Earl had suggested that all presents be of a modest nature, "He doesn't want any more coronets I suppose," being Fred's considered opinion.

Christmas dinner was served at noon and lasted until three o'clock.

The servants then were able to get to their homes, or to the servants' quarters downstairs for their festivities, the cold evening buffet meal already having been laid out and covered in another room. On Boxing Day men from the village, marshalled by the Earls' keepers, beat a section of the estate for those who wished to take part in the shoot. In the meantime Eric and young John decided that this was a good time to explore the forbidden territory. They checked the internal doors to the west wing, finding them firmly locked. It would have to be an outside expedition, so Eric got young John's coat and boots from Moira on the pretext they were going for a little walk. They went out of the main door, that in itself a major obstacle as it was very very heavy, down the front steps, a quick look round to see if anyone was watching, followed by a furtive, half doubled up run across the face of the main building, round the corner, finding themselves in a short while at their objective. It looked quite ordinary, whereas they had expected it to look a bit frightening. True, there was a very close-wired barbed wire fence about six feet high standing some yards from the building itself which effectively prevented any approach to the windows of the building, which were shuttered anyway, but this proved no hindrance to our two adventurers who discovered a shallow channel, dug by a fox probably, under the wire of which they immediately made use, to find themselves inside the compound. They crept along the side of the wall, keeping their heads down beneath window sills as they progressed, until they reached a door, adjacent to which were several bins.

Eric tried the door. It opened noiselessly on well oiled hinges. They went in, closed the door quietly behind them and ascended the flight of stairs in front of them. There was nobody about, it was, after all, Boxing Day. The flight of stairs ended on a landing running left and right, they turned right. At the end of the landing was another door at which they listened, there was no sound so Eric turned the handle, and in they went. They studied the contents of the room.

Up on the wall was a huge map whilst in front of them was a table with what looked to them a picture of the seaside with land and rivers and houses and trees and farms and all sorts of things they couldn't recognise. They pulled up a couple of chairs, making a good deal of noise in the process, standing on them to look at this exciting landscape. Chattering away excitedly they failed to hear the door open, nor know they were not alone, until a voice enquired "and who might you be?"

They turned quickly, young John falling off the chair in the process, then picking himself up ruefully rubbing an injured knee, to see a POLICEMAN, a GIGANTIC POLICEMAN in fact, as they described him later, standing between them and the door. Thoughts of running for it were quickly discarded.

"I think you had better come with me."

"Are you going to put us in the dungeons?" Eric asked.

"What makes you think that?"

"The Earl said we were not to come here or you would put us in the dungeons."

"In that case perhaps we better had. First though I want to know how you got in here."

"We crawled under the wire and came in the door by the bins."

"The door was unlocked?" the War Department policeman asked incredulously.

"Yes, Sir. It opened easily."

"And what did you see in the room you were in?"

Young John broke in excitedly. He was famous for being able to produce an incredible volume of the spoken word without having to draw breath.

"Well we saw this seaside and lovely countryside and churches and farms and there were hedges and some funny bumps we couldn't think what they were and two windmills and that's all I can remember." His piping, just six-year-old voice, his excitement, his enthusiasm, and the fact that as he was reciting all this he was literally dancing from one leg to the other, amused their captor to such an extent he said.

"Well, I think you had better go back the way you came. But listen to me, you must not tell anybody, anybody at all, do you hear? of what you saw in here. It's a secret."

The two boys looked at each other wide-eyed.

"A Secret?"

"Yes, a secret between you and me. Now hold your hand like this." He placed his hand on his heart, "and repeat after me."

The lads did as they were told.

"God's Honour, I will not tell anybody what I saw in that room, or I will go to prison."

They repeated the solemn promise.

"Right, we will go back the way you came in." He led them down the stairway to the door by the bins, took a quick look outside to make sure no eyes were watching, and said, "Right, show me where you got through the wire."

The two boys hurried towards the front of the Grange looking for the depression they had used to get in. Finding it, the policeman said "Right, back you go, and don't forget what you swore on God's Honour."

"We won't forget," they chorused. Eric led the way, keeping his tummy close to the ground, John was not so fortunate. He had his bottom stuck up in the air, as a result caught his flannel shorts on the wire not only producing a rent in them but also scratching his backside, which made him yelp.

"Right away you go, Happy Christmas."

Eric turned, somewhat bewildered. "But that was yesterday."

"Well, if you want to be awkward about it, Happy Boxing Day," grinned the policeman, adding, "and don't forget what I said."

They trotted off. Boys never walk. They might take two or three paces, then they will jump, jog, scamper, skip, hop, run, or a combination of any of those, or they will run with their arms out turning themselves into aeroplanes or they will look down at the ground, still proceeding forward but turning their bodies until they are walking backwards, all these things, but they never just walk. I wonder why that is, and when it stops and they decide to behave like grown ups? In any event our lads proceeded by a variety of methods to the steps to the front door, where once again they had to use their combined strengths to push it open. The first person they saw was the Earl.

"Hallo boys, what have you been up to?" They looked at each other.

"Nothing Sir, we've been for a walk."

"It looks to me as if you have been having a crawl," answered the Earl. It was then they realised that crawling under the wire had left indelible evidence in the form of reddish mud that they had at some time at least, descended from the vertical.

"What on earth?" An astonished Mrs Treharne, having arranged to meet the Earl in the main entrance hall, regarded the two boys.

"How on earth did you get like that Eric?"

"We had to crawl under a fence grandmother."

"Well, you had better take John up to Auntie Moira's room, she's still up there, and then go and take that muddy coat off. And take those muddy boots off both of you before you make any more mess. Oh, I am sorry Christopher.

The Earl was laughing his head off.

"This is the sort of thing that turns a building into a house," he answered "children, mud and torn trousers," he pointed to John's pants, a decided rip showing a sizeable bit of John for all to see.

"Oh, I ought to go and apologise to Moira, Eric is probably to blame for all this."

The Earl held her arms, kissed her lightly, and replied, "Let them sort it out for themselves, it will be good practice for them, my dear."

Strangely enough, not a soul asked them where they had been.

Eric told Moira they crawled under a fence, but there were barbed wire fences everywhere so the mishap caused no unusual interest or comment other than 'don't do it again,' a typical example of motherly phraseology designed purely to put an end to an incident.

In the meantime the policeman locked the offending door, which had been his responsibility in the first place, and the reason he let the lads out the way they came instead of drawing attention to their incursion. You don't have twenty years in the police force, War Department or any other, without learning how to cover your tracks.

Chapter Thirty Six

It was Friday 29th December. After the festivities of the last few days what would, to the Chandlers and their close friends, a great sadness would prevail. All had gathered in various homes, Chandlers Lodge, The Hollies, Megan's House, The Bungalow and with Anni and Ernie. New Year's Eve was, on Sunday, the first anniversary of the death of Ruth Chandler. Canon Rosser, he and his wife being also among the countless numbers of Ruth's friends, had suggested they had a short service of remembrance after matins on Sunday morning to which Rose and Fred had agreed and with grateful thanks. Among the many people to attend the service were past friends and acquaintances who had heard of the proposed service by one means or another. Old friends from Mountfield days, including Frank Lovell, the landlord of the Prince of Orange and his wife. It was the first time in thirty years Frank had been to church except for weddings and funerals. Doctor Power came, the Boltons, Doctor and Mrs Carew, and many, many more. Even the major who used to billet the officers at Chandlers Lodge heard of the service and came with his wife. Virtually every Rotarian was there with his family; Ruth would have been amazed at the number of people, who in many cases had travelled considerable distances in difficult circumstances, to remember her.

Canon Rosser commenced the service by addressing the congregation.

"I need to say nothing of the love and friendship engendered by our dear Ruth over the years than to look at the mass of people gathered here today. This gathering speaks louder than any words I could express."

He went on to say they all had been affected by Ruth's passing in one way or another. Her kindness, her help for those in trouble or needing advice, her boundless hospitality, her generosity and selfless help to Fred and the rest of the family were models of Christian spirit, which would be difficult to equal. He continued:–

"Remembrance services can often be occasions of assemblies of platitudes at which the shortcomings of the person concerned are mercifully overlooked. It is true to say that in Ruth's case it would be difficult to find one person in this large congregation who could, or indeed would, want to find an adverse criticism of her. She was, simply, a good person, the epitome of selflessness.

In concluding the service, the Canon asked God to, "Look kindly on all here who grieve for our dear departed Ruth. Give them strength to carry on their lives to Thy greater glory. Protect her son Harry in the

Asian jungle, and keep her nearest and dearest and all others here safe in the struggle we know there is to come. Through Jesus Christ our Lord, Amen."

There was a very large gathering in Chandlers Lodge that evening. Fred and Rose had specifically used the word 'gathering' when sending out the invitations rather than call it a party. Nevertheless, when most of the visitors had arrived, Jack called the assembly to order, people appearing in the sitting room from the kitchen, the hallway, even a couple who had been sitting on the stairs, namely Charlie Crew and Emma.

"Ladies and gentlemen, Fred would like to say a few words."

An interjection from the crowd, suspected to have come from Ernie, "He's always saying a few words," followed by a general giggle and a momentary halt in the proceedings on Fred's part as he smiled at the pleasantry.

"Ladies and gentlemen, although this is a sad day for all of us, Ruth would be the very last person to deny us the pleasure and enjoyment of each others' company. So eat, drink and be merry as the Bible tells us in St Luke's gospel. You may wonder how I know that, my not being exactly of an ecclesiastical bent, it is probably the only thing I remember from my Bible class, and that was a very long time ago. Anyway I am sure that Ruth is looking down on us and will expect us to see this new year in, in the manner in which it has always been welcomed in Chandlers Lodge in most of the past years."

Prolonged applause greeted Fred's little homily, the applause motivated in part by the relief of knowing they were at a party now, not just a gathering.

As the evening wore on, Rose came over to David and Maria.

"I wonder what Harry is doing now?"

Harry was never far from Rose's mind. As she spoke, Megan joined them.

"Did I hear Harry mentioned?"

David instinctively put his arm around his sister-in-law.

"Rose was wondering what he was doing at this moment."

"Fast asleep I would imagine. It is already new year there, they are eight hours ahead of us, well, seven or eight I am not quite sure."

"Well given we are one hour ahead of Greenwich Time, even in the middle of winter, it is probably eight hours. In which case it will be."

Maria looked at her watch, "It will be almost five o'clock in the morning." They were all silent for a moment.

"By jove, he will have some stories to tell us when he comes home, won't he?" David asked.

"We haven't heard everything you have been up to either," Megan pointed out.

"And with my wife here you are not likely to," David quickly answered, only to receive a thump in the ribs for his pains and a smile from the others. The reply had achieved its purpose, he had made Megan laugh, and Megan really had so little to laugh at these days despite the delight of her children and the closeness of her family, the centre of her life, her Harry, was incarcerated in a green hell thousands of miles away, with no prospect of release as far as could be seen, for a very long time.

In the meantime Charlie and Emma had resumed their somewhat incommodious seat on the stairs, stairs after all, even if covered by carpeting of any sort, being designed to be trodden on not sat on. It would be fair to say though that neither felt any undue punishment to their nether regions. It is positively amazing how love transcends all other feelings. They sat for a while in silence, Charlie with his arm around her waist, she holding his other hand, not because he was trying to be familiar with it, you understand, but because she enjoyed his touch.

After a while he said, "I loved Ruth you know; she was so kind to me." Emma kissed him lightly on the cheek.

"She would have loved you too." A further short silence.

"I love you too, so much. Will you marry me?"

"If you will promise to stay the same as you are now, even if you become an Earl, yes I will marry you."

They kissed. And so under Ruth's roof with Ruth looking down upon them they sat in silence again for a while.

"Do you know darling Emma, nearly everyone here tonight has had his or her life altered by knowing David. First and foremost as far as we are concerned, he gave you my name for you to write to me. Because he met dear, dear Pat his family met the Hoopers, and at their wedding, David and Pat's that is, the general met his wife. When he was in hospital ..."

"What was he in hospital for?"

"He was hurt saving the life of a cowman, George Berry, who was being gored by a bull. Anyway, when he was in hospital, Megan was his nurse, Harry came to visit him and that is how he and Megan met, then at Megan's wedding Jack Hooper met Moira. Then he went to Germany, found Anni would be put in a camp and got her back here, to be looked after by dear Ruth."

They sat again in silence.

"I had better go and ask your parents if they will have me for a son-in-law. If they say yes I will then inform pater and grandfather. They too appear to be on David's connection list, pater is obviously very struck on Cecely Coates and grandfather adores Mrs Treharne, they wouldn't have known them if it had not been for David."

There was a small flaw in that last statement. David would not have known Charlie's father and grandfather if it had not been that he had roomed with Charlie at Octu, so the connection could, arguably, be traced back to Charlie!

He kissed her again. "Wish me luck," descended the stairs into the crowded sitting room, spotted his quarry talking to the general and waiting a few seconds until the general was called away, made his approach. Strangely enough he did not feel nervous in the slightest, having already, somewhat romantically it must be said, decided that if the answer was no, he and Emma would elope!!

"Sir." Mr Langham turned.

"Charlie, where's Emma?"

Without answering the question, Charlie plunged on.

"Sir. I have asked Emma to marry me. She has said she will. We would like your permission." Having got that off his chest, he was lost for words, a state in which it must be said he rarely found himself.

"Mary dear." His wife turned from talking to Megan, apologised and came to his side. "This young man has just asked for our daughter's hand in marriage, though by the looks of things they've already got it sorted out already."

Rose and Maria were talking together nearby when they saw Mary Langham's face light up in delight. Now Rose was not known to David as 'Hawkeye' for nothing, come to that Maria was not at all slow on the uptake. They looked at each other, looked for Emma, saw her in the doorway watching excitedly at Charlie's confrontation of her parents, simultaneously jumped to the only possible solution to be arrived at and swiftly made their way through the throng to her. "What's going on?" asked Maria.

"Is it what we think it is?" Rose queried.

They all three switched their attention to Charlie, noted that Mary Langham had released Charlie from her embrace and that Maurice was shaking hands with him. The three girls turned in to each other, put their arms round each other and did a little jig in the doorway. Charlie went across to the corner of the room where his father and grandfather were talking to Jack Hooper.

"Pater, I have asked Emma to marry me. Astonishingly enough she said yes. Mr Langham has given the go ahead. We would like your blessing and that of Grandfather."

They both shook hands with him. "Gorgeous girl, you're damned lucky" from Grandfather.

"Best of luck Charlie" from Pater.

Charlie made his way to the doorway; put his arm around Emma saying, "Your father said he would have preferred me to have been in the navy, but yes!"

The company began to suspect something was afoot, as a result Fred came over, put his arm around Charlie's shoulders saying, "Now then Charlie, what's going on?"

"Mr Chandler, I have pleasure in informing you that Emma and I are to be wed."

"Quiet please," bellowed Fred. The room hushed. "I have pleasure in announcing that Emma and ... what was your name again? Oh, I remember, Emma and Charlie are engaged to be married."

A tremendous cheer went up, after which a milling throng endeavoured to shake the hands of the two young people. Eventually Charlie was able to head his bride-to-be over to where his father and grandfather were by now talking to the Langhams. The Earl took Emma in his arms and said, "You will bring a breath of fresh air into the Otbournes."

Lord Ramsford said simply as he kissed her on both cheeks, "Welcome to the family."

Midnight approached. Fred called for all to charge their glasses. The radio was switched on to its top volume. Big Ben boomed out its chimes. As the hour struck there was a chorus of Happy New Year's followed by the inevitable Auld Lang Syne sung with gusto. Fred had asked the Earl if he would say a few words to start the new year off, calling the party to order he asked for silence for the Earl of Otbourne.

"Ladies and gentlemen, sadly our dear Ruth, who I got to know with great affection, is not with us. Neither is Harry who I did not know but who has been presented to me as a true Chandler, and there can be no more honourable appellation than that. We comfort our dear Cecely and Greta in their sadness. So, firstly, ladies and gentlemen, I ask you to raise your glasses and drink a toast to past and absent friends and loved ones."

They each murmured the toast, thinking of those they had lost. Ruth, Pat, Jeremy, Colonel Tim, Jim, Trudi Reisner – Anni's mother, Cedric – there were so many.

"And now ladies and gentlemen, I would like for us to look forward to 1944. There is no doubt that this year will herald a great adventure. It could see the end of this terrible war in Europe, although we still have those evil people in the Far East to overcome. A number of our nearest and dearest will be involved, for that matter already are involved, in one way or another in preparation for this great crusade. I ask you therefore to again raise your glasses and drink to 1944 – to the liberation of Europe – and for God to protect our loved ones."

There was loud applause at the end of this stirring utterance. On the debit side was the sinking feeling in the stomachs of Rose, Maria, Emma, and Deborah that their loved ones were to play a part, a leading part in this 'great adventure;' whilst Moira, alone with her thoughts which she could not share with anyone – not even her husband, agonised whether the Germans, who boasted already of having a 'secret weapon,' had, in fact, mastered the construction of the atomic bomb. She knew from her own privileged position in the War Department and Defence Council that the US/UK project in Nevada was well advanced, but if the Germans were a month ahead??? She shrugged off the thought, took a large swallow from her glass of scotch and soda and rejoined the throng.

1944 was to be a very important year for all the Chandlers.